A FORCE OF NATURE

Boundary Lines

and

Untamed

Sign of Seven Trilogy
Blood Brothers • The Hollow • The Pagan Stone

Bride Quartet
*Vision in White • Bed of Roses • Savor the Moment • Happy
Ever After*

The Inn Boonsboro Trilogy
The Next Always • The Last Boyfriend • The Perfect Hope

The Cousins O'Dwyer Trilogy
Dark Witch • Shadow Spell • Blood Magick

The Guardians Trilogy
Stars of Fortune • Bay of Sighs • Island of Glass

Chronicles of The One
Year One • Of Blood and Bone • The Rise of Magicks

The Dragon Heart Legacy
The Awakening • The Becoming

EBOOKS BY NORA ROBERTS

Cordina's Royal Family
*Affaire Royale • Command Performance • The Playboy
Prince • Cordina's Crown Jewel*

The Donovan Legacy
Captivated • Entranced • Charmed • Enchanted

The O'Hurleys
*The Last Honest Woman • Dance to the Piper •
Skin Deep • Without a Trace*

Night Tales
*Night Shift • Night Shadow • Nightshade • Night Smoke •
Night Shield*

• *Witness in Death* • *Judgment in Death* • *Betrayal in Death*
• *Seduction in Death* • *Reunion in Death* • *Purity in Death*
• *Portrait in Death* • *Imitation in Death* • *Divided in Death*
• *Visions in Death* • *Survivor in Death* • *Origin in Death*
• *Memory in Death* • *Born in Death* • *Innocent in Death* •
Creation in Death • *Strangers in Death* • *Salvation in Death*
• *Promises in Death* • *Kindred in Death* • *Fantasy in Death* •
Indulgence in Death • *Treachery in Death* • *New York to Dallas*
• *Celebrity in Death* • *Delusion in Death* • *Calculated in Death*
• *Thankless in Death* • *Concealed in Death* • *Festive in Death* •
Obsession in Death • *Devoted in Death* • *Brotherhood in Death*
• *Apprentice in Death* • *Echoes in Death* • *Secrets in Death* •
Dark in Death • *Leverage in Death* • *Connections in Death* •
Vendetta in Death • *Golden in Death* • *Shadows in Death* •
Faithless in Death • *Forgotten in Death* •
Abandoned in Death • *Desperation in Death*

ANTHOLOGIES

From the Heart • *A Little Magic* • *A Little Fate*

Moon Shadows
(with Jill Gregory, Ruth Ryan Langan, and Marianne Willman)

The Once Upon Series
(with Jill Gregory, Ruth Ryan Langan, and Marianne Willman)
Once Upon a Castle • *Once Upon a Star* • *Once Upon a
Dream* • *Once Upon a Rose* • *Once Upon a Kiss* • *Once Upon
a Midnight*

Silent Night
(with Susan Plunkett, Dee Holmes, and Claire Cross)

Out of This World
(with Laurell K. Hamilton, Susan Krinard, and Maggie Shayne)

Bump in the Night
(with Mary Blayney, Ruth Ryan Langan, and Mary Kay McComas)

Dead of Night
(with Mary Blayney, Ruth Ryan Langan, and Mary Kay McComas)

Three in Death

Suite 606
(with Mary Blayney, Ruth Ryan Langan, and Mary Kay McComas)

In Death

The Lost
(with Patricia Gaffney, Ruth Ryan Langan, and Mary Blayney)

The Other Side
(with Mary Blayney, Patricia Gaffney, Ruth Ryan Langan,
and Mary Kay McComas)

Time of Death

The Unquiet
(with Mary Blayney, Patricia Gaffney, Ruth Ryan Langan,
and Mary Kay McComas)

Mirror, Mirror
(with Mary Blayney, Elaine Fox, Mary Kay McComas, and
R. C. Ryan)

Down the Rabbit Hole
(with Mary Blayney, Elaine Fox, Mary Kay McComas, and
R. C. Ryan)

ALSO AVAILABLE . . .

The Official Nora Roberts Companion
(edited by Denise Little and Laura Hayden)

A FORCE OF NATURE

Boundary Lines

and

Untamed

TWO NOVELS IN ONE

NORA ROBERTS

St. Martin's Paperbacks

This is a work of fiction. All of the characters, organizations, and events portrayed in this book are either products of the author's imagination or are used fictitiously.

Published in the United States by St. Martin's Paperbacks, an imprint of St. Martin's Publishing Group

For information, address St. Martin's Publishing Group, 120 Broadway, New York, NY 10271.

www.stmartins.com

ISBN: 978-1-250-84973-1

Our books may be purchased in bulk for promotional, educational, or business use. Please contact your local bookseller or the Macmillan Corporate and Premium Sales Department at 1-800-221-7945, ext. 5442, or by email at MacmillanSpecialMarkets@macmillan.com.

Printed in the United States of America

St. Martin's Paperbacks edition / November 2022

10 9 8 7 6 5 4 3 2 1

Boundary Lines

For Ruth Langan,
for all the years.

CHAPTER 1

The wind whipped against her cheeks. It flowed through her hair, smelling faintly of spring and growing things. Jillian lifted her face to it, as much in challenge as in appreciation. Beneath her, the sleek mare strained for more speed. They'd ride, two free spirits, as long as the sun stayed high.

Short, tough grass was crushed under hooves, along with stray wildflowers. Jillian gave no thought to the buttercups as she crossed to the path. Here the soil was hard, chestnut in color, and bordered by the silver-gray sage.

There were no trees along this rough, open plain, but Jillian wasn't looking for shade. She galloped by a field of wheat bleaching in the sun with hardly a stray breeze to rustle it. Farther on there was hay, acres of it, nearly ready for the first harvesting. She heard and recognized the call of a meadowlark. But she wasn't a farmer. If someone had termed her one, Jillian would have laughed or bristled, depending on her mood.

The crops were grown because they were needed, in the same way the vegetable patch was sown and tended. Growing your own feed made you self-reliant. There was nothing more important than that in Jillian's estimation. In a good year there were enough crops left over to bring in a few extra dollars. The few extra dollars would buy more cattle. It was always the cattle.

She was a rancher—like her grandfather had been, and his father before him.

The land stretched as far as she could see. Her land. It was rolling and rich. Acre after acre of grain sprouted up, and beyond it were the plains and pastures where the cattle and horses grazed. But she wasn't riding fence today, counting head, or poring over the books in her grandfather's leather-and-oak office. Today she wanted freedom, and was taking it.

Jillian hadn't been raised on the rugged, spacious plains of Montana. She hadn't been born in the saddle. She'd grown up in Chicago because her father had chosen medicine over ranching, and east over west. Jillian hadn't blamed him as her grandfather had—it was a matter of choice. Everyone was entitled to the life they chose. That was why she'd come here, back to her heritage, five years before when she'd turned twenty.

At the top of the hill Jillian stopped the mare. From here she could see over the planted fields to the pastures, fenced in with wire that could hardly be seen from that distance. It gave the illusion of open range where the cattle could roam at will. Once, it would've been like that, she mused as she tossed her hair back over her shoulder. If she narrowed her eyes, she could almost see it—open, free—the way it had been when her ancestors had first come to settle. The gold rush had brought them, but the land had kept them. It kept her.

Gold, she thought with a shake of her head. Who needed gold when there was priceless wealth in space alone? She preferred the spread of land with its isolated mountains and valleys. If her people had gone farther west, into the higher mountains, her great-great-grandparents might have toiled in the streams and the mines. They might have staked their claim there, plucking out nuggets and digging out gold dust, but they would never have found anything richer than this. Jillian had understood the land's worth and its allure the first moment she'd seen it.

She'd been ten. At her grandfather's invitation—command, Jillian corrected with a smirk—both she and her brother, Marc, had made the trip west, to Utopia. Marc had been there before, of course. He'd been sixteen and quietly capable in the way of their father. And no more interested in ranching than his father had been.

Her first glimpse of the ranch hadn't surprised her, though it wasn't what many children might've expected after years of exposure to western cinema. It was vast, and somehow tidy. Paddocks, stables, barns, and the sturdy charm of the ranch house itself. Even at ten, even after one look, Jillian had known she hadn't been meant for the streets and sidewalks of Chicago, but for this open sky and endless land. At ten, she'd had her first experience with love at first sight.

But it wasn't love at first sight with her grandfather. He'd been a tough, weathered, opinionated old man. The ranch and his herd had been his life. He hadn't the least idea what to do with a spindly girl who happened to be his son's daughter. They'd circled each other warily for days, until he'd made the mistake of letting out some caustic remark about her father and his choice of pills and needles. Quick-tempered, Jillian had flown to her father's defense. They'd ended up shouting at each other, Jillian red-faced and dry-eyed even after being threatened with a razor strap.

They'd parted at the end of that visit with a combination of mutual respect and dislike. Then he'd sent her a custom-made, buff-colored Stetson for her birthday. And it began . . .

Perhaps they'd grown to love one another so deeply because they'd taken their time about it. Those sporadic weeks during her adolescence he'd taught her everything, hardly seeming to teach at all: how to gauge the weather by the smell of the air, the look of the sky; how to deliver a breech calf;

how to ride fence and herd a steer. She'd called him Clay because they'd been friends. And when she'd tried her first and only plug of tobacco, he'd held her head when she'd been sick. He hadn't lectured.

When his eyes had grown weak, Jillian had taken over the books. They'd never discussed it—just as they'd never discussed that her move there in the summer of her twentieth year would be permanent. When his illness had begun to take over, she'd gradually assumed the responsibilities of the ranch, though no words had passed between them to make it official.

When he died, the ranch was hers. Jillian hadn't needed to hear the will read to know it. Clay had known she would stay. She'd left the east behind—and if there were memories from there that still twisted inside her, she buried them. More easily than she'd buried her grandfather.

It was herself she grieved for, and knowing it made her impatient. Clay had lived long and hard, doing as he chose the way he chose. His illness had wasted him, and would have brought him pain and humiliation had it continued. He would have hated that, would have railed at her if he could have seen how she'd wept over him.

God Almighty, girl! What're you wasting time here for? Don't you know there's a ranch to run? Get some hands out to check the fence in the west forty before we've got cattle roaming all over Montana.

Yes, she thought with a half smile. He'd have said something like that—cursed her a bit, then would've turned away with a grunt. Of course, she'd have cursed right back at him.

"You mangy old bear," she muttered. "I'm going to turn Utopia into the best ranch in Montana just to spite you." Laughing, she threw her face up to the sky. "See if I don't!"

Sensing her change of mood, the mare began to dance impatiently, tossing her head. "All right, Delilah." Jillian leaned over to pat her creamy neck. "We've got all afternoon." In a deft move she turned the mare around and started off at an easy lope.

There weren't many free hours like this, so they were prized. As it was, Jillian knew she'd stolen them. That made it all the sweeter. If she had to work eighteen hours tomorrow to make up for it, she'd do it without complaint. Even the bookwork, she thought with a sigh. Though there was that sick heifer that needed watching, and the damn Jeep that'd broken down for the third time this month. And the fence along the boundary line. The Murdock boundary line, she thought with a grimace.

The feud between the Barons and the Murdocks stretched back to the early 1900s when Noah Baron, her great-grandfather, came to southeast Montana. He'd meant to go on, to the mountains and the gold, but had stayed to homestead. The Murdocks had already been there, with their vast, rich ranch. The Barons had been peasants to them, intruders doomed to fail—or to be driven out. Jillian gritted her teeth as she remembered the stories her grandfather had told her: cut fences, stolen cattle, ruined crops.

But the Barons had stayed, survived, and succeeded. No, they didn't have the amount of land the Murdocks did, or the money, but they knew how to make the best use of what they did have. If her grandfather had struck oil as the Murdocks had, Jillian thought with a smirk, they could have afforded to specialize in purebred beef as well. That had been a matter of chance, not skill.

She told herself she didn't care about the purebred part of it. Let the Murdock clan wave their blue ribbons and shout about improving the line. She'd raise her Herefords and shorthorns and get the best price for them at the Exchange. Baron beef was prime, and everyone knew it.

When was the last time one of the high-and-mighty Murdocks rode the miles of fence, sweating under the sun while checking for a break? When was the last time one of them had eaten dust on a drive? Jillian knew for a fact that Paul J. Murdock, her grandfather's contemporary, hadn't bothered to ride fence or flank cattle in more than a year.

She let out a short, derisive laugh. All they knew about were the figures in the account books and politicking. By the time she was finished, Utopia would make the Double M look like a dude ranch.

The idea put her in a better mood, so that the line between her brows vanished. She wouldn't think of the Murdocks today, or of the backbreaking work that promised to begin before the sun came up tomorrow. She would think only of the sweetness of these stolen hours, of the rich smell of spring . . . and the endless hard blue of the sky.

Jillian knew this path well. It ran along the westernmost tip of her land. Too tough for the plow, too stubborn for grazing, it was left alone. It was here she always came when she wanted both a sense of solitude and excitement. No one else came here, from her own ranch or from the Murdock spread that ran parallel to it. Even the fence that had once formed the boundary had fallen years before, and had been forgotten. No one cared about this little slice of useless land but her, which made her care all the more.

Now there were a few trees, the cottonwood and aspen just beginning to green. Over the sound of the mare's hooves she heard a warbler begin to sing. There might be coyotes too, and certainly rattlesnakes. Jillian wasn't so enchanted she didn't remember that. There was a rifle, oiled and loaded, strapped to the back of her saddle.

The mare scented the water from the pond, and Jillian let her have her head. The thought of stripping off her sweaty clothes and diving in appealed immensely. Five minutes in that clear, icy water would be exhilarating, and Delilah could rest and drink before they began the long trip back. Spotting the glistening water, Jillian let the reins drop, relaxing. Her grandfather would have cursed her for her lack of attention, but she was already thinking about the luxury of sliding naked into the cold water, then drying in the sun.

But the mare scented something else. Abruptly she reared, plunging so that Jillian's first thought was rattler. While she struggled to control Delilah with one hand, she reached behind for the rifle. Before she could draw a breath, she was hurtling through space. Jillian only had time for one muttered oath before she landed bottom first in the pond. But she'd seen that the rattlesnake had legs.

Sputtering and furious, she struggled to her feet, wiping her wet hair out of her eyes so that she could glare at the man astride a buckskin stallion. Delilah danced nervously while he held the glistening stallion still.

He didn't need to have his feet on the ground for her to see that he was tall. His hair was dark, waving thick and long beneath a black Stetson that shadowed a raw-boned, weathered face. His nose was straight and aristocratic, his mouth well shaped and solemn. Jillian didn't take the time to admire the way he sat the stallion—with a casual sort of control that exuded confidence and power. What she did see was that his eyes were nearly as black as his hair. And laughing.

Narrowing her own, she spat at him, "What the hell are you doing on my land?"

He looked at her in silence, the only movement a very slow lifting of his left brow. Unlike Jillian, he was taking the time to admire. Her fiery hair was darkened almost to copper with the water and clung wetly to accent the elegance of bone and skin—fine boned, honey-toned skin. He could see the flash of green that was her eyes, dark as jade and dangerous as a cat's. Her mouth, clamped together in fury, had a luxuriously full, promising lower lip that contrasted with the firm stubborn chin.

Casually he let his gaze slide down. She was a long one, he thought, with hardly more curves than a boy. But just now, with the shirt wet and snug as a second skin . . . Slowly his gaze climbed back to hers. She didn't blush at the survey, though she recognized it. There wasn't apprehension or fear in her eyes. Instead, she shot him a hard look that might have withered another man.

"I said," Jillian began in a low, clipped voice, "what the hell are you doing on my land?"

Instead of answering he swung out of the saddle—the move smooth and economic enough to tell her he'd been in and out of one most of his life. He walked toward her with a loose, easy stride that still carried the air of command. Then he smiled. In one quick flash his face changed from dangerously sexy to dangerously charming. It was a smile that said, you can trust me . . . for the moment. He held out a hand.

"Ma'am."

Jillian drew in one deep breath and let it out again. Ignoring the offered hand, she climbed out of the water by herself. Dripping, cold, but far from cooled off, Jillian stuck her hands on her hips. "You haven't answered my question."

Nerve, he thought, still studying her. She's got plenty of that. Temper and—he noticed the way her chin was thrown up in challenge—arrogance. He liked the combination. Hooking his thumbs in his pockets, he shifted his weight, thinking it was a shame she'd dry off quickly in the full sun.

"This isn't your land," he said smoothly, with only a hint of a western drawl. "Miss . . ."

"Baron," Jillian snapped. "And who the hell are you to tell me this isn't my land?"

He tipped his hat with more insolence than respect.

"Aaron Murdock." His lips twitched at her hiss of breath. "Boundary runs straight up through here." He looked down at the toes of his boots inches away from the toes of hers as if he could see the line drawn there. "Cuts about clean down the middle of the pond." He brought his gaze back to hers— mouth solemn, eyes laughing. "I think you landed on my side."

Aaron Murdock, son and heir. Wasn't he supposed to be out in Billings playing in their damn oil fields? Frowning, Jillian decided he didn't look like the smooth college boy her grandfather had described to her. That was something she'd think about later. Right now, it was imperative she make her stand, and make it stick.

"*If* I landed on your side," she said scathingly, "it was because you were lurking around with that." She jerked her thumb at his horse. Gorgeous animal, she thought with an admiration she had to fight to conceal.

"Your hands were slack on the reins," he pointed out mildly.

The truth of it only added fuel to the fire. "His scent spooked Delilah."

"Delilah." A flicker of amusement ran over his face as he pushed back his hat and studied the smooth clean lines of Jillian's mare. "Must've been fate," he murmured. "Samson." At the sound of his name the stallion walked over to nuzzle Aaron's shoulder.

Jillian choked back a chuckle, but not in time to conceal the play of a small dimple at the side of her mouth. "Just remember what Samson's fate was," she retorted. "And keep him away from my mare."

"A mighty pretty filly," Aaron said easily. While he stroked his horse's head his eyes remained on Jillian. "A bit highstrung," he continued, "but well built. She'd breed well."

Jillian's eyes narrowed again. Aaron found he liked the way they glinted through the thick, luxurious lashes. "I'll worry about her breeding, Murdock." She planted her feet in the ground that soaked up the water still dripping from her. "What're you doing up here?" she demanded. "You won't find any oil."

Aaron tilted his head. "I wasn't looking for any. I wasn't looking for a woman either." Casually he reached over and lifted a strand of her heavy hair. "But I found one."

Jillian felt that quick, breathless pressure in her chest and recognized it. Oh, no, she'd let that happen to her once before. She let her gaze drop down to where his long brown fingers toyed with the ends of her hair, then lifted it to his face again. "You wouldn't want to lose that hand," she said softly.

For a moment, his fingers tightened, as if he considered picking up the challenge she'd thrown down. Then, as casually as he'd captured her hair, he released it. "Testy, aren't you?" Aaron said mildly. "But then, you Barons've always been quick to draw."

"To defend," Jillian corrected, standing her ground.

They measured each other a moment, both surprised to find the opposition so attractive. Tread carefully. The command went through each of their minds, though it was an order both habitually had trouble carrying out.

"I'm sorry about the old man," Aaron said at length. "He'd have been your—grandfather?"

Jillian's chin stayed up, but Aaron saw the shadow that briefly clouded her eyes. "Yes."

She'd loved him, Aaron thought with some surprise. From his few run-ins with Clay Baron, he'd found a singularly unlovable man. He let his memory play back with the snatches of information he'd gleaned since his return to the Double M. "You'd be the little girl who spent some summers here years back," he commented, trying to remember if he'd ever caught sight of her before. "From back east." His hand came back to stroke his chin, a bit rough from the lack of razor that morning. "Jill, isn't it?"

"Jillian," she corrected coldly.

"Jillian." The swift smile transformed his face again. "It suits you better."

"Miss Baron suits me best," she told him, damning his smile.

Aaron didn't bother to acknowledge her deliberate unfriendliness, instead giving in to the urge to let his gaze slip briefly to her mouth again. No, he didn't believe he'd seen her before. That wasn't a mouth a man forgot. "If Gil Haley's running things at Utopia, you should do well enough."

She bristled. He could almost see her spine snap straight. "I run things at Utopia," she said evenly.

His mouth tilted at one corner. "You?"

"That's right, Murdock, me. I haven't been pushing papers in Billings for the last five years." Something flashed in his eyes, but she ignored it and plunged ahead. "Utopia's mine, every inch of ground, every blade of grass. The difference is I work it instead of strutting around the State Fair waving my blue ribbons."

Intrigued, he took her hands, ignoring her protest as he turned them over to study the palms. They were slender, but hard and capable. Running his thumb over a line of callus, Aaron felt a ripple of admiration—and desire. He'd grown very weary of pampered helpless hands in Billings. "Well, well," he murmured, keeping her hands in his as he looked back into her eyes.

She was furious—that his hands were so strong, that they held hers so effortlessly. That her heartbeat was roaring in her ears. The warbler had begun to sing again, and she could hear the gentle swish of the horses' tails as they stood.

He smelled pleasantly of leather and sweat. Too pleasantly. There was a rim of amber around the outside of his irises that only accented the depth of brown. A scar, very thin and white, rode along the edge of his jaw. You wouldn't notice it unless you looked very closely. Just as you might not notice how strong and lean his hands were unless yours were caught in them.

Jillian snapped back quickly. It didn't pay to notice things like that. It didn't pay to listen to that roaring in your head. She'd done that once before and where had it gotten her? Dewy-eyed, submissive, and softheaded. She was a lot smarter than she'd been five years before. The most important thing was to remember who he was—a Murdock. And who she was—a Baron.

"I warned you about your hands before," she said quietly.

"So you did," Aaron agreed, watching her face. "Why?"

"I don't like to be touched."

"No?" His brow lifted again, but he didn't yet release her hands. "Most living things do—if they're touched properly." His eyes locked on hers abruptly, very direct, very intuitive. "Someone touch you wrong once, Jillian?"

Her gaze didn't falter. "You're trespassing, Murdock."

Again, that faint inclination of the head. "Maybe. We could always string the fence again."

She knew he hadn't misunderstood her. This time, when she tugged on her hands, he released them. "Just stay on your side," she suggested.

He adjusted his hat so that the shadow fell over his face again. "And if I don't?"

Her chin came up. "Then I'll have to deal with you." Turning her back, she walked to Delilah and gathered the reins. It took an effort not to pass her hand over the buckskin stallion, but she resisted. Without looking at Aaron, Jillian swung easily into the saddle, then fit her own damp, flat-brimmed hat back on her head. Now she had the satisfaction of being able to look down at him.

In a better humor, Jillian leaned on the saddle horn. Leather creaked easily beneath her as Delilah shifted her weight. Her shirt was drying warm on her back. "You have a nice vacation, Murdock," she told him with a faint smile. "Don't wear yourself out while you're here."

He reached up to stroke Delilah's neck. "Now, I'm going to try real hard to take your advice on that, Jillian."

She leaned down a bit closer. "Miss Baron."

Aaron surprised her by tugging the brim of her hat down to her nose. "I like Jillian." He grabbed the string tie of the hat before she could straighten, then gave her a long, odd look.

"I swear," he murmured, "you smell like something a man could just close his eyes and wallow in."

She was amused. Jillian told herself she was amused while she pretended not to feel the quick trip of her pulse. She removed his hand from the string of her hat, straightened, and smiled. "You disappoint me. I'd've thought a man who'd spent so much time in college and the big city would have a snappier line and a smoother delivery."

He slipped his hands into his back pockets as he looked up at her. It was fascinating to watch the way the sun shot into her eyes without drawing out the smallest fleck of gold or gray in that cool, deep green. The eyes were too stubborn to allow for any interference; they suited the woman. "I'll practice," Aaron told her with the hint of a smile. "I'll do better next time."

She gave a snort of laughter and started to turn her horse. "There won't be a next time."

His hand was firm on the bridle before she could trot off. The look he gave her was calm, and only slightly amused. "You look smarter than that, Jillian. We'll have a number of next times before we're through."

She didn't know how she'd lost the advantage so quickly, only that she had. Her chin angled. "You seem determined to lose that hand, Murdock."

He gave her an easy smile, patted Delilah's neck, then turned toward his own horse. "I'll see you soon, Jillian."

She waited, seething, until he'd swung into the saddle. Delilah sidestepped skittishly until the horses were nearly nose to nose. "Stay on your own side," Jillian ordered, then pressed in her heels. The straining mare lunged forward.

Samson tossed his head and pranced as they both watched Jillian race off on Delilah. "Not this time," Aaron murmured to himself, soothing his horse. "But soon." He gave a quick laugh, then pointed his horse in the opposite direction. "Damn soon."

Jillian could get rid of a lot of anger and frustration with the speed and the wind. She rode as the mare wanted—fast. Perhaps Delilah needed to outrace her blood as well, Jillian thought wryly. Both male animals had been compelling. If the stallion had belonged to anyone but a Murdock, she would've found a way to have Delilah bred with him—no matter what the stud fee. If she had any hope of increasing and improving Utopia's line of horses, the bulk of the burden rested with her own mare. And there wasn't a stallion on her ranch that could compare with Murdock's Samson.

It was a pity Aaron Murdock hadn't been the smooth, fastidious, boring businessman she'd envisioned him to be. That type would never have made her blood heat. A woman in her position couldn't afford to acknowledge that kind of attraction, especially with a rival. It would put her at an immediate disadvantage when she needed every edge she could get.

So much depended on the next six months if she was going to have the chance to expand. Oh, the ranch could go on, making its cozy little profit, but she wanted more. The fire of her grandfather's ambition hadn't dimmed so much with age as it had been transferred to her. With her youth and energy, and with that fickle lady called luck, she could turn Utopia into the empire her ancestors had dreamed about.

She had the land and the knowledge. She had the skill and the determination. Already, Jillian had poured the cash portion of her inheritance back into the ranch. She'd put a down payment on the small plane her grandfather had been too stubborn to buy. With a plane, the ranch could be patrolled in hours, stray cattle spotted, broken fences reported. Though she still believed in the necessity of a skilled puncher and cow pony, Jillian understood the beauty of mixing new techniques with the old.

Pickups and Jeeps roamed the range as well as horses. CBs could be used to communicate over long distances, while the lariat was still carried by every hand—in the saddle or behind the wheel. The cattle would be driven to feed lots when necessary and the calves herded into the corral for branding, though the iron would be heated by a butane torch rather than an open fire. Times had changed, but the spirit and the code remained.

Above all, the rancher, like any other country person, depended on two things: the sky and the earth. Because the first was always fickle and the second often unyielding, the rancher had no choice but to rely, ultimately, on himself. That was Jillian's philosophy.

With that in mind, she changed directions without changing her pace. She'd ride along the Murdock boundary and check the fences after all.

She trotted along an open pasture while broad-rumped, white-faced Herefords barely glanced up from their grazing. The spring grass was growing thick and full. Hearing the rumble of an engine, she stopped. In almost the same manner as her mount, Jillian scented the air. Gasoline. It was a shame to spoil the scent of grass and cattle with it. Philosophically she turned Delilah in the direction of the sound and rode.

It was easy to spot the battered pickup in the rolling terrain. Jillian lifted her hand in half salute and rode toward it. Her mood had lifted again, though her jeans were still damp and her boots soggy. She considered Gil Haley one of the few dyed-in-the-wool cowboys left on her ranch or any other. A hundred years before, he'd have been happy riding the range with his saddle, bedroll, and plug of tobacco. If he had the chance, she mused, he'd be just as happy that way today.

"Gil." Jillian stopped Delilah by the driver's window and grinned at him.

"You disappeared this morning." His greeting was brusque in a voice that sounded perpetually peppery. He didn't expect an explanation, nor would she have given one.

Jillian nodded to the two men with him, another breed of cowhand, distinguished by their heavy work shoes. Gil might give in to the pickup because he could patrol fifty thousand acres quicker and more thoroughly than on horseback, but he'd never give up his boots. "Any problem?"

"Dumb cow tangled in the wire a ways back." He shifted his tobacco plug while looking up at her with his perpetual squint. "Got her out before she did any damage. Looks like we've got to clear out some of that damn tumbleweed again. Knocked down some line."

Jillian accepted this with a nod. "Anyone check the fence along the west section today?"

There was no change in the squint as he eyed her. "Nope."

"I'll see to it now, then." Jillian hesitated. If there was anyone who knew the gossip, it would be Gil. "I happened to run into Aaron Murdock about an hour ago," she put in casually. "I thought he was in Billings."

"Nope."

Jillian gave him a mild look. "I realize that, Gil. What's he doing around here?"

"Got himself a ranch."

Gamely Jillian hung on to her temper. "I realize that too. He's also got himself an oil field—or his father does."

"Kid sister married herself an oil man," Gil told her. "The old man did some shifting around and got the boy back where he wants him."

"You mean . . ." Jillian narrowed her eyes. "Aaron Murdock's staying on the Double M?"

"Managing it," Gil stated, then spit expertly. "Guess things've simmered down after the blowup a few years back. Murdock's getting on, you know, close on to seventy or more. Maybe he wants to sit back and relax now."

"Managing it," Jillian muttered. So she was going to be plagued with a Murdock after all. At least she and the old man had managed to stay out of each other's way. Aaron had already invaded what she considered her private haven—even if he did own half of it. "How long's he been back?"

Gil took his time answering, tugging absently at the grizzled gray mustache that hung over his lip—a habit Jillian usually found amusing. "Couple weeks."

And she'd already plowed into him. Well, she'd had five years of peace, Jillian reminded herself. In country with this much space, she should be able to avoid one man without too much trouble. There were other questions she wanted to ask, but they'd wait until she and Gil were alone.

"I'll check the fence," she said briefly, then turned the mare and rode west.

Gil watched her with a twinkle. He might squint, but his eyesight was sharp enough to have noticed her damp clothes. And the fire in her eyes. Ran into Aaron Murdock, did she? With a wheeze and a chuckle, he started the pickup. It gave a man something to speculate on.

"Keep your eyes front, son," he grumbled to the young hand who was craning his neck to get a last look of Jillian as she galloped over the pasture.

CHAPTER 2

The day began before sunrise. There was stock to be fed, eggs to be gathered, cows to be milked. Even with machines, capable hands were needed. Jillian had grown so accustomed to helping with the early-morning chores, it never occurred to her to stop now that she was the owner. Ranch life was a routine that varied only in the number of animals to be tended and the weather in which you tended them.

It was pleasantly cool when Jillian made the trip from the ranch house to the stables, but she'd crossed the same ground when the air had been so hot and thick it seemed to stick to her skin, or when the snow had been past her boot tops. There was only a faint lessening in the dark, a hint of color in the eastern sky, but the ranch yard already held signs of life. She caught the scent of grilled meat and coffee as the ranch cook started breakfast.

Men and women went about their chores quietly, with an occasional oath, or a quick laugh. Because all of them had just been through a Montana winter, this sweet spring morning was prized. Spring gave way to summer heat, and summer drought, too quickly.

Jillian crossed the concrete passageway and opened

Delilah's stall. As always, she would tend her first before going on to the other horses, then the dairy cows. A few of the men were there before her, measuring out grain, filling troughs. There was the click of boot heels on concrete, the jingle of spurs.

Some of them owned their own horses, but the bulk of them used Utopia's line. All of them owned their own saddles. Her grandfather's hard-and-fast rule.

The stables smelled comfortably of horses and hay and sweet grain. By the time the stock had been fed and led out to the corrals, it was nearly light. Automatically, Jillian headed for the vast white barn where cows waited to be milked.

"Jillian."

She stopped, waiting for Joe Carlson, her herdsman, to cross the ranch yard. He didn't walk like a cowboy, or dress like one, simply because he wasn't one. He had a smooth, even gait that suited his rather cocky good looks. The early sun teased out the gold in his curling hair. He rode a Jeep rather than a horse and preferred a dry wine to beer, but he knew cattle. Jillian needed him if she was to make a real success out of what was now just dabbling in the purebred industry. She'd hired him six months before over her grandfather's grumbles, and didn't regret it.

"Morning, Joe."

"Jillian." He shook his head when he reached her, then pushed back the powder-gray hat he kept meticulously clean. "When are you going to stop working a fifteen-hour day?"

She laughed and started toward the dairy barn again, matching her longer, looser stride with his. "In August, when I have to start working an eighteen-hour day."

"Jillian." He put a hand on her shoulder, stopping her at the entrance of the barn. His hand was neat and well shaped, tanned but not callused. For some reason it reminded her of a stronger hand, a harder one. She frowned at the horizon.

"You know it's not necessary for you to tie yourself down to every aspect of this ranch. You've got enough hands working for you. If you'd hire a manager . . ."

It was an old routine and Jillian answered it in the usual way. "I am the manager," she said simply. "I don't consider the ranch a toy or a tax break, Joe. Before I hire someone to take over for me, I'll sell out."

"You work too damn hard."

"You worry too much," she countered, but smiled. "I appreciate it. How's the bull?"

Joe's teeth flashed, straight, even, and white. "Mean as ever, but he's bred with every cow we've let within ten feet of him. He's a beauty."

"I hope so," Jillian murmured, remembering just what the purebred Hereford bull had cost her. Still, if he was everything Joe had claimed, he was her start in improving the quality of Utopia's beef.

"Just wait till the calves start dropping," Joe advised, giving her shoulder a quick squeeze. "You want to come take a look at him?"

"Mmmm, maybe later." She took a step inside the barn, then shot a look over her shoulder. "I'd like to see that bull take the blue ribbon over the Murdock entry in July." She grinned, quick and insolent. "Damned if I wouldn't."

By the time the stock had been fed and Jillian had bolted down her own breakfast, it was full light. The long hours and demands should have kept her mind occupied. They always had. Between her concerns over feed and wages and fence, there shouldn't have been room for thoughts of Aaron Murdock. But there was. Jillian decided that once she had the answers to her questions she'd be able to put him out of her mind. So she'd better see about getting them. She hailed Gil before he could climb into his pickup.

"I'm going with you today," she told him as she hopped into the passenger's seat.

He shrugged and spit tobacco out the window. "Suit yourself."

Jillian grinned at the greeting and pushed her hat back on her head. A few heavy red curls dipped over her brow. "Why is it you've never gotten married, Gil? You're such a charmer."

Beneath his grizzled mustache his lips quivered. "Always was a smart aleck." He started the engine and aimed his squint at her. "What about you? You might be skinny, but you ain't ugly."

She propped a booted foot on his dash. "I'd rather run my own life," she said easily. "Men want to tell you what to do and how to do it."

"Woman ain't got no business out here on her own," Gil said stubbornly as he drove out of the ranch yard.

"And men do?" Jillian countered, lazily examining the toe of her boot.

"Men's different."

"Better?"

He shifted, knowing he was already getting out of his depth. "Different," he said again and clamped his lips.

Jillian laughed and settled back. "You old coot," she said fondly. "Tell me about this blowup at the Murdocks'."

"Had a few of them. They're a hardheaded bunch."

"So I've heard. The one that happened before Aaron Murdock went to Billings."

"Kid had lots of ideas when he come back from college." He snorted at education in the way of a man who considered the best learning came from doing. "Maybe some of them were right enough," he conceded. "Always was smart, and knew how to sit a horse."

"Isn't that why he went to college?" Jillian probed. "To get ideas?"

Gil grunted. "Seems the old man felt the boy was taking over too quick. Rumor is the boy agreed to work for his father for three years, then he was supposed to take over. Manage the place like."

Gil stopped at a gate and Jillian climbed out to open it, waiting until he'd driven through before closing and locking it behind her. Another dry day, she thought with a glance at the sky. They'd need some rain soon. A pheasant shot out of the field to her right and wheeled with a flash of color into the sky. She could smell sweet clover.

"So?" she said when she hopped into the truck again.

"So when the three years was up, the old man balked. Wouldn't give the boy the authority they'd agreed on. Well, they got tempers, those Murdocks." He grinned, showing off his dentures. "The boy up and quit, said he'd start his own spread."

"That's what I'd've done," Jillian muttered. "Murdock had no right to go back on his word."

"Maybe not. But he talked the boy into going to Billings 'cause there was some trouble there with the books and such. Nobody could much figure why he did it, unless the old man made it worth his while."

Jillian sneered. Money, she thought derisively. If Aaron had had any guts, he'd've thumbed his nose at his father and started his own place. Probably couldn't handle the idea of starting from the ground up. But she remembered his face, the hard, strong feel of his hand. Something, she thought, puzzled, just didn't fit.

"What do you think of him, Gil—personally?"

"Who?"

"Aaron Murdock," she snapped.

"Can't say much," Gil began slowly, rubbing a hand over his face to conceal another grin. "Was a bright kid and full of sass, like one or two others I've known." He gave a hoot when Jillian narrowed her eyes at him. "Wasn't afraid of work neither. By the time he'd grown whiskers, he had the ladies sighing over him too." Gil put a hand to his heart and gave

an exaggerated sigh of his own. Jillian punched him enthusi-
astically in the arm.

"I'm not interested in his love life, Gil," she began and then
immediately changed gears. "He's never married?"

"Guess he figured a woman might want to tell him what
to do and how to do it," Gil returned blandly.

Jillian started to swear at him, then laughed instead.
"You're a clever old devil, Gil Haley. Look here!" She put a
hand on his arm. "We've got calves."

They got out to walk the pasture together, taking a head
count and enjoying one of the first true pleasures of spring:
new life.

"These'd be from the new bull." Jillian watched a calf
nurse frantically while its mother half dozed in the sun.

"Yep." Gil's squint narrowed further while he skimmed
over the grazing herd and the new offspring. "I reckon Joe
knows what he's about," he murmured and rubbed his chin.
"How many younguns you count?"

"Ten and looks like twenty more cows nearly ready to
drop." She frowned over the numbers a moment. "Wasn't
there—" Jillian broke off as a new sound came over the bored
mooing and rustling. "Over there," she said even as Gil started
forward.

They found him collapsed and frightened beside his dying mother. A day old, no more than two, Jillian estimated
as she gathered up the calf, crooning to him. The cow lay
bleeding, barely breathing. The birth had gone wrong. Jillian
didn't need Gil to tell her that. The cow had survived the
breech, then had crawled off to die.

If the plane had been up . . . Jillian thought grimly as Gil
walked silently back to the pickup. If the plane had been
up, someone would've spotted her from the air, and . . . She
shook her head and nuzzled the calf. This was the price of it,
she reminded herself. You couldn't mourn over every cow or
horse you lost in the course of a year. But when she saw Gil

returning with his rifle, she gave him a look of helpless grief. Then she turned and walked away.

One shudder rippled through her at the sound of the shot, then she forced herself to push the weakness away. Still carrying the calf, she went back to Gil.

"Going to have to call for some men on the CB," he told her. "It's going to take more than you and me to load her up." He cupped the calf's head in his hand and studied him. "Hope this one's got some fight in him or he ain't going to make it."

"He'll make it," Jillian said simply. "I'm going to see to it." She went back to the truck, murmuring to soothe the new-born in her arms.

By nine o'clock that evening she was exhausted. Antelope had raced through a hay field and damaged half an acre's crop. One of her men fractured his arm when his horse was spooked by a snake. They'd found three breaks in the wire along the Murdock boundary and some of her cows had strayed. It had taken the better part of the day to round them up again and repair the fence.

Every spare minute Jillian had been able to scrape together had been dedicated to the orphaned calf. She'd given him a warm, dry stall in the cattle barn and had taken charge of his feeding herself. She ended her day there, with one low light burning and the scent and sound of animals around her.

"Here, now." She sat cross-legged on the fresh hay and stroked the calf's small white face. "You're feeling better." He let out a high, shaky sound that made her laugh. "Yes, Baby, I'm your momma now."

To her relief he took the nipple easily. Twice before, she'd had to force-feed him. This time, she had to take a firm hold on the bottle to prevent him from tugging it right out of her hand. He's catching on, she thought, stroking him as he sucked. It's a tough life, but the only one we've got.

"Pretty Baby," she murmured, then laughed when he wob-bled and sat down hard, back legs spread, without releasing the nipple. "Go ahead and be greedy." Jillian tilted the bottle higher. "You're entitled." His eyes clung to hers as he pulled in his feed. "In a few months you'll be out in the pasture with the rest of them, eating grass and raising hell. I've got a feeling about you, Baby," she said thoughtfully as she scratched his ears. "You might just be a real success with the ladies."

When he started to suck air, Jillian pulled the nipple away. The calf immediately began to nibble at her jeans. "Idiot, you're not a goat." Jillian gave him a gentle shove so that he rolled over and lay, content to have her stroke him.

"Making a pet out of him?"

She whipped her head around quickly and stared up at Aaron Murdock. While he watched, the laughter died out of her eyes. "What are you doing here?"

"One of your favorite questions," he commented as he stepped inside the stall. "Nice-looking calf." He crouched beside her.

Sandalwood and leather. Jillian caught just a whiff of it on him and automatically shifted away. She wanted no scent to creep up and remind her of him when he was gone. "Did you take a wrong turn, Murdock?" she asked dryly. "This is my ranch."

Slowly, he turned his head until their eyes met. Aaron wasn't certain just how long he'd stood watching her—he hadn't intended to watch at all. Maybe it had been the way she'd laughed, that low, smoky sound that had a way of rippling along a man's skin. Maybe it had been the way her hair had glistened—firelike in the low light. Or maybe it had just been that softness he'd seen in her eyes when she'd murmured to the calf. There'd been something about that look that had had tiny aches rushing to the surface. A man needed a woman to look at him like that—first thing in the morning, last thing at night.

There was no softness in her eyes now, but a challenge, a defiance. That stirred something in him as well, something he recognized with more ease. Desire was so simple to label. He smiled.

"I didn't take a wrong turn, Jillian. I wanted to talk to you."

She wouldn't allow herself the luxury of shifting away from him again, or him the pleasure of knowing how badly she wanted to. She sat where she was and tilted her chin. "About what?"

His gaze skimmed over her face. He was beginning to wish he hadn't stayed in Billings quite so long. "Horse breeding— for a start."

Excitement flickered into her eyes and gave her away even though she schooled her voice to casual disinterest. "Horse breeding?"

"Your Delilah." Casually he wound her hair around his finger. What kind of secret female trick did she use to make it so soft? he wondered. "My Samson. I'm too romantic to let a coincidence like that pass."

"Romantic, my foot." Jillian brushed his hand aside only to find her fingers caught in his.

"You'd be surprised," Aaron said softly. So softly only a well-tuned ear would have heard the steel in it. "I also know a"—his gaze skimmed insolently over her face again— "prime filly when I see one." He laughed when her eyes flashed at him. "Are you always so ready to wrestle, Jillian?"

"I'm always ready to talk business, Murdock," she countered. *Don't be too anxious.* Jillian remembered her grandfather's schooling well. *Always play your cards close to your chest.* "I might be interested in breeding Delilah with your stallion, but I'll need another look at him first."

"Fair enough. Come by tomorrow—nine."

She wanted to jump at it. Five years in Montana and she'd never seen the Murdock spread. And that stallion . . . Still, she'd been taught too well. "If I can manage it. Middle of the morning's a busy time." Then she was laughing because the calf, weary of being ignored, was butting against her knee. "Spoiled already." Obligingly she tickled his belly.

"Acts more like a puppy than a cow," Aaron stated, but reached over to scratch the calf's ears. It surprised her how gentle his fingers could be. "How'd he lose his mother?"

"Birthing went wrong." She grinned when the calf licked the back of Aaron's hand. "He likes you. Too young to know better."

Amused, Aaron lifted a brow. "Like I said, it's a matter of touching the right way." He slid one lean hand over the calf's head and massaged its neck. "There's one technique for soothing babies, another for breaking horses, and another for gentling a woman."

"Gentling a woman?" Jillian sent him an arch look that held humor rather than annoyance. "That's a remarkable phrase."

"An apt one, in certain cases."

She watched as the calf, satisfied, his belly full, curled up on the hay to sleep. "A typical male animal," Jillian remarked, still smiling, "Apparently, you're another."

There wasn't any heat in the comment, but an acceptance. "Could be," he agreed, "though I wouldn't say you were typical."

Unconsciously relaxed, Jillian studied him. "I don't *think* you meant that as a compliment."

"No, it was an observation. You'd spit a compliment back in my face."

Delighted, Jillian threw back her head and laughed. "Whatever else you are, Murdock, you're not stupid." Still chuckling, she leaned back against the wall of the stall, bringing up one knee and circling it with her hands. At the moment she didn't want to question why she was pleased to have his company.

"I have a first name." A trick of the angle had the light slanting over her eyes, highlighting them and casting her face in shadow. He felt the stir again. "Ever thought of using it?"

"Not really." But that was a lie, she realized. She already thought of him as Aaron. The real trouble was that she thought of him at all. Yet she smiled again, too comfortable to make an issue of it. "Baby's asleep," she murmured.

Aaron glanced over, grinning. Would she still call him Baby when he was a bull weighing several hundred pounds? Probably. "It's been a long day."

"Mmmm." She stretched her arms to the ceiling, feeling her muscles loosen. The exhaustion she dragged into the barn with her had become a rather pleasant fatigue. "They're never long enough. If I had just ten hours more in a week, I'd catch up."

With what? he wondered. Herself? "Ever heard of overachievement, Jillian?"

"Ambition," she corrected. Her eyes met his again and held. "I'm not the one who's willing to settle for what's handed to her."

Temper surged into him so quickly he clenched at the hay under him. It was clear she was referring to his father's ranch and his own position there. His expression remained completely passive as he battled back the need to strike out where he was struck. "Each of us does what he has to do," Aaron said mildly and let the hay sift through his hands.

It annoyed her that he didn't defend himself. She wanted him to give her his excuses, his reasons. It shouldn't matter, Jillian reminded herself. He shouldn't matter. He didn't, she assured herself with something perilously close to panic. Of course he didn't. Rising, she dusted off her jeans.

"I've got paperwork to see to before I turn in."

He rose too, more slowly, so that it was too late when she realized she was backed into the corner of the stall. "Not even going to offer me a cup of coffee, Jillian?"

There was a band of tension at the back of her neck, a thudding at her ribs. She recognized the temper in his eyes, and though she wondered that she hadn't noticed it before, it wasn't his temper that worried her. It was her own shaky pulse. "No," she said evenly. "I'm not."

He hooked his thumbs through his belt loops and studied her lazily. "You've got a problem with manners."

Her chin came up. "Manners don't concern me."

"No?" He smiled then, in a way that made her brace herself. "Then we'll drop them."

In a move too quick for her to evade, he gathered her shirt-front in one hand and yanked her against him. The first shock came from the feel of that long, hard body against hers. "Damn you, Murdock—" The second shock came when his mouth closed over hers.

Oh, no . . . It was that sweet, weak thought that drifted through her mind even as she fought back like a tiger. Oh, no. He shouldn't feel so good, taste so wonderful. She shouldn't want it to go on and on and on.

Jillian shoved against him and found herself caught closer so that she couldn't shove again. She squirmed and only succeeded in driving herself mad at the feel of her body rubbing against his. Stop it! her mind shouted as the fire began to flicker inside her. She couldn't—wouldn't—let it happen. She knew how to outwit desire. For five years she'd done so with hardly an effort. But now . . . now something was sprinting inside her too fast, twisting and turning so that she couldn't grab on and stop it from getting further and further out of her reach.

Her blood began to swim, her hands began to clutch. And her mouth began to answer.

He'd expected her temper. Because his own had peaked, he'd wanted it. He'd known she'd be furious, that she'd fight against him for outmaneuvering her and taking something without her permission. His anger demanded that she fight, just as his desire demanded that he take.

He'd expected her mouth to be soft. Why else would he have wanted to taste it so badly that he'd spent two days thinking of little else? He'd known her body would be firm with only hints of the subtle dips and curves of a woman. It fit unerringly to his as though it had been fashioned to do so. She strained away from him, shifting, making his skin tingle at the friction her movements caused.

Then, abruptly, her arms were clasped around him. Her lips parted, not in surrender but with an urgency that rocked him. If her passion had been simmering, she'd concealed it well. It seemed to explode in one blinding white flash of heat that came from nowhere. Shaken, Aaron drew back, trying to judge his own reaction, fighting to keep his own needs in perspective.

Jillian stared up at him, her breath coming in jerks. Her hair streamed behind her back, catching the light while her eyes glinted in the dark. Her mind was reeling and she shook her head as if to clear it. Just as she began to draw her first coherent thought, he swore and crushed his mouth to hers again.

There was no hint of struggle this time, nor any hint of sur-render. Passion for passion she met him, matching his need with hers, degree by degree. Sandalwood and leather. Now she drew it in, absorbed the aroma as she absorbed the hard, relentless texture of his lips. She let her tongue toy with his while she drank up all those hot, heady male tastes. There was something unapologetically primitive in the way he held her, kissed her. Jillian reveled in it. If she was to take a man, she neither needed nor wanted any polish or gloss that clouded or chipped away so easily.

She let her body take control. How long had she yearned for this? To have someone hold her, spin her away so that she couldn't think, couldn't worry? There were no responsi-bilities here, and the only demands were of the flesh. Here, with a warm, moist mouth on hers, with a hard body against her, she was finally and ultimately only a woman. Selfishly a woman. She'd forgotten just how glorious it could feel, or perhaps she'd never fully known the sensation before.

What was she doing to him? Aaron tried to pull himself back and found his hands were trapped in the thick softness of her hair. He tried to think and found his senses swimming with the scent of her. And the taste . . . A low sound started in his throat as he ravaged her mouth. How could he have known she'd taste like this? Seductive, pungent, alluring. Her flavor held all the lushness her body lacked, and the combination was devastating. He wondered how he'd ever lived without it. With that thought came the knowledge that he was getting in much too deep much too fast.

Aaron drew away carefully because the hands on her shoulders weren't as steady as he'd have liked.

Jillian started to sway and caught herself. Good God, what was she doing? What had she done? As the breath rushed swiftly and unevenly through her lips, she stared up at him. Those dark, wicked looks and clever mouth . . . She'd forgotten. She'd forgotten who she was, and who he was. Forgotten everything but that heady feeling of freedom and heat. He'd use that against her, she thought grimly. If she let him. But something had happened when—

Don't think now! she ordered herself. Just get him out of here before you make a complete fool of yourself. Very carefully, Jillian brushed Aaron's hands from her shoulders. Tilting her chin, she prayed her voice would be steady.

"Well, Murdock, you've had your fun. Now clear out."

Fun? he thought, staring at her. Whatever had happened it didn't have anything to do with fun. The room was tilting a bit, like it had when he'd downed his first six-pack of beer a hundred years before. That hadn't been much fun either, but it'd been a hell of an experience. And he'd paid for it the next day. He supposed he'd pay for this one as well.

He wouldn't apologize, he told himself as he forced

himself to relax. Damned if he would, but he would back off while he still could. Casually he bent down to pick up the hat that had fallen off when her fingers had combed through his hair. He took his time putting it on.

"You're right, Jillian," he said mildly—when he could. "A man would have a hard time resisting a woman like you." He grinned at her and tipped his hat. "But I'll do my best."

"See that you do, Murdock!" she called out after him, then hugged herself because she'd begun to tremble.

Even after his footsteps died away, she waited five full minutes before leaving the barn. When Jillian stepped outside, the ranch yard was dark and quiet. She thought she could just hear the murmur of a television or radio from the bunkhouse. There were a few lights farther down the road where her grandfather had built quarters for the married hands. She stopped and listened, but couldn't hear the engine of whatever vehicle Aaron had used to drive from his ranch to hers.

Long gone, she thought, and turned on her heel to stride to the house. It was a two-story stone-and-wood structure. All native Montana material. The rambling building had been constructed on the site of the original homestead. Her grandfather had been fond of bragging that he'd been born in a house that would have fit into the kitchen of this one. Jillian entered by the front door, which was still never locked.

She'd always loved the space, and the clever use of wood and tile and stone that made up the living area. You could roast one of Utopia's steers in the fireplace. Her grandmother's ivory lace curtains still hung at the windows. Jillian often wished she'd known her. All she knew was that she'd been an Irishwoman with dainty looks and a strong back. Jillian had inherited her coloring and, from her grandfather's accounting, her temper. And perhaps, Jillian thought wryly as she climbed the stairs, her back.

God, she wished she had a woman to talk to. Halfway up the stairs she paused and pressed her fingers to her temple.

Where did that come from? she wondered. As far back as she could remember, she'd never sought out the company of women. So few of them were interested in the same things she was. And, when there was no niggling sexual problem to overcome, she found men easier to deal with.

But now, with the house so empty around her, with her blood still churning, she wished for a woman who might understand the war going on inside her. Her mother? With a quiet laugh, Jillian pushed open the door to her bedroom. If she called her mother and said she was burning up with desire and had no place to put it, the gentle doctor's wife would blush crimson and stammer out a recommendation for a good book on the subject.

No, as fond as she was of her mother, she wasn't a woman who would understand—well, cravings, Jillian admitted, stripping out of her work shirt. If she was going to be honest, that's what she'd felt in Aaron's arms. Perhaps it was all she was capable of feeling. Frowning, she dropped her jeans into a heap on top of her work shirt and walked naked to the bath.

She should probably be grateful she'd felt that. With a jerk of the wrist, she turned the hot water on full, then added a trickle of cold. She'd felt nothing at all for any man in years. Five years, Jillian admitted and dumped in bath salts with a lavish hand. With an expert twist and a couple of pins, she secured her hair to the top of her head.

It was a good thing she remembered Kevin and that very brief, very unhappy affair. Did one night in bed equal an affair? she wondered ruefully, then lowered herself into the steaming water. Whatever you called it, it had been a fiasco. That's what she had to remember. She'd been so young. Jillian could almost—almost—think of it with amusement now.

The young, dewy-eyed virgin, the smooth, charming intern with eyes as clear as a lake. He hadn't talked her into bed, hadn't pressured her. No, Jillian had to admit that she'd wanted to go with him. And he'd been gentle and sweet with her. It had simply been that the words *I love you* had meant two different things to each of them. To Jillian, they'd been a pledge. To him, they'd been a phrase.

She'd learned the hard way that making love didn't equal love or commitment or marriage. He'd laughed at her, perhaps not unkindly, when she'd naively talked of their future together. He hadn't wanted a wife, or even a partner, but a companion willing to share his bed from time to time. His casualness had devastated her.

She'd been willing to mold herself into whatever he'd wanted—a tidy, socially wise doctor's wife like her mother; a clever, dedicated housewife; an organized marriage partner who could juggle career and family. It had taken her months before she'd realized that she'd made a fool of herself over him, taking every compliment or sweet word literally, because that's what she'd wanted to hear. It had taken more time and several thousand miles of distance before she'd been able to admit that he'd done her a favor.

Not only had he saved her from trying to force her personality into a mold that would never have fit, but he'd given her a solid view of the male species. They weren't to be trusted on a personal level. Once you gave them your love, the power to hurt you, you were lost, ready to do anything to please them even at the loss of self.

When she was young, she'd tried to please her father that way and had failed because she was too like her grandfather. The only man she'd ever loved who'd accepted her for what she was had been Clay Baron. And he was gone.

Jillian lay back, closed her eyes, and let the hot water steam away her fatigue. Aaron Murdock wasn't looking for a partner and neither was she. What had happened between them in the barn was a mistake that wouldn't be repeated. He might be looking for a lover, but she wasn't.

Jillian Baron was on her own, and that's the way she liked it.

CHAPTER 3

He wondered if she would come. Aaron drove back from a line camp on a road that had once been fit only for horses or mules. It wasn't in much better shape now. The Jeep bucked along much like a bad-tempered bronc might, dipping into ruts, bounding over rocks. He rather liked it. Just as he'd enjoyed the early morning visit with five of his men at the line camp. If he could spare the time, he would appreciate a few days at one of the camps in unabashedly male company. Hard, sweaty work during the day, a few beers and a poker game at night. Riding herd far enough from the ranch so that you could forget there was civilization anywhere. Yes, he'd enjoy that, but . . .

He appreciated the conservative, traditional ways of his father—particularly when they were mixed with his own experimental ideas. The men would still rope and flank cattle in the open pasture, but two tractors dragging a cable would clear off more brush in a day than axmen could in a month. And a plane . . .

With a wry smile Aaron remembered how he'd fought six years before for the plane his father had considered a foolish luxury. He'd ended up paying for it himself and flying it himself. His father had never admitted that the plane had become indispensable. That didn't matter to Aaron, as long as it was used. He had no desire to push the cowboy out of existence, just to make him sweat a little less.

Downshifting for the decline, he let the Jeep bump its way down the hill. The differences with his father that had come to a head five years before had eased, but not vanished. Aaron knew he'd have to fight for every change, every improvement, every deviation. And he'd win. Paul Murdock might be stubborn, but he wasn't stupid. And he was sick. In six months . . .

Aaron rammed the Jeep back into fourth. He didn't like to dwell on the battle his father was losing. A battle Aaron could do nothing about. Helplessness was something Aaron wasn't accustomed to. He was too much like his father. Perhaps that's why they spent most of their time arguing.

He pushed his father and mortality out of his mind and thought of Jillian. There was life, and youth, and vitality.

Would she come? Grinning, Aaron sped past a pasture covered with mesquite grass. Damn right she would. She'd come if for no other reason than to prove to him that she couldn't be intimidated. She'd throw her chin up and give him one of those cool go-to-hell looks. No wonder he wanted her so badly it caused an ache in the pit of his belly. The ache had burned like fire when he'd kissed her.

There hadn't been a female who'd made him come so close to stammering since Emma Lou Swanson had initiated him into life's pleasures in the hayloft. It was one thing for a teenager to lose the power of speech and reason with soft arms around him, and quite another for it to happen to a grown man who'd made a study of the delights and frustrations of women. Aaron couldn't quite account for it, but he knew he was going to have to have more. Soon.

She was a typical Baron, he decided. Hotheaded, stubborn, opinionated. Aaron grinned again. He figured the main reason the Barons and Murdocks had never gotten on was that they'd been too much alike. She wasn't going to have an easy time taking over the ranch, but he didn't doubt she'd do it. He didn't doubt he was going to enjoy watching her. Almost as much as he was going to enjoy bedding her.

Whistling between his teeth, Aaron braked in front of the ranch house. Over near the cattle barn a dog was barking half-heartedly. Someone was playing a radio by the feed lot—a slow, twangy country lament. There were asters popping up in the flower bed and not a weed in sight. As he climbed out of the Jeep he heard the porch door open and glanced over. His mother walked out, lips curved, eyes weary.

She was so beautiful—he'd never gotten used to it. Very small, very slender, Karen Murdock walked with the gliding step of a runway model. She was twenty-two years younger than her husband, and neither the cold winters nor the bright sun of Montana had dimmed the luster of her skin. His sister had those looks, Aaron mused, the classic blond beauty that went on and on with the years. Karen wore slimming slacks, a rose-colored blouse, with her hair loosely coiled at the neck. She could've walked into the Beverly Wilshire without changing a stitch. If the need had arisen, she could've saddled up a horse and ridden out to string wire.

"Everything all right?" she asked him, holding out a hand.

"Fine. They've rounded up the strays we were losing through the south fence." Studying her face, Aaron took her hand. "You look tired."

"No." She squeezed his fingers as much for support as reassurance. "Your father didn't sleep well last night. You didn't come by to see him."

"That wouldn't've made him sleep any better."

"Arguing with you is about all the entertainment he has these days."

Aaron grinned because she wanted him to. "I'll come in later and tell him about the five hundred acres of mesquite I want to clear."

Karen laughed and put her hands on her son's shoulders.

With her standing on the porch and him on the ground, their eyes were level. "You're good for him, Aaron. No, don't raise your brow at me," she told him mildly.

"When I saw him yesterday morning, he told me to go to the devil."

"Exactly." Her fingers kneaded absently at his shoulders. "I tend to pamper him, even though I shouldn't. He needs you around to make him angry enough to live a bit longer. He knows you're right—that you've been right all along. He's proud of you."

"You don't have to explain him to me." The steel had crept into his voice before he could prevent it. "I know him well enough."

"Almost well enough," Karen murmured, laying her cheek against Aaron's.

When Jillian drove into the ranch yard, she saw Aaron with his arms around a slim, elegant blonde. The surge of jealousy stunned, then infuriated her. He was a man after all, she reminded herself, gripping the steering wheel tightly for a moment. It was so easy for a man to enjoy quick passion in a horse stall one evening, then a sweet embrace in the sunshine the next day. True emotion never entered into it. Why should it? she thought, setting her teeth. She braked sharply beside Aaron's Jeep.

He turned, and while she had the disadvantage of the sun in her eyes, she met his amused look with ice. Not for a moment would she give him the satisfaction of knowing she'd spent a restless, dream-disturbed night. Jillian stepped out of her aging compact and managed not to slam the door.

"Murdock," she said curtly.

"Good morning, Jillian." He gave her a bland smile with something sharper hovering in his eyes.

She walked to him, since he didn't seem inclined to drop

the blonde's hand and come to her. "I've come to see your stud."

"We talked about manners last night, didn't we?" His grin only widened when she glared at him. "I don't think you two have met."

"No, indeed." Karen came down the porch steps, amused by the gleam in her son's eye, and the fire in the woman's. "You must be Jillian Baron. I'm Karen Murdock, Aaron's mother."

As her mouth fell open Jillian turned to look at Mrs. Murdock. Soft, elegant, beautiful. "Mother?" she repeated before she could stop herself.

Karen laughed, and rested a hand on Aaron's shoulder. "I think I've just been given a wonderful compliment."

He grinned down at her. "Or I have."

Laughing again, she turned back to Jillian. Karen filed away her quick assessment. "I'll leave you two to go about your business. Please, stop in for coffee before you go if you've time, Jillian. I have so little opportunity these days to talk with another woman."

"Yes, ah—thank you." With her brows drawn together, Jillian watched her go back through the porch door.

"I don't think you're often at a loss for words," Aaron commented.

"No." With a little shake of her head she looked up at him. "Your mother's beautiful."

"Surprised?"

"No. That is, I'd heard she was lovely, but . . ." Jillian shrugged and wished he'd stop looking down at her with that infernal smile on his face. "You don't look a thing like her."

Aaron swung his arm around her shoulders as they turned away from the house. "You're trying to charm me again, Jillian."

She had to bite down on her lip to keep the chuckle back.

"I've better uses for my time." Though the weight felt good, she plucked his arm away.

"You smell of jasmine," he said lazily. "Did you wear it for me?"

Rather than dignify the question with an answer, Jillian stopped, tilted her chin, and gave him one long icy look that only wavered when he began to laugh. With a careless flick he knocked the hat from her head, pulled her against him, and gave her a hard, thorough kiss. She felt her legs dissolve from the knees down.

Though he released her before she'd even thought to demand it, Jillian gathered her wits quickly enough. "What the hell do you think—"

"Sorry." His eyes were laughing, but he held his hands up, palms out in a gesture of peace. "Lost my head. Something comes over me when you look at me as though you'd like to cut me into small pieces. *Very* small pieces," he added as he took the hat from where it hung at her back and placed it back on her head.

"Next time I won't just look," she said precisely, wheeling away toward the corral.

Aaron fell into step beside her. "How's the calf?"

"He's doing well. Vet's coming by to check him over this afternoon, but he took the bottle again this morning."

"Was he sired by that new bull of yours?" When Jillian sent him a sharp look, Aaron smiled blandly. "Word gets around. As it happens, you snatched him up from under my nose. I was making arrangements to go to England to check him out for myself when I heard you'd bought him."

"Really?" It was news—and news she couldn't help but be pleased to hear.

"Thought that might make your day," Aaron said mildly.

"Nasty of me," Jillian admitted as they came to the corral fence. Resting a foot on the lower rail, she smiled at him. "I'm not a nice person, Murdock."

He gave her an odd look and nodded. "Then we'll deal well enough together. What's the nickname your hands have dubbed that bull?"

Her smile warmed so that the dimple flickered. He was going to have to find out what it felt like to put his lips just there. "The Terror's the cleanest in polite company."

He chuckled. "I don't think that was the one I heard. How many calves so far?"

"Fifty. It's early yet."

"Mmm. Are you using artificial insemination?"

Her eyes narrowed. "Why?"

"Just curious. We are in the same business, Jillian."

"That's not something I'll forget," she said evenly.

Annoyance tightened his mouth. "Which doesn't mean we have to be opponents."

"Doesn't it?" Jillian shifted her hat lower on her forehead. "I came to look at your stud, Murdock."

He stood watching her a moment, long enough, directly enough, to make Jillian want to squirm. "So you did," Aaron said quietly. Plucking a halter from the fence post, he swung lithely over the corral fence.

Rude, Jillian condemned herself. It was one thing to be cautious, even unfriendly, but another to be pointedly rude. It wasn't like her. Frowning, Jillian leaned on the fence and rested her chin in her open hand. Yet she'd been rude to Aaron almost continually since their first encounter. Her frown cleared as she watched him approach the stallion.

Both males were strong and well built, and each was inclined to want his own way. At the moment the stallion wasn't in the mood for the halter. He pranced away from Aaron to lap disinterestedly at his water trough. Aaron murmured something that had Samson shaking his head and trotting off again.

"You devil," she heard Aaron say, but there was a laugh in

his voice. Aaron crossed to him again, and again the stallion danced off in the opposite direction.

Laughing, Jillian climbed the fence and sat on the top rung. "Round 'em up, cowboy," she drawled.

Aaron flashed her a grin, then shrugged as though he'd given up and turned his back on the stallion. By the time he'd crossed the center of the corral, Samson had come up behind him to nudge his head into Aaron's back.

"Now you wanna make up," he murmured, turning to ruffle the horse's mane before he slipped on the halter. "After you've made me look like a greenhorn in front of the lady."

Greenhorn, hell, Jillian thought, watching the way he handled the skittish stallion. If he cared about impressing anyone, he'd have made the difficult look difficult instead of making it look easy. With a sigh, she felt her respect for him go up another notch.

Automatically she reached out to stroke the stallion's neck as Aaron led him to her. He had a coat like silk, and eyes that were wary but not mean. "Aaron . . ." She glanced down in time to see his brow lift at her voluntary use of his name. "I'm sorry," she said simply.

Something flickered in his eyes, but they were so dark it was difficult to read it. "All right," he said just as simply and held out a hand. She took it and hopped down.

"He's beautiful." Jillian ran her hands along Samson's wide chest and sleek flank. "Have you bred him before?"

"Twice in Billings," he said, watching her.

"How long have you had him?" She went to Samson's head, then passed under him to the other side.

"Since he was a foal. It took me five days to catch his father." Jillian looked up and caught the light in his eyes. "There must've been a hundred and fifty mustangs in his herd. He was a cagey devil, damn near killed me the first time I got a rope around him. Then he busted down the stall and nearly got away again. You should've seen him, blood spurting out of his leg, fire in his eyes. It took six of us to control him when we bred him to the mare."

"What did you do with him?" Jillian swallowed, thinking how easy it would be to breed the wild stallion again and again, then geld him. Break his spirit.

Aaron's eyes met hers over Samson's withers. "I let him go. Some things you don't fence."

She smiled. Before she realized it, she reached over Samson for Aaron's hand. "I'm glad."

With his eyes on hers, Aaron stroked a thumb over her knuckles. The palm of his hand was rough, the back of hers smooth. "You're an interesting woman, Jillian, with a few rather appealing soft spots."

Disturbed, she tried to slip her hand from his. "Very few."

"Which is why they're appealing. You were beautiful last night, sitting in the hay, crooning to the calf, with the light in your hair."

She knew about clever words. Why were these making her pulse jerky? "I'm not beautiful," she said flatly. "I don't want to be."

He tilted his head when he realized she was perfectly serious. "Well, we can't have everything we want, can we?"

"Don't start again, Murdock," she ordered, sharply enough that the stallion moved restlessly under their joined hands.

"Start what?"

"You know, I wondered why I always end up being rude to you," she began. "I realize it's simply because you don't understand anything else. Let go of my hand."

His eyes narrowed at her tone. "No." Tightening his hold, he gave the stallion a quick pat that sent him trotting off, leaving nothing between himself and Jillian. "I wondered why I always end up wanting to toss you over my knee—or my shoulder," he added thoughtfully. "Must be for the same reason."

"Your reasons don't interest me, Murdock."

His lips curved slowly, but his eyes held something entirely different from humor. "Now, I might've believed that, Jillian, if it hadn't been for last night." He took a step closer. "Maybe I kissed you first, but, lady, you kissed me right back. I had a whole long night to think about that. And about just what I was going to do about it."

Maybe it was because he'd spoken the truth when she didn't care to hear it. Maybe it had something to do with the wicked gleam in his eyes or the insolence of his smile. It might have been a combination of all three that loosened Jillian's temper. Before she had a chance to think about it, or Aaron a chance to react, she'd drawn back her fist and plunged it hard into his stomach.

"That's what *I* intend to do about it!" she declared as he grunted. She had only a fleeting glimpse of the astonishment on his face before she spun on her heel and strode away. She didn't get far.

Jillian's breath was knocked out of her as he brought her down in a tackle. She found herself flat on her back, pinned under him with a face filled with fury rather than astonishment looming over hers. It only took her a second to fight back, and little more to realize she was outmatched.

"You hellion," Aaron grunted as he held her down. "You've been asking for a thrashing since the first time I laid eyes on you."

"It'll take a better man than you, Murdock." She nearly succeeded in bringing her knee up and scoring a very important point. Instead he shifted until her position was only more vulnerable. Heat that had nothing to do with temper surged into her stomach.

"By God, you tempt me to prove you wrong." She squirmed again and stirred something dangerous in him. "Woman, if you want to fight dirty, you've come to the right place." He closed his mouth over hers before she could swear at him. At the instant of contact he felt the pulse in her wrist bound under his hands. Then he felt nothing but the hot give of her mouth.

If she was still struggling beneath him, he wasn't aware of it. Aaron felt himself sinking, and sinking much deeper than he'd expected. The sun was warm on his back, she was soft under him, yet he felt only that moist, silky texture that was her lips. He thought he could make do with that sensation alone for the rest of his life. It scared him to death.

Pulling himself back, he stared down at her. She'd stolen the breath from him much more successfully this time than she had with the quick jab to the gut. "I ought to beat you," he said softly.

Somehow in her prone position she managed to thrust her chin out. "I'd prefer it." It wasn't the first lie she'd told, but it might have been the biggest.

She told herself a woman didn't want to be kissed by a man who tossed her on the ground. Yet her conscience played back that she'd deserved that at the least. She wasn't a fragile doll and didn't want to be treated like one. But she shouldn't want him to kiss her again . . . want it so badly she could already taste it. "Will you get off me?" she said between her teeth. "You're not as skinny as you look."

"It's safer talking to you this way."

"I don't want to talk to you."

The gleam shot back in his eyes. "Then we won't talk."

Before Jillian could protest, or Aaron could do what he'd intended, Samson lowered his head between their faces.

"Get your own filly," Aaron muttered, shoving him aside.

"He's got a smoother technique than you," Jillian began, then choked on a laugh as the horse bent down again. "Oh, for God's sake, Aaron, let me up. This is ridiculous."

Instead of obliging he looked back down at her. Her eyes were bright with laughter now, her dimple flashing. Her hair spread like fire in the dust. "I'm beginning to like it. You don't do that enough."

She blew the hair out of her eyes. "What?"

"Smile at me."

She laughed again and he felt the arms under his hands relax. "Why should I?"

"Because I like it."

She tried to give a long-winded sigh, but it ended on a chuckle. "If I apologize for hitting you, will you let me up?"

"Don't spoil it—besides, you won't catch me off guard again."

No, she didn't imagine she would. "Well, in any case you deserved it—and you paid me back. Now, get up, Murdock. This ground's hard."

"Is it? You're not." He lifted a brow as he shifted into a more comfortable position. He wondered if her legs would look as nice as they felt. "Anyway, we still have to discuss that remark about my technique."

"The best I can say about it," Jillian began as Aaron pushed absently at Samson's head again, "is that it needs some polishing. If you'll excuse me, I really have to get back. Some of us work for a living."

"Polishing," he murmured, ignoring the rest. "You'd like something a little—smoother." His voice dropped intimately as he brushed his lips over her cheek, light as a whisper. He heard the quick, involuntary sound she made as he moved lazily toward her mouth.

"Don't." Her voice trembled on the word so that he looked down at her again. Vulnerability. It was in her eyes. That, and a touch of panic. He hadn't expected to see either.

"An Achilles' heel," he murmured, moved, aroused. "You've given me an advantage, Jillian." Lifting a hand, he traced her mouth with a fingertip and felt it tremble. "It's only fair to warn you that I'll use it."

"Your only advantage at the moment is your weight."

He grinned, but before he could speak a shadow fell over them.

"Boy, what're you doing with that little lady on the ground?"

Jillian turned her head and saw an old man with sharp, well-defined features and dark eyes. Though he was pale and had an air of fragility, she saw the resemblance. Astonished, she stared at him. Could this bent old man who leaned heavily on a cane, who was so painfully thin, be the much feared and respected Paul Murdock? His eyes, dark and intense as Aaron's, skimmed over her. The hand on the cane had the faintest of tremors.

Aaron looked up at his father and grinned. "I'm not sure yet," he said easily. "It's a choice between beating her or making love."

Murdock gave a wheezing laugh and curled one hand around the rail of the fence. "It's a stupid man who wouldn't know which choice to make, but you'll do neither here. Let the filly up so I can have a look at her."

Aaron obliged, taking Jillian by the arm and hauling her unceremoniously to her feet. She slanted him a killing glare before she looked back at his father. What nasty twist of fate had decided that she would meet Paul J. Murdock for the first time with corral dust clinging to her and her body still warm from his son's? she wondered as she silently cursed Aaron. Then she tossed back her hair and lifted her chin.

Murdock's face remained calm and unexpressive. "So, you're Clay Baron's granddaughter."

She met his steady hawklike gaze levelly. "Yes, I am."

"You look like your grandmother."

Her chin lifted a fraction higher. "So I've been told."

"She was a fire-eater." A ghost of a smile touched his eyes. "Hasn't been a Baron on my land since she marched over here to pay her respects to Karen after the wedding. If some young buck had tried to wrestle with her, she'd have blackened his eye."

Aaron leaned on the fence, running a hand over his stomach. "She hit me first," he drawled, grinning at Jillian. "Hard."

Jillian slipped her hat from her back and meticulously began to dust it off and straighten it. "Better tighten up those muscles, Murdock," she suggested as she set the hat back on her head. "I can hit a lot harder." She glanced over as Paul Murdock began to laugh.

"I always thought I should've thrashed him a sight more. What's your name, girl?"

She eyed him uncertainly. "Jillian."

"You're a pretty thing," he said with a nod. "And it doesn't appear you lack for sense. My wife would be glad for some company."

For a minute she could only stare at him. This was the fierce Murdock—her grandfather's archrival—inviting her into his home? "Thank you, Mr. Murdock."

"Come in for coffee, then," he said briskly, then shot a look at Aaron. "You and I have some business to clear up."

Jillian felt something pass between the two men that wasn't entirely pleasant before Murdock turned to walk back toward the house. "You'll come in," Aaron said as he unlatched the gate. It wasn't an invitation but a statement. Curious, Jillian let it pass.

"For a little while. I've got to get back."

They walked through the gate together and relatched it. Though they moved slowly, they caught up with Murdock as he reached the porch steps. Seeing his struggle to negotiate them with the cane, Jillian automatically started to reach out for his arm. Aaron grabbed her wrist. He shook his head, then waited until his father had painstakingly gained the porch.

"Karen!" It might have been a bellow if it hadn't been so breathless. "You've got company." Murdock swung open the front door and gestured Jillian in.

It was more palatial than Utopia's main building, but had the same western feel that had first charmed a little girl from

Chicago. All the wood was highly polished—the floor, the beams in the ceilings, the woodwork—all satiny oak. But here was something Utopia lacked. That subtle woman's touch.

There were fresh flowers arranged in a pottery bowl, and softer colors. Though Jillian's grandfather had kept the ivory lace curtains at the windows, his ranch house had reverted to a man's dwelling over the years. Until she walked into the Murdock home and felt Karen's presence, Jillian hadn't realized it.

There was a huge Indian rug spread over the floor in the living area and glossy brass urns beside the fireplace that held tall dried flowers. A seat was fashioned into a bow window and piled with hand-worked pillows. The room had a sense of order and welcome.

"Aren't either of you men going to offer Jillian a chair?" Karen asked mildly as she wheeled in a coffee cart.

"She seems to be Aaron's filly," Murdock commented as he lowered himself into a wing-backed chair and hooked his cane over the arm.

Jillian's automatic retort was stifled as Aaron nudged her onto the sofa. Gritting her teeth, she turned to Karen. "You have a lovely home, Mrs. Murdock."

Karen didn't attempt to disguise her amusement. "Thank you. I believe I saw you at the rodeo last year," she continued as she began to pour coffee. "I remember thinking you looked like Maggie—your grandmother. Do you plan to compete again this year?"

"Yes." Jillian accepted the cup, declining cream or sugar. "Even though my foreman squawked quite a bit when I beat his time in the calf roping."

Aaron reached over to toy with her hair. "That tempts me to enter myself."

"It'd be a pretty sorry day when a son of mine couldn't rope a calf quicker than a female," Murdock muttered.

Aaron sent him a bland look. "That would depend on the female."

"You might be out of practice," Jillian said coolly as she sipped her coffee. "After five years behind a desk." As soon as she'd said it, Jillian felt the tension between father and son, a bit more strained, a bit more unpleasant than she'd felt once before.

"I suppose things like that are in the blood," Karen said smoothly. "You've taken to ranch life, but you were raised back east, weren't you?"

"Chicago," Jillian admitted, wondering what she'd stirred up. "I never fit in." It was out before she realized it. A frown flickered briefly in her eyes before she controlled it. "I suppose ranching just skipped a generation in my family," she said easily.

"You have a brother, don't you?" Karen stirred the slightest bit of cream into her own coffee.

"Yes, he's a doctor. He and my father share a practice now."

"I remember the boy—your father," Murdock told her, then chugged down half a cup of coffee. "Quiet, serious fellow who never said three words if two would do."

Jillian had to smile. "You remember him well."

"Easy to understand why Baron left the ranch to you instead." Murdock held out his cup for more coffee, but Jillian noticed that Karen only filled it halfway. "Guess you can't do much better than Gil Haley for running things."

Her dimple flickered. It was, she supposed, a compliment of sorts. "Gil's the best foreman I could ask for," Jillian said mildly. "But I run Utopia."

Murdock's brows drew together. "Women don't run ranches, girl."

Her chin angled. "This one does."

"Nothing but trouble when you start having cowboys in skirts," he said with a snort.

"I don't wear them when I'm hazing cattle."

He set down his cup and leaned forward. "Whatever I felt about your grandfather, it wouldn't sit well with me to see what he worked for blown away because of some female."

"Paul," Karen began, but Jillian was already rolling.

"Clay wasn't so narrow-minded," Jillian shot back. "If a person was capable, it didn't matter what sex they were. I run Utopia, and before I'm done you'll be watching your back door." She rose, unconsciously regal. "I've got work to do. Thank you for the coffee, Mrs. Murdock." She shot a look at Aaron, who was still lounging back on the sofa. "We still have to discuss your stud."

"What's this?" Murdock demanded, banging his cane.

"I'm breeding Samson to one of Jillian's mares," Aaron said easily.

Color surged into Murdock's pale face. "A Murdock doesn't do business with a Baron."

Aaron unfolded himself slowly and stood. "I do business as I please," Jillian heard him say as she started for the door. She was already at her car when Aaron caught up with her.

"What's your fee?" she said between her teeth.

He leaned against the car. If he was angry, she couldn't see it. "You spark easily, Jillian. I'm usually the only one who can put my father in a rage these days."

"Your father," she said precisely, "is a bigot."

With his thumbs hooked idly in his pockets, Aaron studied the house. "Yeah. But he knows his cows."

She let out a long breath because she wanted to chuckle. "About the stud fee, Murdock."

"Come to dinner tonight, we'll talk about it."

"I haven't time for socializing," she said flatly.

"You've been around long enough to know the advantages of a business dinner."

She frowned at the house. An evening with the Murdocks? No, she didn't think she could get through one without throwing something. "Look, Aaron, I'd like to breed Delilah with

Samson—if the terms are right. I'm not interested in anything more to do with you or your family."

"Why?"

"There's been bad blood between the Barons and Murdocks for almost a century."

He gave her a lazy look under lowered lids. "Now who's a bigot?"

Bull's-eye, she thought and sighed. Putting her hands on her hips, she tried to bring her temper to order. Murdock was an old man, and from the looks of him, a sick one. He was also, though she'd choke rather than admit it, a great deal like her grandfather. She'd be a pretty poor individual if she couldn't drum up some understanding. "All right, I'll come to dinner." She turned back to him. "But I won't be responsible if it ends up with a lot of shouting."

"I think we might avoid that. I'll pick you up at seven."

"I know the way," she countered and started to push him aside to open her door. His hand curled over her forearm.

"I'll pick you up, Jillian." The steel was back, in his eyes, his voice.

She shrugged. "Suit yourself."

He cupped the back of her head and kissed her before she could prevent it. "I intend to," he told her easily, then left her to walk back into the house.

CHAPTER 4

Jillian was still smarting when she returned to Utopia. Murdock's comments, and Aaron's arrogance, had set her back up. She wasn't the sort of woman who made a habit of calming down gracefully. She told herself the only reason she was going back to the Double M to deal with the Murdocks again was because she was interested in a breeding contract. She wanted to believe it.

Dust flew out from her wheels as she drove up the hard-packed road to the ranch yard. It was nearly deserted now at mid-morning, with most of the men out on the range, others busy in the outbuildings. But even an audience wouldn't have prevented her from springing out of her car and slamming the door with a vicious swing. She'd never been a woman who believed in letting her temper simmer if it could boil.

The sound of the door slam echoed like a pistol shot.

Fleetingly she thought of the paperwork waiting for her in the office, then brushed it aside. She couldn't deal with ledgers and numbers at the moment. She needed something physical to drain off the anger before she tackled the dry practicality of checks and balances. Spinning on her heel, she headed for the stables. There'd be stalls to muck out and tack to clean.

"Anybody in particular you'd like to mow down?"

With her eyes still sparkling with anger, Jillian whipped her head around. Joe Carlson walked toward her, his neat hat shading his eyes, a faint, friendly smile on his lips.

"*Murdocks.*"

He nodded after the short explosion of the word. "Figured it was something along those lines. Couldn't come to an agreement on the stud fee?"

"We haven't started negotiating yet." Her jaw clenched. "I'm going back this evening."

Joe scanned her face, wondering that a woman who played poker so craftily should be so utterly readable when riled. "Oh?" he said simply and earned a glare.

"That's right." She bit off each word. "If Murdock didn't have such a damn beautiful horse, I'd tell him to go to the devil and to take his father with him."

This time Joe grinned. "You met Paul Murdock, then."

"He gave me his opinion on cowboys in skirts." Her teeth shut with an audible click.

"Really?"

The dry tone was irresistible. Jillian grinned back at him. "Yes, really." Then she sighed, remembering how difficult it had been for Paul Murdock to climb the four steps to his own porch. "Oh, hell," she murmured, cooling off as quickly as she'd flared. "I shouldn't have let him get under my skin. He's an old man and—"

She broke off, stopping herself before she added *ill*. For some indefinable reason she found it necessary to allow Murdock whatever illusions he had left. Instead she shrugged and glanced toward the corral. "I suppose I'm just used to the way Clay was. If you could ride and drive cattle, he didn't care if you were male or female."

Joe gave her one sharp glance. It wasn't what she'd started to say, but he'd get nothing out of her by probing. One thing he'd learned in the past six months was that Jillian Baron was a woman who did things her way. If a man got too close, one freezing look reminded him how much distance was expected.

"Maybe you'd like to take another look at the bull now, if you've got a few minutes."

"Hmm?" Abstracted, she looked back at him.

"The bull," Joe repeated.

"Oh, yeah." Hooking her thumbs in her pockets, she began to walk with him. "Gil told you about the calves we counted yesterday?"

"Took a look in the south section today. You've got some more."

"How many?"

"Oh, thirty or so. In another week all the calves should be dropped."

"You know, when we were checking the pasture yesterday, I thought the numbers were a little light." Frowning, she went over the numbers in her head again. "I'm going to need someone to go out there and see that some of the bred cows haven't strayed."

"I'll take care of it. How's the orphan?"

With a grin Jillian glanced back toward the cattle barn. "He's going to be fine." Attachments were a mistake, she knew. But it was already too late between her and Baby. "I'd swear he's grown since yesterday."

"And here's Poppa," Joe announced as they came to the bull's paddock.

After angling the hat farther over her eyes, Jillian leaned on the fence. Beautiful, she thought. Absolutely beautiful.

The bull eyed them balefully and snorted air. He didn't have the bulk or girth of an Angus but was built, Jillian thought, like a sleek tank. His red hide glistened as he stood in the full sun. She didn't see boredom in his expression as she'd seen in so many of the steers or cows, but arrogance. His horns curved around the wide white face and gave him a sense of dangerous royalty. It occurred to her that the little orphan she had sheltered in the cattle barn would look essentially the same in a year's time. The bull snorted again and pawed the ground as if daring them to come inside and try their luck.

"His personality's grim at best," Joe commented.

"I don't need him to be polite," Jillian murmured. "I just need him to produce."

"Well, you don't have any problem there." His gaze skimmed over the bull. "From the looks of the calves in this first batch, he's already done a good job for us. Since we're using artificial insemination now, he should be able to service every Hereford cow on the ranch this spring. Your shorthorn bull's a fine piece of beef, Jillian, but he doesn't come up to this one."

"No." Smiling, she rested her elbows on the rail. "As a matter of fact, I found out today that Aaron Murdock was interested in our, ah, Casanova. I can't help but pat myself on the back when I remember how I sent off to England for him on a hunch. Damned expensive hunch," she added, thinking of the hefty dent in the books. "Aaron told me today that he was planning on going over to England to take a look at the bull himself when he learned we'd bought him."

"That was a year ago," Joe commented with a frown. "He was still in Billings."

Jillian shrugged. "I guess he was keeping his finger in the pie. In any case, we've got him." She pushed away from the rail. "I meant what I said about the fair in July, Joe. I can't say I cared much about competition and ribbons before. This year I want to win."

Joe brought his attention from the bull and studied her. "Personal?"

"Yeah." She gave him a grim smile. "You could say it's personal. In the meantime, I'm counting on this guy to give me the best line of beef cattle in Montana. I need a good price in Miles City if I'm going to keep the books in the black. And next year when some of his calves are ready . . ." She trailed off with a last look at the bull. "Well, we'll just take it a bit at a time. Get back to me on those numbers, Joe. I want to take a look at Baby before I go into the office."

"I'll take care of it," he said again and watched her walk away.

* * *

By five Jillian had brought the books up to date and was, if not elated with the figures, at least satisfied. True, the expenses had taken a sharp increase over the last year, but by roundup time, she anticipated a tidy profit from the Livestock Auction Saleyard in Miles City. The expenses had been a gamble, but a necessary one. The plane would be in use within the week and the bull had already proved himself.

Tipping back in her grandfather's worn leather chair, she studied the ceiling. If she could find the time, she'd like to learn how to fly the plane herself. As owner she felt it imperative that she have at least a working knowledge of every aspect of the ranch. In a pinch she could shoe a horse or stitch up a rent hide. She'd learned to operate a hay baler and a bulldozer during a summer visit when she'd still been a teenager—the same year she'd wielded her first and last knife to turn a calf into a steer.

When and if she could afford the luxury, she thought, she'd hire someone to take over the books. Grimacing, she closed the ledger. She had more energy left after ten hours on horseback than she did after four behind a desk.

For now it couldn't be helped. She could justify adding another puncher to the payroll, but not a paper pusher. Next year . . . She laughed at herself and rested her feet on the desk.

Trouble was, she was counting too heavily on next year and too many things could happen. A drought could mean the loss of crops, a blizzard the loss of cattle. And that was just nature. If feed prices continued to rise, she was going to have to seriously consider selling off a larger portion of the calves as baby beef. Then there was the repair bill for the Jeep, the vet bill, the food bill for the hands. The bill for fuel that would rise once the plane was in use. Yes, she was going to need top dollar in Miles City and a blue ribbon or two wouldn't hurt.

In the meantime she was going to keep an eye on her spring calves. And Aaron Murdock. With a half smile, Jillian thought of him. He was an arrogant son of a bitch, she mused with something very close to admiration, and sharp as they came. It was a pity she didn't trust him enough to discuss ranch business with him and kick around ideas. She'd missed that luxury since her grandfather died. The men were friendly enough, but you didn't talk about your business with a hand who might be working for someone else next year. And Gil was . . . Gil was Gil, she thought with a grin. He was fond of her, even respected her abilities, though he wouldn't come out and say so. But he was too steeped in his own ways to talk about ideas and changes. So that left—no one, Jillian admitted.

There had been times in Chicago when she could have screamed for privacy, for solitude. Now there were times she ached just to have someone to share an hour's conversation with. With a shake of her head she rose. She was getting foolish. She had dozens of people to talk to. All she had to do was go down to the barn or the stables. Wherever this sudden discontent had come from it would fade again quickly enough. She didn't have time for it.

Her boots clicked lightly on the floor as she walked through the house and up the stairs. From outside she could hear the ring of the triangle, those quick three notes that ran faster and faster until it was one high sound. Her hands would be sitting down to their meal. She'd better get ready for her own.

Jillian toyed with the idea of just slipping into clean jeans and a shirt. The deliberate casualness of such an outfit would be pointedly rude. She was still annoyed enough at both Aaron and his father to do it, but she thought of Karen Murdock. With a sigh, Jillian rejected the idea and hunted through her closet.

It was a matter of her own choice that she had few dresses. They were relegated to one side of her closet, and she rooted them out on the occasions when she entertained other ranchers or businessmen. She stuck with simple styles, having found it to her advantage not to call her femininity to attention. Standing in a brief teddy, she skimmed over her options.

The oversized white cotton shirt wasn't precisely masculine in cut, but it was still casual. Matched with a full white wrap skirt with yards of sash, it made an outfit she thought not only suitable but understated. She made a small concession with a touch of makeup, hesitated over jewelry, then, shrugging, clipped small swirls of gold at her ears. Her mother, Jillian thought, would have badgered her to do something more sophisticated with her hair. Instead she ran a brush through it and left it down. She didn't need elegant styles to discuss breeding contracts.

When she heard the sound of a car drive up outside, she stopped herself from going to the window to peer out. Deliberately she took her time going back downstairs.

Aaron wasn't wearing a hat. Without it Jillian realized he still looked like what he was—a rugged outdoorsman with touches of the aristocracy. He didn't need the uniform to show it.

Looking at him, she wondered how he had found the patience to sit in Billings behind a desk. Trim black slacks and a thin black sweater fit him as truly as his work clothes, yet they seemed to accent the wickedness of his dark looks. She felt an involuntary stir and met his eyes coolly.

"You're prompt," she commented and let the door swing shut behind her. It might not be wise to be alone with him any longer than necessary.

"So are you." He let his gaze move over her slowly, appreciating the simplicity of her outfit—the way the sash accented her small waist and narrow hips, the way the unrelieved white made her skin glow and her hair spark like fire. "And beautiful," he added, taking her hand. "Whether you like it or not."

Because her pulse reacted immediately, Jillian knew she had to tread carefully. "You keep risking that hand of yours, Murdock." When she tried to slip hers from it, he merely tightened his fingers.

"One thing I've learned is that nothing's worth having if you don't have trouble getting it." Very deliberately he brought her hand to his lips, watching her steadily.

It wasn't a gesture she expected from him. Perhaps that was why she did nothing but stare at him as the sun dipped lower in the sky. She should've jerked her hand away—she wanted to spread her fingers so that she could touch that high curve of cheekbone, that lean line of jaw. She did nothing—until he smiled.

"Maybe I should warn you," Jillian said evenly, "that the next time I hit you, I'm going to aim a bit lower."

He grinned, then kissed her hand again before he released it. "I believe it."

Because she couldn't stop her own smile, she gave up. "Are you going to feed me, Murdock, or not?" Without waiting for an answer, she walked down the steps in front of him.

His car was more in tune with the oil man she'd first envisioned. A low, sleek Maserati. She admired anything well built and fast and settled into her seat with a little sigh. "Nice toy," she commented with a hint of the smile still playing around her mouth.

"I like it," Aaron said easily when he started the engine. It roared into life, then settled down to a purr. "A man doesn't always like to take a woman out in a Jeep or pickup."

"This isn't a date," she reminded him but skimmed her fingers over the smooth leather of the upholstery.

"I admire your practical streak—most of the time."

Jillian turned in her seat to watch the way he handled the car. As well as he handles a horse, she decided. As well as she was certain he handled a woman. The smile curved her lips again. He was going to discover that she wasn't a woman who took to being handled. She settled back to enjoy the ride.

"How does your father feel about me coming to dinner?" she asked idly. Those last slanting rays of the sun were tipping the grass with gold. She heard a cow moo lazily.

"How should he feel about it?" Aaron countered.

"He was amiable enough when I was simply Clay Baron's granddaughter," Jillian pointed out. "But once he found out I was *the* Baron, so to speak, he changed his tune. You're fraternizing with the enemy, aren't you?"

Aaron took his eyes off the road long enough to meet her amused look with one of his own. "So to speak. Aren't you?"

"I suppose I prefer to look at it as making a mutually advantageous bargain. Aaron . . ." She hesitated, picking her way carefully over what she knew was none of her business. "Your father's very ill, isn't he?"

She could see his expression draw inward, though it barely changed at all. "Yes."

"I'm sorry." Jillian turned to look out the side window. "It's hard," she murmured, thinking of her grandfather. "It's so hard for them."

"He's dying," Aaron said flatly.

"Oh, but—"

"He's dying," he repeated. "Five years ago they told him he had a year, two at most. He outfoxed them. But now . . ."

His fingers contracted briefly on the wheel, then relaxed again. "He might make it to the first snow, but he won't make it to the last."

He sounded so matter-of-fact. Perhaps she'd imagined that quick tension in his fingers. "There hasn't even been a rumor of his illness."

"No, we intend to keep it that way."

She frowned at his profile. "Then why did you tell me?"

"Because you understand about pride and you don't play games."

Jillian studied him another moment, then turned away. No soft words or whispered compliments could have moved her more than that brisk, emotionless statement. "It must be difficult for your mother."

"She's tougher than she looks."

"Yes." Jillian smiled again. "She'd have to be to put up with him."

They drove under the high-arched *Double M* at the entrance to the ranch. The day was hovering at dusk when the light grew lazy and the air soft. Cattle stood slack-hipped in the pasture to the right. She saw a mother licking patiently to clean her baby's hide while other calves were busy at their evening feeding. In another few months they'd be heifers and steers, the maternal bond forgotten, but for now they were just babies with awkward legs and demanding stomachs.

"I like this time of day," she murmured, half to herself. "When work's over and it isn't time to think about tomorrow yet."

He glanced down at her hand that lay relaxed against the seat. Competent, unpampered, with narrow bones and slender fingers. "Did you ever consider that you work too hard?"

Jillian turned and met his gaze calmly. "No."

"I didn't think you did."

"Cowboys in skirts again, Murdock?"

"No." But he'd made a few discreet inquiries. Jillian Baron

had a reputation for working a twelve-hour day—on a horse, in a pickup, on her feet. If she wasn't riding fence or hazing cattle, she was feeding her stock, overseeing repairs, or poring over the books. "What do you do to relax?" he asked abruptly. Her blank look gave him the answer before she did.

"I don't have a lot of time for that right now. When I do, there are books or the toy Clay bought a couple years ago."

"Toy?"

"Videotape machine," she said with a grin. "He loved the movies."

"Solitary entertainments," Aaron mused.

"It's a solitary way of life," Jillian countered, then glanced over curiously when he stopped in front of a simple white frame house. "What's this?"

"It's where I live," Aaron told her easily before he stepped from the car.

She sat where she was, frowning at the house. She'd taken it for granted that he lived in the sprawling main house another quarter mile or so up the road. Just as she'd taken it for granted that they were having dinner there, with his parents. Jillian turned her head as he opened her door and sent him an uncompromising look. "What are you up to, Murdock?"

"Dinner." Taking her hand, he pulled her from the car. "Isn't that what we'd agreed on?"

"I was under the impression we were having it up there." She gestured in the general direction of the ranch house.

Aaron followed the movement of her hand. When he turned back to her, his mouth was solemn, his eyes amused. "Wrong impression."

"You didn't do anything to correct it."

"Or to promote it," he countered. "My parents don't have anything to do with what's between us, Jillian."

"Nothing is."

Now his lips smiled as well. "There's a matter of the horses—yours and mine." When she continued to frown, he stepped closer, his body just brushing hers. "Afraid to be alone with me, Jillian?"

Her chin came up. "You overestimate yourself, Murdock."

He saw from the look in her eyes that she wouldn't back down no matter what he did. The temptation was too great. Lowering his head, he nipped at her bottom lip. "Maybe," he said softly. "Maybe not. We can always ride on up to the main house if you're—nervous."

Her heart had already risen to the base of her throat to pound. But she knew what it was to deal with a stray wildcat. "You don't worry me," she said mildly, then turned to walk to the house.

Oh, yes, I do, Aaron thought, and admired her all the more because she was determined to face him down. He decided, as he moved to open the front door, that it promised to be an interesting evening.

She couldn't fault his taste. Jillian glanced around his living quarters, wondering just how much she could learn about him from his choice of furnishings. Apparently, he had his mother's flair for style and color, though there were no subtle feminine touches here. Buffs and creams were offset by a stunning wall hanging slashed with vivid blues and greens. He favored antiques and clean lines. Though the room was small, there was no sense of clutter. Curious, she wandered to a curved mahogany shelf and studied his collection of pewter.

The mustang at full gallop caught her attention, though all the animals in the miniature menagerie were finely crafted. For a moment she wished he wasn't a man who appreciated what appealed to her quite so much. Then, remembering the stand she had to take, she turned around. "This is very nice. Though it is a bit simple for a man who grew up the way you did."

His brow lifted. "I'll take the compliment. How do you like your steak?"

Jillian dipped her hands in the wide pockets of her skirt. "Medium rare."

"Keep me company while I fix them." He curled a hand around her arm and moved through the house with her.

"So, I get Murdock beef prepared by a Murdock." She shot him a look. "I suppose I should be complimented."

"We might consider it a peace offering."

"We might," Jillian said cautiously, then smiled. "Providing you know how to cook. I haven't eaten since breakfast."

"Why not?"

He gave her such a disapproving look that she laughed. "I got bogged down in paperwork. I can't work up much of an appetite sitting at a desk. Well, well," she added, glancing around his kitchen. Its simplicity suited the house, with its hardwood floor and plain counters. There wasn't a crumb out of place. "You're a tidy one, aren't you?"

"I lived in the bunkhouse for a while." Aaron uncorked a bottle of wine that stood on the counter next to two glasses. "It either corrupts or reforms you."

"Why the bunkhouse when—" She cut herself off, annoyed that she'd begun to pry again.

"My father and I deal together better when there's some distance." He poured wine into both glasses. "You'd have heard by now that we don't always agree."

"I heard you'd had a falling-out a few years ago, before you went to Billings."

"And you wondered why I buckled under instead of telling him to go to hell and starting my own place."

Jillian accepted the wine he handed her. "All right, yes, I wondered. It's none of my business."

He looked into his glass a moment, as if studying the dark red color of the wine. "No." Aaron glanced back up and sipped. "It's not."

Without another word he turned to take two hefty steaks out of the refrigerator. Jillian sipped her wine and remained

quiet, watching him as he began preparation of the meal with
the deft, economical moves that were characteristic of him.
Five years ago they'd given his father a year, perhaps two, to
live. Aaron had told her that without even a hint of emotion
in his voice. And he'd gone to Billings five years before.

To wait his father out? she wondered and winced at the
thought. No, she couldn't believe that of him—a man cool and
calculating enough to wait for his father to die? Even if his
feelings for his father didn't run deep, it was too cold, too
heartless. With a shudder, Jillian took a deep swallow of her
wine, then set it down. She wouldn't believe it of him.

"Anything I can do?"

Aaron glanced over his shoulder to see her calmly watching him. He knew what direction her thoughts had taken—
the logical direction. Now he saw she'd decided in his favor.
He told himself he didn't give a damn one way or the other. It
wasn't just astonishing to find out he did, it was enervating. He
could feel the emotion stir, and drain him. To give himself a
moment to settle, he slipped the steaks under the broiler and
turned it on.

"Yeah, there's something you can do." Crossing to her,
Aaron framed her face in his hands, seeing her eyes widen in
surprise just before his mouth closed over hers. He meant to
keep it hard and brief. A gesture—a gesture only to rid him
of whatever emotion had suddenly sprung up in him. But as
his lips moved over hers the emotion swelled, threatening to
take over as the kiss lingered.

She stiffened, and lifted her hands to his chest in automatic
defense. Aaron found he didn't want the struggle that usually
appealed to him, but the softness he knew she'd give to very
few. "Jillian, don't." His fingers tangled in her hair. His voice
had roughened with feelings—mysterious, unnamed—he
didn't pause to question. "Don't fight me—just this once."

Something in his voice, that quiet hint of need, had her

hands relaxing against him before the thought to do so had registered. So she yielded, and in yielding brought herself a moment of sweet, mindless pleasure.

His mouth gentled on hers even as he took her deeper. Her hands crept up to his shoulders, her head tilted back so that he might take what he needed and bring her more of that soft, soft delight she hadn't been aware existed. With a sigh that came from discovery, she gave.

He hadn't known he was capable of tenderness. There'd never been a woman who'd drawn it from him before. He hadn't been aware that desire could ever be calm and easy. Yet while the need built inside of him, he felt a quiet wave of contentment. Aaron basked in it until it made him light-headed. Shaken, he eased her away, studying her face like a man who had seen something he didn't quite understand. And wasn't sure he wanted to.

Jillian took a step back, regaining her balance by placing her palm down on the scrubbed wooden table. She found sweetness in the last place she expected to. There was nothing she was more determined to fight. "I came here for dinner," she began, eyeing him just as warily as he was eyeing her. "And to talk business. Don't do that again."

"You've got a point," he murmured before he turned back to the stove to tend the steaks. "Drink your wine, Jillian. We'll both be safer."

She did as he suggested only because she wanted something to calm her nerves. "I'll set the table," she offered.

"Dishes're up there." Aaron pointed to a cabinet without looking up. The steaks sizzled when he flipped them. "There's salad in the refrigerator."

They finished up the cooking and preparation in silence, with only the sound of sizzling meat and frying potatoes. Jillian finished off her first glass of wine and looked at the food with real enthusiasm.

"Either you know what you're doing, or I'm starved."

"Both." Aaron passed her some ranch dressing. "Eat. When you're skinny you can't afford to miss meals."

Unoffended, she shrugged. "Metabolism," she told him as she speared into the salad. "It doesn't matter how much I eat, nothing sticks."

"Some people call it nervous energy."

She glanced up as he tilted more wine into her glass. "I call it metabolism. I'm never nervous."

"Not often, in any case," he acknowledged. "Why did you leave Chicago?" Aaron asked before she could formulate a response.

"I didn't belong there."

"You could have, if you'd chosen to."

Jillian gave him a long neutral look, then nodded. "I didn't choose to, then. I felt at home here the first summer I visited."

"What about your family?"

She laughed. "They didn't."

"I mean, how do they feel about you living here, running Utopia?"

"How should they feel?" Jillian countered. She frowned into her wine a moment, then shrugged again. "I suppose you could say my father feels about Chicago the way I feel about Montana. It's where he belongs. You'd think he'd been born and raised there. And of course, my mother was, so . . . We just never worked out as a family."

"How?"

Jillian dashed some salt on her steak and cut into it. "I hated my piano lessons," she said simply.

"As easy as that?"

"As basic as that. Marc—my brother—he just melded right in. I suppose it helped that he developed an interest in medicine early, and he loves opera. My mother's quite a fan," she said with a smile. "Anyway, I still cringe a bit when I have to use a needle on a cow, and I've never been able to appreciate *La Traviata*."

"Is that what it takes to suit as a family?" Aaron wondered.

"It was important in mine. When I came here the first time, things started to change. Clay understood me. He yelled and swore instead of lecturing."

Aaron grinned, offering her more steak fries. "You like being yelled at?"

"Patient lecturing is the worst form of punishment."

"I guess I've never had to deal with it. We had a wood shed." He liked the way she laughed, low, appreciative. "Why didn't you come out to stay sooner?"

She moved her shoulders restlessly as she continued to eat. "I was in college. Both my parents thought a degree was vital, and I felt it was important to try to please them in that if nothing else. Then I got involved with—" She stopped herself, stunned that she'd almost told him of her relationship with that long-ago intern. Meticulously she cut a piece of steak. "It just didn't work out," she concluded, "so I came out here."

The someone who touched her wrong, Aaron decided. The astonishment in her eyes had been brief, her cover-up swift and smooth, but not smooth enough. He wouldn't probe there, not on a spot that was obviously tender. But he wondered who it had been who had touched her, and hurt her while she'd still been too young to build defenses.

"I think my mother was right," he commented. "Some things are just in the blood. You belong here."

There was something in the tone that made her look up carefully. She wasn't certain at that moment whether he referred to the ranch or to himself. His eyes reminded her just how ruthless he could be when he wanted something. "I belong at Utopia," she said precisely. "And I intend to stay. Your father said something today too," she reminded him. "That a Murdock doesn't do business with a Baron."

"My father doesn't run my life, personally or professionally."

"Are you going to breed your stallion with Delilah to spite him?"

"I don't waste time with spite." It was said very simply, with that undercurrent of steel that made her think if he wanted revenge, he'd choose a very direct route. "I want the mare"—his dark eyes met hers and held—"for reasons of my own."

"Which are?"

Lifting his wine, he drank. "My own."

Jillian opened her mouth to speak, then shut it again. His reasons didn't matter. Business was business. "All right, what fee are you asking?"

Aaron took his time, calmly watching her face. "You seem to be finished."

Distracted, Jillian looked down to see that she'd eaten every bite on her plate. "Apparently," she said with a half laugh. "Well, I almost hate to admit it, Murdock, but it was good—almost as good as Utopia beef."

He answered her grin as he rose to clear off the table. "Why don't we take the wine in the other room, unless you'd like some coffee."

"No." She got up to help him stack the dishes. "I drank a full pot when I was fooling with the damn books."

"Don't care for paperwork?" Aaron picked up the half-full bottle of wine as they walked out of the kitchen.

"Putting it mildly," she murmured. "But someone has to do it."

"You could get a bookkeeper."

"The thought's crossed my mind. Maybe next year," she said with a move of her shoulders. "I've gotten used to keeping my finger on the pulse, let's say."

"Rumor is you rope a steer with the best of them."

Jillian sat on the couch, the full white skirt billowing

around her. "Rumor's fact, Murdock," she said with a cocky smile. "Anytime you want to put some money on it, we'll go head-to-head."

He sat down beside her and toyed with the end of her sash. "I'll keep that in mind. But I have to admit, it isn't a hardship to look at you in a skirt."

Over the rim of her glass she watched him. "We were talking stud fees. What'd you have in mind for Samson?"

Idly he twisted a lock of her hair around his finger. "The first foal."

CHAPTER 5

For a moment there was complete silence in the room as they measured each other. She'd thought she had him pegged. It infuriated her to realize he was still a step ahead of her. "The first—" Jillian set down her glass of wine with a snap. "You're out of your mind."

"I'm not interested in cash. Two guaranteed breedings. I take the first foal, colt or filly. You take the second. I like the looks of your mare."

"You expect me to breed Delilah, cover all the expenses while she's carrying a foal, lose the use of her for three to four months, deal with the vet fees, then turn the result over to you?"

Relaxed, Aaron leaned back. He'd almost forgotten how good it was to haggle. "You'd have the second for nothing. I'd be willing to negotiate on the expenses."

"A flat fee," Jillian said, rising. "We're not talking about dogs, where you can take the pick of the litter."

"I don't need cash," Aaron repeated, lounging back on the couch. "I want a foal, take it or leave it."

Oh, she'd like to leave it. She'd like to have tossed it back in his face. Simmering, she stalked over to the window and stared out. It surprised her that she didn't. Until that moment Jillian hadn't realized just how much she wanted to breed those two horses. Another hunch, she thought, remembering the bull. She could feel that something special would come out of it. Clay had often told her she had a feel. More than once she'd singled out an animal for no other reason than a feeling. Now she had to weigh that with the absurdity of Aaron's suggestion.

She stared hard out of the window into the full night, full dark. Behind her, Aaron remained silent, waiting, watching her with a faint smile. He wondered if she knew just how lovely she was when she was annoyed. It was tempting to keep her that way.

"I get the first foal," she said suddenly. "You get the second. It's my mare who's taking the risk in pregnancy, who won't be any use for working when she's at term and nursing. I'm the one bearing the brunt of the expense."

Aaron considered a moment. She was playing it precisely as he'd have done himself if the situation was reversed. He found it pleased him. "We breed her back as soon as she's weaned the foal."

"Agreed. You pay half the vet bills—on both foalings."

His brows raised. Whatever she knew about cattle, she wasn't a fool when it came to horse trading. "Half," he agreed. "We breed them as soon as she comes in season."

With a nod, Jillian offered her hand on it. "Do you want to draw up the papers or shall I?"

Standing, Aaron took her hand. "I'm not particular. A handshake's binding enough for me."

"Agreed," she said again. "But it never hurts to have words written down."

He grinned, skimming his thumb over her knuckles. "Don't you trust me, Jillian?"

"Not an inch," she said easily, then laughed because he seemed more pleased than offended. "No, not an inch. And you'd be disappointed if I did."

"You have a way of cutting through to the heart of things.

It's a pity I've been away for five years." He inclined his head. "But I have a feeling we'll be making up for lost time."

"I haven't lost any time," Jillian countered. "Now that we've concluded our business successfully, Murdock, I have a long day tomorrow."

He tightened his fingers on hers before she could turn away. "Not all our business."

"All I came for." Her voice was cool, even when he stepped closer. "I don't want to make a habit out of hitting you."

"You won't connect this time." He took her other hand and held both lightly, though not so lightly she could draw away. "I'm going to have you, Jillian."

She didn't try to pull her hands away. She didn't back up. Her eyes stayed level with his and her voice just as matter-of-fact. "The hell you are."

"And when I do," he went on as if she hadn't spoken, "it's not going to be something either one of us is going to forget. You stirred something in me"—he yanked her closer so that the unrelieved white of her skirt flowed against the stark black of his slacks—"from the first minute I saw you. It hasn't settled yet."

"Your problem." She angled her chin, but her voice was breathless. "You don't interest me, Murdock."

"Tell me that again," he challenged, "in just a minute."

He brought his mouth down on hers, harder than he'd intended. His emotions seemed to have no middle ground with her. It was either all soft tenderness or raw passion. Her arms strained against his hold, her body jerked as if to reject him. Then he felt it—the instant she became as consumed as he. In seconds his arms were around her, and hers around him.

It felt just as she'd wanted it to. Heady, overpowering. She could forget everything but that delicious churning within her own body. The rich flavor of wine that lingered on his tongue would make her drunk, but it didn't matter. Her head could whirl and spin, but she could only be grateful for the giddiness. With unapologetic passion, she met his demand with demand.

When his mouth left hers, she would have protested, but the sound became a moan as his lips raced down her throat. Instinctively she tilted her head back to give him more freedom, and the sharp scent of soap drifted over her, laced with a hint of sandalwood. Then his mouth was at her ear, his teeth tugging and nipping before he whispered something she didn't understand. The words didn't matter, the sound alone made her tremble. With a murmur of desperation, she dragged his lips back to hers.

Jillian was demanding he take more. Aaron could feel the strain of her body against his and knew she was aching to be touched. But his hands were still tangled in her hair as they tumbled onto the couch. Then his hands were everywhere, and he couldn't touch enough fast enough. Her body was so slender under all those yards of thin white cotton. So responsive. Her breast was almost lost under the span of his hand, yet it was so firm. And her heartbeat pounded like thunder beneath it.

His legs tangled with hers before he slipped between them. When she sank into the cushions, he nearly lost himself in the simple give of her body. His mouth ravaged hers—he couldn't prevent it, she didn't protest. She only answered and demanded until he was half mad again. Her scent, part subtle, part sultry, enveloped him so that he knew he'd be able to smell her when she was miles from him. He could hear her breath rush from between her lips into his mouth, where it whispered warm and sweet and promising.

Her body was responding of its own accord while her mind raced off in a dozen directions. His weight, that hard, firm press of his body, felt so good, so natural against hers. Those ruthless kisses gave her everything she needed long before she knew she needed it. He threatened her with words of passion that were only whispered madness in a world of color without form.

His cheek grazed hers as his lips raced over her face. No one had ever wanted her like this. But more, she'd never wanted this wildly. Her only taste of lovemaking had been so mild, so quiet. Nothing had prepared her for a violence of need that came from within herself. She wanted to fly with it. Too much.

His hand skimmed up her leg, seeking, and everything that was inside her built to a fever pitch. If it exploded, she'd be lost. Pieces of herself might scatter so that she'd never be strong enough to stand on her own again.

In a panic, she began to struggle while part of her fought to yield. And to take.

"No." Moaning, she pushed against him.

"Jillian, for God's sake." Her name came out in a gasp as he felt himself drowning.

"No!" Somehow she managed to shove him aside and scramble up. Before either of them could think, she was dashing outside, running away from something that followed much too closely. Aaron was cursing steadily when he caught her.

"What the hell's wrong with you?" he demanded as he whipped her back around.

"Let me go! I won't be pawed that way."

"Pawed? Damn you," he said under his breath. "You were doing some pawing of your own, if that's what you want to call it."

"Just let me go," she said unsteadily. "I told you I don't like to be touched."

"Oh, you like to be touched," he grated, then caught the glint of uncertainty in her eyes. There was pride there as well, a kind of terrorized pride laced with passion.

No, he wasn't a gentle man, but she was the first and only

woman who'd caused him to lose control. Carefully he loosened his hold without releasing her.

"Jillian." His voice was still rough, only slightly calmer. "You can postpone what's going to happen between us, but you can't stop it." She opened her mouth, but he shook his head in warning. "No, you'd be much better off not to say anything just now. I want you, and at the moment it's a damned uncomfortable feeling. I'm going to take you home while I've got myself convinced I play by the rules. It wouldn't take me long to remember I've never followed any."

He pulled open the passenger door, then strode around to the driver's seat without another word. They drove away in a silence that remained thick for miles. Because her body was still throbbing, Jillian sat very straight. She cursed Aaron, then when she began to calm, she cursed herself. She'd wanted him, and every time he touched her, her initial restraint vanished within moments.

The hands in her lap balled into fists. There was a name for a woman who was willing and eager one moment and hurling accusations the next. It wasn't pleasant. She'd never played that kind of game and had nothing but disdain for anyone who did.

He had a right to be furious, Jillian admitted, but then, so did she. He was the one who'd come barging into her life, stirring things up she wanted left alone. She didn't want to feel all those hungers, all those aches that raged through her when he held her.

She couldn't give in to them. Once she did, she'd start depending. If that happened, she'd start chipping away at her own self-reliance until he had more of who and what she was than she did. It had happened before and the need had been nothing like this. She'd gotten a hint, during that strangely gentle kiss in his kitchen, just how easily she could lose herself to him. And yet . . . Yet when it was all said and done,

Jillian was forced to admit, she'd acted like an idiot. The one thing she detested more than anything else was finding herself in the wrong.

A deer bounded over the fence to the left, pausing in the road, as it was trapped in the headlights. Even as Aaron braked, it was sprinting off, slender legs lifting as it took the next fence and disappeared into the darkness. The sight warmed Jillian as it always did. With a soft laugh, she turned back to see the smile in Aaron's eyes. The flood of emotion swamped her.

"I'm sorry." The words came quickly, before she realized she would say them. "I overreacted."

He gave her a long look. He'd wanted to stay angry. Somehow it was easier—now it was impossible. "Maybe we both did. We have a tendency to spark something off each other."

She couldn't deny that, but neither did she want to think about it too carefully just then. "Since we're going to have to deal with each other from time to time, maybe we should come to some kind of understanding."

A smile began to tug at his mouth. "That sounds reasonable. What kind of understanding did you have in mind?"

"We're business associates," she said very dryly because of the amusement in his question.

"Uh-huh." Aaron rested his arm on the back of the seat as he began to enjoy himself.

"Do you practice being an idiot, Murdock, or does it come naturally?"

"Oh, no, no insults, Jillian. We're coming to an understanding."

Jillian fought against a grin and lost. "You have a strange sense of humor."

"A keen sense of the ridiculous," he countered. "So we're business associates. You forgot neighbors."

"And neighbors," she agreed with a nod. "Colleagues, if you want to belabor a point."

"Belabor it," Aaron suggested. "But can I ask you a question?"

"Yes." She drew out the word cautiously.

"What *is* the point?"

"Damn it, Aaron," she said with a laugh. "I'm trying to put things in order so I don't end up apologizing again. I hate apologizing."

"I like the way you do it, very simple and sincere right before you lose your temper again."

"I'm not going to lose my temper again."

"I'll give you five to one."

"Damn it, Aaron." Her laugh rippled, low and smooth. "If I took that bet, you'd go out of your way to make me mad."

"You see, we understand each other already. But you were telling me your point." He pulled into the darkened ranch yard. The light from Jillian's front porch spilled into the car and cast his face in shadows.

"We could have a successful business association *if* we both put a lot of effort into it."

"Agreed." He turned and in the small confines of the car was already touching her. Just the skim of his fingers over her shoulder, the brush of leg against leg.

"We'll continue to be neighbors because neither of us is moving. As long as we remember those things, we should be able to deal with each other without too much fighting."

"You forgot something."

"Did I?"

"You've said what we are to each other, not what we're going to be." He watched her eyes narrow.

"Which is?"

"Lovers." He ran his finger casually down the side of her neck. "I still mean to have you."

Jillian let out a long breath and worked on keeping her temper in check. "It's obvious you can't carry on a reasonable conversation."

"A lot of things are obvious." He put his hand over hers as she reached for the handle. With their faces close, he let his gaze linger on her mouth just long enough for the ache to spread. "I'm not a patient man," Aaron murmured. "But there are some things I can wait for."

"You'll have a long wait."

"Maybe longer than I'd like," he agreed. "But shorter than you think." His hand was still over hers as he pressed down the handle to release the door. "Sleep well, Jillian."

She swung out of the car, then gave him a smoldering look. "Don't cross the line until you're invited, Murdock." Slamming the door, she sprinted up the steps, cursing the low, easy laughter that followed her.

* * *

In the days that followed, Jillian tried not to think about Aaron. When she couldn't stop him from creeping into her mind, she did her best to think of him with scorn. Occasionally she was successful enough to dismiss him as a spoiled, willful man who was used to getting what he wanted by demanding it. If she were successful, she could forget that he made her laugh, made her want.

Her days were long and full and demanding enough that she had little time to dwell on him or her feelings. But though the nights were growing shorter, she swore against the hours she spent alone and unoccupied. It was then she remembered exactly how it felt to be held against him. It was then she remembered how his eyes could laugh while the rest of his face remained serious and solemn. And how firm and strong his mouth could be against hers.

She began to rise earlier, to work later. She exhausted herself on the range or in the outbuildings until she could tumble boneless into bed. But still there were dreams.

Jillian was out in the pasture as soon as it was light. The sky was still tipped with the colors of sunrise so that gold and rose tinted the hazy blue. Like most of her men, she wore a light work jacket and chaps as they began the job of rounding up the first hundred calves and cows for corral branding. This part of the job would be slow and easy. It was too common to run twenty-five pounds off a cow with a lot of racing and roping. A good deal of the work could be done on foot, the rest with experienced horses or four wheels. If they hazed the mothers along gently, the babies would follow.

Jillian turned Delilah, keeping her at a walk as she urged a cow and calf away from a group of heifers. She looked forward to a long hard morning and the satisfaction of a job well done. When she saw Joe slowly prodding cows along on foot, she tipped her hat to him.

"I always thought branding was a kind of stag party," he commented as he came alongside of her.

Looking down, she laughed. "Not on Utopia." She looked around as punchers nudged cows along with soft calls and footwork. "When we brand again in a couple of days, the plane should be in. God knows it'll be easier to spot the strays."

"You've been working too hard. No, don't give me that look," he insisted. "You know you have. What's up?"

Aaron sneaked past her defenses, but now she just shook her head. "Nothing. It's a busy time of year. We'll be haying soon, first crop should come in right after the spring branding. Then there's the rodeo." She glanced down again as Delilah shifted under her. "I'm counting on those blue ribbons, Joe."

"You've been working from first light to last for a week," he pointed out. "You're entitled to a couple days off."

"The boss is the last one entitled to a couple days off." Satisfied that her cows had joined the slowly moving group headed for the pasture, she wheeled Delilah around. She spotted a calf racing west, spooked by the number of men, horses, and trucks. Sending Delilah into an easy lope, Jillian went after him.

Her first amusement at the frantic pace the dogie was setting faded as she saw he was heading directly for the wire. With a soft oath, she nudged more speed out of her mare and reached for her rope. With an expert movement of arm and wrist, she swung it over her head, then shot it out to loop over the maverick's neck. Jillian pulled him up a foot from the wire where he cried and struggled until his mother caught up.

"Dumb cow," she muttered as she dismounted to release him. "Fat lot of good you'd've done yourself if you'd tangled in that." She cast a glance at the sharp points of wire before she slipped the rope from around his head. The mother eyed her with annoyance as she began to recoil the rope. "Yeah, you're welcome," Jillian told her with a grin. Glancing over, she saw Gil crossing to her on foot. "Still think you can beat my time in July?" she demanded.

"You put too much fancy work on the spin."

Though his words were said in his usual rough-and-ready style, something in his eyes alerted her. "What is it?"

"Something you oughta see down here a ways."

Without a word, she gathered Delilah's reins in her hand and began to walk beside him. There was no use asking, so she didn't bother. Part of her mind still registered the sights and sounds around her—the irritated mooing, the high sound of puzzled calves, the ponderous majestic movements of their mothers, the swish of men and animals through grass. They'd start branding by mid-morning.

"Look here."

Jillian saw the small section of broken fence and swore.

"Damn it, we just took care of this line a week ago. I rode this section myself." Jillian scowled into the opposite pasture wondering how many of her cattle had strayed. That would account for the fact that though the numbers reported to her were right, her eye had told her differently that morning. "I'll need a few hands to round up the strays."

"Yeah." Reaching over, he caught a strand of wire in his fingers. "Take a look."

Distracted, she glanced down. Almost immediately, Jillian stiffened and took the wire in her own fingers. The break was much too sharp, much too clean. "It's been cut," she said quietly, then looked up and over into the next pasture. Murdock land.

She expected to feel rage and was stunned when she felt hurt instead. Was he capable? Jillian thought he could be ruthless, even lawless if it suited him. But to deliberately cut wire . . . Could he have found his own way to pay her back for their personal differences and professional enmity? She let the wire fall.

"Send three of the men over to check for strays," she said flatly. "I'd like you to see to this wire yourself." She met Gil's eyes coolly and on level. "And keep it to yourself."

He squinted at her, then spit. "You're the boss."

"If I'm not back by the time the cattle are ready in the corral, get started. We don't have any time to waste getting brands on the calves."

"Maybe we waited a few days too long already."

Jillian swung into the saddle. "We'll see about that." She led Delilah carefully through the break in the wire, then dug in her heels.

It didn't take her long to come across her first group of men. Delilah pulled up at the Jeep and Jillian stared down her nose. "Where's Murdock?" she demanded. "Aaron Murdock."

The man tipped his hat, recognizing an outraged female when he saw one. "In the north section, ma'am, rounding up calves."

"There's a break in the fence," she said briefly. "Some of my men are coming over to look for strays. You might want to do the same."

"Yes, ma'am." But he said it to her back as she galloped away.

The Murdock crew worked essentially the same way her own did. She saw them fanned out, moving slowly, steadily, with the cows plodding along in front of them. A few were farther afield, outflanking the mavericks and driving them back to the herd.

Jillian saw him well out to the right, twisting and turning Samson around a reluctant calf. Ignoring the curious glances of his men, Jillian picked her way through them. She heard them laugh, then shout something short and rude at the calf before he saw her.

The brim of his hat shaded his face from the early-morning sun. She couldn't see his expression, only that he watched her come toward him. Delilah pricked up her ears as she scented the stallion and sidestepped skittishly.

Aaron waited until they were side by side. "Jillian." Because he could already see that something was wrong, he didn't bother with any more words.

"I want to talk to you, Murdock."

"So talk." He nudged the calf, but Jillian reached over to grip his saddle horn. His eyes flicked down to rest on her restraining hand.

"Alone."

His expression remained placid—but she still couldn't see his eyes. Signaling to one of his men to take charge of the maverick, Aaron turned his horse and walked farther north. "You'll have to keep it short, I haven't got time to socialize right now."

"This isn't a social call," she bit off, controlling Delilah as the mare eyed the stallion cautiously.

"So I gathered. What's the problem?"

When she was certain they were out of earshot, Jillian pulled up her mount. "There's a break in the west boundary line."

He looked over her head to watch his men. "You want one of my hands to fix it?"

"I want to know who cut it."

His eyes came back to hers quickly. She could see only that they were dark. The single sign of his mood was the sudden nervous shift of his stallion. Aaron controlled him without taking his eyes off Jillian. "Cut it?"

"That's right." Her voice was even now, with rage bubbling just beneath. "Gil found it, and I saw it myself."

Very slowly he tipped back his hat. For the first time she saw his face unshadowed. She'd seen that expression once before—when it had loomed over her as he pinned her to the ground in Samson's corral. "What are you accusing me of?"

"I'm telling you what I know." Her eyes caught the slant of the morning sun and glittered with it. "You can take it from there."

In what seemed to be a very calm, very deliberate motion, he reached over and gathered the front of her jacket in his hand. "I don't cut fence."

She didn't jerk away from him and her gaze remained steady. A single stray breeze stirred the flame-colored curls that flowed from her hat. "Maybe you don't, but you've got a lot of men working your place. Three of my men are in your pasture now, rounding up my strays. I'm missing some cows."

"I'll send some men to check your herd for any of mine."

"I already suggested that to one of your hands in the border pasture."

He nodded, but his eyes remained very intense and very angry. "A wire can be cut from either side, Jillian."

Dumbfounded, she stared at him. Rage boiled out as she knocked his hand away from her jacket. "That's ridiculous. I wouldn't be telling you about the damn wire if I'd cut it."

Aaron watched her settle her moody mare before he gave her a grim smile. "You have a lot of men working your place," he repeated.

As she continued to stare her angry color drained. Hurt and anger hadn't allowed her to think through the logic of it. Some of her men she'd known and trusted for years. Others—they came and they went, earning a stake, then drifting to another ranch, another county. You rarely knew their names, only their faces. But it was her count that was short, she reminded herself.

"You missing any cattle?" she demanded.

"I'll let you know."

"I'll be doing a thorough count in the west section." She turned away to stare at the rising sun. It could've been one of her men just as easily as it could've been one of his. And she was responsible for everyone who was on Utopia's payroll. She had to face that. "I've no use for your beef, Aaron," she said quietly.

"Any more than I do for yours."

"It wouldn't be the first time." When she looked back at him, her chin stayed up. "The Murdocks made a habit out of cutting Baron wire."

"You want to go back eighty years?" he demanded. "There's two sides to a story, Jillian, just like there's two sides to a line. You and I weren't even alive then, what the hell difference does it make to us?"

"I don't know, but it happened—it could happen again. Clay may be gone, but your father still has some bad feelings."

Temper sprang back into his eyes. "Maybe he dragged himself out here and cut the wire so he could cause you trouble."

"I'm not a fool," she retorted.

"No?" Furious, he wheeled his horse so that they were face-to-face. "You do a damn good imitation. I'll check the west line myself and get back to you."

Before she could throw any of her fury back at him, he galloped away. Teeth gritted, Jillian headed south, back to Utopia.

CHAPTER 6

By the time Jillian galloped into the ranch yard the cattle were already penned. A glance at the sun told her it was only shortly after eight. Cows and calves were milling and mooing in the largest board pen and the workmen had already begun to separate them. No easy task. Listening to the sounds of men and cattle, Jillian dismounted and unsaddled her mare. There wasn't time to brood over the cut wire when branding was under way.

Some of the men remained on horseback, keeping the cows moving as they worked to chase the frantic mothers into a wire pen while the calves were herded into another board corral. The air was already peppered with curses that were more imaginative than profane.

With blows and shouts, a cow and her calf were driven out of the big corral. Men on foot were strung out in a line too tight to allow the cow to follow as the calf slipped through. Relying mostly on arm waving, shrieks, and whistles, the men propelled the cow into the wire pen. Then the process repeated itself. She watched Gil spinning his wiry little body and cheering with an energy that promised to see him through the day despite his years. With a half laugh, Jillian settled her hat firmly on her head and went to join them, lariat in hand.

Calves streaked like terriers back into the cow pen. Dust flew. Cows bullied their way through the line for a reunion with their offspring. Men ran them back with shouts, brute force, or ropes. Men might be outnumbered and outweighed, but the cattle were no match for western ingenuity.

Gil singled a calf out in the cow pen, roped it, and dragged it to him, cursing all the way. With a swat on the flank, he sent it into the calf corral, then squinted at Jillian.

"Fence repaired?" she asked briefly.

"Yep."

"I'll see to the rest myself." She paused, then swung her lariat. "I'm going to want to talk to you later, Gil."

He removed his hat, swiped the sweat off his brow with the arm of his dusty shirt, then perched it on his head again. "When you're ready." He glanced around as Jillian pulled in a calf. "Just about done—time to gang up on 'em."

So saying, he joined the line of men who closed in on the unruly cows to drive the last of them into their proper place. Inside the smaller corral calves bawled and crowded together.

"It isn't pleasant," Jillian muttered to them. "But it'll be quick."

The gate creaked as it was swung across to hold them in. The rest wasn't a business she cared for, though she never would've admitted it to anyone but herself. Knife and needle and iron were used with precision, with a rhythm that started off uneven, then gained fluidity and speed. Calves came through the chute one at a time, dreaming of liberation, only to be hoisted onto the calf table.

She watched the next calf roll his big eyes in astonishment as the table tilted, leaving him helpless on his side, as high as a man's waist. Then he was dealt with as any calf is at a roundup.

It was hot, dirty work. There was a smell of sweat, blood, smoking hide, and medicine. Throughout the steady action reminiscences could be heard—stories no one would believe and everyone tried to top. Cows surged in the wire pen; their babies squealed at the bite of needle or knife. The language grew as steamy as the air in the pen.

It wasn't Jillian's first branding, and yet each one—for all the sweat and blood—made her remember why she was here instead of on one of the wide busy streets back east. It was hard work, but honest. It took a special brand of person to do it. The cattle milling and calling in the corral were hers. Just as the land was. She relieved a man at the table and began her turn at the vaccinations.

The sun rose higher, heading toward afternoon before the last calf was released. When it was done, the men were hungry, the calves exhausted and bawling pitifully for their mothers.

Hot and hungry herself, Jillian sat on a handy crate and wiped the grime from her face. Her shirt stuck to her with patches of wet cutting through the dirt. That was only the first hundred, she thought as she arched her back. They wouldn't finish with the spring brandings until the end of that week or into the next. She waited until nearly all the men had made their way toward the cookhouse before she signaled to Gil. He plucked two beers out of a cooler and went to join her.

"Thanks." Jillian twisted off the cap, then let the cold, yeasty taste wash away some of the dust. "Murdock's going to check the rest of the line himself," she began without pre-amble. "Tell me straight"—she held the bottle to her brow a moment, enjoying the chill—"is he the kind of man who'd play this sort of game?"

"What do you think?" he countered.

What could she think? Jillian asked herself. No matter how hard she tried, her feelings kept getting in the way. Feelings she'd yet to understand because she didn't dare. "I'm asking you."

"Kid's got class," Gil said briefly. "Now, the old man . . ."

He grinned a bit, then squinted into the sun. "Well, he might've done something of the sort years back, just for devilment. Give your grandpaw something to swear about. But the kid—don't strike me like his devilment runs that way. Another thing . . ." He spit tobacco and shifted his weight. "I did a head count in the pasture this morning. Might be a few off, seeing as they were spread out and scattered during roundup."

Jillian took another swig from the bottle, then set it aside. "But?"

"Looked to me like we were light an easy hundred."

"A hundred?" she repeated in a whisper of shock. "That many cattle aren't going to stray through a break in the fence, not on their own."

"Boys got back midway through the branding. Only rounded up a dozen on Murdock land."

"I see." She let out a long breath. "Then it doesn't look like the wire was cut for mischief, does it?"

"Nope."

"I want an accurate head count in the morning, down to the last calf. Start with the west pasture." She looked down at her hands. They were filthy. Her fingers ached. It was as innate in her to work for what was hers as it was to fight for it. "Gil, the chances are pretty good that someone on the Murdock payroll's rustling our cattle, maybe for the Double M, but more likely for themselves."

He tugged on his ear. "Maybe."

"Or, it's one of our own."

He met her eyes calmly. He'd wondered if that would occur to her. "Just as likely," he said simply. "Murdock might find his numbers light too."

"I want that head count by sundown tomorrow." She rose to face him. "Pick men you're sure of, no one that's been here less than a season. Men who know how to keep their thoughts to themselves."

He nodded, understanding the need for discretion. Rustling wasn't any less deadly a foe than it had been a century before. "You gonna work with Murdock on this?"

"If I have to." She remembered the fury on his face— something she recognized as angry pride. She had plenty of that herself. The sigh came before she could prevent it and spoke of weariness. "Go get something to eat."

"You coming?"

"No." She walked back to Delilah and hefted the saddle. Mechanically she began to hook cinches and tighten them. In the corral the cattle were beginning to calm.

When she'd finished, Gil tapped her on the shoulder. Turning her head, she saw him hold out a thick biscuit crammed with meat.

"You eat this, damn it," he said gruffly. "You're going to blow away in a high wind if you keep it up."

Accepting the biscuit, she took a huge bite. "You mangy old dog," she muttered with her mouth full. Then, because no one was around to see and razz him, she kissed both his cheeks. Though it pleased him, he cursed her for it and made her laugh as she vaulted into the saddle.

Jillian trotted the mare out of the ranch yard, then, turning toward solitude, rode her hard.

To satisfy her own curiosity, she headed for the west pasture first. Riding slowly now, she checked the repaired fence, then began to count the cattle still grazing. It didn't take long for her to conclude that Gil's estimate had been very close to the mark. A hundred head. Closing her eyes, she tried to think calmly.

The winter had only cost her twenty—that was something every rancher had to deal with. But it hadn't been nature who'd taken these cows from her. She had to find out who, and quickly, before the losses continued. Jillian glanced over the boundary line. On both sides cattle grazed placidly, at peace now that man had left them to their own pursuits. As far as she could see there was nothing but rolling grass and the cattle growing sleek on it. A hundred head, she thought again. Enough to put a small but appreciable dent in her herd—and her profit. She wasn't going to sit still for it.

Grimly she sent Delilah into a gallop. She couldn't afford the luxury of panicking. She'd have to take it step-by-step, ascertaining a firm and accurate account of her losses before she went to the authorities. But for now she was tired, dirty, and discouraged. The best thing to do was to take care of that before she went back to the ranch.

It had been only a week since she'd last ridden out to the pond, but even in that short time the aspen and cottonwood were greener. She could see hints of bitterroot and of the wild roses that were lovely and so destructive when they sprang up in the pastures. The sun was beginning its gradual decline westward. Jillian judged it to be somewhere between one and two. She'd give herself an hour here to recharge before she went back to begin the painstaking job of checking and rechecking the number of cattle in her books, and their locations. Dismounting, she tethered her mare to a branch of an aspen and let her graze.

Carelessly Jillian tossed her hat aside, then sat on a rock to pull off her boots. As her jeans and shirt followed she listened to the sound of a warbler singing importantly of spring and sunshine. Black-eyed Susans were springing up at the edge of the grass.

The water was deliciously cool. When she lowered herself into it, she could forget about the aches in her muscles, the faint, dull pain in her lower back, and the sense of despair that had followed her out of the west pasture. As owner and boss of Utopia, she'd deal with what needed to be dealt with. For now, she needed to be only Jillian. It was spring, the sun was warm. If the breeze was right, she could smell the young roses. Dipping her head back, she let the water flow over her face and hair.

Aaron didn't ask himself how he'd known she'd be there. He didn't ask himself why knowing it, he'd come. Both he and the stallion remained still as he watched her. She didn't splash around but simply drifted quietly so that the water made soft lapping sounds that didn't disturb the birdsong. He thought he could see the fatigue drain from her. It was the first time he'd seen her completely relaxed without the light of adventure or temper or even laughter in her eyes. This was something she did for herself, and though he knew he intruded, he stayed where he was.

Her skin was milky pale where the sun hadn't touched it. Beneath the rippling water, he could see the slender curves of her body. Her hair clung to her head and shoulders and burned like fire. So did the need that started low in his stomach and spread through his blood.

Did she know how exquisite she was with that long, limber body and creamy skin? Did she know how seductive she looked with that mass of chestnut hair sleek around a face that held both delicacy and strength? No, he thought as she sank beneath the surface, she wouldn't know—wouldn't allow herself to know. Perhaps it was time he showed her. With the slightest of signals, he walked Samson to a tree on his side of the boundary.

Jillian surfaced and found herself looking directly up into Aaron's eyes. Her first shock gave way to annoyance and annoyance to outrage when she remembered her disadvantage. Aaron saw all three emotions. His lips twitched.

"What're you doing here?" she demanded. She knew she could do nothing about modesty and didn't attempt to. Instead she relied on bravado.

"How's the water?" Aaron asked easily. Another woman, he mused, would've made some frantic and useless attempt to conceal herself. Not Jillian. She just tossed up her chin.

"It's cold. Now, why don't you go back to wherever you came from so I can finish what I'm doing."

"It was a long, dusty morning." He sat on a rock near the edge of the pool and smiled companionably. Like Jillian's, his clothes and skin were streaked with grime and sweat. The signs of hard work and effort suited him. Aaron tilted back his hat. "Looks inviting."

"I was here first," she said between her teeth. "If you had any sense of decency, you'd go away."

"Yep." He bent over and pulled off his boots.

Jillian watched first one then the other hit the grass. "What the hell do you think you're doing?"

"Thought I'd take a dip." He gave her an engaging grin as he tossed his hat aside.

"Think again."

He rose, and his brow lifted slowly as he unbuttoned his shirt. "I'm on my own land," he pointed out. He tossed the shirt aside so that Jillian had an unwanted and fascinating view of a hard, lean torso with brown skin stretched tight over the rib cage and a dark vee of hair that trailed down to the low-slung waist of his jeans.

"Damn you, Murdock," she muttered, and judged the distance to her own clothes. Too far to be any use.

"Relax," he suggested, enjoying himself. "We can pretend there's wire strung clean down the middle." With this he unhooked his belt.

His eyes stayed on hers. Jillian's first instinct to look away was overruled by the amusement she saw there. Coolly she watched him strip. If she had to swallow, she did it quietly.

Damn, did he have to be so beautiful? she asked herself and kept well to her own side as he slid into the water. The ripples his body made spread out to tease her own skin. Shivering, she sank a little deeper.

"You're really getting a kick out of this, aren't you?"

Aaron gave a long sigh as the water rinsed away dust and cooled his blood. "Have to admit I am. View from in here's no different from the one I had out there," he reminded her easily. "And I'd already given some thought to what you'd look like without your clothes. Most redheads have freckles."

"I'm just lucky, I guess." Her dimple flickered briefly. At least they were on equal ground again. "You're built like most cowboys," she told him in a drawl. "Lots of leg, no hips." She let her arms float lazily. "I've seen better," she lied. Laughing, she tilted her head and let her legs come up, unable to resist the urge to tease him.

He had only to reach out to grab her ankle and drag her to him. Aaron rubbed his itchy palm on his thigh and relaxed. "You make a habit of skinny-dipping up here?"

"No one comes here." Tossing the hair out of her eyes, she shot him a look. "Or no one did. If you're going to start using the pond regularly, we'll have to work out some kind of schedule."

"I don't mind the company." He drifted closer so that his body brushed the imaginary line.

"Keep to your own side, Murdock," she warned softly, but smiled. "Trespassers still get shot these days." To show her lack of concern, she closed her eyes and floated. "I like to come here on Sunday afternoons, when the men are in the ranch yard, pitching horseshoes and swapping lies."

Aaron studied her face. No, he'd never seen her this relaxed. He wondered if she realized just how little space she gave herself. "Don't you like to swap lies?"

"Men tend to remember I'm a woman on Sunday afternoons. Having me around puts a censor on the—ah, kind of lies."

"They only remember on Sunday afternoons?"

"It's easy to forget the way a person's built when you're out on the range or shoveling out stalls."

He let his eyes skim down the length of her, covered by only a few inches of water. "You say so," he murmured.

"And they need time to complain." With another laugh, she let her legs sink. "About the food, the pay, the work. Hard to do all that when the boss is there." She spun her hand just under the surface and sent the water waving all the way to the edge. He thought it was the first purely frivolous gesture he'd ever seen her make. "Your men complain, Murdock?"

"You should've heard them when my sister decided to fix up the bunkhouse six or seven years back." The memory made him grin. "Seems she thought the place needed some pretty paint and curtains—gingham curtains, baby-blue paint."

"Oh, my God." Jillian tried to imagine what her crew's reaction would be if they were faced with gingham. Throwing back her head, she laughed until her sides ached. "What did they do?"

"They refused to wash anything, sweep anything, or throw anything away. In two weeks' time the place looked like the county dump—smelled like it too."

"Why'd your father let her do it?" Jillian asked, wiping her eyes.

"She looks like my mother," Aaron said simply.

Nodding, she sighed from the effort of laughing. "But they got rid of the curtains."

"I—let's say they disappeared one night," he amended.

Jillian gave him a swift appraising look. "You took them down and burned them."

"If I haven't admitted that in seven years, I'm not going to admit it now. It took damned near a week to get that place cleared out," he remembered. She was smiling at him in such an easy, friendly way it took all his willpower not to reach over and pull her to his side. "Did you do the orphan today?"

"Earmarked, vaccinated, and branded," Jillian returned, trailing her hands through the water again.

"Is that all?"

She grinned, knowing his meaning. "In a couple of years Baby's going to be giving his poppa some competition." She shrugged, so that her body shifted and the water lapped close at the curve of her breast. The less she seemed concerned about her body, the more he became fascinated by it. "I have a feeling about him," she continued. "No use making a steer out of a potential breeder." A cloud of worry came into her eyes. "I rode the west fence before I came up here. I didn't see any more breaks."

"There weren't any more." He'd known they had to discuss it, but it annoyed him to have the few moments of simple camaraderie interrupted. He couldn't remember sharing that sort of simplicity with a woman before. "My men rounded up six cows that had strayed to your side. Seemed like you had about twice that many on mine."

She hesitated a moment, worrying her bottom lip. "Then your count balances?"

He heard the tension in her voice and narrowed his eyes. "Seems to. Why?"

She kept her eyes level and expressionless. "I'm a good hundred head short."

"Hundred?" He'd grabbed her arm before he realized it. "A hundred head? Are you sure?"

"As sure as I can be until we count again and go over the books. But we're short, I'm sure of that."

He stared at her as his thoughts ran along the same path hers had. That many cows didn't stray on their own. "I'll do a count of my own herd in the morning, but I can tell you, I'd know if I had that much extra cattle in my pasture."

"I'm sure you would. I don't think that's where they are."

Aaron reached up to touch her cheek. "I'd like to help you—if you need some extra hands. We can take the plane up. Maybe they wandered in the other direction."

She felt something soften inside her that shouldn't have. A simple offer of help when she needed it—and his hand was gentle on her face. "I appreciate it," Jillian began unsteadily. "But I don't think the cattle wandered any more than you do."

"No." He combed the hair away from her face. "I'll go with you to the sheriff."

Unused to unselfish support, she stared at him. Neither was aware that they were both drifting to the line, and each other. "No—I . . . it isn't necessary, I can deal with it."

"You don't have to deal with it alone." How was it he'd never noticed how fragile she was? he wondered. Her eyes were so young, so vulnerable. The curve of her cheek was so delicate. He ran his thumb over it and felt her tremble. Somehow his hand was at her lower back, bringing her closer. "Jillian . . ." But he didn't have the words, only the needs. His mouth came to hers gently.

Her hands ran up his back, skimming up wet, cool skin. Her lips parted softly under his. The tip of his tongue ran lazily around the inside of her mouth, stopping to tease hers. Jillian relaxed against him, content for the long, moist kiss to go on and on. She couldn't remember ever feeling so pliant, so much in tune with another's movements and wishes. His lips grew warmer and heated hers. Against her own, she could feel his heartbeat—quick and steady. His mouth left hers only long enough to change the angle before he began to slowly deepen the kiss.

It happened so gradually she had no defense. It was an emptiness that started in her stomach like a hunger, then spread until it was an ache to be loved. Her body yearned for it. Her heart began to tell her he was the one she could share herself with, not without risk, not without pain, but with something she'd almost forgotten to ask for: hope.

But when her mind started to cloud, she struggled to clear it. It wasn't sharing, she told herself even as his lips slanted over hers to persuade her. It was giving, and if she gave, she could lose. Only a fool would forget the boundary line that stood between them.

She pulled out of his hold and stared at him. Was she mad?

Making love to a Murdock when her fence had been cut and a hundred of her cows were missing? Was she so weak that a gentle touch, a tender kiss, made her forget her responsibilities and obligations?

"I told you to stay on your own side," she said unsteadily. "I meant it." Turning away, she cut through the water and scrambled up the bank.

Breathing fast, Aaron watched her. She'd been so soft, so giving in his arms. He'd never wanted a woman more—never felt just that way. It came like a blow that she was the first who'd really mattered, and the first to throw his own emotion back in his face. Grimly he swam back to his own side.

"You're one tough lady, aren't you?"

Jillian heard the water lap as he pulled himself from it. Without bothering to shake it out, she dragged on her dusty shirt. "That's right. God knows why I was fool enough to think I could trust you." Why did she want so badly to weep when she never wept? she wondered and buttoned her shirt with shaky fingers. "All that talk about helping me, just so you could get what you wanted." Keeping her back to him, she pulled up her brief panties.

Aaron's hands paused on the snap of his jeans. Rage and frustration tumbled through him so quickly he didn't think he'd be able to control it. "Be careful, Jillian."

She whirled around, eyes brilliant, breasts heaving. "Don't you tell me what to do. You've been clear right from the beginning about what you wanted."

Muscles tense, he laid a hand on the saddle of his stallion. "That's right."

The calm answer only filled her with more fury. "I might've respected your honesty if it wasn't for the fact that I've got a cut fence and missing cattle. Things like that didn't happen when you were in Billings waiting for your father to—" She cut herself off, appalled at what she'd been about to say.

Whatever apology she might have made was swallowed at the murderous look he sent her.

"Waiting for him to what?" Aaron said softly—too softly.

The ripple of fear made her lift her chin. "That's for you to answer."

He knew he didn't dare go near her. If he did, she might not come out whole. His fingers tightened on the rope that hung on his saddle. "Then you'd better keep your thoughts to yourself."

She'd have given half her spread to have been able to take those hateful, spiteful words back. But they'd been said. "And you keep your hands to yourself," she said evenly. "I want you to stay away from me and mine. I don't need soft words, Murdock. I don't want them from you or anyone. You're a damn sight easier to take without the pretense." She stalked away to grab at her jeans.

He acted swiftly. He didn't think. His mind was still reeling from her words—words that had stung because he'd never felt or shown that kind of tenderness to another woman. What had flowed through him in the pond had been much more than a physical need and complex enough to allow him to be hurt for the first time by a woman.

Jillian gave out a gasp of astonishment as the circle of rope slipped around her, snapping snugly just about her waist and pinning her arms above the elbows. Whirling on her heel, she grabbed at the line. "What the hell do you think you're doing?"

With a jerk, Aaron brought her stumbling forward. "What I should've done a week ago." His eyes were nearly black with fury as she fell helplessly against him. "You won't get any more soft words out of me."

She struggled impotently against the rope, but her eyes were defiant and fearless. "You're going to pay for this, Murdock."

He didn't doubt it, but at that moment he didn't give a damn. Gathering her wet hair in one hand, he dragged her closer. "By God," he muttered. "I think it'll be worth it. You make a man ache, Jillian, in the middle of the night when he should have some peace. One minute you're so damn soft, and the next you're snarling. Since you can't make up your mind, I'll do it for you."

His mouth came down on hers so that she could taste enraged desire. She fought against it even as it found some answering chord in her. His chest was still naked, still wet, so that her shirt soaked up the moisture. The air rippled against her bare legs as he scooped them out from under her. With her mouth still imprisoned by his, she found herself lying on the sun-warmed grass beneath him. Her fury didn't leave room for panic.

She squirmed under him, kicking and straining against the rope, cursing him when he released her mouth to savage her neck. But an oath ended on a moan when his mouth came back to hers. He nipped into her full bottom lip as if to draw out passion. Her movements beneath him altered in tone from protest to demand, but neither of them noticed. Jillian only knew her body was on fire, and that this time she'd submit to it no matter what the cost.

He was drowning in her. He'd forgotten about the rope, forgotten his anger and his hurt. All he knew was that she was warm and slender beneath him and that her mouth was enough to drive a man over the line of reason. Nothing about her was calm. Her lips were avid and seeking; her fingers dug into his waist. He could feel the thunder of her heart race to match his. When she caught his lip between her teeth and drew it into her mouth, he groaned and let her have her way.

Jillian flew with the sensations. The grass rubbed against her legs as she shifted them to allow him more intimacy. His hair smelled of the water that ran from it onto her skin. She tasted it, and the light flavor of salt and flesh when she pressed her lips to his throat. Her name shivered in a desperate whisper against her ear. No soft words. There was nothing soft, nothing gentle about what they brought to each other now. This was a raw, primitive passion that she understood even as it was tapped for the first time. She felt his fingers skim down her shirt, releasing buttons so that he could find her. But it was his mouth not his hand that closed over the taut peak, hot and greedy. The need erupted and shattered her.

Lips, teeth, and tongue were busy on her flesh as she lay dazed from the first swift, unexpected crest. While she fought to catch her breath, Aaron tugged on her shirt to remove it, cursing when it remained tight at her waist. In an urgent move his hand swept down. His fingers touched rope. He froze, his breath heaving in his lungs.

Good God, what was he doing? Squeezing his eyes tight, he fought for reason. His face was nuzzled in the slender valley between her breasts so that he could feel as well as hear the frantic beat of her heart.

He was about to force himself on a helpless woman. No matter what the provocation, there could be no absolution for what he was on the edge of doing. Cursing himself, Aaron tugged on the rope, then yanked it over her head. After he'd tossed it aside, he looked down at her.

Her mouth was swollen from his. Her eyes were nearly closed and so clouded he couldn't read them. She lay so still he could feel each separate tremor from her body. He wanted her badly enough to beg. "You can make me pay now," he said softly and rolled from her onto his back.

She didn't move, but looked up into the calm blue sky while needs churned inside her. The warbler was still singing, the roses still blooming.

Yes, she could make him pay—she'd recognized the look of self-disgust in his eyes. She had only to get up and walk away to do it. She'd never considered herself a fool. Deliberately she rolled over on top of him. Aaron automatically put his hands on her arms to steady her. Their eyes met so that desire stared into desire.

"You'll pay—if you don't finish what you've started." Diving her hands into his hair, she brought her mouth down on his.

Her shirt fluttered open so that her naked skin slid over his. Jillian felt his groan of pleasure every bit as clearly as she heard it. Then it was all speed and fire, so fast, so hot, there wasn't time for thought. Tasting, feeling was enough as they raced over each other in a frenzy of demand. Her shirt fell away just before she pulled at the snap of his jeans.

She tugged them down, then lost herself in the long lean line of his hips. Her fingers found a narrow raised scar that ran six inches down the bone. She felt a ripple of pain as if her own skin had been rent. Then he was struggling out of his jeans and the feel of him, hot and ready against her, drove everything else out of her mind. But when she reached for him, he shifted so she was beneath him again.

"Aaron . . ." What she would have demanded ended in a helpless moan as he slid a finger under the elastic riding high on her thigh. With a clever, thorough touch of fingertips he brought her to a racking climax.

She was pulsing all over, inside and out. No longer was she aware that she clung to him, her hands bringing him as much torturous pleasure as his brought her. She only knew that her need built and was met time and time again while he held off that last, that ultimate fulfillment. With eyes dazed with passion, she watched his mouth come toward hers again. Their lips met—he plunged into her, swallowing her gasps.

For a long time she lay spent. The sky overhead was still calm. With her hands on Aaron's shoulders, she could feel each labored breath. There seemed to be no peace for them even in the aftermath of passion. Was this the way it was supposed to be? she wondered. She'd known nothing like this before. Needs that hurt and remained unsettled even after they'd been satisfied. She still wanted him—that moment when her body was hot and trembling from their merging.

After all the years she'd been so careful to distance herself from any chance of an involvement, she found herself needing a man she hardly knew. A man she'd been schooled to distrust. Yet she did trust him . . . that's what frightened her most of all. She had no reason to—no logical reason. He'd made her forget her ambitions, her work, her responsibilities, and reminded her that beneath it all, she was first a woman. More, he'd made her glory in it.

Aaron raised his head slowly, for the first time in his memory unsure of himself. She'd gotten to a place inside him no one had ever touched. He realized he didn't want her to walk away and leave it empty again—and that he'd never be able to hold her unless she was willing. "Jillian . . ." He brushed her damp, tangled hair from her cheek. "This was supposed to be easy. Why isn't it?"

"I don't know." She held onto the weakness another moment, bringing his cheek down to hers so that she could draw in his scent and remember. "I need to think."

"About what?"

She closed her eyes a moment and shook her head. "I don't know. Let me go now, Aaron."

His fingers tightened in her hair. "For how long?"

"I don't know that either. I need some time."

It would be easy to keep her—for the moment. He had only to lower his mouth to hers again. He remembered the wild mustang—the hell he'd gone through to catch it, the hell he'd gone through to set it free. Saying nothing, he released her.

They dressed in silence—both of them too battered by feelings they'd never tried to put into words. When Jillian reached for her hat, Aaron took her arm.

"If I told you this meant something to me, more than I'd expected, maybe more than I'd wanted, would you believe me?"

Jillian moistened her lips. "I do now. I have to be sure I do tomorrow."

Aaron picked up his own hat and shaded his face with it. "I'll wait—but I won't wait long." Lifting a hand, he cupped her chin. "If you don't come to me, I'll come after you."

She ignored the little thrill of excitement that rushed up her spine. "If I don't come to you, you won't be able to come after me." Turning away, she untied her mare and vaulted into the saddle. Aaron slipped his hand under the bridle and gave her one long look.

"Don't bet on it," he said quietly. He walked back over the boundary line to his own mount.

CHAPTER 7

If you don't come to me, I'll come after you.

They weren't words Jillian would forget. She hadn't yet decided what to do about them—any more than she'd decided what to do about what had happened between her and Aaron. There'd been more than passion in that fiery afternoon at the pond, more than pleasure, however intense. Perhaps she could have faced the passion and the pleasure, but it was the something more that kept her awake at nights.

If she went to him, what would she be going to? A man she'd yet to scratch the surface of—an affair that promised to have more hills and valleys than she knew how to negotiate. The risk—she was beginning to understand the risk too well. If she relaxed her hands on the reins this time, she'd tumble into love before she could regain control. That was difficult for her to admit, and impossible for her to understand.

She'd always believed that people fell in love because they wanted to, because they were looking for, or were ready for, romance. Certainly she'd been ready for it once before, open for all those soft feelings and heightened emotions. Yet now, when she believed she was on the border of love again, she was neither ready for it, nor was she experiencing any soft feelings. Aaron Murdock didn't ask for them—and in not asking, he demanded so much more.

If she went to him . . . could she balance her responsibilities, her ambitions, with the needs he drew out of her? When she was in his arms, she didn't think of the ranch, or her position there that she had to struggle every day to maintain.

If she fell in love with him . . . could she deal with the imbalance of feelings between them and cope when the time came for him to go his own way? She never doubted he would. Other than Clay, there'd never been a man who'd remained constant to her.

Indecision tore at her, as it would in a woman accustomed to following her own route in her own way.

And while her personal life was in turmoil, her professional one fared no better. Five hundred of her cattle were missing. There was no longer any doubt that her herd had been systematically and successfully rustled.

Jillian hung up the phone, rubbing at the headache that drummed behind her temples.

"Well?" Hat in lap, Joe Carlson sat on the other side of her desk.

"They can't deliver the plane until the end of the week." Grimly she set her jaw as she looked over at him. "It hardly matters now. Unless they're fools, they've got the cattle well away by this time. Probably transported them over the border into Wyoming."

He studied the brim of his neat Stetson. "Maybe not, that would make it federal."

"It's what I'd do," she murmured. "You can't hide five hundred head of prime beef." Rising, she dragged her hands through her hair. *Five hundred.* The words continued to flash in her mind—a sign of failure, impotence, vulnerability. "Well, the sheriff's doing what he can, but they've got the jump on us, Joe. There's nothing I can do." On a sound of frustration, she balled her fists. "I hate being helpless."

"Jillian . . ." Joe ran the brim of his hat through his hands, frowning down at it another moment. During his silence she could hear the old clock on her grandfather's desk tick the time away. "I wouldn't feel right if I didn't bring it up," he said at length and looked back at her. "It wouldn't be too difficult to hide five hundred head if they were scattered through a few thousand."

Her eyes chilled. "Why don't you speak plainly, Joe?"

He rose. After more than six months on Utopia, he still looked more businessman than outdoorsman. And she understood it was the businessman who spoke now. "Jillian, you can't just ignore the fact that the west boundary line was cut. That pasture leads directly onto Murdock land."

"I know where it leads," she said coolly. "Just as I know I need more than a cut line to accuse anyone, particularly the Murdocks, of rustling."

Joe opened his mouth to speak again, met her uncompromising look, then shut it. "Okay."

The simplicity of his answer only fanned her temper. And her doubts. "Aaron told me he was going to take a thorough head count. He'd know if there were fifty extra head on his spread, much less five hundred."

It was her tone much more than her words that told him where the land lay now. "I know."

Jillian stared at him. His eyes were steady and compassionate. "Damn it, he doesn't need to steal cattle from me."

"Jillian, you lose five hundred head now and your profit dwindles down to nothing. Lose that much again, half that much again, and . . . you might have to start thinking about selling off some of your pasture. There're other reasons than the price per head for rustling."

She spun around, shutting her eyes tight. She'd thought of that—and hated herself for it. "He would've asked me if he wanted to buy my land."

"Maybe, but your answer would've been no. Rumor is he

was going to start his own place a few years back. He didn't—
but that doesn't mean he's content to make do with what his
father has."

She couldn't contradict him, not on anything he'd said. But
she couldn't live with it either. "Leave the investigating to the
sheriff, Joe. That's his job."

He drew very straight and very stiff at the clipped tone of
her voice. "All right. I guess I better get back to mine."

On a wave of frustration and guilt, she turned before he
reached the door. "Joe—I'm sorry. I know you're only thinking about Utopia."

"I'm thinking about you, too."

"I appreciate it, I really do." She picked up her worn leather
work glove from the desk and ran it through her hands. "I
have to handle this my own way, and I need a little more time
to decide just what that is."

"Okay." He put his hat on and lowered the brim with his
finger. "Just so you know you've got support if you need it."

"I won't forget it."

When he'd gone, Jillian stopped in the center of the office. God, she wanted so badly to panic. Just to throw up her
hands and tell whoever'd listen that she couldn't deal with it.
There had to be someone else, somewhere, who could take
over and see her through until everything was back in order.
But she wasn't allowed to panic, or to turn over her responsibilities even for a minute. The land was hers, and all that
went with it.

Jillian picked up her hat and her other glove. There was
work to be done. If they cleaned her out down to the last hundred head, there would still be work to be done, and a way to
build things back up again. She had the land, and her grandfather's legacy of determination.

Even as she opened the front door to go out, she saw Karen
Murdock drive up in front of the house. Surprised, Jillian hesitated, then went out on the porch to meet her.

"Hello, I hope you don't mind that I just dropped by."

"No, of course not." Jillian smiled, marveling for the second time at the soft, elegant looks of Aaron's mother. "It's nice to see you again, Mrs. Murdock."

"I've caught you at a bad time," she said, glancing down at the work gloves in Jillian's hand.

"No." Jillian stuck the gloves in her back pocket. "Would you like some coffee?"

"I'd love it."

Karen followed Jillian into the house, glancing around idly as they walked toward the kitchen. "Lord, it's been years since I've been in here. I used to visit your grandmother," she said with a rueful smile. "Of course your grandfather and Paul both knew, but we were all very careful not to mention it. How do you feel about old feuds, Jillian?"

There was a laugh in her voice that might have set Jillian's back up at one time. Now it simply nudged a smile from her. "Not precisely the same way I felt a few weeks ago."

"I'm glad to hear it." Karen took a seat at the kitchen table while Jillian began to brew a fresh pot of coffee. "I realize Paul said some things the other day that were bound to rub you the wrong way. I have to confess he does some of it on purpose. Your reaction was the high point of his day."

Jillian smiled a little as she looked over her shoulder. "Maybe he's more like Clay than I'd imagined."

"They were out of the same mold. There aren't many of them," she murmured. "Jillian—we've heard about your missing cattle. I can't tell you how badly I feel. I realize the words *if there's anything I can do* sound empty, but I mean them."

Turning back to the coffeepot, Jillian managed to shrug. She wasn't sure she could deal easily with sympathy right then. "It's a risk we all take. The sheriff's doing what he can."

"A risk we all take," Karen agreed. "When it happens to one of us, all of us feel it." She hesitated a moment, knowing the ground was delicate. "Jillian, Aaron mentioned the cut line to me, though he's kept it from his father."

"I'm not worried about the cut line," Jillian told her quietly. "I know Aaron didn't have any part in it—I'm not a fool."

No, Karen thought, studying the clean-lined profile. A fool you're not. "He's very concerned about you."

"He needn't be." She swung open a cupboard door for cups. "It's my problem, I have to deal with it."

Karen watched calmly as Jillian poured. "No support accepted?"

With a sigh, Jillian turned around. "I don't mean to be rude, Mrs. Murdock. Running a ranch is a difficult, chancy business. When you're a woman, you double those stakes." Bringing the coffee to the table, she sat across from her. "I have to be twice as good as a man would be in my place because this is still a man's world. I can't afford to cave in."

"I understand that." Karen sipped and glanced around the room. "There's no one here you have to prove anything to."

Jillian looked up from her own cup and saw the compassion, and the unique bond one woman can have with another. As she did, the tight band of control loosened. "I'm so scared," she whispered. "Most of the time I don't dare admit it to myself because there's so much riding on this year. I've taken a lot of gambles—if they pay off . . . Five hundred head." She let out a long breath as the numbers pounded in her mind. "It won't put me under, I can't let it put me under, but it's going to take a long time to recover."

Reaching out, Karen covered her hand with her own. "They could be found."

"You know the chances of that now." For a moment she sat still, accepting the comfort of the touch before she put her hand back on her cup. "Whichever way it goes, I'm still boss at Utopia. I have a responsibility to make what was passed on to me work. Clay trusted me with what was his. I'm going to make it work."

Karen gave her a long, thorough look very much like one of her son's. "For Clay or for yourself?"

"For both of us," Jillian told her. "I owe him for the land, and for what he taught me."

"You can put too much of yourself into this land," Karen said abruptly. "Paul would swear I'd taken leave of my senses if he heard me say so, but it's true. Aaron—" She smiled, indulgent, proud. "He's a great deal like his father, but he doesn't have Paul's rigidity. Perhaps he hasn't needed it. You can't let the land swallow you, Jillian."

"It's all I have."

"You don't mean that. Oh, you think you do," she murmured when Jillian said nothing. "But if you lost every acre of this land tomorrow, you'd make something else. You've the guts for it. I recognize it in you just as I've always seen it in Aaron."

"He had other options." Agitated, Jillian rose to pour coffee she no longer wanted.

"You're thinking of the oil." For a moment Karen said nothing as she weighed the pros and cons of what she was going to say. "He did that for me—and for his father," she said at length. "I hope I don't ever have to ask anything like that of him again."

Jillian came back to the table but didn't sit. "I don't understand."

"Paul was wrong. He's a good man and his mistakes have always been made with the same force and vigor as he does everything." A smile flickered on her lips, but her eyes were serious. "He'd promised something to Aaron, something that had been understood since Aaron was a boy. The Double M would be his, if he'd earned it. By God, he did," she whispered. "I think you understand what I mean."

"Yes." Jillian looked down at her cup, then set it down. "Yes, I do."

"When Aaron came back from college, Paul wasn't ready

to let go. That's when Aaron agreed to work it his father's way for three years. He was to take over as manager after that—with full authority."

"I've heard," Jillian began, then changed her tack. "It can't be easy for a man to give up what he's worked for, even to his own son."

"It was time for Paul to give," Karen told her, but she held her head high. "Perhaps he would have if . . ." She gestured with her hands as though she were slowing herself down. "When he refused to stick to the bargain, Aaron was furious. They had a terrible argument—the kind that's inevitable between two strong, self-willed men. Aaron was determined to go down to Wyoming, buy some land for himself, and start from scratch. As much as he loved the ranch, I think it was something he'd been itching to do in any case."

"But he didn't."

"No." Karen's eyes were very clear. "Because I asked him not to. The doctors had just diagnosed Paul as terminal. They'd given him two years at the outside. He was infuriated that age had caught up with him, that his body was betraying him. He's a very proud man, Jillian. He'd beaten everything he'd ever gone up against."

She remembered the hawklike gaze and trembling hands. "I'm sorry."

"He didn't want anyone to know, not even Aaron. I can count the times I've gone against Paul on one hand." She glanced down at her own palms. Something in her expression told Jillian very clearly that if the woman had acquiesced over the years, it had been because of strength and not weakness. "I knew if Aaron went away like that, Paul would stop fighting for whatever time he had left. And then Aaron, once he knew, would never be able to live with it. So I told him." She let out a long sigh and turned her hands over. "I asked him to give up what he wanted. He went to Billings, and though I'm sure he's always thought he did it for me, I know he did it for his father. I don't imagine the doctors would agree, but Aaron gave his father five years."

Jillian turned away as her throat began to ache. "I've said some horrible things to him."

"You wouldn't be the first, I'm sure. Aaron knew what it would look like. He's never given a damn what people think of him. What most people think," she corrected softly.

"I can't apologize," Jillian said as she fought to control herself. "He'd be furious if I told him I knew."

"You know him well."

"I don't," Jillian returned with sudden passion. "I don't know him, I don't understand him, and—" She cut herself off, amazed that she was about to bare her soul to Aaron's mother.

"I'm his mother," Karen said, interpreting the look. "But I'm still a woman. And one who understands very well what it is to have feelings for a man that promise to lead to difficulties." This time she didn't weigh her words but spoke freely. "I was barely twenty when I met Paul, he was past forty. His friends thought he was mad and that I wanted his money." She laughed, then sat back with a little sigh. "I can promise you, I didn't see the humor in it thirty years ago. I'm not here to offer advice on whatever's between you and Aaron, but to offer support if you'll take it."

Jillian looked at her—the enduring beauty, the strength that showed in her eyes, the kindness. "I'm not sure I know how."

Rising, Karen placed her hands on Jillian's shoulders. So young, she thought wistfully. So dead set. "Do you know how to accept friendship?"

Jillian smiled and touched Karen's hands, still resting on her shoulders. "Yes."

"That'll do. You're busy," she said briskly, giving Jillian a quick squeeze before she released her. "But if you need a woman, as we sometimes do, call me."

"I will. Thank you."

Karen shook her head. "No, it's not all unselfish. I've lived over thirty years in this man's world." Briefly she touched Jillian's cheek. "I miss my daughter."

*   *   *

Aaron stood on the porch and watched the moon rise. The night was so still he heard the whisk of a hawk's wings over his head before it dove after its night prey. In one hand he held a can of iced beer that he sipped occasionally, though he wasn't registering the taste. It was one of those warm spring nights when you could taste the scent of the flowers and smell the hint of summer, which was creeping closer.

He'd be damned if he'd wait much longer.

It had been a week since he'd touched her. Every night after the long, dusty day was over, he found himself aching to have her with him, to fill that emptiness inside him he'd become so suddenly aware of. It was difficult enough to have discovered he didn't want Jillian in the same way he'd wanted any other woman, but to have discovered his own vulnerabilities . . .

She could hurt him—had hurt him. That was a first, Aaron thought grimly and lifted his beer. He hadn't yet worked out how to prevent it from happening again. But that didn't stop him from wanting her.

She didn't trust him. Though he'd once agreed that he didn't want her to, Aaron had learned that was a lie. He wanted her to give him her trust—to believe in him enough to share her problems with him. She must be going through hell now, he thought as his fingers tightened on the can. But she wouldn't come to him, wouldn't let him help. Maybe it was about time he did something about that—whether she liked it or not.

Abruptly impatient, angry, he started toward the steps. The

sound of an approaching car reached him before the head-lights did. Glancing toward the sound, he watched the twin beams cut through the darkness. His initial disinterest became a tension he felt in his shoulder and stomach muscles.

Aaron set the half-empty beer on the porch rail as Jillian pulled up in front of his house. Whatever his needs were, he still had enough sense of self-preservation to prevent himself from just rushing down the stairs and grabbing her. He waited.

She'd been so sure her nerves would calm during the drive over. It was difficult for her, as a woman who simply didn't permit herself to be nervous, to deal with a jumpy stomach and dry throat. Not once since his mother had left her that morning had Aaron been out of her thoughts. Yet Jillian had gone through an agony of doubt before she'd made the final decision to come. In coming, she was giving him something she'd never intended to—a portion of her private self.

With the moon at her back she stood by her car a moment, looking up at him. Perhaps because her legs weren't as strong as they should've been, she kept her chin high as she walked up the porch steps.

"This is a mistake," she told him.

Aaron remained where he was, one shoulder leaning against the rail post. "Is it?"

"It's going to complicate things at a time when my life's complicated enough."

His stomach had twisted into a mass of knots that were only tugging tighter as he looked at her. She was pale, but there wasn't a hint of a tremor in her voice. "You took your sweet time coming here," he said mildly, but he folded his fingers into his palm to keep from touching her.

"I wouldn't have come at all if I could've stopped myself."

"That so?" It was more of an admission than he'd expected. The first muscles began to relax. "Well, since you're here, why don't you come a little closer?"

He wasn't going to make it easy for her, Jillian realized. And she'd have detested herself if she'd let him. With her eyes on his, she stepped forward until their bodies brushed. "Is this close enough?"

His eyes skimmed her face, then he smiled. "No."

Jillian hooked her hands behind his head and pressed her lips to his. "Now?"

"Closer." He allowed himself to touch her—one hand at the small of her back rode slowly up to grip her hair. His eyes glittered in the moonlight, touched with triumph, amusement, and passion. "A damn sight closer, Jillian."

Her eyes stayed open as she fit her body more intimately to his. She felt the answering response of his muscles against her own, the echoing thud of his heart. "If we get much closer out here on the porch," she murmured with her mouth a whisper from his, "we're going to be illegal."

"Yeah." He traced her bottom lip, moistening it, and felt her little jerk of breath on his tongue. "I'll post bond if you're worried."

Her lips throbbed from the expert flick of his tongue. "Shut up, Murdock," she muttered and crushed her mouth to his. Jillian let all the passions, all the emotions that had been chasing her around for days, have their way. Even as they sprang out of her, they consumed her. Mindlessly she pressed against him so that he was caught between her body and the post.

The thrill of pleasure was so intense it almost sliced through his skin. Aaron's arm came around her so that he could cup the back of her head and keep that wildly aggressive mouth on his own. Then, swiftly, his arm scooped under her knees and lifted her off her feet.

"Aaron—" Her protest was smothered by another ruthless kiss before he walked across the porch to the door. Though she admired the way he could swing the screen open, and slam the heavy door with his arms full, she laughed. "Aaron, put me down. I can walk."

"Don't see how when I'm carrying you," he pointed out as he started up the narrow steps to the second floor.

"Is this the sort of thing you do to express male dominance?"

She was rewarded with a narrow-eyed glare and smiled sweetly.

"No," Aaron said in mild tones. "This is the sort of thing I do to express romance. Now, when I want to express male dominance . . ." As he drew near the top of the steps he shifted her quickly so that she hung over his shoulder.

After the initial shock Jillian had to acknowledge a hit. "Had that one coming," she admitted, blowing the hair out of her face. "I think my point was that I wasn't looking for romance or dominance."

Aaron's brow lifted as he walked into the bedroom. The words had been light enough, but he'd caught the sincerity of tone. Slowly he drew her down so that before her feet had touched the floor every angle of her body had rubbed against his. Weakened by the maneuver, she stared up at him with eyes already stormy with desire. "Don't you like romance, Jillian?"

"That's not what I'm asking for," she managed, reaching for him.

He grabbed her wrists, holding her off. "That's too bad, then." Very lightly he nipped at her ear. "You'll just have to put up with it. Do you reckon straight passion's safer?"

"As anything could be with you." She caught her breath as his tongue traced down the side of her throat.

Aaron laughed, then began lazily, determinedly, to seduce her with his mouth alone. "This right here," he murmured, nibbling at a point just above her collar. "So soft, so delicate. A man could almost forget there're places like this on you until he finds them for himself. You throw up that damn-the-devil chin and it's tempting to give it one good clip, but then"—he tilted his head to a new angle and his lips skimmed along her skin—"right under it's just like silk."

He tugged with his teeth at the cord of her neck and felt her arms go boneless. That's what he wanted, he thought with rising excitement. To have her melting and pliant and out of control, if only for a few minutes. Hot blood and fire were rewards in themselves, but this time, perhaps only this time, he wanted the satisfaction of knowing he could make her as weak as she could make him.

He slanted his mouth over hers, teasing her tongue with the tip of his until her breath was short and shallow. Her pulse pounded into his palms. He was going to take his time undressing her, he thought. A long, leisurely time that would drive them both crazy.

Without hurry Aaron backed her toward the bed, then eased her down until she sat on the edge. In the moonlight he could see that her eyes had already misted with need, her skin softly flushed with it. Watching her, he ran a long finger down her throat to the first button on her shirt. His eyes remained steady as he undid it, then the second—then the third. He stopped there to move his hands down her, lightly over her breasts, the nipped waist, and narrow hips to the long, slender thighs. She was very still but for the quiver of her flesh.

Turning, he tucked her leg between his and began pulling off her boot. The first hit the floor, but when he took the other and tugged, Jillian gave him some assistance with a well-placed foot.

Surprised, he glanced back to see her shoot him a cocky smile. She recovered quickly, he thought. It would be all the more exciting to turn her to putty again. "You might do the same for me," Aaron suggested, then dropped on the bed, leaned back on his elbows, and held out a booted foot.

Jillian rose to oblige him and straddled his leg. This—the wicked grin, the reckless eyes—she knew how to deal with. It might light a fire in her, but it didn't bring on that uncontrollable softness. When she'd finally made her decision to come, she'd made it to come on equal terms, with no quiet promises or tender phrases that meant no more than the breath it took to make them. She'd told herself she wouldn't fall in love with him as long as she listened to her body and blocked off her heart.

The minute his second boot hit the floor, Aaron grabbed her around the waist and swung her back so that she fell onto the bed, laughing. "You're a tough guy, Murdock." Jillian hooked her arms around his neck and grinned up at him. "Always tossing women around."

"Bad habit of mine." Lowering his head, he nibbled idly at her lips, resisting her attempt to deepen the kiss. "I like your mouth," he murmured. "It's another of those soft, surprising places." Gently he sucked on her lower lip until he felt the hands at his neck grow lax.

The mists were closing in again and she forgot the ways and means to hold them off. This wasn't what she wanted . . . was it? Yet it seemed to be everything she wanted. Her mind was floating, out of her body, so that she could almost see herself lying languorous and pliant under Aaron. She could see the tension and anxieties of the past days drain out of her own face until it was soft and relaxed under the lazy touch of his mouth and tongue. She could feel her heartbeat drop to a light pace that wasn't quite steady but not yet frantic. Perhaps this was what it felt like to be pampered, to be prized. She wasn't sure, but knew she couldn't bear to lose the sensation. Her sigh came slowly with the release of doubts.

When he bent to whisper something foolish in her ear, she could smell his evening shower on him. His face was rough with the stubble of a long day, but she rubbed her cheek against it, enjoying the scrape. Then his lips grazed across the skin that was alive and tingling until they found their way back to hers.

She felt the brush of strong, clever fingers as they trailed down to release the last buttons of her shirt. Then they skimmed over her rib cage, lightly, effortlessly drawing her deeper into the realm of sensation. He barely touched her. The kisses remained soft, his hands gentle. All coherent thought spun away.

"My shirt's in the way," he murmured against her ear. "I want to feel you against me."

She lifted her hands, and though her fingers didn't fumble, she couldn't make them move quickly. It seemed like hours before she felt the press of his flesh against hers. With a sigh, she slid her hands up to his shoulders and back until she'd drawn the shirt away. The ridge of muscle was so hard. As she rubbed her palms over him, Jillian realized she'd only had flashes of impressions the first time they'd made love. Everything had been so fast and wild she hadn't been able to appreciate just how well he was formed.

Tight sinew, taut flesh. Aaron was a man used to using his back and his hands to do a day's work. She didn't stop to reason why that in itself was a pleasure to her. Then she could reason nothing because his mouth had begun to roam.

He hadn't known he could gain such complete satisfaction in thinking of another's pleasure. He wanted her—wanted her quick and fast and furious, and yet it was a heady feeling to know he had the power to make her weak with a touch.

The underside of her breast was so soft . . . and he lingered. The skin above the waistband of her jeans was white and smooth . . . and his hand was content to move just there. He felt her first trembles; they rippled under his lips and hands until his senses swam. Denim strained against denim until he pulled the jeans down over her hips to find her.

Jillian wasn't certain when the languor had become hunger. She arched against him, demanding, but he continued to move without haste. She couldn't understand his fascination with her body when she'd always considered it too straight, too slim and practical. Yet now he seemed anxious to touch, to taste every inch. And the murmurs that reached her whispered approval. His hand cupped her knee so that his fingers trailed over the sensitive back. Years of riding, walking, working, had made her legs strong, and very susceptible.

When his teeth scraped down her thigh, she cried out, stunned to be catapulted to the taut edge of the first peak. But he didn't allow her to go over. Not yet. His warm breath teased her, then the light play of his tongue. She felt the threat of explosion building, growing in power and depth. Yet somehow he knew the instant before it shattered her, and retreated. Again and again he took her to the verge and brought her back until she was weak and desperate.

Jillian shifted beneath Aaron, willing him to take anything, all that he wanted—not even aware that he'd removed the last barrier of clothing until he was once more lying full length on her. She felt each warm, unsteady breath on her face just before his lips raced over it.

"This time . . ." Aaron pulled air into his lungs so that he could speak. "This time you tell me—you tell me that you want me."

"Yes." She locked herself around him, shuddering with need. "Yes, I want you. Now."

Something flashed in his eyes. "Not just now," he said roughly and drove into her.

Jillian slid over the first edge and was blinded. But there was more, so much more.

CHAPTER 8

It was the scent of her hair that slowly brought him back to reason. His face was buried in it. The fragrance reminded him of the wildflowers his mother would sometimes gather and place in a little porcelain vase on a window ledge. It was tangled in his hands, and so soft against his skin he knew he'd be content to stay just as he was through the night.

She lay still beneath him, her breathing so quiet and even she might have been asleep. But when he turned his head to press his lips to her neck, her arms tightened around him. Lifting his head, he looked down at her.

Her eyes were nearly closed, heavy. He'd seen the shadows beneath them when she'd first walked toward him on the porch. With a small frown, Aaron traced his thumb over them. "You haven't been sleeping well."

Surprised by the statement, and his tone, she lifted her brows. After where they'd just gone together, she might've expected him to say something foolish or arousing. Instead his brows had drawn together and his tone was disapproving. She wasn't sure why it made her want to laugh, but it did.

"I'm fine," she said with a smile.

"No." He cut her off and cupped her chin in his hand. "You're not."

She stared up, realizing how easy it would be to just pour

out her thoughts and feelings. The worries, the fears, the problems, that seemed to build up faster than she could cope with them—how reassuring it would be to say it all out loud, to him.

She'd done too much of that with his mother, but somehow Jillian could justify that. It was one thing to confess fears and doubts to another woman, and another to give a man an insight on your weaknesses. At dawn they'd both be ranchers again, with a boundary line between them that had stood for nearly a century.

"Aaron, I didn't come here to—"

"I know why you came," he interrupted. His voice was much milder than his eyes. "Because you couldn't stay away. I understand that. Now you're just going to have to accept what comes with it."

It was difficult to drum up a great deal of dignity when she was naked and warm beneath him, but she came close to succeeding. "Which is?"

The annoyance in his eyes lightened to amusement. "I like the way you say that—just like my third grade teacher."

Her lips quivered. "It's one of the few things I managed to pick up from my mother. But you haven't answered the question, Murdock."

"I'm crazy about you," he said suddenly and the mouth that had curved into a smile fell open. She wasn't ready to hear that one, Aaron mused. He wasn't sure he was ready for the consequences of it himself, and decided to play it light. "Of course, I've always been partial to nasty-tempered females. I mean to help you, Jillian." His eyes were abruptly sober. "If I have to climb over your back to do it."

"There isn't anything you can do even if I wanted you to."

He didn't comment immediately but shifted, pulling the pillows up against the headboard, then leaning back before he drew her against him. Jillian didn't stiffen as much as go still. There was something quietly possessive about the move, and irresistibly sweet. Before she could stop it, she'd relaxed against him.

Aaron felt the hesitation but didn't comment. When you went after trust, you did it slowly. "Tell me what's been done."

"Aaron, I don't want to bring you into this."

"I am in it, if for no other reason than that cut line."

She could accept that, and let her eyes close. "We did a full head count and came up five hundred short. As a precaution, we branded what calves were left right away. I estimate we lost fifty or sixty of them. The sheriff's been out."

"What'd he find?"

She moved her shoulders. "Can't tell where they took them out. If they'd cut any more wire, they'd fixed it. Very neat and tidy," she murmured, knowing something died inside her each time she thought of it. "It seems as though they didn't take them all at once, but skimmed a few head here and there."

"Seems odd they left the one line down."

"Maybe they didn't have time to fix it."

"Or maybe they wanted to throw your attention my way until they'd finished."

"Maybe." She turned her face into his shoulder—only slightly, only for an instant—but for Jillian it was a large step toward sharing. "Aaron, I didn't mean the things I said about you and your father."

"Forget it."

She tilted her head back and looked at him. "I can't."

He kissed her roughly. "Try harder," he suggested. "I heard you were getting a plane."

"Yes." She dropped her head on his shoulder and tried to order her thoughts. "It doesn't look like it's going to be ready until next week."

"Then we'll go up in mine tomorrow."

"But why—"

"Nothing against the sheriff," he said easily. "But you know your land better."

Jillian pressed her lips together. "Aaron, I don't want to be obligated to you. I don't know how to explain it, but—"

"Then don't." Taking hold of her hair, he jerked it until her face came up to his. "You're going to find I'm not the kind who'll always give a damn about what you want. You can fight me, sometimes you might even win. But you won't stop me."

Her eyes kindled. "Why do you gear me up for a fight when I'm trying to be grateful?"

In one swift move he shifted so that they lay crosswise across the bed. "Maybe I like you better that way. You're a hell of a lot more dangerous when you soften up."

She threw up her chin. "That's not something that's going to happen very often around you."

"Good," he said and crushed his mouth onto hers. "You'll stay with me tonight."

"I'm not—" Then he silenced her with a savage kiss that left no room for thought, much less words.

"Tonight," he said with a laugh that held more challenge than humor, "you stay with me."

And he took her in a fury that whispered of desperation.

* * *

The birds woke her. There was a short stretch of time during the summer when the sun rose early enough that the birds were up before her. With a sigh, Jillian snuggled into the pillow. She could always fool her system into thinking she'd been lazy when she woke to daylight and birdsong.

Groggily she went over the day's workload. She'd have to check Baby before she went in to the horses. He liked to have his bottle right off. With one luxurious stretch, she rolled over, then stared blankly around the room. Aaron's room. He'd won that battle.

Lying back for a moment, she thought about the night with a mixture of pleasure and discomfort. He'd said once before that it wasn't as easy as it should've been. But could he have any idea what it had done to her to lie beside him through the night? She'd never known the simple pleasure of sleeping with someone else, sharing warmth and quiet and darkness. What had made her believe that she could have an affair and remain practical about it?

But she wasn't in love with him. Jillian reached over to touch the side of the bed where he'd slept. She still had too much sense to let that happen. Her fingers dug into the sheet as she closed her eyes. Oh, God, she hoped she did.

The birdcalls distracted her so that she looked over at the window. The sun poured through. But it wasn't summer, Jillian remembered abruptly. What was she still doing in bed when the sun was up? Furious with herself, she sat up just as the door opened. Aaron walked in, carrying a mug of coffee.

"Too bad," he commented as he crossed to her. "I was looking forward to waking you up."

"I've got to get back," she said, tossing her hair from her eyes. "I should've been up hours ago."

Aaron held her in place effortlessly with a hand on her shoulder. "What you should do is sleep till noon," he corrected as he studied her face. "But you look better."

"I've got a ranch to run."

"And there isn't a ranch in the country that can't do without one person for one day." He sat down beside her and pushed the cup into her hand. "Drink your coffee."

She might've been annoyed by his peremptory order, but the scent of coffee was more persuasive. "What time is it?" she asked between sips.

"A bit after nine."

"Nine!" Her eyes grew comically wide. "Good God, I've got to get back."

Again Aaron held her in bed without effort. "You've got to drink your coffee," he corrected. "Then you've got to have some breakfast."

After a quick, abortive struggle, Jillian shot him an exasperated look. "Will you stop treating me as though I were eight years old?"

He glanced down to where she held the sheet absently at her breasts. "It's tempting," he agreed.

"Eyes front, Murdock," she ordered when her mouth twitched. "Look, I appreciate the service," Jillian continued, gesturing with her cup, "but I can't sit around until midday."

"When's the last time you had eight hours' sleep?" He watched the annoyance flicker into her eyes as she lifted the coffee again, sipping rather than answering. "You'd have had more than that last night if you hadn't—distracted me."

She lifted her brows. "Is that what I did?"

"Several times, as I recall." Something in her expression, a question, a hint of doubt, made him study her a bit more carefully. Was it possible a woman like her would need reassurance after the night they'd spent together? What a strange mixture of tough and vulnerable she was. Aaron bent over and brushed his lips over her brow, knowing what would happen if he allowed himself just one taste of her mouth. "Apparently, you don't have to try very hard," he murmured. His lips trailed down to her temple before he could prevent them. "If you'd like to take advantage of me . . ."

Jillian let out an unsteady breath. "I think—I'd better have pity on you this morning, Murdock."

"Well . . ." He hooked a finger under the sheet and began to draw it down. "Can't say I've ever cared much for pity."

"Aaron." Jillian tightened her hold on the sheet. "It's nine o'clock in the morning."

"Probably a bit past that by now."

When he started to lean closer, she lifted the mug and held it against his chest. "I've got stock to check and fences to ride," she reminded him. "And so do you."

He had a woman to protect, he thought, surprising himself. But he had enough sense not to mention it to the woman. "Sometimes," he began, then gave her a friendly kiss, "you're just no fun, Jillian."

Laughing, she drained the coffee. "Why don't you get out of here so I can have a shower and get dressed?"

"See what I mean." But he rose. "I'll fix your breakfast," he told her, then continued before she could say it wasn't necessary. "And neither of us is riding fence today. We're going up in the plane."

"Aaron, you don't have to take the time away from your own ranch to do this."

He hooked his hands in his pockets and studied her for so long her brows drew together. "For a sharp woman, you can be amazingly slow. If it's easier for you, just remember that rustling is every rancher's business."

She could see he was annoyed; she could hear it in the sudden coolness of tone. "I don't understand you."

"No." He inclined his head in a gesture that might've been resignation or acceptance. "I can see that." He started for the door, and Jillian watched him, baffled.

"I . . ." What the devil did she want to say? "I have to drive over and let Gil know what I'm doing."

"I sent a man over earlier." Aaron paused at the door and turned back to her. "He knows you're with me."

"He knows—you sent—" She broke off, her fingers tightening on the handle of the mug. "You sent a man over to tell him I was here, this morning?"

"That's right."

She dragged a hand through her hair and sunlight shimmered gold at the ends. "Do you realize what that looks like?"

His eyes became very cool and remote. "It looks like what it is. Sorry, I didn't realize you wanted an assignation."

"Aaron—" But he was already closing the door behind him. Jillian brought the mug back in a full swing and barely prevented herself from following through. With a sound of disgust, she set it down and pulled herself from bed. That had been clumsy of her, she berated herself. How was he to understand that it wasn't shame, but insecurity? Perhaps it was better if he didn't understand.

Aaron could cheerfully have strangled her. In the kitchen, he slapped a slice of ham into the skillet. His own fault, he thought as it began to sizzle. Damn it, it was his own fault. He'd had no business letting things get beyond what they were meant to. If he stretched things, he could say that she had a wary sort of affection for him. It was unlikely it would ever go beyond that. If his feelings had, he had only himself to blame, and himself to deal with.

Since when did he want fences around him? Aaron thought savagely as he plunged a kitchen fork into the grilling meat. Since when did he want more from a woman, any woman, than companionship, intelligence, and a warm bed? Maybe his feelings had slipped a bit past that, but he wasn't out of control yet.

Pouring coffee, he drank it hot and black. He'd been around too long to lose his head over a firebrand who didn't want anything more than a practical, uncomplicated affair. After all, he hadn't been looking for any more than that himself. He'd just let himself get caught up because of the problems she was facing, and the unwavering manner with which she faced them.

The coffee calmed him. Reassured, he pulled a carton of eggs out of the refrigerator. He'd help her as much as he could over the rustling, take her to bed as often as possible, and that would be that.

When she came into the room, he glanced over casually. Her hair was still wet, her face naked and glowing with health and a good night's sleep.

Oh, God, he was in love with her. And what the hell was he going to do?

The easy comment she'd been about to make about the smell of food vanished. Why was he staring at her as if he'd never seen her before? Uncharacteristically self-conscious, she shifted her weight. He looked as though someone had just knocked the wind from him. "Is something wrong?"

"What?"

His answer was so dazed she smiled. What in the world had he been thinking about when she'd interrupted him? she wondered. "I said, is something wrong? You look like you've just taken a quick fall from a tall horse."

He cursed himself and turned away. "Nothing. How do you want your eggs?"

"Over easy, thanks." She took a step toward him, then hesitated. It wasn't a simple matter for her to make an outward show of affection. She'd met with too many lukewarm receptions in her life. Drawing up her courage, she crossed the room and touched his shoulder. He stiffened. She withdrew. "Aaron . . ." How calm her voice was, she mused. But then, she'd grown very adept very early at concealing hurt. "I'm not very good at accepting support."

"I've noticed." He cracked an egg and let it slide into the pan.

She blinked because her eyes had filled. Stupid! she railed at herself. Never put your weaknesses on display. Swallowing pride came hard to her, but there were times it was necessary. "What I'd like to say is that I appreciate what you're doing. I appreciate it very much."

Emotions were clawing him. He smacked another egg on the side of the pan. "Don't mention it."

She backed away. What else did you expect? she asked herself. You've never been the kind of person who inspires tender feelings. You don't want to be. "Fine," she said carelessly. "I won't." Moving to the coffeepot, she filled her mug again. "Aren't you eating?"

"I ate before." Aaron flipped the eggs, then reached for a plate.

She eyed his back with dislike. "I realize I'm keeping you from a lot of pressing matters. Why don't you just send me up with one of your men?"

"I said I'd take you." He piled her plate with food, then dropped it unceremoniously on the table.

Chin lifted, Jillian took her seat. "Suit yourself, Murdock."

He turned to see her hack a slice from the ham. "I always do." On impulse he grabbed the back of her head and covered her mouth in a long, ruthlessly thorough kiss that left them both simmering with anger and need.

When it was done, Jillian put all her concentration into keeping her hands steady. "A man should be more cautious," she said mildly as she cut another slice, "when a woman's holding a knife."

With a short laugh, he dropped into the chair across from her. "Caution doesn't seem to be something I hold on to well around you." Sipping his coffee, Aaron watched her as she worked her way systematically through the meal. Maybe it was too late to realize that intimacy between them had been a mistake, but if he could keep their relationship on its old footing otherwise, he might get his feelings back in line.

"You know, you should've bought a plane for Utopia years ago," he commented, perfectly aware that it would annoy her.

Her gaze lifted from her plate, slow and deliberate. "Is that so?"

"Only an idiot argues with progress."

Jillian tapped her fork against her empty plate. "What a

fascinating statement," she said sweetly. "Do you have any other suggestions on how I might improve the running of Utopia?"

"As a matter of fact"—Aaron drained his coffee—"I could come up with several."

"Really." She set down the fork before she stabbed him with it. "Would you like me to tell you what you can do with each and every one of them?"

"Maybe later." He rose. "Let's get going. The day's half gone already."

Grinding her teeth, Jillian followed him out the back door. She thought it was a pity she'd wasted even a moment on gratitude.

The small two-seater plane gave her a bad moment. She eyed the propellers while Aaron checked the gauges before takeoff. She trusted things with four legs or four wheels. There, she felt, you had some control—a control she'd be relinquishing the moment Aaron took the plane off the ground. With a show of indifference, she hooked her seat belt while he started the engine.

"Ever been up in one of these?" he asked idly. He slipped on sunglasses before he started down the narrow paved runway.

"Of course I went up in the one I bought." She didn't mention the jitters that one ride had given her. As much as she hated to agree with him, a plane was a necessary part of ranch life in the late twentieth century.

The engine roared and the ground tilted away. She'd just have to get used to it, she reminded herself, since she was going to learn to fly herself. She let her hands lie loosely on her knees and ignored the rolling pitch of her stomach.

"Are you the only one who flies this?" This tuna can with propellers, she thought dismally.

"No, two of our men are licensed pilots. It isn't smart to have only one person who can handle a specific job."

She nodded. "Yes. I've had a man on the payroll for over a month who can fly, but I'm going to have to get a license myself."

He glanced over. "I could teach you." Aaron noticed that her fingers were moving back and forth rhythmically over her knees. Nerves, he realized with some surprise. She hid them very well. "These little jobs're small," he said idly. "But the beauty is maneuverability. You can set them down in a pasture if you have to and hardly disturb the cattle."

"They're very small," Jillian muttered.

"Look down," he suggested. "It's very big."

She did so because she wouldn't, for a moment, have let him know how badly she wanted to be safe on the ground. Oddly her stomach stopped jumping when she did. Her fingers relaxed.

The landscape rolled under them, green and fresh, with strips of brown and amber so neat and tidy they seemed laid out with a ruler. She saw the stream that ran through her property and his, winding blue. Cattle were clumps of black and brown and red. Two young foals frolicked in a pasture while adult horses sunned themselves and grazed. She saw men riding below. Now and again one would take off his hat and wave it in a salute. Aaron dipped his wings in answer. Laughing, Jillian looked farther, to the plains and isolated mountains.

"It's fabulous. God, sometimes I look at it and I can't believe it belongs to me."

"I know." He skimmed the border line and banked the plane over her land. "You can't get tired of looking at it, smelling it."

She rested her head against the window. He loves it as much as I do, she thought. Those five years in Billings must have eaten at him. Every time she thought of it, of the five years he'd given up, her admiration for him grew.

"Don't laugh," she told him and watched him glance over

curiously. No, he wouldn't laugh, she realized. "When I was little—the first time I came out—I got a box and dug up a couple handfuls of pasture to take home with me. It didn't stay sweet for long, but it didn't matter."

Good God, sometimes she was so totally disarming it took his breath away. "How long did you keep it?"

"Until my mother found it and threw it away."

He had to bite back an angry remark on insensitivity and ignorance. "She didn't understand you," Aaron said instead.

"No, of course not." She gave a quick laugh at the idea. Who could've expected her to? "Look, that's Gil's truck." The idea of waving down to him distracted her so that she missed Aaron's smoldering look. He'd had some rocky times with his own father, some painful times, but he'd always been understood.

"Tell me about your family."

Jillian turned her head to look at him, not quite trusting the fact that she couldn't see his eyes through his tinted sunglasses. "No, not now." She looked back out the window. "I wish I knew what I was looking for," she murmured.

So do I, he thought grimly and banked down his frustration. It wasn't going to work, he decided. He wasn't going to be able to talk himself out of needing her, all of her, any time soon. "Maybe you'll know when you see it. Could you figure if they took more cattle from any specific section?"

"It seems the north section was the hardest hit. I can't figure out how it got by me. Five hundred head, right under my nose."

"You wouldn't be the first," he reminded her. "Or the last. If you were going to drive cattle out of your north section, where would you go with them?"

"If they weren't mine," she said dryly, "I suppose I'd load them up and get them over the border."

"Maybe." He wondered if his own idea would be any harder for her to take. "Packaged beef's a lot easier to transport than it is on the hoof."

Slowly she turned back to him. She'd thought of it herself—more than once. But every time she'd pushed it aside. The last fragile hope of recovering what was hers would be lost. "I know that." Her voice was calm, her eyes steady. "If that's what was done, there's still the matter of catching who did it. They're not going to get away with it."

Aaron grinned in pure admiration. "Okay. Then let's think about it from this angle a minute. You've got the cattle—the cows are worth a lot more than the calves at this point, so maybe you're going to ship them off to greener pastures for a while. Unless we're dealing with a bunch of idiots, they're not going to slaughter a registered cow for the few hundred the calf would bring."

"A bunch of idiots couldn't have rustled my cattle," she said precisely.

"No." He nodded in simple agreement. "The steers, now . . . it might be a smart choice to pick out a quiet spot and butcher them. The meat would bring in some quick cash while you worked out the deal for the rest." He made a slight adjustment in course and headed north.

"If you were smarter still, you'd have already set up a deal for the cows and the yearlings," Jillian pointed out. "That accounts for nearly half of what I lost. If I were using a trailer, and slipping them out a few head at a time, I'd make use of one of the canyons in the mountains."

"Yeah. Thought we'd take a look."

Her euphoria was gone, though the landscape below was a rambling map of color and texture. The ground grew more uneven, with the asphalt two-lane road cutting through the twists and angles. The barren clump of mountain wasn't majestic like its brothers farther west, but sat alone, inhabited by coyotes and wildcats who preferred to keep man at a distance.

Aaron took the plane higher and circled. Jillian looked down at jagged peaks and flat-bottomed canyons. Yes, if she had butchering in mind, no place made better sense. Then she saw the vultures, and her heart sank down to her stomach.

"I'm going to set her down," Aaron said simply.

Jillian said nothing but began to check off her options if they found what she thought they would. There were a few economies she could and would have to make before winter, even after the livestock auction at the end of the summer. The old Jeep would simply have to be repaired again instead of being replaced. There were two foals she could sell and keep her books in the black. Checks and balances, she thought as the plane bumped on the ground. Nothing personal.

Aaron shut off the engine. "Why don't you wait here while I take a look?"

"My cattle," she said simply and climbed out of the plane.

The ground was hard and dusty from the lack of rain. She could smell its faintly metallic odor, so unlike the scent of grass and animals that permeated her own land. With no trees for shade, the sun beat down hard and bright. She heard the flap of a vulture's wings as one circled in and settled on a ridge.

It wasn't difficult going over the low rocky ground through the break in the mountain. No problem at all for a four-wheel drive, she thought and angled the brim of her hat to compensate for the glare of sunlight.

The canyon wasn't large and was cupped between three walls of rock, worn gray with some stubborn sage clinging here and there. Their boots made echoing hollow sounds. From somewhere, surprisingly, she heard a faint tinkling of water. The spring must be small, she mused, or she'd smell it. All she smelled here was . . .

She stopped and let out a long breath. "Oh, God."

Aaron recognized the odor, sickeningly hot and sweet, even as she did. "Jillian—"

She shook her head. There was no longer room for comfort or hope. "Damn. I wonder how many."

They walked on and saw, behind a rock, the bones a coyote had dug up and picked clean.

Aaron swore in a low soft stream that was all the more pungent in its control. "There's a shovel in the plane," he began. "We can see what's here, or go back for the sheriff."

"It's my business." Jillian wiped her damp hands on her jeans. "I'd rather know now."

He knew better than to suggest she wait at the plane again. In her place, he'd have done precisely what she was ready to do. Without another word, he left her alone.

When she heard his footsteps die away, she squeezed her eyes tight, doubled her hands into fists. She wanted to scream out the useless, impotent rage. What was hers had been stolen, slaughtered, and sold. There could be no restitution now, no bringing back this part of what she'd worked for. Slowly, painfully, she brought herself under tight control. No restitution, but she'd have justice. Sometimes it was just a cleaner word for revenge.

When Aaron returned with the shovel, he saw the anger glittering in her eyes. He preferred it to that brief glimpse of despair he'd seen. "Let's just make sure. After we know, we go into town for the sheriff."

She agreed with a nod. If they found one hide, it would be one too many. The shovel bit into the ground with a thud.

Aaron didn't have to dig long. He glanced up at Jillian to see her face perfectly composed, then uncovered the first stack of hides. Though the stench was vile, she crouched down and made out the *U* of her brand.

"Well, this should be proof enough," she murmured and stayed where she was because she wanted to drop her head to her knees and weep. "How many—"

"Let the sheriff deal with it," Aaron bit off, as infuriated by their find as he would have been if the hide had borne his own brand. With an oath, he scraped the shovel across the loosened dirt and dislodged something.

Jillian reached down and picked it up. The glove was filthy, but the leather was quality—the kind any cowhand would need for working with the wire. A bubble of excitement rose in her. "One of them must've lost it when they were burying these." She sprang to her feet, holding the glove in both hands. "Oh, they're going to pay for it," she said savagely. "This is one mistake they're going to pay for. Most of my hands score their initials on the inside." Ignoring the grime, she turned the bottom of the glove over and found them.

Aaron watched her color drain as she stared at the inside flap of the glove. Her fingers whitened against the leather before she lifted her eyes to his. Without a word, she handed it to him. Watching her, he took the soiled leather in his hand, then glanced down. There were initials inside. His own.

His face was expressionless when he looked back at her. "Well," he said coolly, "it looks like we're back to square one, doesn't it?" He passed the glove back to her. "You'll need this for the sheriff."

She sent him a look of smoldering anger that cut straight through him. "Do you think I'm stupid enough to believe you had anything to do with this?" Spinning around, she stalked away before he had a chance to understand, much less react. Then he stood where he was for another instant as it struck him, forcibly.

He caught her before she had clambered over the last rocks leading out of the canyon. His hands weren't gentle as he whirled her around, his breath wasn't steady.

"Maybe I do." She jerked away only to have him grab her again. "Maybe I want you to tell me why you don't."

"I might believe a lot of things of you, I might not like everything I believe. But not this." Her voice broke and she fought to even it. "Integrity—integrity isn't something that has to be polite. You wouldn't cut my lines and you wouldn't butcher my cattle."

Her words alone would've shaken him, but he saw her eyes

were swimming with tears. What he knew about comforting a woman could be said in one sentence: get out of the way. Aaron held on to her and lifted a hand to her cheek. "Jillian . . ."

"No! For God's sake don't be kind now." She tried to turn away, only to find herself held close, her face buried against his shoulder. His body was like a solid wall of support and understanding. If she leaned against it now, what would she do when he removed it? "Aaron, don't do this." But her hands clutched at him as he held on.

"I've got to do something," he murmured, stroking her hair. "Lean on me for a minute. It won't hurt you."

But it did. She'd always found tears a painful experience. There was no stopping them, so she wept with the passion they both understood while he held her near the barren mountain under the strong light of the sun.

CHAPTER 9

Jillian didn't have time to grieve over her losses. Over two hundred hides had been unearthed from the canyon floor, all bearing the Utopia brand. She'd had interviews with the sheriff, talked to the Cattlemen's Association, and dealt with the visits and calls from neighboring ranchers. After her single bout of weeping, her despair had iced over to a frigid rage she found much more useful. It carried her through each day, pushing her to work just that much harder, helping her not to break down when she was faced with sympathetic words.

For two weeks she knew there was little talk of anything else, on her ranch or for miles around. There hadn't been a rustling of this size in thirty years. It became easier for her when the talk began to die down, though it became equally more difficult to go on believing that the investigation would yield fruit. She had accepted the loss of her cattle because she had no choice, but she couldn't accept the total victory of the thieves.

They were clever—she had to admit it. They'd pulled off a rustling as smooth as anything the old-timers in the area claimed to remember. The cut wire, Aaron's glove; deliberate and subtle "mistakes" that were designed to turn her attention toward Murdock land. Perhaps the first of them had worked well enough to give the rustlers just enough extra time to cover their tracks. Jillian's only comfort was that she hadn't fallen for the second.

Aaron had given her no choice but to accept his support. She'd balked, particularly after recovering from her lapse in the canyon, but he'd proven to be every bit as obstinate as she. He'd taken her to the sheriff himself, stood by her with the Cattlemen's Association, and one evening had come by to drag her forty miles to a movie. Through it all he wasn't gentle with her, didn't pamper. For that more than anything else, Jillian felt she owed him. Kindness left her no defense and edged her back toward despair.

As the days passed, Jillian forced herself to take each one of them separately. She could fill the hours with dozens of tasks and worries and responsibilities. Then there wouldn't be time to mourn. For now, her first concern was the breeding of her mare with Aaron's stallion.

He'd brought two of his own men with him. With Gil and another of Jillian's hands, they would hold the restraining ropes on the stallion. Once he caught the scent of Jillian's mare in heat, he'd be as wild as his father had been, and as dangerous.

When Jillian brought Delilah into the paddock, she cast a look at the stallion surrounded by men. A gorgeous creature, she thought, wholly male—not quite tamed. Her gaze flicked over to Aaron, who stood at the horse's head.

His dark hair sprang from under his hat to curl carelessly over his neck and ears. His body was erect and lean. One might look at him and think he was perfectly relaxed. But Jillian saw more—the coiled tension beneath, the power that was always there and came out unexpectedly. Eyes nearly as dark as his hair were half hidden by the brim of his hat as he both soothed and controlled his stallion.

No mount could've suited him more. Her lover, she realized with the peculiar little jolt that always accompanied the thought. Would her nerves ever stop skidding along whenever she remembered what it was like to be with him—or imagined what it would be like to be with him again? He'd opened up so many places inside of her. When she was alone, it came close to frightening her; when she saw him, her feelings had nothing to do with fear.

Maybe it was the thick, heavy air that threatened rain or the half-nervous, half-impatient quiverings of her mare, but Jillian's heart was already pounding. The horses caught each other's scent.

Samson plunged and began to fight against the ropes. With his head thrown back, his mane flowing, he called the mare. One of the men cursed in reflex. Jillian tightened her grip on Delilah's bridle as the mare began to struggle—against the restraint or against the inevitable, Jillian would never be sure. She soothed her with words that weren't even heard. Samson gave a long, passionate whinny that was answered. Delilah reared, nearly ripping the bridle from Jillian's hand. Watching the struggle and flying hooves, Aaron felt his heart leap into his throat.

"Help her hold the mare," he ordered.

"No." Jillian fought for new purchase and got it. "She doesn't trust anyone but me. Let's get it done." A long line of sweat held her shirt to her back.

The stallion was wild, plunging and straining, his coat glossy with sweat, his eyes fierce. With five men surrounding him, he reared back, hanging poised and magnificent for a heartbeat before he mounted the mare.

The horses were beyond any thought, any fear, any respect for the humans now. Instinct drove them, primitive and consuming. Jillian forgot her aching arms and the rivulets of sweat that poured down her sides. Her feet were planted, her leg muscles taut as she pitted all her strength toward keeping the mare from bolting or rearing and injuring herself.

She was caught up in the fire and desperation of the horses, and the elemental beauty. The air was ripe with the scent of sweat and animal passion. She couldn't breathe but that she drew it in. Since she'd been a child she'd seen animals breed, helped with the matings whenever necessary, but now, for the first time, she understood the consuming force that drove them. The need of a woman for a man could be equally un-restrained, equally primitive.

Then it began to rain, slowly, heavily, coolly over her skin. With her face lifted to the mare's, Jillian let it flow over her cheeks. Another of the men swore as the ropes grew wet and slippery.

When her eyes met Aaron's, she found her heart was still in her throat, the beat as lurching and uneven as the mare's would be. She felt the flash of need that was both shocking and basic. He saw and recognized. As the rain poured over him, he smiled. Her thigh muscles went lax so quickly she had to fight to strengthen them again and maintain her con-trol of the mare. But she didn't look away. Excitement was nearly painful, knowledge enervating. As if his hands were on her, she felt the need pulse from him.

Gradually a softer feeling drifted in. There was a strange sensation of being safe even though the safety was circled with dangers. This time she didn't question it or fight against it. They were helping to create new life. Now there was a bond between them.

The horses' sides were heaving when they drew them apart. The rain continued to sluice down. She heard Gil give a cackle of laughter over something one of the men said un-der his breath. Jillian forgot them, giving her full attention to the mare. Soothing and murmuring, she walked her back into the stables.

The light was dim, the air heavy with the scent of dry hay and oiled leather. After removing the bridle, Jillian began to groom the mare with long slow strokes until the quivering stopped.

"There now, love." Jillian nuzzled her face into Delilah's neck. "There's not much any of us can do about their bodies."

"Is that how you look at it?"

Jillian turned her head to see Aaron standing at the entrance to the stall. He was drenched and apparently unconcerned about it. She saw his eyes make a short but very thorough scan of her face—a habit he'd developed since their discovery in the canyon. She knew he looked for signs of strain and somewhere along the line had stopped resenting it.

"I'm not a horse," she returned easily and patted Delilah's neck.

Aaron came into the stall and ran his hands over the mare himself. She was dry and still. "She all right?"

"Mmmm. We were right not to field breed them," she added. "Both of them are spirited enough to have done damage." Laughing, she turned to him. "The foal's going to be a champion. I can feel it. There was something special out there just now, something important." On impulse, she threw her arms around Aaron's neck and kissed him ardently.

Surprise held him very still. His hands came to her waist more in instinct than response. It was the first time she'd given him any spontaneous show of affection or offered him any part of herself without reluctance. The ache of need wove through him, throbbing with what he now understood was connected to passion but not exclusive of it.

She was still smiling when she drew away, but he wasn't. Before the puzzlement over what was in his eyes had fully registered with her, Aaron drew her back against him and just held on. Jillian found the unexpected sweetness disconcerting and wonderful.

"Hadn't you better see to Samson?" she murmured.

"My men have already taken him back."

She rubbed her cheek against his wet shirt. They'd steal some time, she thought. An hour, a moment—just some time. "I'll fix you some coffee."

"Yeah." He slipped an arm around her shoulders as they went back into the rain. "Heard anything from the sheriff?"

"Nothing new."

They crossed the ranch yard together, both too accustomed to the elements to heed the rain as anything but necessary.

"It's got the whole county in an uproar."

"I know." They paused at the kitchen door to rid themselves of muddy boots. Jillian ran a careless hand through her hair and scattered rain. "It might do more good than anything else. Every rancher I know or've heard of in this part of Montana's got his eyes open. And any number over the border, from what I'm told. I'm toying with offering a reward."

"Not a bad idea." Aaron sat down at the table and stretched out long legs as Jillian brewed coffee. The rain was a constant soothing sound against the roof and windows. He found an odd comfort there in the gloomy light, in the warm kitchen. It might be like this if it were their ranch they were in rather than hers, or his. It might be like this if he could ever make her a permanent part of his life.

It took only a second for the thoughts to go through his head, and another for him to be jolted by them. Marriage. He was thinking marriage. He sat for a moment while the idea settled over him, not uncomfortably but inevitably. I'll be damned, he thought and nearly laughed before he brought himself back to what she'd been saying.

"Let me do it," he said briskly. She turned, words of refusal on the tip of her tongue. "Wait," Aaron ordered. "Hear me out. My father got wind of the cut wire." He watched her subside before she turned away for mugs. "Obviously it didn't set well with him. These old stories between the Murdocks and Barons don't need much fanning to come to life again. Some people are going to think, even if they don't say, that he's eating your beef."

Jillian poured the coffee, then turned with a mug in each hand. "I don't think it."

"I know." He gave her an odd look, holding out a hand. She placed a mug in it, but Aaron set it down on the table and lightly took her fingers. "That means a great deal to me." Because she didn't know how to respond to that tone, she didn't respond at all but only continued to look down at him. "Jillian, this has set him back some. A few years ago the idea of people thinking he'd done something unethical or illegal would probably have pleased him. He's not as strong as he was. Your grandfather was a rival, but he was also a contemporary, someone he understood, even respected. It would help if he could do something. I don't like to ask for favors any more than you like to accept them."

She looked down at their joined hands, both tanned, both lean and strong, yet hers was so easily swallowed up by his. "You love him very much."

"Yes." It was said very simply, in the same emotionless tone he'd used to tell her his father was dying. This time Jillian understood him better.

"I'd appreciate it if you'd stake the reward."

He laced his fingers with hers. "Good."

"Want some more coffee?"

"No." That wicked light of humor shot into his eyes. "But I was thinking I should help you out of those wet clothes."

With a laugh, Jillian sat down. "You know I'm still planning on beating out the Double M on July Fourth."

"I was hoping you were planning on it," Aaron returned easily. "But about doing it . . ."

"You a gambling man, Murdock?"

He lifted his brow. "It's been said."

"I've got fifty that says my Hereford bull will take the blue ribbon over anything you have to put against him."

Aaron contemplated the dregs of his coffee as if considering. If everything he'd heard about Jillian's bull was true, he was tolerably sure he was throwing money away. "Fifty," he agreed and smiled. "And another fifty that says I beat your time in the calf roping."

"My pleasure." Jillian held out a hand to seal it.

"Are you competing in anything else?"

"I don't think so." She stretched her back, thinking what a luxury it was to sit stone still in the middle of the afternoon. "The barrel racing doesn't much interest me and I know better than to try bronc riding."

"Know better?"

"Two reasons. First the men would do a lot of muttering and complaining if I did. And second"—she grinned and shrugged—"I'd probably break my neck."

It occurred to him that she wouldn't have admitted the second to him even a week before. Laughing, he leaned over and kissed her. But the friendly kiss stirred something, and cupping the back of her neck, he kissed her again, lingeringly. "It's your mouth," he murmured while his fingertips toyed with her skin. "Once I get started on it, I can't find a single reason to stop."

Her breath fluttered unevenly through her lips, through his. "It's the middle of the day."

He smiled, then teased her tongue with the tip of his. "Yeah. Are you going to take me to bed?"

The eyes that were nearly closed opened again. In them he saw desire and confusion, a combination he found very much to his liking. "I have to check the—" His teeth nipped persuasively into her bottom lip.

"The what?" he whispered as her words ended on a little shiver.

"The, uh . . ." His lips were skimming over hers in something much more provocative than a kiss. The lazy caress of his tongue kept them moist. His fingers were very light on the back of her neck. Their knees were brushing. Somehow she could already feel the press of his body against hers and the issuing warmth the pressure always brought. "I can't think," she murmured.

It was what he wanted. Or he wanted her to think of him and only him. For himself, he needed to know that she put him first this time, or at least her need for him. Over her ranch, her men, her cattle, her ambitions. If he could draw her feelings out to match his once, he might be able to do so again and again until she was as rashly in love with him as he was with her. "Why do you have to?" he asked and, rising, drew her to her feet. "You can feel."

Yes, with her arms around him and her head cradled against his chest, she could feel. Emotions nudging at her, urging her to acknowledge them—needs, pressing and searingly urgent, demanding that she fulfill them. They were all connected to him, the hungers, the tiny fears, the wishes. She couldn't deny them all. Perhaps, just this once, she didn't need to.

"I want to make love with you." She sighed with the words and nuzzled closer. "I can't seem to stop wanting to."

He tilted her head back so that he could see her face, then, half smiling, skimmed his thumb over her jaw. "In the middle of the day?"

She tossed the hair out of her eyes and settled her linked hands comfortably behind his neck. "I'm going to have you now, Murdock. Right now."

He glanced at the tidy kitchen table and his grin was wicked. "Right now?"

"Your mind takes some unusual turns," she commented. "I think I can give you time enough to get upstairs." Releasing him, she walked over and flicked off the coffeepot. "If you hurry." Even as he grinned, she crossed back to him. Putting her hands on his shoulders, she leaped up, locking her legs around his waist, her arms around his neck. "You know where the stairs are?"

"I can find them."

She pressed her lips to his throat. "Top of the stairs, second door on the right," she told him as she began to please herself with his taste.

As Aaron wound through the house Jillian wondered what he would think or say if he knew she'd never done anything quite like this before. She'd come to realize that the man from her youth hadn't been a lover, but an incident. It took more than one night to make a lover. She'd feel much too foolish telling Aaron he was the first—much too inadequate. How could she tell him that the first rush of passion had loosened the locks she'd put on parts of herself? How could she trust her own feelings when they were so muddled and new?

She rested her head on his shoulder a moment and closed her eyes. For once in her life she was going to enjoy without worrying about the consequences. Shifting, she leaned back so that she could smile at him. "You're out of shape, Murdock. One flight of stairs and your heart's pounding."

"So's yours," he pointed out. "And you had a ride up."

"Must be the rain," she said loftily.

"Your clothes're still damp." He moved into the room she'd directed him to and glanced around briefly.

It was consistent with her style—understated femininity, practicality. It was a room without frills or pastels, but he'd have known it for a woman's. It had none of the feminine disorder of his sister's old room at the ranch, nor the subtle elegance of his mother's. Like the woman he still held, Aaron found the room unique.

Plain walls, plain floors, easy colors, no clutter. No, Jillian wasn't a woman to clutter her life. She wouldn't give herself the time. Perhaps it was the few indulgences she'd allowed herself that gave him the most insight.

A stoneware vase with fluted edges held pussy willow—soft brown nubs that wouldn't quite be considered a flower. There was a small carved box on her dresser he was certain would play some soft tune when the top was lifted. She might lift it sometimes when she was alone, or lonely. On the wall was a watercolor with all the bleeding passion of sunset. How carefully, how painstakingly, he thought, she'd controlled whatever romanticism she was prone to. How surprised she'd be to know that because she did, it only shouted out louder.

Recognizing his survey, Jillian cocked her head. "There's not a lot to see in here."

"You'd be surprised," he murmured.

The enigmatic answer made her glance around herself. "I don't spend a lot of time in here," she began, realizing it was rather sparse even compared to his room in the white frame house.

"You misunderstood me." Aaron let his hands run up her sides as she slid down. "I'd've known this was your room. It even smells like you."

She laughed, pleased without knowing why. "Are you being poetic?"

"Maybe."

Lifting a hand, she toyed with the top button of his shirt. "Want me to help you out of those wet clothes?"

"Absolutely."

She began to oblige him, then shot him an amused look as she slid the shirt over his shoulders. "If you expect me to seduce you, you're going to be disappointed."

His stomach muscles were already knotted with need. "I am?"

"I don't know any tricks." Before he could comment, she

launched herself at him, overbalancing him so that they tumbled back onto the bed. "No wiles," she continued. "No subtlety."

"You're a pushy lady, all right." He could feel the heat of her body through her damp shirt.

"I like the way you look, Murdock." She trailed her fingers through his thick dark hair as she studied his face. "It used to annoy the hell out of me, but now it's kind of nice."

"The way I look?"

"That I like the way you look. It's ruthless," she decided, skimming a finger down his jawline. "And when you smile, it can be very charming—the kind of charm a smart woman recognizes as highly dangerous."

He grinned, cupping her hips in his hands. "Did you?"

"I'm a smart woman." With a little laugh, she rubbed her nose against his. "I know a rattlesnake when I see one."

"But not enough to keep your distance."

"Apparently not—then I don't always look for a long, safe ride."

But a short, rocky one, he thought as her lips came down to his. He'd be happy to give her the wisps of danger and trouble, he decided, drawing her closer. But she was going to find out he intended it to last.

He started to shift her, but then her lips were racing over his face. Soft, light, but with a heat that seeped right into him. Her long, limber body seemed almost weightless over his, yet he could feel every line and curve. Moisture still clung to her hair and reminded him of the first time, when he'd dragged her to the ground, consumed with need and fury. Now he was helpless against her rapid assault on his senses. No, she had no wiles, nor he the patience for them.

He could hear the rain patter rhythmically against the window. He could smell it on her. When his lips brushed through her hair, he could taste it. It was almost as though they were alone in a quiet field, with the scent of wet grass and the rain slipping over their skin. The light was gray and indistinct; her mouth was vivid wherever it touched him.

She hadn't known it could be so exciting to weaken a man with herself. Feeling the strength drain from him made her almost light-headed with power. She'd met him on equal terms, and from time to time to her disadvantage, but never when she'd been so certain she could dominate. Her laugh was low and confident as it whispered along his skin, warm and sultry as it brushed over his lips.

He seemed content to lie still while she learned of him. She thought the air grew thicker. Perhaps that alone weighed him down and kept him from challenging her control. Her hands were eager, rushing here then there to linger over some small fascination: tight cords of muscle that ran down his upper arms to bunch and gather at her touch; smooth, taut skin that was surprisingly soft over his rib cage; the narrow, raised scar along his hipbone.

"Where'd you get this?" she murmured, outlining it with a fingertip.

"Brahma," he managed as she tugged his jeans down infinitesimally lower. "Jillian—" But her lips drifted over his again and silenced him.

"A bull?"

"Rodeo, when I had more guts than brains."

She heard the sound of pleasure in his throat as her mouth journeyed down. His body was a treasure of delight to her. In the soft rainy light she could see it, brown and hard against the plain, serviceable bedspread. Rangy and loose limbed, it was made for riding well and long, toughened by physical work, burnished by the elements. Tiny jumping thrills coursed through her as she thought that it was hers to touch and taste, to look at as long as she liked.

She took a wandering route down him, feeling his skin heat and pulse as she stripped him. The room was filled with the sound of rain and quickening breathing. It was all she heard. The sweet scent of passion enveloped her—a fragrance mixed of the essence of both of them. Intimate. She could taste desire on his skin, a heady flavor that made her greedy when she felt the thud of his heart under her tongue. Even when her excitement grew until her blood was racing, she could have luxuriated in him for hours. The sharp urgency she'd once felt had mellowed into a glowing contentment. She pleasured him. It was more than she'd believed she could do for anyone.

There were flames in his stomach, spreading. God, she was like a drug and he was lost, half dreaming while his flesh was burning up. Her fingers were so cool as they tortured him, her mouth so hot. He'd never explored his own vulnerabilities; it had always been more important to work around them or ignore them altogether. Now he had no choice and he found the sensation incredible.

She aroused, teased, and withdrew only to arouse again. Her enervating, openmouthed kisses ranged over him while her hands stroked and explored lazily, finding point after sensitive point until he trembled. No woman had ever made him tremble. Even as this thought ran through his ravaged mind, she caused him to do so again. Then he knew she was driving him mad.

The wind kicked up, hurling rain against the window, then retreating with a distant howl. Something crazed sprang into him. Roughly he grabbed her, rolling over and pinning her, her arms above her head. His breathing was labored as he looked down.

Her chin was up, her hair spread out, her eyes glowing. There was no fear on her face, and nothing of submission. Though her own breathing came quickly, there was challenge in the look she gave him. A dare. He could take her, take her anyway he chose. And when he did so, he'd be taken as well.

So be it, he thought with a muffled oath. His mouth devoured hers.

She matched his urgency, aroused simply by knowing she had taken him to the edge. He wanted her. Her. In some ways he knew her better than anyone ever had, and still he wanted her. She'd waited so long for that, not even knowing that she'd waited at all. She couldn't think of this, or what the effects might be when his long desperate kisses were rousing her, when she could see small, silvery explosions going on behind her closed lids.

She felt him tug at the buttons of her shirt, heard him swear. When she felt the material rip away, she knew only that at last she could feel his flesh against hers. As it was meant to be. His hands wouldn't be still and drove her as she had driven him. He pulled clothes from her in a frenzy as his mouth greedily searched. Somewhere in her hazy brain she felt wonder that she could bring him to this just by being.

Their bodies pressed, their limbs entwined. Their mouths joined. He thought the mixing of their tastes the most intimate thing he'd ever known. Under him she arched, more a demand than an offer. He raised himself over her, wanting to see her, wanting her to see him when he made her his.

Her eyes were dark, misted with need. Need for him. He knew he had what he'd wanted: she thought of nothing and no one else. "I wanted you from the first minute," he murmured as he slipped inside her.

He saw the change in her face as he moved slowly, the flicker of pleasure, the softening that came just before delirium. Pushing back the rushing need in his blood, he drew out the sensations with a control so exquisite it burned in his muscles. Lowering his head, he nibbled at her lips.

She couldn't bear it. She couldn't stop it. When she thought she finally understood what passion was, he showed her there was more. Sensation after sensation slammed into her, leaving her weak and gasping. Even as the pressure built inside her, drumming under her skin and threatening to implode, she wanted it to go on. She could have wept from the joy of it, moaned from the ache. Unwittingly it was she who changed things simply by breathing his name as if she knew no other.

The instant his control snapped, she felt it. There was time only for a tingle of nervous excitement before he was catapulting her with him into a dark, frantic sky where it was all thunder and no air.

CHAPTER 10

The lengthy, dusty drive into town and the soaring temperatures couldn't dull the spirit. It was the Fourth of July, and the long, raucous holiday had barely begun.

By early morning the fairgrounds were crowded—ranchers, punchers, wives and sweethearts, and those looking for a sweetheart to share the celebration with. Prized animals were on display to be discussed, bragged about, and studied. Quilts and pies and preserves waited to be judged. As always, there was a pervasive air of expectancy.

Cowboys wore their best uniform—crisp shirts and pressed jeans, with the boots and hats that were saved and cherished for special occasions. Belt buckles gleamed. Children sported their finest, which promised to be dirt streaked and grass stained by the end of the long day.

For Jillian, it was the first carefree day in the season, and one she was all the more determined to enjoy because of her recent problems. For twenty-four hours she was going to forget her worries, the numbers in her account books, and the title of boss she worked day after day to earn. On this one sun-filled, heat-soaked day, she was going to simply enjoy the fact that she was part of a unique group of men and women who both lived and played off the land.

There was an excited babble of voices near the paddock

and stable areas. The pungent aroma of animals permeated the air. From somewhere in the distance she could already hear fiddle music. There'd be more music after sundown, and dancing. Before then, there'd be games for young and old, the judgings, and enough food to feed the entire county twice over. She could smell the spicy aroma of an apple pie, still warm, as someone passed her with a laden basket. Her mouth watered.

First things first, she reminded herself as she wandered over to check out her bull's competition.

There were six entries altogether, all well muscled and fierce to look at. Horns gleamed, sharp and dangerous. Hides were sleek and well tended. Objectively Jillian studied each one, noting their high points and their weaknesses. There wasn't any doubt that her stiffest competitor would be the Double M's entry. He'd taken the blue ribbon three years running.

Not this year, she told him silently as her gaze skimmed over him. Pound for pound, he probably had her bull beat, but she thought hers had a bit more breadth in the shoulders. And there was no mistaking that her Hereford's coloring and markings were perfect, the shape of his head superior.

Time for you to move over and make room for new blood, she told the reigning champion. Rather pleased with herself, she hooked her thumbs in her back pockets. First place and that little swatch of blue ribbon would go a long way to making up for everything that'd gone wrong in the past few weeks.

"Know a winner when you see one?"

Jillian turned at the thready voice that still held a hint of steel. Paul Murdock was dressed to perfection, but his hawk-like face had little color under his Stetson. His cane was elegant and tipped with gold, but he leaned on it heavily. As they met hers, however, his eyes were very much alive and challenging.

"I know a winner when I see one," she agreed, then let her gaze skim over to her own bull.

He gave a snort of laughter and shifted his weight. "Been hearing a lot about your new boy." He studied the bull with a faint frown and couldn't prevent a twinge of envy. He, too, knew a winner when he saw one.

He felt the sun warm on his back and for a moment, for just a moment, wished desperately for his youth again. Years ate at strength. If he were fifty again and owned that bull . . . But he wasn't a man to sigh. "Got possibilities," he said shortly.

She recognized something of the envy and smiled. Nothing could've pleased her more. "Nothing wrong with second place," she said lightly.

Murdock glanced over sharply, pinned her eyes with his, then laughed when she didn't falter. "Damn, you're quite a woman, aren't you, Jillian Baron? The old man taught you well enough."

Her smile held more challenge than humor. "Well enough to run Utopia."

"Could be," he acknowledged. "Times change." There wasn't any mistaking the resentment in the statement, but she understood it. Sympathized with it. "This rustling . . ." He glanced over to see her face, impassive and still. Murdock had a quick desire to sit across a poker table from her with a large, juicy pot in between. "It's a damn abomination," he said with a savagery that made him momentarily breathless. "There was a time a man'd have his neck stretched for stealing another man's beef."

"Hanging them won't get my cattle back," Jillian said calmly.

"Aaron told me about what you found in the canyon." Murdock stared at the well-muscled bulls. These were the life's blood of their ranches—the profit and the status. "A hard thing for you—for all of us," he added, shifting his eyes to hers again. "I want you to understand that your grandfather and I had our problems. He was a stubborn, stiff-necked bastard."

"Yes," Jillian agreed easily, so easily Murdock laughed. "You'd understand a man like that," she added.

Murdock stopped laughing to fix her with a glittering look. She returned it. "I understand a man like that," he acknowledged. "And I want you to know that if this had happened to him, I'd've been behind him, just as I'd've expected him to be behind me. Personal feelings don't come into it. We're ranchers."

It was said with a sting of pride that made her own chin lift. "I do know it."

"It'd be easy to say the cattle could've been driven over to my land."

"Easy to say," Jillian said with a nod. "If you knew me better, Mr. Murdock, you'd know I'm not a fool. If I believed you'd had my beef on your table, you'd already be paying for it."

His lips curved in a rock-hard, admiring smile. "Baron did well by you," he said after a moment. "Though I still think a woman needs a man beside her if she's going to run a ranch."

"Be careful, Mr. Murdock, I was just beginning to think I could tolerate you."

He laughed again, so obviously pleased that Jillian grinned. "Can't change an old dog, girl." His eyes narrowed fractionally as she'd seen his son's do. It occurred to her that in forty years Aaron would look like this—that honed-down strength that was just a little bit mean. It was the kind of strength you'd want behind you when there was trouble. "I've heard my boy's had his eye on you—can't say I fault his taste."

"Have you?" she returned mildly. "Do you believe everything you hear?"

"If he hasn't had his eye on you," Murdock countered, "he's not as smart as I give him credit for. Man needs a woman to settle him down."

"Really?" Jillian said very dryly.

"Don't get fired up, girl," Murdock ordered. "There'd've been a time when I'd have had his hide for looking twice at a Baron. Times change," he repeated with obvious reluctance. "Our land has run side by side for most of this century, whether we like it or not."

Jillian took a moment to brush off her sleeve. "I'm not looking to settle anyone, Mr. Murdock. And I'm not looking for a merger."

"Sometimes we wind up getting things we're not looking for." He smiled as she stared at him. "You take my Karen— never figured to hitch myself with a beauty who always made me feel like I should wipe my feet whether I'd been in the pastures or not."

Despite herself Jillian laughed, then surprised them both by hooking her arm through his as they began to walk. "I get the feeling you're trying to bury the hatchet." When he stiffened, she muffled a chuckle and continued. "Don't *you* get fired up," she said easily. "I'm willing to try a truce. Aaron and I have . . . we understand each other," she decided. "I like your wife, and I can just about tolerate you."

"You're your grandmother all over again," Murdock muttered.

"Thanks." As they walked Jillian noted the few speculative glances tossed their way. Baron and Murdock arm in arm; times had indeed changed. She wondered how Clay would feel and decided, in his grudging way, he would've approved. Especially if it caused talk.

When Aaron saw them walking slowly toward the arena area, he broke off the conversation he'd been having with a puncher. Jillian tossed back her hair, tilted her head slightly toward his father's, and murmured something that made the old man hoot with laughter. If he hadn't already, Aaron would've fallen in love with her at that moment.

"Hey, isn't that Jillian Baron with your paw?"

"Hmmm? Yeah." Aaron didn't waste time glancing back at the puncher when he could look at Jillian.

"She sure is easy on the eyes," the puncher concluded a bit wistfully. "Heard you and her—" He broke off, chilled by the cool, neutral look Aaron aimed at him. The cowboy coughed into his hand. "Just meant people wonder about it, seeing as the Murdocks and Barons never had much dealings with each other."

"Do they?" Aaron relieved the cowboy by grinning before he walked off. Murdocks, the puncher thought with a shake of his head. You could never be too sure of them.

"Life's full of surprises," Aaron commented as he walked toward them. "No blood spilled?"

"Your father and I've reached a limited understanding." Jillian smiled at him, and though they touched in no way, Murdock was now certain the rumors he'd heard about Jillian and his son were true. Intimacy was something people often foolishly believed they could conceal, and rarely did.

"Your mother's got me judging the mincemeat," Murdock grumbled. This time he didn't feel that twinge of regret for what he'd lost, but an odd contentment at seeing his slice of immortality in his son. "We'll be in the stands later to watch you." He gave Jillian an arch look. "Both of you."

He walked off slowly. Jillian had to stuff her hands in her pockets to keep from helping him. That, she knew, would be met with cold annoyance. "He came over to the pens," Jillian told Aaron when Murdock was out of earshot. "I think he did it on purpose so that he could talk to me. He was very kind."

"Not many people see him as kind."

"Not many people had a grandfather like Clay Baron." She turned to Aaron and smiled.

"How are you?" He couldn't have resisted the urge to touch her if he'd wanted to. His fingertips skimmed along her jaw.

"How do I look?"

"You don't like me to tell you you're beautiful."

She laughed, and the under-the-lashes look she sent him was the first flirtatious move he'd ever seen from her. "It's a holiday."

"Spend it with me?" He held out a hand, knowing if she put hers in it, in public, where there were curious eyes and tongues that appreciated a nice bit of gossip, it would be a commitment of sorts.

Her fingers laced with his. "I thought you'd never ask."

They spent the morning doing what couples had done at county fairs for decades. There was lemonade to be drunk, contests to be watched. It was easy to laugh when the sky was clear and the sun promised a dry, golden day.

Children raced by with balloons held by sticky fingers. Teenagers flirted with the nonchalance peculiar to their age. Old-timers chewed tobacco and out-lied each other. The air was touched with the scent of food and animals, and the starch in bandbox shirts had not yet wilted with sweat.

With Aaron's arm around her, Jillian crowded to the fence to watch the greased pig contest. The ground had been flooded and churned up so that the state of the mud was perfection. The pig was slick with lard and quick, so that he eluded the five men who lunged after him. The crowd called out suggestions and hooted with laughter. The pig squealed and shot, like a bullet, out of capturing arms. Men fell on their faces and swore good-naturedly.

Jillian shot him a look, then inclined her head toward the pen where the activity was still wild and loud. "Don't you like games, Murdock?"

"I like to make up my own." He swung her around. "Now, there's this real quiet hayloft I know of."

With a laugh, she eluded him. He'd never known her to be deliberately provocative and found himself not quite certain how to deal with it. The glitter in her eyes made him decide. In one smooth move, Aaron gathered her close and kissed her soundly. There was an approving whoop from a group of cowboys behind them. When Jillian managed to untangle herself, she glanced over to see two of her own men grinning at her.

"It's a holiday," Aaron reminded her when she let out a huff of breath.

She brought her head back slowly and took his measure. Oh, he was damn proud of himself, she decided. And two could play. Her smile had him wondering just what she had up her sleeve.

"You want fireworks?" she asked, then threw her arms around him and silenced him before he could agree or deny.

While his kiss had been firm yet still friendly, hers whispered of secrets only the two of them knew. Aaron never heard the second cheer go up, but he wouldn't have been surprised to feel the ground move.

"I missed you last night, Murdock," she whispered, then went from her toes to her flat feet so that their lips parted. She took a step back before she offered her hand, and the smile on those fascinating lips was cocky.

Carefully Aaron drew air into his lungs and released it. "You're going to finish that one later, Jillian."

She only laughed again. "I certainly hope so. Let's go see if Gil can win the pie-eating contest again this year."

He went wherever she wanted and felt foolishly, and appealingly, like a kid on his first date. It was the sudden carefree aura around her. Jillian had dropped everything, all worries and responsibilities, and had given herself a day for fun. Perhaps because she felt a slight twinge of guilt, like a kid playing hooky, the day was all the sweeter.

She would have sworn the sun had never been brighter, the sky so blue. In all of her life, she couldn't remember ever laughing so easily. A slice of cherry pie was ambrosia. If she could have concentrated the day down, section by section, she would have put it into a box where she could have taken out an hour at a time when she was alone and tired. Because she was too practical to believe that possible, Jillian chose to live each moment to the fullest.

By the time the rodeo officially opened, Jillian was nearly drunk on freedom. As the Fourth of July Queen and her court rode sedately around the arena, she still clutched her bull's blue ribbon in her hand. "That's fifty you owe me," she told Aaron with a grin.

He sat on the ground exchanging dress boots for worn, patched riding favorites. "Why don't we wait and see how the second bet comes out?"

"Okay." She perched on a barrel and listened to the crowd cheer from the stands. She was riding high and knew it. Her luck had turned—there wasn't a problem she could be hit with that she couldn't handle.

A lot of cowboys and potential competitors had already collected behind the chutes. Though it all seemed very casual—the lounging, the rigging bags set carelessly against the chain-link fence—there was an air of suppressed excitement. There was the scent of tobacco from the little cans invariably carried in the right rear pocket of jeans, and mink oil on leather. Already she heard the jingle of spurs and harnesses as equipment was checked. The bareback riding was first. When she heard the announcement, Jillian rose and wandered to the fence to watch.

"I'm surprised you didn't give this one a try," Aaron commented.

She tilted her head so that it brushed his arm—one of the rare signs of affection that made him weak. "Too much energy," she said with a laugh. "I'm dedicating the day to laziness. I noticed you were signed up for the bronc riding." Jillian nudged her hat back as she looked up at him. "Still more guts than brains?"

He grinned and shrugged. "Worried about me?"

Jillian gave a snort of laughter. "I've got some good

liniment—it'll take the soreness out of the bruises you're going to get."

He ran a fingertip down her spine. "The idea tempts me to make sure I get a few. You know"—he turned her into his arms in a move both smooth and possessive—"it wouldn't take much for me to forget all about this little competition." Lowering his head, he nibbled at her lips, oblivious of whoever might be milling around them. "It's not such a long drive back to the ranch. Not a soul there. Pretty day like this—I start thinking about taking a swim."

"Do you?" She drew her head back so their eyes met.

"Mmmm. Water'd be cool, and quiet."

Chuckling, she pressed her lips to his. "After the calf roping," she said and drew away.

Jillian preferred the chutes to the stands. There she could listen to the men talk of other rodeos, other rides, while she checked over her own equipment. She watched a young girl in a stunning buckskin suit rev up her nerves before the barrel racing. An old hand worked rosin into the palm of a glove with tireless patience. The little breeze carried the scent of grilled meat from the concessions.

No, she thought, her family could never understand the appeal of this. The earthy smells, the earthy talk. They'd be just as much out of their element here as she'd always been at her mother's box at the opera. It was times like these, when she was accepted for simply being what she was, that she stopped remembering the little twinges of panic that had plagued her while she grew up. No, there was nothing lacking in her as she'd often thought. She was simply different.

She watched the bull riding, thrilling to the danger and daring as men pitted themselves against a ton of beef. There were spills and close calls and clowns who made the terrifying seem amusing. Half dreaming, she leaned on the fence as a riderless bull charged and snorted around the arena, poking bad temperedly at a clown in a barrel. The crowd was loud, but she could hear Aaron in an easy conversation with Gil from somewhere behind her. She caught snatches about the little sorrel mare Aaron had drawn in the bronc riding. A fire-eater. Out of the chute, then a lunge to the right. Liked to spin. Relaxed, Jillian thought she'd enjoy watching Aaron pit himself against the little fire-eater. After she'd won another fifty from him.

She thought the day had simply been set aside for her, warm and sunny and without demands. Perhaps she'd been this relaxed before, this happy, but it was difficult to remember when she'd shared the two sensations so clearly. She savored them.

Then everything happened so quickly she didn't have time to think, only to act.

She heard the childish laughter as she stretched her back muscles. She saw the quick flash of red zip through the fence and bounce on the dirt without fully registering it. But she saw the child skim through the rungs of the fence and into the arena. He was so close his jeans brushed hers as he scrambled through after his ball. Jillian was over the fence and running before his mother screamed. Part of her registered Aaron's voice, either furious or terrified, as he called her name.

Out of the corner of her eye Jillian saw the bull turn. His eyes, already wild from the ride, met hers, though she never paused. Her blood went cold.

She didn't hear the chaos as the crowd leaped to their feet or the mass confusion from behind the chutes as she sprinted after the boy. She did feel the ground tremble as the bull began its charge. There wasn't time to waste her breath on shouting. Running on instinct, she lunged, letting the momentum carry her forward. She went down hard, full length on the boy, and knocked the breath out of both of them. As the bull skimmed by them, she felt the hot rush of air.

Don't move, she told herself, mercilessly pinning the boy beneath her when he started to squirm. Don't even breathe. She could hear shouting, very close by now, but didn't dare move her head to look. She wasn't gored. Jillian swallowed on the thought. No, she'd know it if he'd caught her with his horns. And he hadn't trampled her. Yet.

Someone was cursing furiously. Jillian closed her eyes and wondered if she'd ever be able to stand up again. The boy was beginning to cry lustily. She tried to smother the sound with her body.

When hands came under her arms, she jolted and started to struggle. "You *idiot*!" Recognizing the voice, Jillian relaxed and allowed herself to be hauled to her feet. She might have swayed if she hadn't been held so tightly. "What kind of a stunt was that?" She stared up at Aaron's deathly white face while he shook her. "Are you hurt?" he demanded. "Are you hurt anywhere?"

"What?"

He shook her again because his hands were trembling. "Damn it, Jillian!"

Her head was spinning a bit like it had when she'd had that first plug of tobacco. It took her a moment to realize someone was gripping her hand. Bemused, she listened to the tearful gratitude of the mother while the boy wept loudly with his face buried in his father's shirt. The Simmons boy, she thought dazedly. The little Simmons boy, who played in the yard while his mother hung out the wash and his father worked on her own land.

"He's all right, Joleen," she managed, though her mouth didn't want to follow the order of her brain. "I might've put some bruises on him, though."

Aaron cut her off, barely suppressing the urge to suggest someone introduce the boy to a razor strap before he dragged Jillian away. She had a misty impression of a sea of faces and Aaron's simmering rage.

". . . get you over to first aid."

"What?" she said again as his voice drifted in and out of her mind.

"I said I'm going to get you over to first aid." He bit off the words as he came to the fence.

"No, I'm fine." The light went gray for a moment and she shook her head.

"As soon as I'm sure of that, I'm going to strangle you."

She pulled her hand from his and straightened her shoulders. "I said I'm fine," she repeated. Then the ground tilted and rushed up at her.

The first thing she felt was the tickle of grass under her palm. Then there was a cool cloth, more wet than damp, on her face. Jillian moaned in annoyance as water trickled down to her collar. Opening her eyes, she saw a blur of light and shadow. She closed them again, then concentrated on focusing.

She saw Aaron first, grim and pale as he hitched her up to a half-sitting position and held a glass to her lips. Then Gil, shifting his weight from foot to foot while he ran his hat through his hands. "She ain't hurt none," he told Aaron in a voice raised to convince everyone, including himself. "Just had herself a spell, that's all. Women do."

"A lot you know," she muttered, then discovered what Aaron held to her lips wasn't a glass but a flask of neat brandy. It burned very effectively through the mists. "I didn't faint," Jillian said in disgust.

"You did a damn good imitation, then," Aaron snapped at her.

"Let the child breathe." Karen Murdock's calm, elegant voice had the magic effect of moving the crowd back. She slipped through and knelt at Jillian's side. Clucking her tongue, she took the dripping cloth from Jillian's brow and wrung it out. "Men'll always try to overcompensate. Well, Jillian, you caused quite a sensation."

Grimacing, Jillian sat up. "Did I?" She pressed her forehead to her knees a minute until she was certain the world wasn't going to do any more spinning. "I can't believe I fainted," she mumbled.

Aaron swore and took a healthy swig from the flask himself. "She almost gets herself killed and she's worried about what fainting's going to do to her image."

Jillian's head snapped up. "Look, Murdock—"

"I wouldn't push it if I were you," he warned and meticulously capped the flask. "If you can stand, I'll take you home."

"Of course I can stand," she retorted. "And I'm not going home."

"I'm sure you're fine," Karen began and shot her son a telling look. For a smart man, Karen mused, Aaron was showing a remarkable lack of sense. Then again, when love was around, sense customarily went out the window. "Trouble is, you're a seven-day wonder," she told Jillian with a brief glance at the gathering crowd. "You're going to be congratulated to death if you stay around here." She smiled as she saw her words sink in.

Grumbling, Jillian rose. "All right." The bruises were beginning to be felt. Rather than admit it, she brushed at the dust on her jeans. "There's no need for you to go," she told Aaron stiffly. "I'm perfectly capable of—"

His fingers were wrapped tight around her arm as he dragged her away. "I don't know what your problem is, Murdock," she said through her teeth. "But I don't have to take this."

"I'd keep a lid on it for a while if I were you." The crowd fell back as he strode through. If anyone considered speaking to Jillian, Aaron's challenging look changed their minds.

After wrenching open the door of his truck, Aaron gave her a none-too-gentle boost inside. Jillian pulled her hat from her back and, taking the brim in both hands, slammed it down on her head. Folding her arms, she prepared to endure the next hour's drive in absolute silence. As Aaron pulled out it occurred to her that she had missed not only the calf roping, but also her sacred right to gloat over her bull's victory at the evening barbecue. The injustice of it made her smolder.

And just what's he so worked up about? Jillian asked herself righteously. He hadn't scared himself blind, wrenched his knee, or humiliated himself by fainting in public. Gingerly she touched her elbow where she'd scraped most of the skin away. After all, if you wanted to be technical, she'd probably saved that kid's life. Jillian's chin angled as her arm began to ache with real enthusiasm. So why was he acting as though she'd committed some crime?

"One of these days you're going to put your chin out like that and someone's going to take you up on it."

Slowly she turned her head to glare at him. "You want to give it a shot, Murdock?"

"Don't tempt me." He punched on the gas until the speedometer hovered at seventy.

"Look, I don't know what your problem is," she said tightly. "But since you've got one, why don't you just spill it? I'm not in the mood for your nasty little comments."

He swung the truck over to the side of the road so abruptly she crashed into the door. By the time she'd recovered, he was out of his side and striding across the tough wild grass of a narrow field. Rubbing her sore arm, Jillian pushed out of the truck and went after him.

"What the hell is all this about?" Anger made her breathless as she caught at his shirtsleeve. "If you want to drive like a maniac, I'll hitch a ride back to the ranch."

"Just shut up." He jerked away from her. Distance, he told himself. He just needed some distance until he pulled himself together. He was still seeing those lowered horns sweeping past Jillian's tumbling body. His rope might've missed the mark, and then—He couldn't afford to think of any *and thens*. As it was, it had taken three well-placed ropes and several strong arms before they'd been able to drag the bull away from those two prone bodies. He'd nearly lost her. In one split second he'd nearly lost her.

"Don't you tell me to shut up." Spinning in front of him, Jillian gripped his shirtfront. Her hat tumbled down her back as she tossed her head and rage poured out of her. "I've had all I'm going to take from you. God knows why I've let you get away with this much, but no more. Now you can just hop back in your truck and head it in whatever direction you like. To hell would suit me just fine."

She whirled away, but before she could storm off she was spun back and crushed in his arms. Spitting mad, she struggled only to have his grip tighten. It wasn't until she stopped to marshal her forces that she realized he was trembling and that his breathing came fast and uneven. Emotion ruled him, yes, but it wasn't anger. Subsiding, she waited. Not certain what she was offering comfort for, she stroked his back. "Aaron?"

He shook his head and buried his face in her hair. It was the closest he could remember to just falling apart. It hadn't been distance he'd needed, he discovered, but this. To feel her warm and safe and solid in his arms.

"Oh, God, Jillian, do you know what you did to me?"

Baffled, she let her cheek rest against his drumming heart and continued to stroke his back. "I'm sorry," she offered, hoping it would be enough for whatever she'd done.

"It was so close. Inches—just inches more. I wasn't sure at first that he hadn't gotten you."

The bull, Jillian realized. It hadn't been anger, but fear. Something warm and sweet moved through her. "Don't," she murmured. "I wasn't hurt. It wasn't nearly as bad as it must've looked."

"The hell it wasn't." His hands came to her face and jerked it back. "I was only a few yards back when I got the first rope around him. He was more'n half crazy by then. Another couple of seconds and he'd've scooped you right up off that ground."

Jillian stared up at him and finally managed to swallow. "I—I didn't know."

He watched as the color her temper had given her fled from her cheeks. And I just had to tell you, he thought furiously. Taking both her hands, he brought them to his lips, burying his mouth in one palm, then the other. The gesture alone was enough to distract her. "It's done," Aaron said with more control. "I guess I overreacted. It's not easy to watch something like that." Because she needed it, he smiled at her. "I wouldn't have cared for it if you'd picked up any holes."

Relaxing a bit, she answered the smile. "Neither would I. As it is, I picked up a few bruises I'm not too fond of."

Still holding her hands, he bent over and kissed her with such exquisite gentleness that she felt the ground tilt for the second time. There was something different here, she realized dimly. Something . . . But she couldn't hold on to it.

Aaron drew away, knowing the time was coming when he'd have to tell her what he felt, whether she was ready to hear it or not. As he led her back to the truck he decided that since he was only going to bare his heart to one woman in his life, he was going to do it right.

"You're going to take a hot bath," he told her as he lifted her into the truck. "Then I'm going to fix you dinner."

Jillian settled back against the seat. "Maybe fainting isn't such a bad thing after all."

CHAPTER 11

By the time they drove into the ranch yard, Jillian had decided she'd probably enjoy a few hours of pampering. As far as she could remember, no one had ever fussed over her before. As a child, she'd been strong and healthy. Whenever she'd been ill, she'd been treated with competent practicality by her doctor father. She'd learned early that the fewer complaints you made the less likelihood there was for a hypodermic to come out of that little black bag. Clay had always treated bumps and blood as a routine part of the life. Wash up and get back to work.

Now she thought it might be a rather interesting experience to have someone murmur over her scrapes and bruises. Especially if he kissed her like he had on the side of the road . . . in that soft, gentle way that made the top of her head threaten to spin off.

Perhaps they wouldn't have the noise and lights and music of the fairgrounds, but they could make their own fireworks, alone, on Utopia.

All the buildings were quiet, bunkhouse, barns, stables. Instead of the noise and action that would accompany any late afternoon, there was simple, absolute peace over acres of land. Whatever animals hadn't been taken to the fair had

been left to graze for the day. It would be hours before anyone returned to Utopia.

"I don't think I've ever been here alone before," Jillian
murmured when Aaron stopped the truck. She sat for a
moment and absorbed the quiet and the stillness. It occurred to her that she could cup her hands and shout if she
liked—no one would even hear the echo.

"It's funny, it even feels different. You always know there're
people around." She stepped out of the truck, then listened
to the echo of the slam. "Somebody in the bunkhouse or the
cookhouse or one of the outbuildings. Some of the wives or
children hanging out clothes or working in the gardens. You
hardly think about it, but it's like a little town."

"Self-sufficient, independent." He took her hand, thinking
that the words described her just as accurately as they described the ranch. They were two of the reasons he'd been
drawn to her.

"It has to be, doesn't it? It's so easy to get cut off—one bad
storm. Besides, it's what makes it all so special." Though she
didn't understand the smile he sent her, she answered it. "I'm
glad I've got so many married hands who've settled," she
added. "It's harder to depend on the drifters." Jillian scanned
the ranch yard, not quite understanding her own reluctance
to go inside. It was as if she were missing something. With
a shrug, she put it down to the oddity of being alone, but she
caught herself searching the area again.

Aaron glanced down and saw the lowered-brow look of
concentration. "Something wrong?"

"I don't know . . . It seems like there is." With another
shrug, she turned to him. "I must be getting jumpy." Reaching up, she tipped back the brim of his hat. She liked the way
it shadowed his face, accenting the angle of bone, adding just
one more shade of darkness to his eyes. "You didn't mention
anything about scrubbing my back when I took that hot bath,
did you?"

"No, but I could probably be persuaded."

Agreeably she went into his arms. She thought she could catch just a trace of rosin on him, perhaps a hint of saddle soap. "Did I mention how sore I am?"

"No, you didn't."

"I don't like to complain . . ." She snuggled against him.

"But?" he prompted with a grin.

"Well, now that you mention it—there are one or two places that sting, just a bit."

"Want me to kiss them and make them better?"

She sighed as he nuzzled her ear. "If it wouldn't be too much trouble."

"I'm a humanitarian," he told her, then began to nudge her slowly toward the porch steps. It was then Jillian remembered. With a gasp, she broke out of his arms and raced across the yard. "Jillian—" Swearing, Aaron followed her.

Oh, God, how could she've missed it! Jillian raced to the paddock fence and leaned breathlessly against it. Empty. *Empty.* She balled her hands into fists as she looked at the bottle she'd left hanging at an angle in the shade. The trough of water glimmered in the sun. The few scoops of grain she'd left were barely touched.

"What's going on?"

"Baby," she muttered, tapping her hand rhythmically against the fence. "They've taken Baby." Her tone started out calm, then became more and more agitated. "They walked right into my backyard, right into my backyard, and stole from me."

"Maybe one of your hands put him back in the barn."

She only shook her head and continued to tap her hand on the fence. "The five hundred weren't enough," she murmured. "They had to come here and steal within a stone's throw of my house. I should've left Joe—he offered to stay. I should've stayed myself."

"Come on, we'll check the barn."

She looked at him, and her eyes were flat and dark. "He's not in the barn."

He'd rather have had her rage, weep, than look so—resigned. "Maybe not, but we'll be sure. Then we'll see if anything else was taken before we call the sheriff."

"The sheriff." Jillian laughed under her breath and stared blindly into the empty paddock. "The sheriff."

"Jillian—" Aaron slipped his arms around her, but she drew away immediately.

"No, I'm not going to fall apart this time." Her voice trembled slightly, but her eyes were clear. "They won't do that to me again."

It might be better if she did, Aaron thought. Her face was pale, but he knew that expression by now. There'd be no backing down. "You check the barn," he suggested. "I'll look in the stables."

Jillian followed the routine, though she knew it was hopeless. Baby's stall was empty. She watched the little motes of hay and dust as they floated in the slant of sunlight. Someone had taken her yearling. Someone. Her hands balled into fists. Somehow, some way, she was going to get a name. Spinning on her heel, she strode back out. Though she itched with impatience, she waited until Aaron crossed the yard to her. There wasn't any need for words. Together, they went into the house.

She's not going to take this one lying down, he decided, with as much admiration as concern. Yes, she was still pale, but her voice was strong and clear as she spoke to the sheriff's office. Resigned—yes, she was still resigned that it had been done. But she didn't consider it over.

He remembered the way she'd nuzzled the calf when it'd been newborn—the way her eyes had softened when she spoke of it. It was always a mistake to make a pet out of one of your stock, but there were times it happened. She was paying for it now.

Thoughtfully he began to brew coffee. Aaron considered it a foolish move for anyone to have stolen Utopia's prize yearling. For butchering? It hardly seemed worth the risk or effort. Yet what rancher in the area would buy a young Hereford so easily identified? Someone had gotten greedy, or stupid. Either way, it would make them easier to catch.

Jillian leaned against the kitchen wall and talked steadily into the phone. Aaron found himself wanting to shield, to protect. She took the coffee from him with a brief nod and continued talking. Shaking his head, he reminded himself he should know better by now. Protection wasn't something Jillian would take gracefully. He drank his own coffee, looking out of the kitchen window and wondering how a man dealt with loving a woman who had more grit than most men.

"He'll do what he can," she said as she hung up the phone with a snap. "I'm going to offer a separate reward for Baby." Jillian drank down half the coffee, hot and black. "Tomorrow I'll go see the Cattlemen's Association again. I want to put the pressure on, and put it on hard. People are going to realize this isn't going to stop at Utopia." She looked into her coffee, then grimly finished it off. "I kept telling myself it wasn't personal. Even when I saw the hides and bones in the canyon. Not this time. They got cocky, Aaron. It's always easier to catch arrogance."

There was relish in the tone of her voice, the kind of relish that made him smile as he turned to face her. "You're right."

"What're you grinning at?"

"I was thinking if the rustlers could see you now, they'd be shaking the dust of this county off their boots in a hurry."

Her lips curved. She hadn't thought it possible. "Thank you." She gestured with the cup, then set it back on the stove. "I seem to be saying that to you quite a bit these days."

"You don't have to say it at all. Hungry?"

"Hmmm." She put her hand on her stomach and thought about it. "I don't know."

"Go get yourself a bath, I'll rustle up something."

Walking to him, Jillian slipped her arms around his waist and rested her head on his chest. How was it he knew her so well? How did he understand that she needed a few moments alone to sort through her thoughts and feelings?

"Why are you so good to me?" she murmured.

With a half laugh, Aaron buried his face in her hair. "God knows. Go soak your bruises."

"Okay." But she gave in to the urge to hug him fiercely before she left the room.

She wished she knew a better way to express gratitude. As she climbed the stairs to the second floor, Jillian wished she were more clever with words. If she were, she'd be able to tell him how much it meant that he offered no more than she could comfortably take. His support today had been steady but unobtrusive. And he was giving her time alone without leaving her alone. Perhaps it had taken her quite some time to discover just how special a man he was, but she had discovered it. It wasn't something she'd forget.

As Jillian peeled off her clothes she found she was a bit more tender in places than she'd realized. Better, she decided, and turned the hot water on in the tub to let it steam. A few bruises were something solid to concentrate on. They were easier than the bruises she felt on the inside. It might have been foolish to feel as though she'd let her grandfather down, but she couldn't rid herself of the feeling. He'd given her something in trust and she hadn't protected it well enough. It would have soothed her if he'd been around to berate her for it.

Wincing a bit, she lowered herself into the water. The raw skin on her elbow objected and she ignored it. One of her own men? she thought with a grimace. It was too possible. Back up a truck to the paddock, load up the calf, and go.

She'd start making a few discreet inquiries herself. Stealing the calf would've taken time. Maybe she could discover just who was away from the fair. Perhaps they'd be confident enough to throw a little extra money around if they thought they were safe and then . . . Then they'd see, she thought as she relaxed in the water.

Poor Baby. No one would spend the time scratching his ears or talking to him now. Sinking farther in the water, she waited until her mind went blank.

It was nearly an hour before she came downstairs again. She'd soaked the stiffness away and nearly all the depression. Nothing practical could be done with depression. She caught the aroma of something spicy that had her stomach juices churning.

Aaron's name was on the tip of her tongue as she walked into the kitchen, but the room was empty. A pot simmered on the stove with little hisses and puffs of steam. It drew her, irresistibly. Jillian lifted the lid, closed her eyes, and breathed deep. Chili, thick, and fragrant enough to make the mouth water. She wouldn't have to give it any thought if he asked if she was hungry now.

Picking up a spoon, she began to stir. Maybe just one little taste . . .

"My mother used to smack my hand for that," Aaron commented. Jillian dropped the lid with a clatter.

"Damn, Murdock! You scared me to—" Turning, she saw the clutch of wildflowers in his hand.

Some men might've looked foolish holding small colorful blooms in a hand roughened by work and weather. Other men might've seemed awkward. Aaron was neither. Something turned over in her chest when he smiled at her.

She looked stunned—not that he minded. It wasn't often you caught a woman like Jillian Baron off-balance. As he watched, she put her hands behind her back and gripped them together. He lifted a brow. If he'd known he could make her nervous with a bunch of wildflowers, he'd have dug up a field of them long before this.

"Feel better?" he asked and slowly crossed to her.

She'd backed into the counter before she'd realized she made the defensive move. "Yes, thanks."

He gave her one of his long, serious looks while his eyes laughed. "Something wrong?"

"No. The chili smells great."

"Something I picked up at one of the line camps a few years back." Bending his head, he kissed the corners of her mouth. "Don't you want the flowers, Jillian?"

"Yes, I—" She found she was gripping her fingers together until they hurt. Annoyed with herself, she loosened them and took the flowers from his hand. "They're very pretty."

"It's what your hair smells like," he murmured and saw the cautious look she threw up at him. Tilting his head, he studied her. "Hasn't anyone ever given you flowers before?"

Not in years, she realized. Not since—florist boxes, ribbons, and soft words. Realizing she was making a fool of herself, she shrugged. "Roses," she said carelessly. "Red roses."

Something in her tone warned him. He kept his touch very light as he wound her hair around his finger. It was the color of flame, the texture of silk. "Too tame," he said simply. "Much too tame."

Something flickered inside her—acknowledgment, caution, need. With a sigh, she looked down at the small bold flowers in her hand. "Once—a long time ago—I thought I could be too."

He tugged on her hair until she looked up at him. "Is that what you wanted to be?"

"Then, I—" She broke off, but something in his eyes demanded an answer. "Yes, I would've tried."

"Were you in love with him?" He wasn't certain why he was hacking away at a wound—his and hers—but he couldn't stop.

"Aaron—"

"Were you?"

She let out a long breath. Mechanically she began to fill a water glass for the flowers. "I was very young. He was a great deal like my father—steady, quiet, dedicated. My father loved me because he had to, never because he wanted to. There's a tremendous difference." The sharp, clean scent of the wild-flowers drifted up to her. "Maybe somewhere along the line I thought if I pleased him, I'd please my father. I don't know, I was foolish."

"That isn't an answer." He discovered jealousy tasted bitter even after it was swallowed.

"I guess I don't have one I'm sure of." She moved her shoulders and fluffed the flowers in the glass. "Shouldn't we eat?" She went very still when his hands came to her shoulders, but she didn't resist when he turned her around.

She had a moment's fear that he would say something gentle, something sweet, and undermine her completely. She saw something of it in his eyes, just as he saw the apprehension in hers. Aaron tugged her against him and brought his mouth down hard on hers.

She could understand the turbulence and let go. She could meet the desire, the violence of needs, without fear of stumbling past her own rules. Her arms went around him to hold him close. Her lips sought his hungrily. If through the relief came a stir of feeling, she could almost convince herself it was nothing more complex than passion.

"Eat fast," Aaron told her. "I've been thinking about making love with you for hours."

"Didn't we eat already?"

With a chuckle he nuzzled her neck. "No, you don't. When I cook for a woman, she eats." He gave her a companionable smack on the bottom as he drew away. "Get the bowls."

Jillian handed him two and watched him scoop out generous portions. "Smells fabulous. Want a beer?"

"Yeah."

Unearthing two from the refrigerator, she poured them into glasses. "You know, if you ever get tired of ranching, you could have a job in the cookhouse here at Utopia."

"Always a comfort to have something to fall back on."

"We've got a woman now," Jillian went on as she took her seat. "The men call her Aunt Sally. She's got a way with biscuits—" She broke off as she took the first bite. Heat spread through her and woke up every cell in her body. Swallowing, she met Aaron's grin. "You use a free hand with the peppers."

"Separates the men from the boys." He took a generous forkful. "Too hot for you?"

Disdainfully she took a second bite. "There's nothing you can dish out I can't take, Murdock."

Laughing, he continued to eat. Jillian decided the first encounter had numbed her mouth right down to the vocal cords. She ate with as much relish as he, cooling off occasionally with sips of cold beer.

"Those people in town don't know what they're missing," she commented as she scraped down to the bottom of the bowl. "It isn't every day you get battery acid this tasty."

He glanced over as she ate the last forkful. "Want some more?"

"I want to live," she countered. "God, Aaron, a steady diet of that and you wouldn't have a stomach lining. It's fabulous."

"We had a Mexican foreman when I was a boy," Aaron told her. "Best damn cattleman I've ever known. I spent the best part of a summer with him up at the line camp. You should taste my flour tortillas."

The man was a constant surprise, Jillian decided as she rested her elbows on the table and cupped her chin in her hand. "What happened to him?"

"Saved his stake, went back to Mexico, and started his own spread."

"The impossible dream," Jillian murmured.

"Too easy to lose a month's pay in a poker game."

She nodded, but her lips curved. "Do you play?"

"I've sat in on a hand or two. You?"

"Clay taught me. We'll have to arrange a game one of these days."

"Any time."

"I'm counting on a few poker skills to bring me out of this rustling business."

Aaron watched her rise to clear the table. "How?"

"People get careless when they think you're ready to fold. They made a mistake with the yearling, Aaron. I'm going to be able to find him—especially if nobody knows how hard I'm looking. I'm thinking about hiring an investigator. Whatever it costs, I'd rather pay it than have the stealing go on."

He sat for a moment, listening to her run water in the sink—a homey, everyday sound. "How hard is all this hitting your books, Jillian?"

She cast a look over her shoulder, calm and cool. "I can still raise the bet."

He knew better than to offer her financial assistance. It irked him. Rising, he paced the kitchen until he'd come full circle behind her. "The Cattlemen's Association would back you."

"They'd have to know about it to do that. The less people who know, the more effective a private investigation would be."

"I want to help you."

Touched, she turned and took him into her arms. "You have helped me. I won't forget it."

"I have to hog-tie you before you'll let me do anything."

She laughed and lifted her face to his. "I'm not that bad."

"Worse," he countered. "If I offered you some men to help patrol your land . . ."

"Aaron—"

"See." He kissed her before she could finish the protest. "I could work for you myself until everything was straightened out."

"I couldn't let you—" Then his mouth was hard and bruising on hers again.

"I'm the one who has to watch you worry and struggle," he told her as his hands began to roam down. "Do you know what that does to me?"

She tried to concentrate on his words, but his mouth—his mouth was demanding all her attention. The hot, spicy kiss took her breath away, but she clung to him and fought for more. Each time he touched her it was only seconds until the needs took over completely. She'd never known anything so liberating, or so imprisoning. Jillian might have struggled against the latter if she'd known how. Instead she accepted the bars and locks even as she accepted the open sky and the wind. He was the only man who could tempt her to.

This was something he could do for her, Aaron knew. Make her forget, thrust her problems away from her, if only temporarily. Even so, he knew, if she had a choice, she would have kept some distance there as well. She'd been hurt, and her trust wasn't completely his yet. The frustration of it made his mouth more ruthless, his hands more urgent. There was still only one way that she was his without question. He swept her up, then silenced her murmured protest.

Jillian was aware she was being carried. Some inner part of her rebelled against it. And yet . . . He wasn't taking her anywhere she wouldn't have gone willingly. Perhaps he needed this—romance he'd once called it. Romance frightened her, as the flowers had frightened her. It was so easy to lie in candlelight, so easy to deceive with fragrant blossoms and soft words. And she was no longer sure the defenses she'd once had were still there. Not with him.

"I want you." The words drifted from her to shimmer against his lips.

He would've taken her to bed. But it was too far. He would have given her the slow, easy loving a cherished woman deserves. But he was too hungry. With his mouth still fused to hers, he tumbled onto the couch with her and let the fire take them both.

She understood desperation. It was honest and real. There could be no doubting the frantic search of his mouth or the urgent pressure of his fingers against her skin. Desire had no shadows. She could feel it pulsing from him even as it pulsed from her. His curses as he tugged at her clothes made her laugh breathlessly. *She* made him clumsy. It was the greatest compliment she'd ever had.

He was relentless, spinning her beyond time and space the moment he could touch her flesh. She let herself go. Every touch, every frenzied caress, every deep, greedy kiss, took her further from the strict, practical world she'd formed for herself. Once she'd sought solitude and speed when she'd needed freedom. Now she needed only Aaron.

She felt his hair brush over her bare shoulder and savored even that simple contact. It brought a sweetness flowing into her while the burn of his mouth brought the fire. Only with him had she realized it was possible to have both. Only with him had she realized the great, yawning need in herself to have both. Her moan came as much from the revelation as from the passion.

Did she know how giving she was? How incredibly arousing? Aaron had to fight the need to take her quickly, ruthlessly, while they were both still half dressed. No woman had ever sapped his control the way she could. One look, one touch, and he was hers so completely—How could she not know?

Her body flowed, fluid as water, heady as wine, under his hands. Her lips had the punch of an electric current and the texture of silk. Could any woman remain unaware of such a deadly combination?

As if to catch his breath, he took his lips to her throat and burrowed there. He drew in the fragrance from her bath, some subtle woman's scent that lingered there, waiting to entice a lover. It was then he remembered the bruises. Aaron shook his head, trying to clear it.

"I'm hurting you."

"No." She drew him back, close. "No, you're not. You never do. I'm not fragile, Aaron."

"No?" He lifted his head so that he could see her face. There was the delicate line of bone she couldn't deny, the honey-touched skin that remained soft after hours in the sun. The frailty that came and went in her eyes at the right word, the right touch. "Sometimes you are," he murmured. "Let me show you."

"No—"

But even as she protested, his lips skimmed hers, so gentle, so reassuring. It did nothing to smother the fire, only banked it while he showed her what magic there could be with mouth to mouth. With his fingers he traced her face as though he might never see it with his eyes again—over the curve of cheekbone, down the slim line of jaw.

Patient, soft, murmuring, he seduced where no seduction was needed. Tender, thorough, easy, he let his lips show her what he hadn't yet spoken. The hand on his shoulder slid bonelessly down to his waist. He touched the tip of her tongue with his, then went deeper, slowly, in a soul-wrenching kiss that left them both limp. Then he began a careful worship of her body. She floated.

Was there any kind of pleasure he couldn't show her? Jillian wondered. Was this humming world just one more aspect to passion? She wanted desperately to give him something in return, yet her body was so heavy, weighed down with sensations. Sandalwood and leather—it would always bring him to her mind. The ridge of callus on his hand where the reins rubbed daily—nothing felt more perfect against her skin. He shifted so that she sank deeper into the cushions, and he with her.

She could taste him—and what she realized must be a wisp of herself on his lips. His cheek grazed hers, not quite smooth. She wanted to burrow against it. He whispered her name and generated a new layer of warmth.

Even when his hands began to roam, the excitement stayed hazy. She couldn't break through the mists, and no longer tried. Her skin was throbbing, but it went deeper, to the blood and bone. His mouth was light at her breast, his tongue clever enough to make her shudder, then settle, then shudder again.

He kept the pace easy, though she began to writhe under him. Time dripped away as he gave himself the pleasure of showing her each new delight. He knew afternoon was ending only by the way the light slanted over her face. The quiet was punctuated only with murmurs and sighs. He'd never felt more alone with her.

He took her slowly, savoring each moment, each movement, until there could be no more.

As she lay beneath him, Jillian watched the light shift toward dusk. It had been like a dream, she thought, like something you sigh over in the middle of the night when your wishes take control. Should it move her more than the fire and flash they usually brought each other? Somehow she knew what she'd just experienced had been more dangerous.

Aaron shifted, and though she made no objection to his weight, sat up, bringing her with him. "I like the way you stay soft and warm after I make love to you."

"It's never been just like that before," she murmured.

The words moved him; he couldn't stop it. "No." Tilting back her head, he kissed her again. "It will be again."

Perhaps because she wanted so badly to hold on, to stay,

to depend, she drew away. "I'm never sure how to take you."
Something warned her it was time to play it light. She was
out of her depth—far, far out of her depth.

"In what way?"

She gave in to the urge to hold him again, just to feel the
way his hand slid easily up and down her bare back. Reluctantly she slipped out of his arms and pulled on her shirt.
"You're a lot of different people, Aaron Murdock. Every time
I think I might get to know who you are, you're someone
else."

"No, I'm not." Before she could button it, Aaron took
her shirtfront and pulled her back to him. "Different moods
don't make different people."

"Maybe not." She disconcerted him by kissing the back of
his hand. "But I still can't get a handle on you."

"Is that what you want?"

"I'm a simple person."

He stared at her a moment as she continued to dress. "Are
you joking?"

Because there was a laugh in his voice, she looked over,
half serious, half embarrassed. "No, I am. I have to know
where I stand, what my options are, what's expected of me.
As long as I know I can do my job and take care of what's
mine, I'm content."

He watched her thoughtfully as he pulled on his jeans.
"Your job's what's vital in your life?"

"It's what I know," she countered. "I understand the land."

"And people?"

"I'm not really very good with people—a lot of people.
Unless I understand them."

Aaron pulled his shirt on but left it open as he crossed to
her. "And I'm one you don't understand?"

"Only sometimes," she murmured. "I guess I understand
you best when I'm annoyed with you. Other times . . ." She
was sinking even deeper and started to turn away.

"Other times," Aaron prompted, holding on to her arms.

"Other times I don't know. I never expected to get involved with you—this way."

He ran his thumbs over the pulses at the inside of her elbows. They weren't steady any longer. "This way, Jillian?"

"I didn't expect that we'd be lovers. I never expected—" Why was her heart pounding like this again, so soon? "To want you," she finished.

"Didn't you?" There was something about the way she looked at him—not quite sure of herself when he knew she was fighting to be—that made him reckless. "I wanted you from the first minute I saw you, riding hell for leather on that mare. There were other things I didn't expect. Finding those soft places, on you, in you."

"Aaron—"

He shook his head when she tried to stop him. "Thinking of you in the middle of the day, the middle of the night. Remembering just the way you say my name."

"Don't."

He felt her start to tremble before she tried to pull away. "Damn it, it's time you heard what I've been carrying around inside of me. I love you, Jillian."

Panic came first, even when she began to build up the reserve. "No, you don't have to say that." Her voice was sharp and fast. "I don't expect to hear those kinds of things."

"What the hell are you talking about?" He shook her once in frustration, and a second time in anger. "I know what I have to say. I don't care if you expect to hear it or not, because you're going to."

She hung on to her temper because she knew it was emotion that brought on betrayal. If she hadn't had her pride, she would have told him just how much those words, that easily said empty phrase hurt her. "Aaron, I told you before I don't need the soft words. I don't even like them. Whatever's between us—"

"What is between us?" he demanded. He hadn't known he could be hurt, not like this. Not so he could all but feel the blood draining out of him where he stood. He'd just told a woman he loved her—the only woman, the first time. And she was answering him with ice. "You tell me what there is between us. Just this?" He swung a hand toward the couch, still rumpled from their bodies. "Is that it for you, Jillian?"

"I don't—" There was a tug-of-war going on inside of her, so fierce she was breathless from it. "It's all I thought you—" Frightened, she dragged both hands through her hair. Why was he doing this now, when she was just beginning to think she understood what he wanted from her, what she needed from him? "I don't know what you want. But I—I just can't give you any more than I already have. It's already more than I've ever given to anyone else."

His fingers loosened on her arms one by one, then dropped away. They were a match in many ways, and pride was one of them. Aaron watched her almost dispassionately as he buttoned his shirt. "You've let something freeze inside you, woman. If all you want's a warm body on a cold night, you shouldn't have much trouble. Personally, I like a little something more."

She watched him walk out of the door, heard the sound of his truck as it broke the silence. The sun was just slipping over the horizon.

CHAPTER 12

He worked until his muscles ached and he could think about little more than easing them. He probably drank too much. He rode the cattle, hours in the saddle, rounded strays, and ate more dust than food. He spent the long, sweaty days of summer at the line camp, driving himself from sunup to sundown. Sometimes, only sometimes, he managed to push her out of his mind.

For three weeks Aaron was hell to be around. Or so his men mumbled whenever he was out of earshot. It was a woman, they told each other. Only a woman could drive a man to the edge, and then give him that gentle tap over. The Baron woman's name came up. Well, Murdocks and Barons had never mixed, so it was no wonder. No one'd expected much to come of that but hot tempers and bad feelings.

If Aaron heard the murmurs, he ignored them. He'd come up to the camp to work—and he was going to do just that until she was out of his system. No woman was going to make him crawl. He'd told her he loved her, and she'd shoved his words, his emotions, right back in his face. Not interested.

Aaron dropped a new fence post into the ground as the sweat rolled freely down his back and sides. Maybe she was the first woman he'd ever loved—that didn't mean she'd be the last. He came down hard on the post with a sledgehammer, hissing with the effort.

He hadn't meant to tell her—not then, not that way. Somehow, the words had started rolling and he hadn't been able to stop them. Had she wanted them all tied up with a ribbon, neat and fancy? Cursing, he came down with the hammer again so that the post vibrated and the noise sang out. Maybe he had more finesse than he'd shown her, and maybe he could've used it. With someone else. Someone who didn't make his feelings come up and grab him by the throat.

Where in God's name had he ever come up with the idea that she had those soft parts, that sweet vulnerability under all that starch and fire? Must've been crazy, he told himself as he began running fresh wire. Jillian Baron was a cold, single-minded woman who cared more about her head count than any real emotion.

And he was almost sick with loving her.

He gripped the wire hard enough so that it bit through the leather of his glove and into his hand. He cursed again. He'd just have to get over it. He had his own land to tend.

Pausing, he looked out. It rolled, oceans of grass, high with summer, green and rippling. The sky was a merciless blue, and the sun beat down, strong and clean. It could be enough for a man—these thousands of acres. His cattle were fat and healthy, the yearlings growing strong. In a few weeks they'd round them up, drive them into Miles City. When those long days were over, the men would celebrate. It was their right to. And so would he, Aaron told himself grimly. So, by God, would he.

He'd have given half of what was his just to get her out of his mind for one day.

At dusk he washed off the day's sweat and dirt. He could smell the night's meal through the open windows of the cabin. Good red meat. Someone was playing a guitar and singing of lonely, lamented love. He found he wanted a beer more than he wanted his share of the steak. Because he knew a man couldn't work and not eat, he piled food on his plate and transferred it to his stomach. But he worked his way through one beer, then two, while the men made up their evening poker game. As they grew louder he took a six-pack and went out on the narrow wood porch.

The stars were just coming out. He heard a coyote call at the moon, then fall silent. The air was as still as it had been all day and barely cooler, but he could smell the sweet clover and wild roses. Resting his back against the porch rail, Aaron willed his mind to empty. But he thought of her . . .

Fully dressed and spitting mad, standing in the pond—crooning quietly to an orphaned calf—laughing up at him with her hair spread out over the earth of the corral—weeping in his arms over her butchered cattle. Soft one minute, prickly the next—no, she wasn't a temperate woman. But she was the only one he wanted. She was the only one he'd ever felt enough for to hurt over.

Aaron took a long swig from the bottle. He didn't care much for emotional pain. The poets could have it. She didn't want him. Aaron swore and scowled into the dark. The hell she didn't—he wasn't a fool. Maybe her needs weren't the same as his, but she had them. For the first time in weeks he began to think calmly.

He hadn't played his hand well, he realized. It wasn't like him to fold so early—then again, he wasn't used to being softheaded over a woman. Thoughtfully he tipped back his hat and looked at the stars. She was too set on having her own way, and it was time he gave her a run for her money.

No, he wasn't going back on his knees, Aaron thought with a grim smile. But he was going back. If he had to hobble and brand her, he was going to have Jillian Baron.

When the screen door opened, he glanced around absently. His mood was more open to company.

"My luck's pretty poor."

Jennsen, Aaron thought, running through a quick mental outline of the man as he offered him a beer. A bit jittery, he mused. On his first season with the Double M, though he wasn't a greenhorn. He was a man who kept to himself and whose past was no more than could be seen in a worn saddle and patched boots.

Jennsen sat on the first step so that his lantern jaw was shadowed by the porch roof. Aaron thought he might be anywhere from thirty-five to fifty. There was age in his eyes— the kind that came from too many years of looking into the sun at another man's land.

"Cards aren't falling?" Aaron said conversationally while he watched Jennsen roll a cigarette. He didn't miss the fact that the fingers weren't quite steady.

"Haven't been for weeks." Jennsen gave a brief laugh as he struck a match. "Trouble is, I've never been much good at staying away from a gamble." He shot Aaron a sidelong look as he drank again. He'd been working his way up to this talk for days and nearly had enough beer in him to go through with it. "Your luck's pretty steady at the table."

"Comes and goes," Aaron said, deciding Jennsen was feeling his way along for an advance or a loan.

"Luck's a funny thing." Jennsen wiped his mouth with the back of his hand. "Had some bad luck over at the Baron place lately. Losing that cattle," he continued when Aaron glanced over at him. "Somebody made a pretty profit off that beef."

He caught the trace of bitterness. Casually he twisted the top from another bottle and handed it over. "It's easy to make a profit when you don't pay for the beef. Whoever skimmed from the Baron place did a smooth job of it."

"Yeah." Jennsen drew in strong tobacco. He'd heard the rumors about something going on between Aaron Murdock and the Baron woman, but there didn't seem to be anything to it. Most of the talk was about the bad blood between the two families. It'd been going on for years, and it seemed as though it would go on for years more. At the moment he needed badly to believe it. "Guess it doesn't much matter on this side of the fence how much cattle slips away from the Baron spread."

Aaron stretched out his legs and crossed them at the ankles. The lowered brim of his hat shadowed his eyes. "People have to look out for themselves," he said lazily.

Jennsen moistened his lips and prodded a bit further. "I've heard stories about your grandpaw helping himself to Baron beef."

Aaron's eyes narrowed to slits, but he checked his temper. "Stories," he agreed. "No proof."

Jennsen took another long swallow of beer. "I heard that somebody waltzed right onto Baron land and loaded up a prize yearling, sired by that fancy bull."

"Did a tidy job of it." Aaron kept his voice expressionless. Jennsen was testing the waters all right, but he wasn't looking for a loan. "It'd be a shame if they took it for baby beef," he added. "The yearling has the look of his sire—a real moneymaker. 'Course, in a few months he'd stand out like a sore thumb on a small spread. Hate to see a good bloodline wasted."

"Man hears things," Jennsen mumbled, accepting the fresh beer Aaron handed him. "You were interested in the Baron bull."

Aaron took a swig from his bottle, tipped back his hat, and grinned agreeably. "I'm always interested in good stock. Know where I can get my hands on some?"

Jennsen searched his face and swallowed. "Maybe."

* * *

Jillian slowed down as she passed the white frame house. Empty. Of course it was empty, she told herself. Even if he'd come back, he wouldn't be home in the middle of the morning. She shouldn't be here on Murdock land when she had her hands full of her own work. She couldn't stay away. If he didn't come back soon, she was going to make a fool of herself and go up to the line camp and . . .

And what? she asked herself. Half the time she didn't know what she wanted to do, how she felt, what she thought. The one thing she was certain of was that she'd never spent three more miserable weeks in her life. It was perilously close to grief.

Something had died in her when he'd left—something she hadn't acknowledged had been alive. She'd convinced herself that she wouldn't fall in love with him. It would be impossible to count the times she'd told herself it wouldn't happen—even after it already had. Why hadn't she recognized it?

Jillian supposed it wasn't always easy to recognize something you'd never experienced before. Especially when it had no explanation. A woman so accustomed to getting and going her own way had no business falling for a man who was equally obstinate and independent.

Falling in love. Jillian thought it an apt phrase. When it happened, you just lost your foothold and plunged.

Maybe he'd meant it, she thought. Maybe they had been more than words to him. If he loved her back, didn't it mean she had someone to hold on to while she was falling? She let out a long breath as she pulled up in front of the ranch house. If he'd meant it, why wasn't he here? Mistake, she told herself with forced calm. It was always a mistake to depend too much. People pulled back or just went away. But if she could only see him again . . .

"Going to just sit there in that Jeep all morning?"

With a jerk, Jillian turned to watch Paul Murdock take a few slow, measured steps out onto the porch. She got out of the Jeep, wondering which of the excuses she'd made up before she'd set out would work the best.

"Sit," Murdock ordered before she could come to a decision. "Karen's fixing up a pitcher of tea."

"Thank you." Feeling awkward, she sat on the edge of the porch swing and searched for something to say.

"He hasn't come down from the camp yet," Murdock told her bluntly as he lowered himself into a rocker. "Don't frazzle your brain, girl," he ordered with an impatient brush of his hand. "I may be old, but I can see what's going on under my nose. What'd the two of you spat about?"

"Paul." Karen carried a tray laden with glasses and an iced pitcher. "Jillian's entitled to her privacy."

"Privacy!" he snorted while Karen arranged the tray on a table. "She's dangling after my son."

"*Dangling!*" Jillian was on her feet in a flash. "I don't dangle after anything or anyone. If I want something, I get it."

He laughed, rocking back and forth and wheezing with the effort as she glared down at him. "I like you, girl, damn if I don't. Got a fetching face, doesn't she, Karen?"

"Lovely." With a smile, Karen offered Jillian a glass of tea.

"Thank you." Stiffly she took her seat again. "I just stopped by to let Aaron know that the mare's doing well. The vet was by yesterday to check her out."

"That the best you could do?" Murdock demanded.

"Paul." Karen sat on the arm of the rocker and laid a hand on his arm.

"If I want manure, all I have to do is walk my own pasture," he grumbled, then pointed his cane at Jillian. "You going to tell me you don't want my boy?"

"Mr. Murdock," Jillian began with icy dignity, "Aaron and I have a business arrangement."

"When a man's dying, he doesn't like to waste time," Murdock said with a scowl. "Now, you want to look me in the eye and tell me straight you've got no feelings for that son of mine, fine. We'll talk about the weather a bit."

Jillian opened her mouth, then closed it again with a

helpless shake of her head. "When's he coming back?" she whispered. "It's been three weeks."

"He'll come back when he stops being as thickheaded as you are," Murdock told her curtly.

"I don't know what to do." After the words had tumbled out, she sat in amazement. She'd never in her life said that out loud to anyone.

"What do you want?" Karen asked her.

Jillian looked over and studied them—the old man and his beautiful wife. Karen's hand was over his on top of the cane. Their shoulders brushed. A few scattered times in her life she'd seen that kind of perfect intimacy that came from deep abiding love. It was easy to recognize, enviable. And a little scary. It came as a shock to discover she wanted that for herself. One man, one lifetime. But if that was ultimately what love equaled for her, she understood it had to be a shared dream.

"I'm still finding out," she murmured.

"That Jeep." Murdock nodded toward it. "You wouldn't have any trouble getting up to the line camp in a four-wheel drive."

Jillian smiled and set her glass aside. "I can't do it that way. It wouldn't work for me if I didn't meet him on equal terms."

"Stubborn young fool," Murdock grumbled.

"Yes." Jillian smiled again as she rose. "If he wants me, that's what he's going to get." The sound of an engine had her glancing over. When she recognized Gil's truck, she frowned and started down the steps.

"Ma'am." He tipped his hat to Karen but didn't even open the door of the truck. "Mr. Murdock. Got a problem," he said briefly, shifting his eyes to Jillian.

"What is it?"

"Sheriff called. Seems your yearling's been identified on a spread 'bout hundred and fifty miles south of here. Wants you to go down and take a look for yourself."

Jillian gripped the bottom of the open window. "Where?"

"Old Larraby spread. I'll take you now."

"Leave your Jeep here," Murdock told her, getting to his feet. "One of my men'll take it back to your place."

"Thanks." Quickly she dashed around to the other side of the truck. "Let's go," she ordered the moment the door shut beside her. "How, Gil?" she demanded as they drove out of the ranch yard. "Who identified him?"

Gil spit out the window and felt rather pleased with himself. "Aaron Murdock."

"Aaron—"

Gil was a bit more pleased when Jillian's mouth fell open. "Yep." When he came to the fork in the road, he headed south at a steady, mile-eating clip.

"But how? Aaron's been up at his line camp for weeks, and—"

"Maybe you'd like to settle down so I can tell you, or maybe you wouldn't."

Seething with impatience, Jillian subsided. "Tell me."

"Seems one of the Murdock men had a hand in the rustling, fellow named Jennsen. Well, he wasn't too happy with his cut and gambled away most of it anyhow. Decided if they could slice off five hundred and get away with it, he'd take one more for himself."

"Baby," Jillian muttered and crossed her arms over her chest.

"Yep. Had himself a tiger by the tail there. Knew the makings of a prize bull when he saw it and took it over to Larraby. Used to work there before Larraby fell on hard times. Anyhow, he started to get nervous once the man who headed up the rustling got wind of who took the little bull, figured he better get it off his hands. Last night he tried to sell him to Aaron Murdock."

"I see." That was one more she owed him, Jillian thought with a scowl. It was hard to meet a man toe to toe when you were piling up debts. "If it is Baby, and this Jennsen was involved, we'll get the rest of them."

"We'll see if it's Baby," Gil said, then eased a cautious look at her. "The sheriff's already rounding up the rest of them. Picked up Joe Carlson a couple hours ago."

"Joe?" Stunned, she turned completely around in her seat to stare at Gil. "Joe Carlson?"

"Seems he bought himself a little place over in Wyoming. From the sound of it, he's already got a couple hundred head of your cattle grazing there."

"Joe." Shifting, Jillian stared straight ahead. So much for trust, she thought. So much for her expert reading of character. Clay hadn't wanted to hire him—she'd insisted. One of her first major independent decisions on Utopia had been her first major mistake.

"Guess he fooled me too," Gil muttered after a moment. "Knew his cattle front and back." He spit again and set his teeth. "Shoulda known better than to trust a man with soft hands and a clean hat."

"I hired him," Jillian muttered.

"I worked with him," Gil tossed back. "Side by side. And if you don't think that sticks in my craw, then you ain't too smart. Bamboozled me," he grumbled. "*Me!*"

It was his insulted pride that made her laugh. Jillian propped her feet up on the dash. What was done was over, she told herself. She was going to get a good chunk of her cattle back and see justice done. And at roundup time her books would shift back into the black. Maybe they'd have that new Jeep after all. "Did you get the full story from the sheriff?"

"Aaron Murdock," Gil told her. "He came by right before I set out after you."

"He came by the ranch?" she asked with a casualness that wouldn't have fooled anyone.

"Stopped by so I'd have the details."

"Did he—ah—say anything else?"

"Just that he had a lot of things to see to. Busy man."

"Oh." Jillian turned her head and stared out the window. Gil took a chance and grinned hugely.

* * *

She waited until it was nearly dark. It was impossible to bank down the hope that he'd come by or call, if only to see that everything had gone well. She worked out a dozen opening speeches and revised them. She paced. When she knew that she'd scream if she spent another minute within four walls, Jillian went out to the stables and saddled her mare.

"Men," she grumbled as she pulled the cinch. "If this is all part of the game, I'm not interested."

Ready for a run, Delilah sniffed the air the moment Jillian led her outside. When Jillian swung into the saddle, the mare danced and strained against the bit. Within moments they'd left the lights of the ranch yard behind.

The ride would clear her head, she told herself. Anyone would be a bit crazed after a day like this one. Getting Baby back had eased the sting of betrayal she'd felt after learning Joe Carlson had stolen from her. Methodically stolen, she thought, while offering advice and sympathy. He'd certainly been clever, she mused, subtly, systematically turning her attention toward the Murdocks while he was slipping her own cattle through her own fences. Until she found a new herdsman, she'd have to add his duties to her own.

It would do her good, she decided, keep her mind off things. Aaron. If he'd wanted to see her, he'd known where to find her. Apparently, she'd done them both a favor by pushing him away weeks before. If she hadn't, they'd have found themselves in a very painful situation. As it was, they were each just going their own way—exactly as she'd known they would from the beginning. Perhaps she'd had a few moments of weakness, like the one that morning on the Double M, but they wouldn't last. In the next few weeks she'd be too busy to worry about Aaron Murdock and some foolish dreams.

Jillian told herself she hadn't deliberately ridden to the pond, but had simply let Delilah go her own way. In any case, it was still a spot she'd choose for solitude, no matter what memories lingered there.

The moon was full and white, the brush silvered with it. She told herself she wasn't unhappy, just tired after a long day of traveling, dealing with the sheriff, answering questions. She couldn't be unhappy when she finally had what was hers back. When the weariness passed, she'd celebrate. She could have wept, and hated herself.

When she saw the moon reflected on the water, she slowed Delilah to an easy lope. There wasn't a sound but the steady hoofbeats of her own mount. She heard the stallion even as her mare scented him. With her own heart pounding, Jillian controlled the now skittish Delilah and brought her to a halt. Aaron stepped out of the shadow of a cottonwood and said nothing at all.

He'd known she'd come—sooner or later. He could've gone to her, or waited for her to come to him. Somehow he'd known they had to meet here on land that belonged to them both.

It was better to face it all now and be done with it, Jillian told herself, then found her hands were wet with nerves as she dismounted. Nothing could've stiffened her spine more effectively. In thrumming silence she tethered her mare. When she turned, she found Aaron had moved behind her, as silently as the wildcat she'd once compared him to. She stood very straight, kept her tone very impassive.

"So, you came back."

His eyes were lazy and amused as he scanned her face. "Did you think I wouldn't?"

Her chin came up as he'd known it would. "I didn't think about it at all."

"No?" He smiled then—it should have warned her. "Did you think about this?" He dragged her to him, one hand at her waist, one at the back of her head, and devoured the mouth he'd starved for. He expected her to struggle—perhaps he would've relished it just then—but she met the demands of his mouth with the strength and verve he remembered.

When he tore his mouth from hers, she clung, burying her face in his shoulder. He still wanted her—the thought pounded inside her head. She hadn't lost him, not yet. "Hold me," she murmured. "Please, just for a minute."

How could she do this to him? Aaron wondered. How could she shift his mood from crazed to tender in the space of seconds? Maybe he'd never figure out quite how to handle her, but he didn't intend to stop learning.

When she felt her nerves come back, she drew away. "I want to thank you for what you did. The sheriff told me that you got the evidence from Jennsen, and—"

"I don't want to talk about the cattle, Jillian."

"No." Linking her hands together, she turned away. No, it was time they put that aside and dealt with what was really important. What was vital. "I've thought about what happened—about what you said the last time we saw each other." Where were all those speeches she'd planned? They'd all been so calm, so lucid. She twisted her fingers until they hurt, then separated them. "Aaron, I meant it when I said that I don't expect to be told those things. Some women do."

"I wasn't saying them to some women."

"It's so easy to say," she told him in a vibrating whisper. "So easy."

"Not for me."

She turned slowly, warily, as if she expected him to make a move she wasn't prepared for. He looked so calm, she thought. And yet the way the moonlight hit his eyes . . . "It's hard," she murmured.

"What is?"

"Loving you."

He could have gone to her then, right then, and pulled her to him until there was no more talk, no more thought. But her chin was up and her eyes were swimming. "Maybe it's supposed to be. I'm not offering you an easy road."

"No one's ever loved me back the way I wanted." Swallowing, she stepped away. "No one but Clay, and he never told me. He never had to."

"I'm not Clay, or your father. And there's no one who's ever going to love you the way I do." He took a step toward her, and though she didn't back up, he thought he could see every muscle brace. "What are you afraid of?"

"I'm not afraid!"

He came closer. "Like hell."

"That you'll stop." It wrenched out of her as she gripped her hands behind her back. Once started, the words rushed out quickly and ran together. "That you'll decide you never really loved me anyway. And I'll have let myself want and start depending and needing you. I've spent most of my life working on not depending on anyone, not for anything."

"I'm not anyone," he said quietly.

Her breath came shuddering out, "Since you've been gone I haven't cared about anything except you coming back."

He ran his hands up her arms. "Now that I am?"

"I couldn't bear it if you didn't stay. And though I think I could stand the hurt, I just can't stand being afraid." She put her hands to his chest when he started to draw her to him.

"Jillian, do you think you can tell me things I've been waiting to hear and have me keep my hands off you? Don't you know there's risk on both sides? Dependence on both sides?"

"Maybe." She made herself breathe evenly until she got it all out. "But people aren't always looking for the same things."

"Such as?"

This time she moistened her lips. "Are you going to marry me?" The surprise in his eyes made her muscles stiffen again.

"You asking?"

She dragged herself out of his hold, cursing herself for being a fool and him for laughing at her. "Go to hell," she told him as she started for her horse.

He caught her around the waist, lifting her off the ground as she kicked out. "Damn, you've got a short fuse," he muttered and ended by pinning her to the ground. "I have a feeling I'm going to spend the best part of my life wrestling with you." Showing an amazing amount of patience, he waited until she'd run out of curses and had subsided, panting. "I'd planned to put the question to you a bit differently," he began. "As in, will you? But as I see it, that's a waste of time." As she stared up at him, he smiled. "God, you're beautiful. Don't argue," he warned as she opened her mouth. "I'm going to tell you that whenever I please so you might as well start swallowing it now."

"You were laughing at me," she began, but he cut her off.

"At both of us." Lowering his head, he kissed her, gently at first, then with building passion. "Now . . ." Cautiously he let her wrists go until he was certain she wasn't going to take a swing at him. "I'll give you a week to get things organized at your ranch."

"A week—"

"Shut up," he suggested. "A week, then we're both taking the next week off to get married."

Jillian lay very still and soaked it in. It was pure joy. "It doesn't take a week to get married."

"The way I do it does. When we get back—"

"Get back from where?"

"From any place where we can be alone," he told her. "We're going to start making some plans."

She reached for his cheek. "So far I like them. Aaron, say it again, while I'm looking at you."

"I love you, Jillian. A good bit of the time I like you as well, though I can't say I mind fighting with you."

"I guess you really mean it." She closed her eyes a moment. When she opened them again, they were laughing. "It's hard to take a Murdock at his word, but I'm going to gamble."

"What about a Baron?"

"A Baron's word's gold," she said, angling her chin. "I love you, Aaron. I'm going to make you a frustrating wife and a hell of a partner." She grinned as his lips pressed against hers. "What about those plans?"

"You've got a ranch, I've got a ranch," he pointed out as he kissed her palm. "I don't much care whether we run them separately or together, but there's a matter of living. Your house, my house—that's not going to work for either of us. So we'll build our house, and that's where we're going to raise our children."

Our. She decided it was the most exciting word in the English language. She was going to use it a dozen times every day for the rest of her life. "Where?"

He glanced over her head, skimming the pool, the solitude. "Right on the damn boundary line."

With a laugh, Jillian circled his neck. "What boundary line?"

Untamed

CHAPTER 1

At the crack of the whip, twelve lions stood on their haunches and pawed the air. On command, they began to leap from pedestal to pedestal in a quick, close-formation, figure eight pattern. This required split-second timing. With voice and hand commands the trainer kept the tawny, springing bodies moving.

"Well done, Pandora."

At her name and the signal, the muscular lioness leaped to the ground and lay down on her side. One by one the others followed suit, until, snarling and baring their teeth, they stretched across the tanbark. A male was positioned beside each female; at a sharp reproof from the trainer, Merlin ceased nibbling on Ophelia's ear.

"Heads up!" They obeyed as the trainer walked briskly in front of them. The whip was tossed aside with a flourish, then, with apparent nonchalance, the trainer reclined lengthwise across the warm bodies. The center cat, a full-maned African, let out a great, echoing bellow. As a reward for his response to the cue, his ear was given a good scratching. The trainer rose from the feline couch, clapped hands and brought the lions to their feet. Then, with a hand signal, each was called by name and sent through the chute and into their cages. One stayed behind, a huge, black-maned cat who, like an ordinary tabby, circled and rubbed up against his trainer's legs.

Deftly, a rope was attached to a chain that was hidden under his mane. Then, with swift agility, the trainer mounted the lion's back. As the door of the big cage opened, lion and rider passed through for a tour of the practice ring. When they reached the back door of the ring barn, Merlin, the obliging lion, was transferred to a wheel cage.

"Well, Duffy." Jo turned after the cage was secured. "Are we ready for the road?"

Duffy was a small, round man with a monk's fringe of chestnut hair and a face that exploded with ginger freckles. His open smile and Irish blue eyes gave him the look of an aging choirboy. His mind was sharp, shrewd and scrappy. He was the best manager Prescott's Circus Colossus could have had.

"Since we open in Ocala tomorrow," he replied in a raspy voice, "you'd better be ready." He shifted his fat cigar stump from the right side of his mouth to the left.

Jo merely smiled, then stretched to loosen muscles grown taut during the thirty minutes in the cage. "My cats are ready, Duffy. It's been a long winter. They need to get back on the road as much as the rest of us."

Duffy frowned. As circumstances had it, he stood only inches higher than his animal trainer. Widely spaced, almond-shaped eyes stared back at him. They were as sharp and green as emeralds, surrounded by thick, inky lashes. At the moment they were fearless and amused, but Duffy had seen them frightened, vulnerable and lost. He shifted his cigar again and took two quick puffs as Jo gave a cage hand instructions.

He remembered Steve Wilder, Jo's father. He had been one of the best cat men in the business. Jo was as good with the cats as Wilder had been. In some ways, Duffy acknowledged, even better. But she had the traits of her mother: deli-

cate build; dark, passionate looks. Jolivette Wilder was as
slender as her aerialist mother had been, with bold green
eyes and straight, raven black hair that fell to just below her
waist. Her brows were delicately arched, her nose small and
straight, her cheekbones high and elegant, while her mouth
was full and soft. Her skin was tawny from the Florida sun;
it added to her bohemian-like appearance. Confidence added
spark to the beauty.

Finishing her instructions, Jo tucked her arm through
Duffy's. She had seen that frown before. "Somebody quit?"
she asked as they began to walk toward Duffy's office.

"Nope."

His monosyllabic reply caused Jo to lift a brow. It was not
often Duffy answered any question briefly. Years of experience told her to hold her tongue as they moved across the
compound.

Rehearsals were going on everywhere. Vito the wire
walker informally sharpened his act on a cable stretched between two trees. The Mendalsons called out to each other
as they tossed their juggling pins high in the air, while the
equestrian act led their horses into the ring barn. She saw one
of the Stevenson girls walking on stilts. She'd be six now,
Jo mused, tossing the hair from her eyes as she watched the
young girl's wavering progress. Jo remembered the year she
had been born. It had been that same year that she had been
allowed to work the big cage alone. She had been sixteen, and
it had been another full year before she had been permitted
to work an audience.

For Jo, there had never been any home but the circus. She
had been born during the winter break, had been tucked into
her parents' trailer the following spring to spend her first year
and each subsequent one of her life thereafter on the road. She
had inherited both her fascination and her flair with animals
from her father, her style and grace of movement from her
mother. Though she had lost both parents fifteen years

before, they continued to influence her. Their legacy to her had been a world of restlessness, a world of fantasies. She had grown up playing with lion cubs, riding elephants, wearing spangles and traveling like a nomad.

Jo glanced down at a cluster of daffodils growing by the side of Prescott's winter office and smiled. She remembered planting them when she had been thirteen and in love with a tumbler. She remembered, too, the man who had stooped beside her, offering advice on bulb planting and broken hearts. As Jo thought of Frank Prescott, her smile grew sad.

"I still can't believe he's gone," she murmured as she and Duffy moved inside.

Duffy's office was sparsely furnished with a wooden desk, metal filing cabinets and two spindly chairs. A collage of posters adorned the walls. They promised the amazing, the astounding, the incredible: elephants that danced, men who flew through the air, beautiful girls who spun by their teeth, raging tigers that rode horseback. Tumblers, clowns, lions, strong men, fat ladies, boys who could balance on their forefingers; they brought the magic of the circus into the drab little room.

As Jo glanced over at a narrow pine door, Duffy followed her gaze. "I keep expecting him to come busting through there with some crazy new idea," he mumbled as he began to fiddle with his prize possession, an automatic coffeemaker.

"Do you?" With a sigh Jo straddled a chair, then rested her chin on its back. "We all miss him. It's not going to seem the same without him this year." She looked up suddenly, and her eyes were angry. "He wasn't an old man, Duffy. Heart attacks should be for old men." She brooded into space, touched again with the injustice of Frank Prescott's death.

He had been barely into his fifties and full of laughter and simple kindness. Jo had loved him and trusted him without reservation. At his death she had grieved for him more acutely than she had for her own parents. In her longest memory he had been the core of her life.

"It's been nearly six months," Duffy said gruffly as he studied her face. When Jo glanced up, he stuck out a mug of coffee.

"I know." She took the mug, letting it warm her hands in the chilly March morning. Resolutely, she shook off the mood. Frank would not have wanted to leave sadness behind. Jo studied the coffee, then sipped. It was predictably dreadful. "Rumor has it we're following last year's route to the letter. Thirteen states." Jo smiled, watching Duffy wince over his coffee before he downed it. "Not superstitious, are you?" She grinned, knowing he kept a four-leaf clover in his billfold.

"Pah!" he said indignantly, coloring under his freckles. He set down his empty cup, then moved around his desk and sat behind it. When he folded his hands on the yellow blotter, Jo knew he was getting down to business. Through the open window she could hear the band rehearsing. "We should be in Ocala by six tomorrow," he began. Dutifully, Jo nodded. "Should have the tents up before nine."

"The parade should be over by ten, and the matinee will start at two," Jo finished with a smile. "Duffy, you're not going to ask me to work the menagerie in the sideshow again, are you?"

"Should be a good crowd," he replied, adroitly skirting her question. "Bonzo predicts clear skies."

"Bonzo should stick with pratfalls and unicycles." She watched as Duffy chewed on the stub of a now dead cigar. "Okay," she said firmly, "let's have it."

"Someone's going to be joining us in Ocala, at least temporarily." He pursed his lips as his eyes met Jo's. His were blue, faded with age. "I don't know if he'll finish out the season with us."

"Oh, Duffy, not some first of mayer we have to break in this late?" Jo demanded, using the circus term for novice. "What is he, some energetic writer who wants an epic on the vanishing tent circus? He'll spend a few weeks as a roust-about and swear he knows all there is to know about it."

"I don't think he'll be working as a roustabout," Duffy muttered. Striking a match, he coaxed the cigar back to life. Jo frowned, watching the smoke struggle toward the ceiling.

"It's a bit late to work in a new act now, isn't it?"

"He's not a performer." Duffy swore lightly under his breath, then met Jo's eyes again. "He owns us."

For a moment Jo said nothing. She sat unmoving, as Duffy had seen her from time to time when she trained a young cat. "No!" She rose suddenly, shaking her head. "Not him. Not now. Why does he have to come? What does he want here?"

"It's his circus," Duffy reminded her. His voice was both rough and sympathetic.

"It'll never be his circus," Jo retorted passionately. Her eyes lit and glowed with a temper she rarely let have sway. "It's Frank's circus."

"Frank's dead," Duffy stated in a quiet, final tone. "Now the circus belongs to his son."

"Son?" Jo countered. She lifted her fingers to press them against her temple. Slowly, she moved to the window. Outside, the sun was pouring over the heads of troupers. She watched the members of the trapeze act, in thick robes worn over their tights, head toward the ring barn. The chatter of mixed languages was so familiar she failed to notice it. She placed her palms on the windowsill and with a little sigh, steadied her temper. "What sort of son is it who never both-ers to visit his father? In thirty years he never came to see Frank. He never wrote. He didn't even come to the funeral." Jo swallowed the tears of anger that rose to her throat and thickened her voice. "Why should he come now?"

"You've got to learn that life's a two-sided coin, kiddo," Duffy said briskly. "You weren't even alive thirty years ago. You don't know why Frank's wife up and left him or why the boy never visited."

"He's not a boy, Duffy, he's a man." Jo turned back, and he saw that she again had herself under control. "He's thirty-one, thirty-two years old now, a very successful attorney with a fancy Chicago office. He's very wealthy, did you know?" A small smile played on her lips but failed to reach her eyes. "And not just from court cases and legal fees. There's quite a lot of money on his mother's side. Nice, quiet, old money. I can't understand what a rich city lawyer would want with a tent circus."

Duffy shrugged his broad, round shoulders. "Could be he wants a tax shelter. Could be he wants to ride an elephant. Could be anything. He might want to take inventory and sell us off, piece by piece."

"Oh, Duffy, no!" Emotion flew back into Jo's face. "He couldn't do that."

"The heck he couldn't," Duffy muttered as he stubbed out his cigar. "He can do as he pleases. If he wants to liquidate, he liquidates."

"But we have contracts through October . . ."

"You're too smart for that, Jo." Duffy frowned, scratching his rim of hair. "He can buy them off or let them play through. He's a lawyer. He can figure the way out of a contract if he wants to. He can wait till August when we start to negotiate again and let them all lapse." Seeing Jo's distress, he backpedaled. "Listen, kiddo, I didn't say he was going to sell, I said he *could*."

Jo ran a hand through her hair. "There must be something we can do."

"We can show a profit by the end of the season," Duffy said wryly. "We can show the new owner what we have to offer. I think it's important that he sees we're not just a mud show but a profitable three-ring circus with class acts. He should see what Frank built, how he lived, what he wanted to do. I think," Duffy added, watching Jo's face, "that you should be in charge of his education."

"Me?" Jo was too incredulous to be angry. "Why? You're better qualified in the public relations department than I am. I train lions, not lawyers." She could not keep the hint of scorn from her voice.

"You were closer to Frank than anyone. And there isn't anyone here who knows this circus better than you." Again he frowned. "And you've got brains. Never thought much use would come of all those fancy books you read, but maybe I was wrong."

"Duffy." Her lips curved into a smile. "Just because I like to read Shakespeare doesn't mean I can deal with Keane Prescott. Even thinking about him makes me furious. How will I act when I meet him face to face?"

"Well." Duffy shrugged before he pursed his lips. "If you don't think you can handle it . . ."

"I didn't say I *couldn't* handle it," Jo muttered.

"Of course, if you're afraid . . ."

"I'm not afraid of anything, and I'm certainly not afraid of some Chicago lawyer who doesn't know sawdust from tanbark." Sticking her hands in her pockets, she paced the length of the small room. "If Keane Prescott, attorney-at-law, wants to spend his summer with the circus, I'll do my best to make it a memorable one."

"Nicely," Duffy cautioned as Jo moved to the door.

"Duffy—" She paused and gave him an innocent smile. "You know what a gentle touch I have." To prove it, Jo slammed the door behind her.

*   *   *

Dawn was hovering over the horizon as the circus caravan drew up in a large grassy field. Colors were just a promise in a pale gray sky. In the distance was grove upon grove of orange trees. As Jo stepped from the cab of her truck, the fragrance met her. It's a perfect day, she decided, then took a long, greedy breath. To her, there was no more beautiful sight than dawn struggling to life.

The air was vaguely chilly. She zipped up her gray sweat jacket as she watched the rest of the circus troupe pouring out of their trucks and cars and trailers. The morning quiet was soon shattered by voices. Work began immediately. As the Big Top canvas was being unrolled out of the spool truck, Jo went to see how her lions had fared the fifty-mile journey.

Three handlers unloaded the traveling cages. Buck had been with Jo the longest. He had worked for her father, and during the interim between his death and Jo's professional debut, he had worked up a small act with four male lions. His shyness had made his retirement from performing a relief. To Buck, two people were a crowd. He stood six foot four, and his build was powerful enough for him to pad the sideshow from time to time as Hercules the Strong Man. He had an impressive head of wild blond hair and a full, curling beard. His hands were wide, with thick, strong fingers, but Jo remembered their gentleness when the two of them had delivered a lioness of a pair of cubs.

Pete's small frame seemed puny beside Buck's. He was of indeterminable age. Jo guessed between forty and fifty, but she was never certain. He was a quiet man with skin like polished mahogany and a rich, low-pitched voice. He had come to Jo five years before, asking for a job. She had never asked where he had come from, and he had never told her. He wore a fielder's cap and was never seen without a wad of gum moving gently in his teeth. He read Jo's books and was the undisputed king of the poker table.

Gerry was nineteen and eager. He was nearly six feet and still carried the lankiness of his youth. His mother sewed, and his father was a souvenir salesman, or a candy butcher, as circus jargon had it. Working the big cage was Gerry's dream, and because it had been hers, Jo had finally agreed to tutor him.

"How are my babies?" she demanded as she approached. At each cage she paused and soothed a nervous cat, calling each by name until they had settled. "They've traveled well. Hamlet's still edgy, but it's his first year on the road."

"He's a mean one," Buck muttered, watching Jo move from cage to cage.

"Yes, I know," she replied absently. "He's smart, too." She had twisted her hair into one thick braid and now tossed it to her back. "Look, here come some towners." A few cars and a smattering of bikes drew into the field.

These were the people from the outlying towns who wanted to see a Big Top raised, who wanted to see the circus, if only for a moment, from the other side. Some would watch while others would lend a hand with tent poles, stretching canvas and rigging. They would earn a show pass and an unforgettable experience.

"Keep them clear of the cages," Jo ordered, nodding to Pete before she moved toward the still-flaccid canvas. Buck lumbered beside her.

The field was alive with ropes and wire and people. Six elephants were harnessed but idle, with their handlers standing by the stake line. As workers pulled on guy ropes, the dusky brown canvas billowed up like a giant mushroom.

The poles were positioned—side, quarter, center—while the canvas muffled the sounds of scrambling workers. In the east the sun was rising fast, streaking the sky with pink. There were shouted instructions from the head canvas man, laughter from adventuresome boys and an occasional oath. As the quarter poles were driven into the sag of canvas, Jo signaled Maggie, the large African elephant. Obligingly, Maggie lowered her trunk. Jo stepped nimbly into the U, then scrambled onto the wide, gray back.

The sun grew higher by the second, shooting the first

streams of light onto the field. The scent of orange blossoms mingled with the odor of leather harnesses. Jo had watched the canvas rise under a lightening sky countless times. Each time it was special, and the first raising each season was the most special of all. Maggie lifted her head and trumpeted as if pleased to be around for another season. With a laugh Jo reached back and swatted her rough, wrinkled rump. She felt free and fresh and incredibly alive. *If there were a moment,* she thought suddenly, *that I could capture and bottle, it would be this one. Then, when I'm very old, I could take it out and feel young again.* Smiling, she glanced down at the people swarming below her.

Her attention was caught by a man who stood by a coil of cable. Typically, she noted his build first. A well-proportioned body was essential to a performer. He was lean and stood straight. She noted he had good shoulders but doubted if there was much muscle in his arms. Though he was dressed casually in jeans, *city* stood out all over him. His hair was a dark, rich blond, and the early breeze had disturbed it so that it teased his forehead. He was clean-shaven, with a narrow, firm-jawed face. It was an attractive face. It was not, Jo mused, smoothly handsome like Vito the wire walker's but more aware, more demanding. Jo liked the face, liked the shape of the long, unsmiling mouth, liked the hint of bone beneath his tawny skin. Most of all she liked the directness of the amber eyes that stared back at her. They're like Ari's, she observed, thinking of her favorite lion. She was certain that he had been watching her long before she had looked down. Knowing this, Jo was impressed with his unselfconsciousness. He continued to stare, making no effort to camouflage his interest. She laughed, unperturbed, and tossed her braid from her shoulder.

"Want a ride?" she called out. Too many strangers had walked in and out of her world for her to be aloof. She watched his brow lift in acknowledgment of her offer. She would see if it was only his eyes that were like Ari's. "Maggie won't hurt you. She's gentle as a lamb, just bigger." Instantly, she saw he had understood the challenge. He walked across the grass until he stood beside her. He moved well, she noted. Jo tapped Maggie's side with the bull hook she carried. Wearily, the elephant knelt down on her trunklike front legs. Jo held out her hand. With an agility that surprised her, the man mounted the elephant and slid into place behind her.

For a moment she said nothing, a bit stunned by the trembling that had coursed up her arm as her palm had met his. The contact had been brief. Jo decided she had imagined it. "Up, Maggie," she said, giving her mount another tap. With an elephantine sigh, Maggie obeyed, rocking her passengers gently from side to side.

"Do you always pick up strange men?" the voice behind her inquired. It was a smooth, well-keyed voice, a good pitchman's voice.

Jo grinned over her shoulder. "Maggie's doing the picking up."

"So she is. Are you aware that she's remarkably uncomfortable?"

Jo laughed with genuine enjoyment. "You should try riding her a few miles in a street parade while keeping a smile on your face."

"I'll pass. Are you in charge of her?"

"Maggie? No, but I know how to handle her. You have eyes like one of my cats," she told him. "I like them. And since you seemed to be interested in Maggie and me, I asked you up."

This time it was he who laughed. Jo twisted her head, wanting to see his face. There was humor in his eyes now, and his teeth were white and straight. Liking his smile, she answered with one of her own. "Fascinating. You asked me to take a ride on an elephant because I have eyes like your cat's. And no offense to the lady beneath me, but I was looking at you."

"Oh?" Jo pursed her lips in thought. "Why?"

For several seconds he studied her in silence. "Strange, I believe you really don't know."

"I wouldn't ask if I did," she returned, shifting her weight slightly. "It would be a waste of time to ask a question if I knew the answer." She shifted again and turned away from him. "Hold on now. Maggie's got to earn her bale of hay."

The poles hung between the canvas and the ground at forty-five-degree angles. Quickly the elephant's chains were hooked to the metal rings at the base of the quarter poles. Jo urged Maggie forward in unison with her coworkers. Poles skidded along the ground, then up into place, pushing the canvas with it. The Big Top billowed to life under the early-morning sky.

Her job done, Maggie moved through the flaps and into the light. "Beautiful, isn't it?" Jo murmured. "It's born fresh every day."

Vito walked by, calling out to Jo in Italian. Sending him a wave, she called back in his own language, then signaled to Maggie to kneel again. Jo waited until her passenger had dismounted before she slid off. It surprised her, when they stood face to face, that he was so tall. Tilting back her head, she judged him to be only two inches shy of Buck.

"You looked shorter when I was up on Maggie," she told him with her usual candor.

"You looked taller."

Jo chuckled, patting Maggie behind the ear. "Will you see the show?" She knew that she wanted him to, knew as well that she wanted to see him again. She found this both strange and intriguing. Men had always taken a second place to her cats, and towners had never interested her.

"Yes, I'm going to see the show." There was a slight smile

on his face, but he was studying her thoughtfully. "Do you perform?"

"I have an act with my cats."

"I see. Somehow I pictured you in an aerial act, flying from the trapeze."

She sent him an easy smile. "My mother was an aerialist." Someone called her name, and looking, Jo saw Maggie was needed for raising the sideshow tent. "I have to go. I hope you like the show."

He took her hand before she could lead Maggie away. Jo stood still, again surprised by a trembling up her arm. "I'd like to see you tonight."

Glancing up, she met his eyes. They were direct and unselfconscious. "Why?" The question was sincere. Jo knew she wanted to see him as well but was unsure why.

This time he did not laugh. Gently, he ran a finger down the length of her braid. "Because you're beautiful, and you intrigue me."

"Oh." Jo considered. She had never thought of herself as beautiful. Striking, perhaps, in her costume, surrounded by her cats, but in jeans, without makeup, she doubted it. Still, it was an interesting thought. "All right, if there's no trouble with the cats. Ari hasn't been well."

A smile played at the corners of his mouth. "I'm sorry to hear that."

There was another loud summons for Jo, and both looked toward it. "I see you're needed," he said with a nod. "Perhaps you could point out Bill Duffy for me before you go."

"Duffy?" Jo repeated, surprised. "You can't be looking for a job?" There was incredulity in her voice, and he grinned.

"Why can't I?"

"Because you don't fit any of the types."

"Are there types?" he asked, both interested and amused. Jo shook her head in annoyance.

"Yes, of course, and you don't fit into any of them."

"Actually, I'm not looking for a job, so to speak," he told her, still smiling. "But I am looking for Bill Duffy."

It was against Jo's nature to probe. Privacy was both guarded and respected in the circus. Shielding her eyes with her hand, Jo looked around until she spotted Duffy supervising the raising of the cookhouse tent. "There," she said, pointing. "Duffy's the one with the red checked jacket. He still dresses like an outside talker."

"A what?"

"You'd call it a barker, I imagine." With easy grace she mounted the patient Maggie. "That's a towner's term, not a circus one." She smiled at him, then urged Maggie into a walk. "Tell Duffy Jo said to give you a pass," she called over her shoulder, then waved and turned away.

Dawn was over, and it was morning.

CHAPTER 2

Jo stood at the back door of the Big Top waiting for her cue. Beside her was Jamie Carter, alias Topo. He was a third generation clown and wore his bright face and orange wig naturally. He was young and limber and used these traits as well as his makeup to bring enthusiasm to his craft. To Jo, Jamie was more brother than friend. He was tall and thin, and under his greasepaint his face was mobile and pleasant. He and Jo had grown up together.

"Did she say anything?" Jamie demanded for the third time. With a sigh, Jo tossed closed the flap of the tent. Inside, clowns were performing around the hippodrome track while hands set up the big cage.

"Carmen said nothing. I don't know why you waste your time." Her voice was sharp, and Jamie bristled.

"I don't expect you to understand," he said with great dignity. His thin shoulders drew straight under his red-polka-dot shirt. "After all, Ari's the closest you've come to being involved with the opposite sex."

"That's very cute," Jo replied, unoffended by the jibe. Her annoyance stemmed from seeing Jamie make a fool of himself over Carmen Gribalti, the middle sister of the flying Gribaltis. She was darkly beautiful, graceful, talented, selfish and sublimely indifferent to Jamie. Looking into his happy, painted face and moody eyes, Jo's irritation dissipated. "She probably hasn't had a chance to answer the note you sent her," she soothed. "The first day of a new season's always wild."

"I suppose," Jamie muttered with a grudging shrug. "I don't know what she sees in Vito."

Jo thought of the wire walker's dark, cocky looks and rippling muscles. Wisely, she refrained from mentioning them. "Who can account for taste?" She gave him a smacking kiss on his round, red nose. "Personally, I get all wobbly when I see a man with thick, orange hair."

Jamie grinned. "Proves you know what to look for in a man."

Turning, Jo lifted the flap again, noting Jamie's cue was nearly upon them. "Did you happen to notice a towner hanging around today?"

"Only a couple dozen of them," Jamie answered drily as he lifted the pail of confetti he used to finish the gag now being performed inside.

Jo shot him a half-hearted glare. "Not the usual type. About thirty, I think," she continued. "Wearing jeans and a T-shirt. He was tall, six-one, six-two," she went on as laughter poured out of the open flap to drown out her words. "He had dark blond straight hair."

"Yeah, I saw him." Jamie nudged her out of his way and prepared to make his entrance. "He was going into the red wagon with Duffy." With a wild, high-pitched scream, Topo the clown bounded into the Big Top in size fifteen tennis shoes, brandishing his bucket of confetti.

Thoughtfully, Jo watched Jamie chase three other clowns around the track. It was odd, she thought, for Duffy to take a towner into the administration trailer. He had said he wasn't looking for a job. He wasn't a drifter; there was an unmistakable air of stability about him. He wasn't a circus hand from another show, either. His palm had been too smooth. And,

her mind added as she vaulted onto Babette, a pure white
mare, there had been an undeniable aura of urbanity about
him. Success, as well, she thought. And authority. No, he
had not been looking for a job.

Jo shrugged, annoyed that a stranger was crowding into
her thoughts. It irritated her further that she had scanned the
crowds for him during the parade and that even now she wondered if he sat somewhere in the circular arena. He hadn't
been at the matinee. Jo patted the mare's neck absently, then
straightened as she heard the ringmaster's whistle.

"Ladies and gentlemen," he called in deep, musical tones.
"Presenting the most spectacular exhibition of animal sub-
jugation under the Big Top. Jovilette, Queen of the Jungle
Cats!"

Jo nudged Babette with her heels and raced into the arena.
The applause rose to meet her as the audience appreciated
the dashing figure she cut. Swathed in a black cape, raven
hair flying free under a glittering tiara, she galloped bareback
on the snow-white mare. In each hand she held a long, thin
whip, which she cracked alternately overhead. At the entrance
to the big cage she leaped from the still-racing horse. While
Babette galloped out of the back door and into the care of a
handler, Jo shifted both whips into one hand, then removed
the cape with a flourish. Her costume was a close-fitting, one-
piece jumpsuit, dazzling in white and spangled with gold
sequins. In dramatic contrast, her hair hung straight and se-
vere down her back.

Make an entrance, Frank had always said. And Jovilette
made an entrance.

The twelve cats were already in the cage, banding its inside edge as they perched on blue and white pedestals. Entering the main cage appeared routine to the audience, but
Jo knew it was one of the most dangerous moments of the
act. To enter, she had to pass directly between two cats as
she moved from the safety cage to the main arena. She

always stationed her best behaved cats there, but if one was irritated, or even playful, he could easily strike out with a powerful paw. Even with sharp claws retracted, the damage could be deadly.

She entered swiftly and was surrounded by cats on all sides. Her spangles and tiara caught the lights and played with them as she began to move around the cage, cracking the whip for showmanship while using her voice to command the cats to rise on their haunches. She moved them through their routine, adjusting the timing to compensate for any feline reluctance, letting one trick begin where the last ended.

Jo disliked overdone propping, preferring action and movement. The contrast of the big, tawny cats and the small white and gold woman were the best props available to her. She used them well. Hers was a *picture act,* relying on style and flash, rather than a *fighting act,* which emphasized the ferocity of the big cats by employing blank-bulleted guns and rehearsed charges, or *bounces.* Her confidence transmitted itself to the audience, making her handling of the cats appear effortless. In truth, her body was coiled for any danger, and her mind was focused so intently on her cats, there might have been no audience at all.

She stood between two high pedestals as the cats leaped over her head from both directions. They set up a light breeze, which stirred her hair. They roared when she cued them, setting up an echoing din. Now and then one reached out to paw at the stock of her whip, and she stopped him with a quick command. She sent her best leaper through a hoop of flame and coaxed her best balancer to walk on a glistening silver ball. She ended to waves of applause by trotting Merlin around the hippodrome track.

At the back door Merlin jumped into a wheel cage and was turned over to Pete. "Nice show," he said as he handed her a long chenille robe. "Smooth as silk."

"Thanks." Cold, she bundled into the robe. The spring night was frigid in contrast to the hot lights and heat in the big cage. "Listen, Pete, tell Gerry he can feed the cats tonight. They're behaving themselves."

Pete snapped his gum and chuckled. "Won't he be riding high tonight." As he moved to the truck that would pull the cage to the cat area, Jo called after him.

"Pete." She bit her lip, then shrugged when he twisted his head. "You'll keep an eye on him, won't you?"

Pete grinned and climbed into the cab of the truck. "Who you worried about, Jo? Those big cats or that skinny boy?"

"Both," she answered. The rhinestones in her tiara sparkled as she tossed her head and laughed. Knowing she had nearly an hour before the finale parade, Jo walked away from the Big Top. She thought of wandering to the cookhouse for some coffee. Mentally, she began replaying every segment of her act. It had gone well, she thought, pleased with the timing and the flow. If Pete had said it had been smooth, Jo knew it had. She had heard his criticisms more than once over the past five years. True, Hamlet had tested her once or twice, but no one knew that but Jo and the cat. She doubted if anyone but Buck would have seen that he had given her trouble. Closing her eyes a moment, Jo rolled her shoulders, loosening tight, tensed muscles.

"That's quite an act you have."

Jo whirled around at the sound of the voice. She could feel her heart rate accelerate. Though she wondered at her interest in a man she barely knew, Jo was aware that she had been waiting for him. There was a quick surge of pleasure as she watched him approach, and she allowed it to show on her face.

"Hello." She saw that he smoked a cigar, but unlike Duffy's, his was long and slim. Again she admired the elegance of his hands. "Did you like the show?"

He stopped in front of her, then studied her face with

a thoroughness that made her wonder if her makeup had smeared. Then he gave a small, surprised laugh and shook his head. "Do you know," he began, "when you told me this morning that you did an act with cats, I had Siamese in mind rather than African."

"Siamese?" Jo repeated blankly, then laughed. "House cats?" He brushed her hair behind her back while Jo giggled at the thought of coaxing a Siamese to jump through a flaming hoop.

"From my point of view," he told her as he let a strand of her hair linger between his fingers, "it made more sense than a little thing like you walking into a cage with a dozen lions."

"I'm not little," Jo corrected good-naturedly. "Besides, size hardly matters to twelve lions."

"No, I suppose it doesn't." He lifted his eyes from her hair and met hers. Jo continued to smile, enjoying looking at him. "Why do you do it?" he asked suddenly.

Jo gave him a curious look. "Why? Because it's my job."

By the way he studied her, Jo could see that he was not satisfied with the simplicity of her answer. "Perhaps I should ask *how* you became a lion tamer."

"Trainer," Jo corrected automatically. To her left, she could hear the audience's muffled applause. "The Beirots are starting," she said with a glance toward the sound. "You shouldn't miss their act. They're first-rate acrobats."

"Don't you want to tell me?" His voice was soft.

She lifted a brow, seeing that he truly wanted to know. "Why, it's not a secret. My father was a trainer, and I have a knack for working with cats. It just followed." Jo had never thought about her career past this point, and she shrugged it aside. "You shouldn't waste your ticket standing out here. You can stand by the back door and watch the rest of the act." Jo turned to lead the way to the performers' entrance but stopped when his hand took hers.

He stepped forward until their bodies were nearly touching. Jo could feel the heat from his as she watched his face. Her heart was thudding in a quick, steady rhythm. She could hear it vibrate through her the same way it did when she approached a new cat for the first time. Here was something new, something untested. She tingled with the excitement of the unknown when he lifted his hand to touch her cheek. She did not move but let the warmth spread while she watched him carefully, gauging him. Her eyes were wide, curious and unafraid.

"Are you going to kiss me?" she asked in a tone that expressed more interest than desire.

His eyes lit with humor and glittered in the dim light. "I had given it some thought," he answered. "Do you have any objections?"

Jo considered a moment, dropping her eyes to his mouth. She liked its shape and wondered how it would feel against hers. He brought her no closer. One hand still held hers while the other slid around to cradle her neck. Jo shifted her gaze until their eyes met again. "No," she decided. "I haven't any objections."

The corners of his mouth twitched as he tightened his hold slightly on the base of her neck. Slowly, he lowered his head toward hers. Curious and a bit wary, Jo kept her eyes open, watching his. She knew from experience that you could tell more about people and about cats from the eyes. To her surprise, his remained open as well, even as their lips met.

It was a gentle kiss, without pressure, only a whisper of a touch. Amazed, Jo thought she felt the ground tremble under her feet. Dimly, she wondered if the elephants were being led by. But it can't be time, she thought in confusion. His lips moved lightly over hers, and his eyes remained steady. Jo's pulse drummed under her skin. They stood, barely touching, as the Big Top throbbed with noise behind them. Lazily, he traced her lips with the tip of his tongue, teasing them open.

Still there was no demand in the kiss, only testing. Unhurried, confident, he explored her mouth while Jo felt her breath accelerating. A soft moan escaped her as her lids fluttered down.

For an instant she surrendered utterly to him, to the new sensations swimming through her. She leaned against him, straining toward pleasure, sighing with it as the kiss lingered.

He drew her away, but their faces remained close. Dizzily, Jo realized that she had risen to her toes to compensate for their difference in height. His hand was still light on the back of her neck. His eyes were gold in the darkening night.

"What an incredible female you are, Jovilette," he murmured. "One surprise after another."

Jo felt stunningly alive. Her skin seemed to tingle with new feelings. She smiled. "I don't know your name."

He laughed, releasing her neck to take her other hand in his. Before he could speak, Duffy called out from the direction of the Big Top. Jo turned to watch as he moved toward them in his quick, rolling walk.

"Well, well, well," he said in his jolly, rough voice. "I didn't know you two had met. Has Jo been showing you around already?" Reaching them, he squeezed Jo's shoulder. "Knew I could count on you, kiddo." Jo glanced at him in puzzlement, but he continued before she could form a question. "Yes, sir, this little girl puts on quite a show, doesn't she? Always a grabber. And she knows this circus like the back of her hand. Born and raised to it," he continued. Jo relaxed. She recognized that Duffy was into one of his spiels, and there was no stopping him. "Yessiree, any questions you got, you just ask our Jo, and she'll tell you. 'Course, I'm always at your disposal, too. Anything I can tell you about the books or accounts or contracts and the like, you just let me know." Duffy puffed twice on his cigar as Jo felt her first hint of unease.

Why was Duffy rambling about books and contracts? Jo

glanced at the man who still held her hands in his. He was watching Duffy with an easy, amused smile.

"Are you a bookkeeper?" Jo asked, perplexed. Duffy laughed and patted her head.

"You know Mr. Prescott's a lawyer, Jo. Don't miss your cue." He gave them both a friendly nod and toddled off.

Jo had stiffened almost imperceptibly at Duffy's offhand information, but Keane had felt it. His brows lowered as he studied her. "Now you know my name."

"Yes." All warmth fled from Jo. Her voice was as cool as her blood. "Would you let go of my hands, Mr. Prescott?"

After a brief hesitation Keane inclined his head and obliged. Jo stuffed her hands quickly into the pockets of her robe. "Don't you think we've progressed to the first name stage of our relationship, Jo?"

"I assure you, Mr. Prescott, if I had known who you were, we wouldn't have progressed at all." Jo's words were stiff with dignity. Inside, though she tried to ignore it, she felt betrayal, anger, humiliation. All pleasure had died from the evening. Now the kiss that had left her feeling clean and alive seemed cheap and shabby. No, she would not use his first name, she vowed. She would never use it. "If you'll excuse me, I have some things to do before my cue."

"Why the turnaround?" he asked, halting her with a hand on her arm. "Don't you like lawyers?"

Coldly, Jo studied him. She wondered how it was possible that she had completely misjudged the man she had met that morning. "I don't categorize people, Mr. Prescott."

"I see." Keane's tone became detached, his eyes assessing. "Then it would appear that you have an aversion to my name. Should I assume you hold a grudge against my father?"

Jo's eyes glittered with quick fury. She jerked her arm from his hold. "Frank Prescott was the most generous, the kindest, most unselfish man I've ever known. I don't even associate you with Frank, Mr. Prescott. You have no right to him."

Though it was nearly impossible, Jo forced herself to speak in a normal tone of voice. She would not shout and draw anyone's attention. This would be kept strictly between Keane Prescott and herself. "It would have been much better if you had told me who you were right away, then there would have been no mix-up."

"Is that what we've had?" he countered mildly. "A mix-up?"

His cool tone was nearly Jo's undoing. He watched her with a dispassionate curiosity that tempted her to slap him. She fought to keep her fury from spilling over into her voice. "You have no right to Frank's circus, Mr. Prescott," she managed quietly. "Leaving it to you is the only thing I've ever faulted him for." Knowing her control was slipping, Jo whirled, running across the grass until she merged with the darkness.

CHAPTER 3

The morning was surprisingly warm. There were no trees to block the sun, and the smell of the earth was strong. The circus had moved north in the early hours. All the usual scents merged into the aroma of circus: canvas, leather, sweating horses, greasepaint and powder, coffee and oilcloth. The trailers and trucks sat in the accustomed spots, forming the "backyard" that would always take the same formation each time the circus made a stop along the thousands of miles it traveled. The flag over the cookhouse tent signaled that lunch was being served. The Big Top stood waiting for the matinee.

Rose hurried along the midway toward the animal cages. Her dark hair was pinned neatly in a bun at the back of her neck. Her big brown eyes darted about searchingly, while her mouth sat softly in a pout. She was wrapped in a terry cloth robe and wore tennis shoes over her tights. When she saw Jo standing in front of Ari's cage, she waved and broke into a half run. Watching her, Jo shifted her attention from Ari. Rose was always a diversion, and Jo felt in need of one.

"Jo!" She waved again as if Jo had not seen her the first time, then came to a breathless halt. "Jo, I only have a few minutes. Hello, Ari," she added out of politeness. "I was looking for Jamie."

"Yes, I gathered." Jo smiled, knowing Rose had set her heart on capturing Topo's alter ego. And if he had any sense, she thought, he'd let himself be caught instead of pining over Carmen. Silly, she decided, dismissing all affairs of the heart. Lions were easier to understand. "I haven't seen him all morning, Rose. Maybe he's rehearsing."

"Drooling over Carmen, more likely," Rose muttered, sending a sulky glare in the direction of the Gribalti trailer. "He makes a fool of himself."

"That's what he's paid for," Jo reminded her, but Rose did not respond to the humor. Jo sighed. She had a true affection for Rose. She was bright and fun and without pretentions. "Rose," she said, keeping her voice both light and kind. "Don't give up on him. He's a little slow, you know," she explained. "He's just a bit dazzled by Carmen right now. It'll pass."

"I don't know why I bother," she grumbled, but Jo saw the dark mood was already passing. Rose was a creature of quick passions that flared and soon died. "He's not so very handsome, you know."

"No," Jo agreed. "But he has a cute nose."

"Lucky for him I like red," Rose returned and grinned. "Ah, now we're speaking of handsome," she murmured as her eyes drifted from Jo. "Who is this?"

At the question, Jo glanced over her shoulder. The humor fled from her eyes. "That's the owner," she said colorlessly.

"Keane Prescott? No one told me he was so handsome. Or so tall," she added, admiring him openly as he crossed the backyard. Jo noted that Rose always became more outgoing around men. "Such shoulders. Lucky for Jamie I'm a one-man woman."

"Lucky for you your mama can't hear you," Jo muttered, earning an elbow in the ribs.

"But he comes here, *amiga,* and he looks at you. La, la, my papa would have Jamie to the altar pronto if he looked at me that way."

"You're an idiot," Jo snapped, annoyed.

"Ah, Jo," Rose said with mock despair. "I am a romantic."

Jo was helpless against the smile that tugged at her lips. Her eyes were laughing when she glanced up and met Keane's. Hastily, she struggled to dampen their brilliance, turning her mouth into a sober line.

"Good morning, Jovilette." He spoke her name too easily, she thought, as if he had been saying it for years.

"Good morning, Mr. Prescott," she returned. Rose gave a loud, none-too-subtle cough. "This is Rose Sanches."

"It's a pleasure, Mr. Prescott." Rose extended a hand, trying out a smile she had been saving for Jamie. "I heard you were traveling with us."

Keane accepted the hand and smiled in return. Jo noticed with annoyance that it was the same easy, disarming smile of the stranger she had met the morning before. "Hello, Rose, it's nice to meet you."

Seeing her friend's blood heat her cheeks, Jo intervened. She would not permit Keane Prescott to make a conquest here. "Rose, you only have ten minutes to get back and into makeup."

"Holy cow!" she said, forgetting her attempt at sophistication. "I've got to run." She began to do so, then called over her shoulder, "Don't tell Jamie I was looking for him, the pig!" She ran a little farther, then turned and ran backward. "I'll look for him later," she said with a laugh, then turned back and streaked toward the midway.

Keane watched her dart across the compound while holding up the long skirts of her robe in one hand. "Charming."

"She's only eighteen," Jo offered before she could stop herself.

When Keane turned to her, his look was one of amusement. "I see," he said. "I'll take that information under advisement. And what does the eighteen-year-old Rose do?" he asked, slipping his thumbs into the front pockets of his jeans. "Wrestle alligators?"

"No," Jo returned without batting an eye. "Rose is Serpentina, your premier sideshow attraction. The snake charmer." She was pleased with the incredulous look that passed over his face. It was replaced quickly, however, with one of genuine humor.

"Perfect." He brushed Jo's hair from her cheek before she could protest by word or action. "Cobras?" he asked, ignoring the flash in her eyes.

"And boa constrictors," she returned sweetly. Jo brushed the dust from the knees of her faded jeans. "Now, if you'll excuse me . . ."

"No, I don't think so." Keane's voice was cool, but she recognized the underlying authority. She did her best not to struggle against it. He *was* the owner, she reminded herself.

"Mr. Prescott," she began, banking down hard on the urge to mutiny. "I'm very busy. I have to get ready for the afternoon show."

"You've got an hour and a half until you're on," he countered smoothly. "I think you might spare me a portion of that time. You've been assigned to show me around. Why don't we start now?" The tone of the question left room for only one answer. Jo's mind fidgeted in search of a way out.

Tilting her head back, she met his eyes. He won't be easy to beat, she concluded, studying his steady, measuring gaze. I'd better study his moves more carefully before I start a battle. "Where would you like to begin?" she asked aloud.

"With you."

Keane's easy answer brought a deep frown to Jo's brows. "I don't understand what you mean."

For a moment Keane watched her. There was no coyness or guile in her eyes as they looked into his. "No, I can see you don't," he agreed with a nod. "Let's start with your cats."

"Oh." Jo's frown cleared instantly. "All right." She watched as he pulled out a thin cigar, waiting until the flame of his lighter licked the tip before speaking. "I have thirteen—seven males, six females. They're all African lions between four-and-a-half and twenty-two years."

"I thought you worked with twelve," Keane commented as he dropped his lighter into his pocket.

"That's right, but Ari's retired." Turning, Jo indicated the large male lion dozing in a cage. "He travels with me because he always has, but I don't work him anymore. He's twenty-two, the oldest. My father kept him, even though he was born in captivity, because he was born the same day I was." Jo sighed, and her voice became softer. "He's the last of my father's stock. I couldn't sell him to a zoo. It seemed like shoving an old relative into a home and abandoning him. He's been with this circus every day of his life, just as I have. His name is Hebrew for *lion*." Jo laughed, forgetting the man beside her as she sifted through memories. "My father always gave his cats names that meant lion somehow or other. Leo, Leonard, Leonara. Ari was a first-class leaper in his prime. He could climb, too. Some cats won't. I could teach Ari anything. Smart cat, aren't you, Ari?" The altered tone of her voice caused the big cat to stir. Opening his eyes, he stared back at Jo. The sound he made was more grumble than roar before he dozed again. "He's tired," Jo murmured, fighting a shaft of gloom. "Twenty-two's old for a lion."

"What is it?" Keane demanded, touching her shoulder before she could turn away. Her eyes were drenched with sadness.

"He's dying," she said unsteadily. "And I can't stop it." Stuffing her hands in her pockets, Jo moved away to the main group of cages. To steady herself, she took two deep breaths while waiting for Keane to join her. Regaining her composure, she began again. "I work with these twelve," she told him, making a sweeping gesture. "They're fed once a day, raw meat six days a week and eggs and milk on the seventh.

They were all imported directly from Africa and were cage broken when I got them."

The faint sound of a calliope reached them, signaling the opening of the midway. "This is Merlin, the one I ride out on at the finish. He's ten, and the most even-tempered cat I've ever worked with. Heathcliff," she continued as she moved down the line of cages, "he's six, my best leaper. And this is Faust, the baby at four and a half." The lions paced their cages as Jo walked Keane down the line. Unable to prevent herself, Jo gave Faust a signal by raising her hand. Obediently, he sent out a huge, deafening roar. To Jo's disappointment, Keane did not scramble for cover.

"Very impressive," he said mildly. "You put him in the center when you lie down on them, don't you?"

"Yes." She frowned, then spoke her thoughts candidly. "You're very observant—and you've got steady nerves."

"My profession requires them, too, to an extent," he returned.

Jo considered this a moment, then turned back to the lions. "Lazareth, he's twelve and a natural ham. Bolingbroke, he's ten, from the same lioness as Merlin. Hamlet," she said stopping again, "he's five. I bought him to replace Ari in the act." Jo stared into the tawny eyes. "He has potential, but he's arrogant. Patient, too. He's just waiting for me to make a mistake."

"Why?" Keane glanced over at Jo. Her eyes were cool and steady on Hamlet's.

"So he can get a good clean swipe at me," she told him without altering her expression. "It's his first season in the big cage. Pandora," Jo continued, pointing out the females. "A very classy lady. She's six. Hester, at seven, my best all-around. And Portia. It's her first year, too. She's mostly a seat warmer."

"Seat warmer?"

"Just what it sounds like," Jo explained. "She hasn't mastered any complicated tricks yet. She evens out the act, does a few basics and warms the seat." Jo moved on. "Dulcinea, the prettiest of the ladies. Ophelia, who had a litter last year, and Abra, eight, a bit bad-tempered but a good balancer."

Hearing her name, the cat rose, stretched her long, golden body, then began to rub it against the bars of the cage. A deep sound rumbled in her throat. Jo scowled and jammed her hands into her pockets. "She likes you," she muttered.

"Oh?" Lifting a brow, Keane studied the three-hundred-pound Abra more carefully. "How do you know?"

"When a lion likes you, it does exactly what a house cat does. It rubs against you. Abra's rubbing against the bars because she can't get any closer."

"I see." Humor touched his mouth. "I must admit, I'm at a loss on how to return the compliment." He drew on his cigar, then regarded Jo through a haze of smoke. "Your choice of names is fascinating."

"I like to read," she stated, leaving it at that. "Is there anything else you'd like to know about the cats?" Jo was determined to keep their conversation on a professional level. His smile had reminded her all too clearly of their encounter the night before.

"Do you drug them before a performance?"

Fury sparked Jo's eyes. "Certainly not."

"Was that an unreasonable question?" Keane countered. He dropped his cigar to the ground, then crushed it out with his heel.

"Not for a first of mayer," Jo decided with a sigh. She tossed her hair carelessly behind her back. "Drugging is not only cruel, it's stupid. A drugged animal won't perform."

"You don't touch the lions with that whip," Keane commented. He watched the light breeze tease a few strands of her hair. "Why do you use it?"

"To get their attention and to keep the audience awake." She smiled reluctantly.

Keane took her arm. Instantly, Jo stiffened. "Let's walk," he suggested. He began to lead her away from the cages. Spotting several people roaming the backyard, Jo refrained from pulling away. The last thing she wanted was the story spreading that she was having a tiff with the owner. "How do you tame them?" he asked her.

"I don't. They're not tame, they're trained." A tall blond woman walked by carrying a tiny white poodle. "Merlin's hungry today," Jo called out with a grin.

The woman bundled the dog closer to her breast in mock alarm and began a rapid scolding in French. Jo laughed, telling her in the same language that Fifi was too tough a mouthful for Merlin.

"Fifi can do a double somersault on the back of a moving horse," Jo explained as they began to walk again. "She's trained just as my cats are trained, but she's also domesticated. The cats are wild." Jo turned her face up to Keane's. The sun cast a sheen over her hair and threw gold flecks into her eyes. "A wild thing can never be tamed, and anyone who tries is foolish. If you take something wild and turn it into a pet, you've stolen its character, blanked out its spark. And still, there's always an essence of the wild that can come back to life. When a dog turns on his master, it's ugly. When a lion turns, it's lethal." She was beginning to become accustomed to his hand on her arm, finding it easy to talk to him because he listened. "A full-grown male stands three feet at the shoulder and weighs over five hundred pounds. One well-directed swipe can break a man's neck, not to mention what teeth and claws can do." Jo gave a smile and a shrug. "Those aren't the virtues of a pet."

"Yet you go into a cage with twelve of them, armed with a whip?"

"The whip's window dressing." Jo discounted it with a gesture of her hand. "It would hardly be a defense against even one cat at full charge. A lion is a very tenacious enemy.

A tiger is more bloodthirsty, but it normally strikes only once. If it misses, it takes it philosophically. A lion charges again and again. Do you know the line Byron wrote about a tiger's spring? 'Deadly, quick and crushing.'" Jo had completely forgotten her animosity and began to enjoy her walk and conversation with this handsome stranger. "It's a true description, but a lion is totally fearless when he charges, and stubborn. He's not the razzle-dazzle fighter the tiger is, just accurate. I'd bet on a lion against a tiger any day. And a man simply hasn't a prayer against one."

"Then how do you manage to stay in one piece?"

The calliope music was just a hint in the air now. Jo turned, noting with surprise that they had walked a good distance from camp. She could see the trailers and tents, hear occasional shouts and laughter, but she felt oddly separated from it all. She sat down cross-legged on the grass and plucked a blade. "I'm smarter than they are. At least I make them think so. And I dominate them, partly by a force of will. In training, you have to develop a rapport, a mutual respect and, if you're lucky, a certain affection. But you can't trust them to the point where you grow careless. And above all," she added, glancing over as he sat down beside her, "you have to remember the basic rule of poker. Bluff." Jo grinned, leaning back on her elbows. "Do you play poker?"

"I've been known to." Her hair trailed out along the grass, and he lifted a strand. "Do you?"

"Sometimes. My assistant handler, Pete . . ." Jo scanned the backyard, then smiled and pointed. "There he is, by the second trailer, sitting with Mac Stevenson, the one with the fielder's cap. Pete organizes a game now and then."

"Who's the little girl on stilts?"

"That's Mac's youngest, Katie. She wants to walk on them in the street parade. She's getting pretty good. There's Jamie," she said, then laughed as he did a pratfall and landed at Katie's wooden stilts.

"Rose's Jamie?" Keane asked, watching the impromptu show in the backyard.

"If she has her way. He's currently dazzled by Carmen Gribalti. Carmen won't give Jamie the time of day. She bats her lashes at Vito, the wire walker. He bats his at everyone."

"A complicated state of affairs," Keane commented. He twisted Jo's hair around his fingers. "Romance seems to be very popular in circus life."

"From what I read," she countered, "it's popular everywhere."

"Who dazzles you, Jovilette?" He gave her hair a tug to bring her face around to his.

Jo hadn't realized he was so close. She need do no more than sway for her mouth to touch his. Her eyes measured his while she waited for her pulse to calm. It was odd, she thought, that he had such an effect on her. With sudden clarity, she could smell the grass, a clean, sweet scent, and feel the sun. The sounds of the circus were muted in the background. She could hear birds call out with an occasional high-pitched trill. She remembered the taste of his mouth and wondered if it would be the same.

"I've been too busy to be dazzled," she replied. Her voice was steady, but her eyes were curious.

For the first time, Jo truly *wanted* to be kissed by a man. She wanted to feel again what she had felt the night before. She wanted to be held, not lightly as he had held her before, but close, with his arms tight around her. She wanted to renew the feeling of weightlessness. She had never experienced a strong physical desire, and for a moment she explored the sensation. There was a quiver in her stomach which was both pleasant and disturbing. Throughout her silent contemplations Keane watched her, intrigued by the intensity of her eyes.

"What are you thinking of?"

"I'm wondering why you make me feel so odd," she told

him with simple frankness. He smiled, and she noticed that it grew in his eyes seconds before it grew on his mouth.

"Do I?" He appeared to enjoy the information. "Did you know your hair catches the sunlight?" Keane took a handful, letting it spill from between his fingers. "I've never seen another woman with hair like this. It's a temptation all in itself. In what way do I make you feel odd, Jovilette?" he asked as his eyes trailed back up to hers.

"I'm not sure yet." Jo found her voice husky. Abruptly, she decided it would not do to go on feeling odd or to go on wanting to be kissed by Keane Prescott. She scrambled up and brushed off the seat of her pants.

"Running away?" As Keane rose, Jo's head snapped up.

"I never run away from anything, Mr. Prescott." Ice sharpened her voice. She was annoyed that she had allowed herself to fall under his charm again. "I certainly won't run from a city-bred lawyer." Her words were laced with scorn. "Why don't you go back to Chicago and get someone thrown in jail?"

"I'm a defense attorney," Keane countered easily. "I get people out of jail."

"Fine. Go put a criminal back on the streets, then."

Keane laughed, bringing Jo's temper even closer to the surface. "That covers both sides of the issue, doesn't it? You dazzle me, Jovilette."

"Well, it's strictly unintentional." She took a step back from the amusement in his eyes. She would not tolerate him making fun of her. "You don't belong here," she blurted out. "You have no business here."

"On the contrary," he disagreed in a cool, untroubled voice. "I have every business here. I own this circus."

"Why?" she demanded, throwing out her hands as if to push his words aside. "Because it says so on a piece of paper? That's all lawyers understand, I imagine—pieces of paper with strange little words. Why did you come? To look us over and calculate the profit and loss? What's the liquidation value of a dream, Mr. Prescott? What price do you put on the human spirit? Look at it!" she demanded, swinging her arm to encompass the lot behind them. "You only see tents and a huddle of trailers. You can't possibly understand what it all means. But Frank understood. He loved it."

"I'm aware of that." Keane's voice was still calm but had taken on a thin edge of steel. Jo saw that his eyes had grown dark and guarded. "He also left it to me."

"I don't understand why." In frustration, Jo stuffed her hands in her pockets and turned away.

"Neither do I, I assure you, but the fact remains that he did."

"Not once in thirty years did you visit him." Jo whirled back around. Her hair followed in a passionate arch. "Not once."

"Quite true," Keane agreed. He stood with his weight even on both legs and watched her. "Of course, some might look at it differently. Not once in thirty years did he visit me."

"Your mother left him and took you to Chicago—"

"I won't discuss my mother," Keane interrupted in a tone of clipped finality.

Jo bit off a retort, spinning away from him again. Still she could not find the reins to her control. "What are you going to do with it?" she demanded.

"That's my business."

"Oh!" Jo spun back, then shut her eyes and muttered in a language he failed to understand. "Can you be so arrogant? Can you be so dispassionate?" Her lashes fluttered up, revealing eyes dark with anger. "Do the lives of all those people mean nothing to you? Does Frank's dream mean nothing? Haven't you enough money already without hurting people to get more? Greed isn't something you inherited from Frank."

"I'll only be pushed so far," Keane warned.

"I'd push you all the way back to Chicago if I could manage it," she snapped.

"I wondered how much of a temper there was behind those sharp green eyes," Keane commented, watching her passion pour color into her cheeks. "It appears it's a full-grown one." Jo started to retort, but Keane cut her off. "Just hold on a minute," he ordered. "With or without your approval, I own this circus. It might be easier for you if you adjusted to that. Be quiet," he added when her mouth opened again. "Legally, I can do with my—" he hesitated a moment, then continued in a mordant tone "—inheritance as I choose. I have no obligation or intention of justifying my decision to you."

Jo dug her nails into her palms to help keep her voice from shaking. "I never knew I could grow to dislike someone so quickly."

"Jovilette." Keane dipped his hands into his pockets, then rocked back on his heels. "You disliked me before you ever saw me."

"That's true," she replied evenly. "But I've learned to dislike you in person in less than twenty-four hours. I have a show to do," she said, turning back toward the lot. Though he did not follow, she felt his eyes on her until she reached her trailer and closed the door behind her.

* * *

Thirty minutes later Jamie sprang through the back door of the Big Top. He was breathless after a lengthy routine and hooked one hand through his purple suspenders as he took in gulps of air. He spotted Jo standing beside the white mare. Her eyes were dark and stormy, her shoulders set and rigid. Jamie recognized the signs. Something or someone had put Jo in a temper, and she had barely ten minutes to work her way out of it before her cue.

He crossed to her and gave a tug on her hair. "Hey."

"Hello, Jamie." Jo struggled to keep her voice pleasant, but he heard the traces of emotion.

"Hello, Jo," he replied in precisely the same tone.

"Cut it out," she ordered before taking a few steps away. The mare followed docilely. Jo had been trying for some time to put her emotions back into some semblance of order. She was not succeeding.

"What happened?" Jamie asked from directly behind her.

"Nothing," Jo snapped, then hated herself for the short nastiness of the word.

Jamie persisted, knowing her too well to be offended. "Nothing is one of my favorite topics of conversation." He put his hands on her shoulders, ignoring her quick, bad-tempered jerk. "Let's talk about it."

"There's nothing to talk about."

"Exactly." He began massaging the tension in her shoulders with his white gloved hands.

"Oh, Jamie." His good-heartedness was irresistible. Sighing, she allowed herself to be soothed. "You're an idiot."

"I'm not here to be flattered."

"I had an argument with the owner." Jo let out a long breath and shut her eyes.

"What're you doing having arguments with the owner?"

"He infuriates me." Jo whirled around. Her cape whipped and snapped with the movement. "He shouldn't be here. If he were back in Chicago . . ."

"Hold it." With a slight shake of her shoulders, Jamie halted Jo's outburst. "You know better than to get yourself worked up like this right before a show. You can't afford to have your mind on anything but what you're doing when you're in that cage."

"I'll be all right," she mumbled.

"Jo." There was censure in his voice mixed with affection and exasperation.

Reluctantly, Jo brought her gaze up to his. It was impossible to resist the grave eyes in the brightly painted face. With something between a sigh and a moan, she dropped her forehead to his chest. "Jamie, he makes me so mad! He could ruin everything."

"Let's worry about it when the time comes," Jamie suggested, patting her hair.

"But he doesn't understand us. He doesn't understand anything."

"Well, then it's up to us to make him understand, isn't it?"

Jo looked up and wrinkled her nose. "You're so logical."

"Of course I am," he agreed and struck a pose. As he wiggled his orange eyebrows, Jo laughed. "Okay?" he asked, then picked up his prop bucket.

"Okay," she agreed and smiled.

"Good, 'cause there's my cue."

When he disappeared behind the flap, Jo leaned her cheek against the mare and nuzzled a moment. "I don't think I'm the one to make him understand, though."

I wish he'd never come, she added silently as she vaulted onto the mare's back. *I wish I'd never noticed how his eyes are like Ari's and how nice his mouth is when he smiles,* she thought. Jo ran the tip of her tongue gingerly over her lips. *I wish he'd never kissed me. Liar.* Her conscience spoke softly in her ear: *Admit it, you're glad he kissed you. You've never felt anything like that before, and no matter what, you're glad he kissed you last night. You even wanted him to kiss you again today.*

She forced her mind clear, taking deep, even breaths until she heard the ringmaster announce her. With a flick of her heels, she sent the mare sprinting into the tent.

It did not go well. The audience cheered her, oblivious to any problem, but Jo was aware that the routine was far from smooth. And the cats sensed her preoccupation. Again and again they tested her, and again and again Jo was forced to alter her timing to compensate. When the act was over, her head throbbed from the strain of concentration. Her hands were clammy as she turned Merlin over to Buck.

The big man came back to her after securing the cage. "What's the matter with you?" he demanded without preamble. By the underlying and very rare anger in his voice, Jo knew he had observed at least a portion of her act. Unlike the audience, Buck would note any deviation. "You go in the cage like that again, one of those cats is going to find out what you taste like."

"My timing was a little off, that's all." Jo fought against the trembling in her stomach and tried to sound casual.

"A little?" Buck glowered, looking formidable behind the mass of blond beard. "Who do you think you're fooling? I've been around these ugly cats since before you were born. When you go in the cage, you've got to take your brain in with you."

Only too aware that he was right, Jo conceded. "I know, Buck. You're right." With a weary hand she pushed back her hair. "It won't happen again. I guess I was tired and a little off-balance." She sent him an apologetic smile.

Buck frowned and shuffled. Never in his forty-five years had he managed to resist feminine smiles. "All right," he muttered, then sniffed and made his voice firm. "But you go take a nap right after the finale. No coffee. I don't want to see you around again until dinnertime."

"Okay, Buck." Jo kept her voice humble, though she was tempted to grin. The weakness was going out of her legs, and the dull buzz of fear was fading from between her temples. Still she felt exhausted and agreeable to Buck's uncharacteristic tone of command. A nap, she decided as Buck drove Merlin away, was just what she needed, not to mention that it was as good a way as any to avoid Keane Prescott for the rest of the day. Shooing this thought aside, Jo decided to while away the time until the finale in casual conversation with Vito the wire walker.

CHAPTER 4

It rained for three days. It was a solid downpour, not heavy but insistent. As the circus wound its way north, the rain followed. Nevertheless, canvas men pitched the tents in soggy fields and muddy lots while straw was laid on the hippodrome track and performers scurried from trailers to tents under dripping umbrellas.

The lot near Waycross, Georgia, was scattered with puddles under a thick, gray sky. Jo could only be grateful that no evening show had been scheduled. By six, it was nearly dark, with a chill teasing the damp air. She hustled from the cookhouse after an early supper. She would check on the cats, she decided, then closet herself in her trailer, draw the curtains against the rain and curl up with a book. Shivering, she concluded that the idea was inspired.

She carried no umbrella but sought questionable shelter under a gray rolled-brim hat and thin windbreaker. Keeping her head lowered, she jogged across the mud, skimming around or hopping over puddles. She hummed lightly, anticipating the simple pleasures of an idle evening. Her humming ended in a muffled gasp as she ran into a solid object. Fingers wrapped around her upper arms. Even before she lifted her head, Jo knew it was Keane who held her. She recognized his touch. Through some clever maneuvering, she had managed to avoid being alone with him since they had walked together and looked back on the circus.

"Excuse me, Mr. Prescott. I'm afraid I wasn't looking where I was going."

"Perhaps the weather's dampened your radar, Jovilette." He made no move to release her. Annoyed, Jo was forced to hold her hat steady with one hand as she tilted her head to meet his eyes. Rain fell cool on her face.

"I don't know what you mean."

"Oh, I think you do," Keane countered. "There's not another soul around. You've been careful to keep yourself in a crowd for days."

Jo blinked rain from her lashes. She admitted ruefully that it had been foolish to suppose he wouldn't notice her ploy. She saw he carried no umbrella either, nor did he bother with a hat. His hair was darkened with rain, much the same color that one of her cats would be if caught in an unexpected shower. It was difficult, in the murky light, to clearly make out his features, but the rain could not disguise his mockery.

"That's an interesting observation, Mr. Prescott," Jo said coolly. "Now, if you don't mind, I'm getting wet." She was surprised when she remained in his hold after a strong attempt on her part to pull away. Frowning, she put both hands against his chest and pushed. She discovered that she had been wrong; under the lean frame was an amazing amount of strength. Infuriated that she had misjudged him and that she was outmatched, Jo raised her eyes again. "Let me go," she demanded between clenched teeth.

"No," Keane returned mildly. "I don't believe I will."

Jo glared at him. "Mr. Prescott, I'm cold and wet and I'd like to go to my trailer. Now, what do you want?"

"First, I want you to stop calling me Mr. Prescott." Jo pouted but she kept silent. "Second, I'd like an hour of your time for going over a list of personnel." He paused. Through her windbreaker Jo could feel his fingers unyielding on her arms.

"Is there anything else?" she demanded, trying to sound bored.

For a moment there was only the sound of rain drumming on the ground and splashing into puddles. "Yes," Keane said quietly. "I think I'll just get this out of my system."

Jo's instincts were swift but they were standing too close for her to evade him. And he was quick. Her protest was muffled against his mouth. Her arms were pinioned to her sides as his locked around her. Jo had felt a man's body against her own before—working out with the tumblers, practicing with the equestrians—but never with such clarity as this. She was aware of Keane in every fiber of her being. His body was whipcord lean and hard, his arms holding the strength she had discounted the first time she had seen him. But more, it was his mouth that mystified her. Now it was not gentle or testing; it took and plundered and demanded more before she could withhold a response.

Jo forgot the rain, though it continued to fall against her face. She forgot the cold. The warmth spread from inside, where her blood flowed fast, as her body was molded to Keane's. She forgot herself, or the woman she had thought herself to be, and discovered another. When he lifted his mouth, Jo kept her eyes closed, savoring the lingering pleasures, inviting fresh ones.

"More?" he murmured as his hand trailed up, then down her spine. Heat raced after it. "Kissing can be a dangerous pastime, Jo." He lowered his mouth again, then nipped at her soft bottom lip. "But you know all about danger, don't you?" He kissed her hard, leaving her breathless. "How courageous are you without your cats?"

Suddenly her heart raced to her throat. Her legs became rubbery, and a tingle sprinted up her spine. Jo recognized the feeling. It was the way she felt when she experienced a close call with the cats. Reaction would set in after the door of the safety cage locked behind her and the crisis had passed. It was then that fear found her. She studied Keane's bold, amber eyes, and her mouth went dry. She shuddered.

"You're cold." His voice was abruptly brisk. "Small wonder. We'll go to my trailer and get you some coffee."

"No!" Jo's protest was sharp and instantaneous. She knew she was vulnerable and she knew as well that she did not yet possess the experience to fight him. To be alone with him now was too great a risk.

Keane drew her away, but his grip remained firm. She could not read his expression as he searched her face. "What happened just now was personal," he told her. "Strictly man to woman. I'm of the opinion that lovemaking should be personal. You're an appealing armful, Jovilette, and I'm accustomed to taking what I want, one way or another."

His words were like a shot of adrenaline. Jo's chin thrust forward, and her eyes flamed. "No one *takes* me, one way or another." She spoke with the deadly calm of fury. "If I make love with anyone, it's only because I want to."

"Of course," Keane agreed with an easy nod. "We're both aware you'll be willing when the time comes. We could make love quite successfully tonight, but I think it best if we know each other better first."

Jo's mouth trembled open and closed twice before she could speak. "Of all the arrogant, outrageous . . ."

"Truthful," Keane supplied, tossing her into incoherency again. "But for now, we have business, and while I don't mind kissing in the rain, I prefer to conduct business in a drier climate." He held up a hand as Jo started to protest. "I told you, the kiss was between a man and a woman. The business we have now is between the owner of this circus and a performer under contract. Understood?"

Jo took a long, deep breath to bring her voice to a normal

level. "Understood," she agreed. Without another word she let him lead her across the slippery lot.

When they reached Keane's trailer, he hustled Jo inside without preliminaries. She blinked against the change in light when he hit the wall switch. "Take off your coat," he said briskly, pulling down her zipper before she could perform the task for herself. Instinctively, her hand reached for it as she took a step backward. Keane merely lifted a brow, then stripped off his own jacket. "I'll get the coffee." He moved down the length of the narrow trailer and disappeared around the corner where the tiny kitchen was set.

Slowly, Jo pulled off her dripping hat, letting her hair tumble free from where it had been piled under its confinement. With automatic movements she hung both her hat and coat on the hooks by the trailer door. It had been almost six months since she had stood in Frank's trailer, and like a woman visiting an old friend, she searched for changes.

The same faded lampshade adorned the maple table lamp that Frank had used for reading. The shade sat straight now, however, not at its usual slightly askew angle. The pillow that Lillie from wardrobe had sewn for him on some long-ago Christmas still sat over the small burn hole in the seat cushion of the couch. Jo doubted that Keane knew of the hole's existence. Frank's pipe stand sat, as always, on the counter by the side window. Unable to resist, Jo crossed over to run her finger over the worn bowl of his favorite pipe.

"Never could pack it right," she murmured to his well-loved ghost. Abruptly, her senses quivered. She twisted her head to see Keane watching her. Jo dropped her hand. A rare blush mantled her cheeks as she found herself caught unguarded.

"How do you take your coffee, Jo?"

She swallowed. "Black," she told him, aware that he was granting her the privacy of her thoughts. "Just black. Thank you."

Keane nodded, then turned to pick up two steaming mugs.

"Come, sit down." He moved toward the Formica table that sat directly across from the kitchen. "You'd better take off your shoes. They're wet."

After squeaking her way down the length of the trailer, Jo sat down and pulled at the damp laces. Keane set both mugs on the table before disappearing into the back of the trailer. When he returned, Jo was already sipping at the coffee.

"Here." He offered her a pair of socks.

Surprised, Jo shook her head. "No, that's all right. I don't need . . ."

Her polite refusal trailed off as he knelt at her feet. "Your feet are like ice," he commented after cupping them in his palms. Briskly, he rubbed them while Jo sat mute, oddly disarmed by the gesture. The warmth was spreading dangerously past her ankles. "Since I'm responsible for keeping you out in the rain," he went on as he slipped a sock over her foot, "I'd best see to it you don't cough and sneeze your way through tomorrow's show. Such small feet," he murmured, running his thumb over the curve of her ankle as she stared wordlessly at the top of his head.

Raindrops still clung to and glistened in his hair. Jo found herself longing to brush them away and feel the texture of his hair beneath her fingers. She was sharply aware of him and wondered if it would always be this way when she was near him. Keane pulled on the second sock. His fingers lingered on her calf as he lifted his eyes. Hers were darkened with confusion as they met his. The body over which she had always held supreme control was journeying into frontiers her mind had not yet explored.

"Still cold?" Keane asked softly.

Jo moistened her lips and shook her head. "No. No, I'm fine."

He smiled a lazy, masculine smile that said as clearly as words that he was aware of his effect on her. His eyes told her he enjoyed it. Unsmiling, Jo watched him rise to his feet.

"It doesn't mean you'll win," she said aloud in response to their silent communication.

"No, it doesn't." Keane's smile remained as his gaze roamed possessively over her face. "That only makes it more interesting. Open and shut cases are invariably boring, hardly worth the trouble of going on if you've won before you've finished your opening statement."

Jo lifted her coffee and sipped, taking a moment to settle her nerves. "Are we here to discuss the law or circus business, Counselor?" she asked, letting her eyes drift to his again as she set the mug back on the table. "If it's law, I'm afraid I'm going to disappoint you. I don't know much about it."

"What do you know about, Jovilette?" Keane slid into the chair beside hers.

"Cats," she said. "And Prescott's Circus Colossus. I'll be glad to let you know whatever I can about either."

"Tell me about you," he countered, and leaning back, pulled a cigar from his pocket.

"Mr. Prescott—" Jo began.

"Keane," he interrupted, flicking on his lighter. He glanced at the tip of his cigar, then back up at her through the thin haze of smoke.

"I was under the impression you wanted to be briefed on the personnel."

"You are a member of this circus, are you not?" Casually, Keane blew smoke at the ceiling. "I have every intention of being briefed on the entire troupe and see no reason why you shouldn't start with yourself." His eyes traveled back to hers. "Humor me."

Jo decided to take the line of least resistance. "It's a short enough story," she said with a shrug. "I've been with the circus all my life. When I was old enough, I started work as a generally useful."

"A what?" Keane paused in the action of reaching for the coffeepot.

"Generally useful," Jo repeated, letting him freshen her cup. "It's a circus term that means exactly what it says. Rose's parents, for instance, are generally usefuls. We get a lot of drifters who work that way, too. It's also written into every performer's contract, after the specific terms, that they make themselves generally useful. There isn't room in most circuses, and certainly not in a tent circus, for performers with star complexes. You do what's necessary, what's needed. Buck, my handler, fills in during a slump at the sideshow, and he's one of the best canvas men around. Pete is the best mechanic in the troupe. Jamie knows as much about lighting as most shandies—electricians," she supplied as Keane lifted a brow. "He's also a better-than-average tumbler."

"What about you?" Keane interrupted the flow of Jo's words. For a moment she faltered, and the hands that had been gesturing became still. "Besides riding a galloping horse without reins or saddle, giving orders to elephants and facing lions?" He lifted his cup, watching her as he sipped. A smile lurked in his eyes. Jo frowned, studying him.

"Are you making fun of me?"

His smile sobered instantly. "No, Jo, I'm not making fun of you."

She continued. "In a pinch, I run the menagerie in the sideshow or I fill in the aerial act. Not the trap," she explained, relaxing again. "They have to practice together constantly to keep the timing. But sometimes I fill in on the Spanish Web, the big costume number where the girls hang from ropes and do identical moves. They're using butterfly costumes this year."

"Yes, I know the one." Keane continued to watch her as he drew on his cigar.

"But mostly Duffy likes to use girls who are more curvy. They double as showgirls in the finale."

"I see." A smile tugged at the corners of Keane's mouth. "Tell me, were your parents European?"

"No." Diverted, Jo shook her head. "Why do you ask?"

"Your name. And the ease with which I've heard you speak both French and Italian."

"It's easy to pick up languages in the circus," Jo said.

"Your accent was perfect in both cases."

"What? Oh." She shrugged and absently shifted in her chair, bringing her feet up to sit cross-legged. "We have a wide variety of nationalities here. Frank used to say that the world could take a lesson from the circus. We have French, Italian, Spanish, German, Russian, Mexican, Americans from all parts of the country and more."

"I know. It's like a traveling United Nations." He tipped his cigar ash in a glass tray. "So you picked up some French and Italian along the way. But if you've traveled with the circus all your life, what about the rest of your schooling?"

The hint of censure in his voice brought up her chin. "I went to school during the winter break and had a tutor on the road. I learned my ABC's, Counselor, and a bit more, besides. I probably know more about geography and world history than you, and from more interesting sources than textbooks. I imagine I know more about animals than a third-year veterinary student and have more practical experience healing them. I can speak seven languages and—"

"Seven?" Keane interrupted. "Seven languages?"

"Well, five fluently," she corrected grudgingly. "I still have a bit of trouble with Greek and German, unless I can really take my time, and I can't read Greek yet at all."

"What else besides French, Italian and English?"

"Spanish and Russian." Jo scowled into her coffee. "The Russian's handy. I use it for swearing at the cats during the act. Not too many people understand Russian cursing, so it's safe."

Keane's laughter brought Jo's attention from her coffee. He was leaning back in his chair, his eyes gold with their mirth. Jo's scowl deepened. "What's so funny?"

"You are, Jovilette." Stung, she started to scramble up,

but his hands on her shoulders stopped her. "No, don't be offended. I can't help but find it amusing that you toss out so offhandedly an accomplishment that any language major would brag about." Carelessly, he ran a finger over her sulky mouth. "You continually amaze me." He brushed a hand through her hair. "You mumbled something at me the other day. Were you swearing at me in Russian?"

"Probably."

Grinning, Keane dropped his hand and settled into his chair again. "When did you start working with the cats?"

"In front of an audience? When I was seventeen. Frank wouldn't let me start any earlier. He was my legal guardian as well as the owner, so he had me both ways. I was ready when I was fifteen."

"How did you lose your parents?"

The question caught her off guard. "In a fire," she said levelly. "When I was seven."

"Here?"

She knew Keane was not referring to their locale but to the circus. Jo sipped her cooling coffee. "Yes."

"Didn't you have any other family?"

"The circus is a family," she countered. "I was never given the chance to be an orphan. And I always had Frank."

"Did you?" Keane's smile was faintly sarcastic. "How was he as a father figure?"

Jo studied him for a moment. Was he bitter? she wondered. Or amused? Or simply curious? "He never took my father's place," she replied quietly. "He never tried to, because neither of us wanted it. We were friends, as close as I think it's possible for friends to be, but I'd already had a father, and he'd already had a child. We weren't looking for substitutes. You look nothing like him, you know."

"No," Keane replied with a shrug. "I know."

"He had a comfortable face, all creases and folds." Jo smiled, thinking of it while she ran a finger absently around the rim of her mug. "He was dark, too, just beginning to gray when . . ." She trailed off, then brought herself back with a quick shake of her head. "Your voice is rather like his, though. He had a truly beautiful voice. I'll ask you a question now."

Keane's expression became attentive, then he gestured with the back of his hand. "Go ahead."

"Why are you here? I lost my temper when I asked you before, but I do want to know." It was against her nature to probe, and some of her discomfort found its way into her voice. "It must have caused you some difficulty to leave your practice, even for a few weeks."

Keane frowned at the end of his cigar before he slowly crushed it out. "Let's say I wanted to see firsthand what had fascinated my father all these years."

"You never came when he was alive." Jo gripped her hands together under the table. "You didn't even bother to come to his funeral."

"I would've been the worst kind of hypocrite to attend his funeral, don't you think?"

"He was your father." Jo's eyes grew dark and her tone sharp in reproof.

"You're smarter than that, Jo," Keane countered calmly. "It takes more than an accident of birth to make a father. Frank Prescott was a complete stranger to me."

"You resent him." Jo felt suddenly torn between loyalty for Frank and understanding for the man who sat beside her.

"No." Keane shook his head thoughtfully. "No, I believe I actively resented him when I was growing up, but . . ." He shrugged the thought aside. "I grew rather ambivalent over the years."

"He was a good man," Jo stated, leaning forward as she willed him to understand. "He only wanted to give people pleasure, to show them a little magic. Maybe he wasn't made to be a father—some men aren't—but he was kind and gentle. And he was proud of you."

"Of me?" Keane seemed amused. "How?"

"Oh, you're hateful," Jo whispered, hurt by his careless attitude. She slipped from her chair, but before she could step away, Keane took her arm.

"No, tell me. I'm interested." His hold on her arm was light, but she knew it would tighten if she resisted.

"All right." Jo tossed her head to send her hair behind her back. "He had the Chicago paper delivered to his Florida office. He always looked for any mention of you, any article on a court case you were involved in or a dinner party you attended. Anything. You have to understand that to us a write-up is very important. Frank wasn't a performer, but he was one of us. Sometimes he'd read me an article before he put it away. He kept a scrapbook."

Jo pulled her arm away and strode past Keane into the bedroom. The oversize wooden chest was where it had always been, at the foot of Frank's bed. Kneeling down, Jo tossed up the lid. "This is where he kept all the things that mattered to him." Jo began to shift through papers and mementos quickly; she had not been able to bring herself to sort through the chest before. Keane stood in the doorway and watched her. "He called it his memory box." She pushed at her hair with an annoyed hand, then continued to search. "He said memories were the rewards for growing old. Here it is." Jo pulled out a dark green scrapbook, then sat back on her heels. Silently, she held it out to Keane. After a moment he crossed the room and took it from her. Jo could hear the rain hissing on the ground outside as their eyes held. His expression was unfathomable as he opened the book. The pages rustled to join the quiet sound of the rain.

"What an odd man he must have been," Keane murmured, "to keep a scrapbook on a son he never knew." There was no rancor in his voice. "What was he?" he asked suddenly, shifting his eyes back to Jo.

"A dreamer," she answered. "His watch was always five

minutes slow. If he hung a picture on the wall, it was always crooked. He'd never straighten it because he'd never notice. He was always thinking about tomorrow. I guess that's why he kept yesterday in this box." Glancing down, she began to straighten the chaos she had caused while looking for the book. A snatch of red caught her eye. Reaching for it, her fingers found a familiar shape. Jo hesitated, then drew the old doll out of the chest.

It was a sad piece of plastic and faded silk with its face nearly washed away. One arm was broken off, leaving an empty sleeve. The golden hair was straggled but brave under its red cap. Ballet shoes were painted on the dainty feet. Tears backed up behind Jo's eyes as she made a soft sound of joy and despair.

"What is it?" Keane demanded, glancing down to see her clutching the battered ballerina.

"Nothing." Her voice was unsteady as she scrambled quickly to her feet. "I have to go." Though she tried, Jo could not bring herself to drop the doll back into the box. She swallowed. She did not wish to reveal her emotions before his intelligent, gold eyes. Perhaps he would be cynical, or worse, amused. "May I have this, please?" She was careful with the tone of the request.

Slowly, Keane crossed the distance between them, then cradled her chin in his hand. "It appears to be yours already."

"It was." Her fingers tightened on the doll's waist. "I didn't know Frank had kept it. Please," she whispered. Her emotions were already dangerously heightened. She could feel a need to rest her head against his shoulder. The evening had been a roller coaster for her feelings, climaxing now with the discovery of her most prized childhood possession. She knew that if she did not escape, she would seek comfort in his arms. Her own weakness frightened her. "Let me by."

For a moment, Jo read refusal in his eyes. Then he stepped

aside. Jo let out a quiet, shaky breath. "I'll walk you back to your trailer."

"No," she said quickly, too quickly. "It isn't necessary," she amended, moving by him and into the kitchen. Sitting down, she pulled on her shoes, too distraught to remember she still wore his socks. "There's no reason for us both to get wet again." She rambled on, knowing he was watching her hurried movement, but unable to stop. "And I'm going to check on my cats before I go in, and . . ."

She stopped short when he took her shoulders and pulled her to her feet. "And you don't want to take the chance of being alone in your trailer with me in case I change my mind."

A sharp denial trembled on her lips, but the knowledge in his eyes crushed it. "All right," she admitted. "That, too."

Keane brushed her hair from her neck and shook his head. He kissed her nose and moved down to pluck her hat and coat from their hooks. Cautiously, Jo followed him. When he held out her coat, she turned and slipped her arms into the sleeves. Before she could murmur her thanks, he turned her back and pulled up the zipper. For a moment his fingers lingered at her neck, his eyes on hers. Taking her hair into his hand, he piled it atop her head, then dropped on her hat. The gestures were innocent, but Jo was rocked by a feeling of intimacy she had never experienced.

"I'll see you tomorrow," he said, pulling the brim of her hat down further over her eyes.

Jo nodded. Holding the doll against her side, she pushed open the door. The sound of rain was amplified through the trailer. "Good night," she murmured, then moved quickly into the night.

CHAPTER 5

The morning scent was clean. In the new lot rainbows glistened in puddles. At last the sky was blue with only harmless white puffs of clouds floating over its surface. In the cookhouse a loud, crowded breakfast was being served. Finding herself without appetite, Jo skipped going to the cookhouse altogether. She was restless and tense. No matter how she disciplined her mind, her thoughts wandered back to Keane Prescott and to the evening they had spent together. Jo remembered it all, from the quick passion of the kiss in the rain to the calmness of his voice when he had said good night. It was odd, she mused, that whenever she began to talk to him, she forgot he was the owner, forgot he was Frank's son. Always she was forced to remind herself of their positions.

Deep in thought, Jo slipped into tights and a leotard. It was true, she admitted, that she had failed to keep their relationship from becoming personal. She found it difficult to corral her urge to laugh with him, to share a joke, to open for him the doorway to the magic of the circus. If he could feel it, she thought, he would understand. Though she could admit her interest in him privately, she could not find a clear reason for his apparent interest in her.

Why me? she wondered with a shake of her head. Turning, she opened her wardrobe closet and studied herself in the full-length glass on the back of the door. There she saw a woman of slightly less-than-average height with a body lacking the generous curves of Duffy's showgirls. The legs, she decided, were not bad. They were long and well-shaped with slim thighs. The hips were narrow, more, she thought with a pout, like a boy's than a woman's; and the bustline was sadly inadequate. She knew many women in the troupe with more appeal and a dozen with more experience.

Jo could see nothing in the mirror that would attract a sophisticated Chicago attorney. She did not note the honesty that shone from her beautiful green eyes or the strength in her chin or the full promise of her mouth. She saw the touch of allure in the tawny complexion and raven hair but remained unaware of the appeal that came from the hint of something wild and untamed just under the surface. The plain black leotard showed her firm, lithe body to perfection, but Jo thought nothing of the smooth satiny sheen of her skin. She was frowning as she pulled her hair back and began to braid it.

He must know dozens of women, she thought as her hands worked to confine her thick mane of hair. He probably takes a different one to dinner every night. They wear beautiful clothes and expensive perfume, she mused, torturing herself with the thought. They have names like Laura and Patricia, and they have low, sophisticated laughs. Jo lifted a brow at the reflection in the mirror and gave a light, low laugh. She wrinkled her brow at the hollowness of the sound. They discuss mutual friends, the Wallaces or the Jamesons, over candlelight and Beaujolais. And when he takes the most beautiful one home, they listen to Chopin and drink brandy in front of the fire. Then they make love. Jo felt an odd tightening in her stomach but pursued the fantasy to the finish. The lovely lady is experienced, passionate and worldly. Her skin is soft. When he leaves, she is not devastated but mature. She doesn't even care if he loves her or not.

Jo stared at the woman in the glass and saw her cheeks were wet. On a cry of frustration, she slammed the door shut. *What's wrong with me?* she demanded, brushing all traces of tears from her face. *I haven't been myself for days! I need to shake myself out of this—this . . . whatever it is that I'm in.* Slipping on gymnastic shoes and tossing a robe over her arm, Jo hustled from the trailer.

She moved carefully, avoiding puddles and any further speculation on Keane Prescott's romantic life. Before she was halfway across the lot, she saw Rose. From the expression on her face, Jo could see she was in a temper.

"Hello, Rose," she said, strategically stepping aside as the snake charmer splashed through a puddle.

"He's hopeless," Rose tossed back. "I tell you," she continued, stopping and wagging a finger at Jo, "I'm through this time. Why should I waste my time?"

"You've certainly been patient," Jo agreed, deciding that sympathy was the wisest course. "It's more than he deserves."

"Patient?" Rose raised a dramatic hand to her breast. "I have the patience of a saint. Yet even a saint has her limits!" Rose tossed her hair behind her shoulders. She sighed heavily. "Adios. I think I hear Mama calling me."

Jo continued her walk toward the Big Top. Jamie walked by, his hands in his pockets. "She's crazy," he muttered. He stopped and spread his arms wide. His look was that of a man ill-used and innocent. Jo shrugged. Shaking his head, Jamie moved away. "She's crazy," he said again.

Jo watched him until he was out of sight, then darted to the Big Top.

Inside, Carmen watched adoringly while Vito practiced a new routine on the incline wire. The tent echoed with the sounds of rehearsals: voices and thumps, the rattle of rigging, the yapping of clown dogs. In the first ring Jo spotted the Six Beirots, an acrobatic act that was just beginning its warm-ups. Pleased with her timing, Jo walked the length of the arena. A raucous whistle sounded over her head, and she glanced up to shake a friendly fist at Vito. He called from fifteen feet above her as he balanced on a slender wire set at a forty-five-degree angle.

"Hey, chickie, you have a nice rear view. You're almost as cute as me."

"No one's as cute as you, Vito," she called back.

"Ah, I know." With a weighty sigh, he executed a neat pivot. "But I have learned to live with it." He sent down a lewd wink. "When you going into town with me, chickie?" he asked as he always did.

"When you teach my cats to walk the wire," Jo answered as she always did. Vito laughed and began a light-footed cha-cha. Carmen fired Jo a glare. She must have it bad, Jo decided, if she takes Vito's harmless flirting seriously. Stopping beside her, Jo leaned close and spoke in a conspirator's whisper. "He'd fall off his wire if I said I'd go."

"I'd go," Carmen said with a lovely pout, "if he'd just ask me."

Jo shook her head, wondering why romances were invariably complicated. She was lucky not to have the problem. Giving Carmen an encouraging pat on the shoulder, Jo set off toward the first ring.

*   *   *

The Six Beirots were brothers. They were all small-statured men who had immigrated from Belgium. Jo worked out with them often to keep herself limber and to keep her reflexes sharp. She liked them all, knew their wives and children, and understood their unique blending of

French and English. Raoul was the oldest, and the stockiest of the six brothers. Because of his build and strength, he was the under-stander in their human pyramid. It was he who spotted Jo and first lifted a hand in greeting.

"Halo." He grinned and ran his palm over his receding hairline. "You gonna tumble?"

Jo laughed and did a quick handspring into the ring. She stuck out her tongue when the unanimous critique was "sloppy." "I just need to warm up," she said, assuming an air of injured dignity. "My muscles need tuning."

For the next thirty minutes Jo worked with them, doing muscle stretches and limbering exercises, rib stretches and lung expanders. Her muscles warmed and loosened, her heart pumped steadily. She was filled with energy. Her mind was clear. Because of her lightened mood, Jo was easily cajoled into a few impromptu acrobatics. Leaving the more compli-cated feats to the experts, she did simple ts, handsprings or twists at Raoul's command. She did a brief, semisuccessful thirty seconds atop the rolling globe and earned catcalls from her comrades at her dismount.

She stood back as they began the leaps. One after another they lined up to take turns running along a ramp, bounding upon a springboard and flying up to do flips or twists before landing on the mat. There was a constant stream of French as they called out to each other.

"Hokay, Jo." Raoul gestured with his hand. "Your turn."

"Oh, no." She shook her head and reached for her robe. "Uh-uh." There was a chorus of coaxing, teasing French. "I've got to give my cats their vitamins," she told them, still shaking her head.

"Come on, Jo. It's fun." Raoul grinned and wiggled his eyebrows. "Don't you like to fly?" As she glanced at the ramp, Raoul knew she was tempted. "You take a good spring," he told her. "Do one forward somersault, then land on my shoul-ders." He patted them to show their ability to handle the job.

Jo smiled and nibbled pensively on her lower lip. It had been a long while since she had taken the time to go up on the trapeze and really fly. It did look like fun. She gave Raoul a stern look. "You'll catch me?"

"Raoul never misses," he said proudly, then turned to his brothers. *"N'est-ce pas?"* His brothers shrugged and rolled their eyes to the ceiling with indistinguishable mutters. "Ah." He waved them away with the back of his hand.

Knowing Raoul was indeed a top flight understander, Jo approached the ramp. Still she gave him one last narrow-eyed look. "You catch me," she ordered, shaking her finger at him.

"Cherie." He took his position with a stylish movement of his hand. "It's a piece of pie."

"Cake," Jo corrected, took a deep breath, held it and ran. When she came off the springboard, she tucked into the somersault and watched the Big Top turn upside down. She felt good. As the tent began to right itself, she straightened for her landing, keeping herself loose. Her feet connected with Raoul's powerful shoulders, and she tilted only briefly before he took her ankles in a firm grip. Straightening her poor posture, Jo styled elaborately with both arms while she received exaggerated applause and whistles. She leaped down nimbly as Raoul took her waist to give her landing bounce.

"When do you want to join the act?" he asked her, giving her a friendly pat on the bottom. "We'll put you up on the sway pole."

"That's okay." Grinning, Jo again reached for her robe. "I'll stick with the cats." After a cheerful wave, she slipped one arm into a sleeve and started back down the hippodrome track. She pulled up short when she spotted Keane leaning up against the front seat rail.

"Amazing," he said, then straightened to move to her. "But then, the circus is supposed to be amazing, isn't it?" He lifted the forgotten sleeve to her robe, then slipped her other arm into it. "Is there anything here you can't do?"

"Hundreds of things," Jo answered, taking him seriously. "I'm only really proficient with animals. The rest is just show and play."

"You looked amazingly proficient to me for the last half hour or so," he countered as he pulled out her braid from where it was trapped by her robe.

"Have you been here that long?"

"I walked in as Vito was commenting on your rear view."

"Oh." Jo laughed, glancing back to where Vito now stood flirting with Carmen. "He's crazy."

"Perhaps," Keane agreed, taking her arm. "But his eyesight's good enough. Would you like some coffee?"

Jo was reminded instantly of the evening before. Leery of being drawn to his charms again, she shook her head. "I've got to change," she told him, belting her robe. "We've got a show at two. I want to rehearse the cats."

"It's incredible how much time you people devote to your art. Rehearsals seem to run into the beginning of a show, and a show seems to run into more rehearsals."

Jo softened when he referred to circus skills as art. "Performers always look for just a bit more in themselves. It's a constant struggle for perfection. Even when a performance goes beautifully and you know it, you start thinking about the next time. How can I do it better or bigger or higher or faster?"

"Never satisfied?" Keane asked as they stepped out into the sunlight.

"If we were, we wouldn't have much of a reason to come back and do it all over again."

He nodded, but there was something absent in the gesture, as if his mind was elsewhere. "I have to leave this afternoon," he said almost to himself.

"Leave?" Jo's heart skidded to a stop. Her distress was overwhelming and so unexpected that she was forced to take an extra moment to steady herself. "Back to Chicago?"

"Hmm?" Keane stopped, turning to face her. "Oh, yes."

"And the circus?" Jo asked, thoroughly ashamed that it had not been her first concern. She didn't want him to leave, she suddenly realized.

Keane frowned a moment, then continued to walk. "I see no purpose in disrupting this year's schedule." His voice was brisk now and businesslike.

"This year's?" Jo repeated cautiously.

Keane turned and looked at her. "I haven't decided its ultimate fate, but I won't do anything until the end of the summer."

"I see." She let out a long breath. "So we have a reprieve."

"In a manner of speaking," Keane agreed.

Jo was silent for a moment but could not prevent herself from asking, "Then you won't—I mean, you'll be staying in Chicago now. You won't be traveling with us?"

They negotiated their way around a puddle before Keane answered. "I don't feel I can make a judicious decision about the circus after so brief an exposure. There's a complication in one of my cases that needs my personal attention, but I should be back in a week or two."

Relief flooded through her. He would be back, a voice shouted in her ear. *It shouldn't matter to you,* another whispered. "We'll be in South Carolina in a couple of weeks," Jo said casually. They had reached her trailer, and she took the handle of her door before she turned to face him. *It's just that I want him to understand what this circus means,* she told herself as she looked up into his eyes. *That's the only reason I want him to come back.* Knowing she was lying to herself made it difficult to keep her gaze steady.

Keane smiled, letting his eyes travel over her face. "Yes, Duffy's given me a route list. I'll find you. Aren't you going to ask me in?"

"In?" Jo repeated. "Oh, no, I told you, I have to change, and . . ." He stepped forward as she talked. Something in his eyes told her a firm stand was necessary. She had seen a similar look in a lion's eyes while he contemplated taking a dangerous liberty. "I simply don't have time right now. If I don't see you before you go, have a good trip." She turned and opened the door. Aware of a movement, she turned back, but not before he had nudged her through the door and followed. As it closed at his back, Jo bristled with fury. She did not enjoy being outmaneuvered. "Tell me, Counselor, do you know anything about a law concerning breaking and entering?"

"Doesn't apply," he returned smoothly. "There was no lock involved." He glanced around at the attractive simplicity of Jo's trailer. The colors were restful earth tones without frills. The beige-and-brown-flecked linoleum floor was spotlessly clean. It was the same basic floor-plan as Frank's trailer, but here there were softer touches. There were curtains rather than shades at the windows; large, comfortable pillows tossed onto a forest green sofa; a spray of fresh wildflowers tucked into a thin, glass vase. Without comment Keane wandered to a black lacquer trunk that sat directly opposite the door. On it was a book that he picked up while Jo fumed. "'The Count of Monte Cristo,'" he read aloud and flipped it open. "In French," he stated, lifting a brow.

"It was written in French," Jo muttered, pulling it from his hand. "So I read it in French." Annoyed, she lifted the lid on the trunk, preparing to drop the book inside and out of his reach.

"Good heavens, are those all yours?" Keane stopped the lid on its downswing, then pushed books around with his other hand. "Tolstoy, Cervantes, Voltaire, Steinbeck. When do you have time in this crazy, twenty-four-hour world you live in to read this stuff?"

"I make time," Jo snapped as her eyes sparked. "My *own* time. Just because you're the owner doesn't mean you can barge in here and poke through my things and demand an account of my time. This is my trailer. I own everything in it."

"Hold on." Keane halted her rushing stream of words. "I wasn't demanding an account of your time, I was simply astonished that you could find enough of it to do this type of reading. Since I can't claim to be an expert on your work, it would be remarkably foolish of me to criticize the amount of time you spend on it. Second," he said, taking a step toward her—and though Jo stiffened in anticipation, he did not touch her, "I apologize for 'poking through your things,' as you put it. I was interested for several reasons. One being I have quite an extensive library myself. It seems we have a common interest, whether we like it or not. As for barging into your trailer, I can only plead guilty. If you choose to prosecute, I can recommend a couple of lousy attorneys who overcharge."

His last comment forced a smile onto Jo's reluctant lips. "I'll give it some thought." With more care than she had originally intended, Jo lowered the lid of the trunk. She was reminded that she had not been gracious. "I'm sorry," she said as she turned back to him.

His eyes reflected curiosity. "What for?"

"For snapping at you." She lifted her shoulders, then let them fall. "I thought you were criticizing me. I suppose I'm too sensitive."

Several seconds passed before he spoke. "Unnecessary apology accepted if you answer one question."

Mystified, Jo frowned at him. "What question?"

"Is the Tolstoy in Russian?"

Jo laughed, pushing loose strands of hair from her face. "Yes, it is."

Keane smiled, enjoying the two tiny dimples that flickered in her cheeks when she laughed. "Did you know that though you're lovely in any case, you grow even more so when you smile?"

Jo's laughter stilled. She was unaccustomed to this sort of compliment and studied him without any idea of how to respond. It occurred to her that any of the sophisticated women she had imagined that morning would have known precisely what to say. She would have been able to smile or laugh as she tossed back the appropriate comment. That woman, Jo admitted, was not Jovilette Wilder. Gravely, she kept her eyes on his. "I don't know how to flirt," she said simply.

Keane tilted his head, and an expression came and went in his eyes before she could analyze it. He stepped toward her. "I wasn't flirting with you, Jo, I was making an observation. Hasn't anyone ever told you that you're beautiful?"

He was much too close now, but in the narrow confines of the trailer, Jo had little room to maneuver. She was forced to tilt back her head to keep her eyes level with his. "Not precisely the way you did." Quickly, she put her hand to his chest to keep the slight but important distance between them. She knew she was trapped, but that did not mean she was defeated.

Gently, Keane lifted her protesting hand, turning it palm up as he brought it to his lips. An involuntary breath rushed in and out of Jo's lungs. "Your hands are exquisite," he murmured, tracing the fine line of blue up the back. "Narrow-boned, long-fingered. And the palms show hard work. That makes them more interesting." He lifted his eyes from her hand to her face. "Like you."

Jo's voice had grown husky, but she could do nothing to alter it. "I don't know what I'm supposed to say when you tell me things like that." Beneath her robe her breasts rose and fell with her quickening heart. "I'd rather you didn't."

"Do you really?" Keane ran the back of his hand along her jawline. "That's a pity, because the more I look at you, the more I find to say. You're a bewitching creature, Jovilette."

"I have to change," she said in the firmest voice she could muster. "You'll have to go."

"That's unfortunately true," he murmured, then cupped her chin. "Come, then, kiss me goodbye."

Jo stiffened. "I hardly think that's necessary . . ."

"You couldn't be more wrong," he told her as he lowered his mouth. "It's extremely necessary." In a light, teasing whisper, his lips met hers. His arms encircled her, bringing her closer with only the slightest pressure. "Kiss me back, Jo," he ordered softly. "Put your arms around me and kiss me back."

For a moment longer she resisted, but the lure of his mouth nibbling at hers was too strong. Letting instinct rule her will, Jo lifted her arms and circled his neck. Her mouth grew mobile under his, parting and offering. Her surrender seemed to lick the flames of his passion. The kiss grew urgent. His arms locked, crushing her against him. Her quiet moan was not of protest but of wonder. Her fingers found their way into his hair, tangling in its thickness as they urged him closer. She felt her robe loosen, then his hands trail up her rib cage. At his touch, she shivered, feeling her skin grow hot, then cold, then hot again in rapid succession.

When his hand took her breast, she shied, drawing in her breath quickly. "Steady," he murmured against her mouth. His hands stroked gently, coaxing her to relax again. He kissed the corners of her mouth, waiting until she quieted before he took her deep again. The thin leotard molded her body. It created no barrier against the warmth of his searching fingers. They moved slowly, lingering over the peak of her breast, exploring its softness, wandering to her waist, then tracing her hip and thigh.

No man had ever touched her so freely. Jo was helpless to stop him, helpless against her own growing need for him to touch her again. Was this the passion she had read of so often? The passion that drove men to war, to struggle against all reason, to risk everything? She felt she could understand it now. She clung to him as he taught her—as she learned—the demands of her own body. Her mouth grew hungrier for the taste of him. She was certain she remained in his arms while seasons flew by, while decades passed, while worlds were destroyed and built again.

But when he drew away, Jo saw the same sun spilling through her windows. Eternity had only been moments.

Unable to speak, she merely stared up at him. Her eyes were dark and aware, her cheeks flushed with desire. But somehow, though it still tingled from his, her mouth maintained a youthful innocence. Keane's eyes dropped to it as his hands loitered at the small of her back.

"It's difficult to believe I'm the first man to touch you," he murmured. His eyes roamed to hers. "And quite desperately arousing. Particularly when I find you've passion to match your looks. I think I'd like to make love with you in the daylight first so that I can watch that marvelous control of yours slip away layer by layer. We'll have to discuss it when I get back."

Jo forced strength back into her limbs, knowing she was on the brink of losing her will to him. "Just because I let you kiss me and touch me doesn't mean I'll let you make love to me." She lifted her chin, feeling her confidence surging back. "If I do, it'll be because it's what I want, not because you tell me to."

The expression in Keane's eyes altered. "Fair enough," he agreed and nodded. "It'll simply be my job to make it what you want." He took her chin in his hand and lowered his mouth to hers for a brief kiss. As she had the first time, Jo kept her eyes open and watched him. She felt him grin against her mouth before he raised his head. "You are the most fascinating woman I've ever met." Turning, he crossed to the door. "I'll be back," he said with a careless wave before it closed behind him. Dumbly, Jo stared into empty space.

Fascinating? she repeated, tracing her still-warm lips with her fingertips. Quickly, she ran to the window, and kneeling on the sofa below it, watched Keane stride away.

She realized with a sudden jolt that she missed him already.

CHAPTER 6

Jo learned that weeks could drag like years. During the second week of Keane's absence she had searched each new lot for a sign of him. She had scanned the crowds of towners who came to watch the raising of the Big Top, and as the days stretched on and on, she balanced between anger and despair at his continued absence. Only in the cage did she manage to isolate her concentration, knowing she could not afford to do otherwise. But after each performance Jo found it more and more difficult to relax. Each morning she felt certain he would be back. Each night she lay restless, waiting for the sun to rise.

Spring was in full bloom. The high grass lots smelled of it. Often there were wildflowers crushed underfoot, leaving their heavy fragrances in the air. Even as the circus caravan traveled north, the days grew warm, sunlight lingering further into evening. While other troupers enjoyed the balmy air and providentially sunny skies, Jo lived on nerves.

It occurred to her that after returning to his life in Chicago, Keane had decided against coming back. In Chicago he had comfort and wealth and elegant women. Why should he come back? Jo closed her mind against the ultimate fate of the circus, unwilling to face the possibility that Keane might close the show at the end of the season. She told herself the only reason she wanted him to come back was to convince him to keep the circus open. But the memory of being in his arms intruded too often into her thoughts. Gradually, she grew resigned, filling the strange void she felt with her work.

Several times each week she found time to give the eager Gerry more training. At first she had only permitted him to work with the two menagerie cubs, allowing him, with the protection of leather gloves, to play with them and to feed them. She encouraged him to teach them simple tricks with the aid of small pieces of raw meat. Jo was as pleased as he when the cats responded to his patience and obeyed.

Jo saw potential in Gerry, in his genuine affection for animals and in his determination. Her primary concern was that he had not yet developed a healthy fear. He was still too casual, and with casualness, Jo knew, came carelessness. When she thought he had progressed far enough, Jo decided to take him to the next step of his training.

* * *

There was no matinee that day, and the Big Top was scattered with rehearsing troupers. Jo was dressed in boots and khakis with a long-sleeved blouse tucked into the waist. She studied Gerry as she ran the stock of her whip through her hand. They stood together in the safety cage while she issued instructions.

"All right, Buck's going to let Merlin through the chute. He's the most tractable of the cats, except for Ari." She paused a moment while her eyes grew sad. "Ari isn't up to even a short practice session." She pushed away the depression that threatened and continued. "Merlin knows you, he's familiar with your voice and your scent." Gerry nodded and swallowed. "When we go in, you're to be my shadow. You move when I move, and don't speak until I tell you. If you get frightened, don't run." Jo took his arm for emphasis. "That's *important,* understand? Don't run. Tell me if you want out, and I'll get you to the safety cage."

"I won't run, Jo," he promised and wiped hands, damp with excitement, on his jeans.

"Are you ready?"

Gerry grinned and nodded. "Yeah."

Jo opened the door leading to the big cage and let Gerry through behind her before securing it. She walked to the center of the arena in easy, confident strides. "Let him in, Buck," she called and heard the immediate rattle of bars. Merlin entered without hurry, then leaped onto his pedestal. He yawned hugely before looking at Jo. "A solo today, Merlin," she said as she advanced toward him. "And you're the star. Stay with me," she ordered as Gerry merely stood still and stared at the big cat. Merlin gave Gerry a disinterested glance and waited.

With an upward move of her arm, she sent Merlin into a sit-up. "You know," she told the boy behind her, "that teaching a cat to take his seat is the first trick. The audience won't even consider it one. The sit-up," she continued while signaling Merlin to bring his front paws back down, "is usually next and takes quite a bit of time. It's necessary to strengthen the cat's back muscles first." Again she signaled Merlin to sit up, then, with a quick command, she had him pawing the air and roaring. "Marvelous old ham," she said with a grin and brought him back down. "The primary move of each cue is always given from the same position with the same tone of voice. It takes patience and repetition. I'm going to bring him down off the pedestal now."

Jo flicked the whip against the tanbark, and Merlin leaped down. "Now I maneuver him to the spot in the arena where I want him to lie down." As she moved, Jo made certain her student moved with her. "The cage is a circle, forty feet in diameter. You have to know every inch of it inside your head. You have to know precisely how far you are from the bars at all times. If you back up into the bars, you've got no room to maneuver if there's trouble. It's one of the biggest mistakes a trainer can make." At her signal Merlin laid down, then shifted to his side. "Over, Merlin," she said briskly, sending him into a series of rolls. "Use their names often—it keeps them in tune with you. You have to know each cat and their individual tendencies."

Jo moved with Merlin, then signaled him to stop. When he roared, she rubbed the top of his head with the stock of her whip. "They like to be petted just like house cats, but they are not tabbies. It's essential that you never give them your complete trust and that you remember always to maintain your dominance. You subjugate not by poking them or beating or shouting, which is not only cruel but makes for a mean, undependable cat, but with patience, respect and will. Never humiliate them. They have a right to their pride. You bluff them, Gerry," she said as she raised both arms and brought Merlin up on his hind legs. "Man is the unknown factor. That's why we use jungle-bred rather than captivity-bred cats. Ari is the exception. A cat born and raised in captivity is too familiar with man, so you lose your edge." She moved forward, keeping her arms raised. Merlin followed, walking on his hind legs. He spread seven feet into the air and towered over his trainer. "They might have a sense of affection for you, but there's no fear and little respect. Unfortunately, this often happens if a cat's been with a trainer a long time. They don't become more docile the longer they're in an act, but they become more dangerous. They test you constantly. The trick is to make them believe you're indestructible."

She brought Merlin down, and he gave another yawn before she sent him back to his seat. "If one swipes at you, you have to stop it then and there, because they try again and again, getting closer each time. Usually, if a trainer's hurt in the cage, it's because he's made a mistake. The cats are quick to spot them. Sometimes they let them pass, sometimes they

don't. This one's given me a good smack on the shoulder now
and again. He's kept his claws retracted, but there's always
the possibility that one time he'll forget he's just playing. Any
questions?"

"Hundreds," Gerry answered, wiping his mouth with the
back of his hand. "I just can't focus on one right now."

Jo chuckled and again scratched Merlin's head when he
roared. "They'll come to you later. It's hard to absorb anything the first time, but it'll come back to you when you're
relaxed again. All right, you know the cue. Make him sit up."

"Me?"

Jo stepped to the side, giving Merlin a clear view of her
student. "You can be as scared as you like," she said easily.
"Just don't let it show in your voice. Watch his eyes."

Gerry rubbed his palm on the thighs of his jeans, then
lifted it as he had seen Jo do hundreds of times. "Up," he told
the cat in a passably firm voice.

Merlin studied him a moment, then looked at Jo. This,
his eyes told her clearly, was an amateur and beneath his notice. Carefully, Jo kept her face expressionless. "He's testing
you," she told Gerry. "He's an old hand and a bit harder to
bluff. Be firm and use his name this time."

Gerry took a deep breath and repeated the hand signal.
"Up, Merlin."

Merlin glanced back at him, then stared with measuring,
amber eyes. "Again," Jo instructed and heard Gerry swallow audibly. "Put some authority into your voice. He thinks
you're a pushover."

"Up, Merlin!" Gerry repeated, annoyed enough by Jo's description to put some dominance into his voice. Though his
reluctance was obvious, Merlin obeyed. "He did it," Gerry
whispered on a long, shaky breath. "He really did it."

"Very good," Jo said, pleased with both the lion and her
student. "Now bring him down." When this was accomplished, Jo had him bring Merlin from the seat. "Here." She

handed Gerry the whip. "Use the stock to scratch his head. He likes it best just behind the ear." She felt the faint tremble in his hand as he took the whip, but he held it steady, even as Merlin closed his eyes and roared.

Because he had performed well, Jo afforded Merlin the liberty of rubbing against her legs before she called for Buck to let him out. The rattle of the bars was the cat's cue to exit, and like a trouper, he took it with his head held high. "You did very well," she told Gerry when they were alone in the cage.

"It was great." He handed her back the whip, the stock damp from his sweaty palms. "It was just great. When can I do it again?"

Jo smiled and patted his shoulder. "Soon," she promised. "Just remember the things I've told you and come to me when you remember all those questions."

"Okay, thanks, Jo." He stepped through the safety cage. "Thanks a lot. I want to go tell the guys."

"Go ahead." Jo watched him scramble away, leaping over the ring and darting through the back door. With a grin, she leaned against the bars. "Was I like that?" she asked Buck, who stood at the opposite end of the cage.

"The first time you got a cat to sit up on your own, we heard about it for a week. Twelve years old and you thought you were ready for the big show."

Jo laughed, and wiping the damp stock of her whip against her pants, turned. It was then she saw him standing behind her. "Keane!" She used the name she had sworn not to use as pleasure flooded through her. It shone on her face. Just as she had given up hope of seeing him again, he was there. She took two steps toward him before she could check herself. "I didn't know you were back." Jo gripped the stock of the whip with both hands to prevent herself from reaching out to touch him.

"I believe you missed me." His voice was as she remembered, low and smooth.

Jo cursed herself for being so naive and transparent. "Perhaps I did, a little," she admitted cautiously. "I suppose I'd gotten used to you, and you were gone longer than you said you'd be." He looks the same, she thought rapidly, exactly the same. She reminded herself that it had only been a month. It had seemed like years.

"*Mmm,* yes. I had more to see to than I had expected. You look a bit pale," he observed and touched her cheek with his fingertip.

"I suppose I haven't been getting much sun," she said with quick prevarication. "How was Chicago?" Jo needed to turn the conversation away from personal lines until she had an opportunity to gauge her emotions; seeing him suddenly had tossed them into confusion.

"Cool," he told her, making a long, thorough survey of her face. "Have you ever been there?"

"No. We play near there toward the end of the season, but I've never had time to go all the way into the city."

Nodding absently, Keane glanced into the empty cage behind her. "I see you're training Gerry."

"Yes." Relieved that they had lapsed into a professional discussion, Jo let the muscles of her shoulders ease. "This was the first time with an adult cat and no bars between. He did very well."

Keane looked back at her. His eyes were serious and probing. "He was trembling. I could see it from where I stood watching you."

"It was his first time—" she began in Gerry's defense.

"I wasn't criticizing him," Keane interrupted with a tinge of impatience. "It's just that he stood beside you, shaking from head to foot, and you were totally cool and in complete control."

"It's my job to be in control," Jo reminded him.

"That lion must have stood seven feet tall when he went

up on his hind legs, and you walked under him without any protection, not even the traditional chair."

"I do a picture act," she explained, "not a fighting act."

"Jo," he said so sharply she blinked. "Aren't you ever frightened in there?"

"Frightened?" she repeated, lifting a brow. "Of course I'm frightened. More frightened than Gerry was—or than you would be."

"What are you talking about?" Keane demanded. Jo noted with some curiosity that he was angry. "I could see that boy sweat in there."

"That was mostly excitement," Jo told him patiently. "He hasn't the experience to be truly frightened yet." She tossed back her hair and let out a long breath. Jo did not like to talk of her fears with anyone and found it especially difficult with Keane. Only because she felt it necessary that he understand this to understand the circus did she continue. "Real fear comes from knowing them, working with them, understanding them. You can only speculate on what they can do to a man. I *know*. I know exactly what they're capable of. They have an incredible courage, but more, they have an incredible guile. I've seen what they can do." Her eyes were calm and clear as they looked into his. "My father almost lost a leg once. I was about five, but I remember it perfectly. He made a mistake, and a five-hundred-pound Nubian sunk into his thigh and dragged him around the arena. Luckily, the cat was diverted by a female in season. Cats are unpredictable when they have sex on their minds, which is probably one of the reasons he attacked my father in the first place. They're fiercely jealous once they've set their minds on a mate. My father was able to get into the safety cage before any of the other cats took an interest in him. I can't remember how many stitches he had or how long it was before he could walk properly again, but I do remember the look in that cat's eyes. You learn quickly about fear when you're in the cage, but you control it, you channel it or you find another line of work."

"Then why?" Keane demanded. He took her shoulders before she could turn away. "Why do you do it? And don't tell me because it's your job. That's not good enough."

It puzzled Jo why he seemed angry. His eyes were darkened with temper, and his fingers dug into her shoulders. As if wanting to draw out her answer, he gave her one quick shake. "All right," Jo said slowly, ignoring the ache in her flesh. "That is part of it, but not all. It's all I've ever known, that's part of it, too. It's what I'm good at." While she spoke, she searched his face for a clue to his mood. She wondered if perhaps he had felt it wrong of her to take Gerry into the cage. "Gerry's going to be good at it, too," she told him. "I imagine everyone needs to be good—really good—at something. And I enjoy giving the people who come to see me the best show I can. But over all, I suppose it's because I love them. It's difficult for a layman to understand a trainer's feeling for his animals. I love their intelligence, their really awesome beauty, their strength, the unquenchable streak of wildness that separates them from well-trained horses. They're exciting, challenging and terrifying."

Keane was silent for a moment. She saw that his eyes were still angry, but his fingers relaxed on her shoulders. "I suppose excitement becomes addicting—difficult to live without once it's become a habit."

"I don't know," Jo replied, grateful that his temper was apparently cooling. "I've never thought about it."

"No, I suppose you'd have little reason to." With a nod, he turned to walk away.

Jo took a step after him. "Keane." His name raced through her lips before she could prevent it. When he turned back to her, she realized she could not ask any of the dozens of questions that flew through her mind. There was only one she felt she had any right to ask. "Have you thought any more about what you're going to do with us . . . with the circus?"

For an instant she saw temper flare again into his eyes. "No." The word was curt and final. As he turned his back on her again, she felt a spurt of anger and reached for his arm.

"How can you be so callous, so unfeeling?" she demanded. "How is it possible to be so casual when you hold the lives of over a hundred people in your hands?"

Carefully, he removed her hand from his arm. "Don't push me, Jo." There was warning in his eyes and in his voice.

"I'm not trying to," she returned, then ran a frustrated hand through her hair. "I'm only asking you to be fair, to be . . . kind," she finished lamely.

"Don't ask me anything," he ordered in a brisk, authoritative tone. Jo's chin rose in response. "I'm here," he reminded her. "You'll have to be satisfied with that for now."

Jo battled with her temper. She could not deny that in coming back he had proved himself true to his word. She had the rest of the season if nothing else. "I don't suppose I have any choice," she said quietly.

"No," he agreed with a faint nod. "You don't."

Frowning, Jo watched him stride away in a smooth, fluid gait she was forced to admire. She noticed for the first time that her palms were as damp as Gerry's had been. Annoyed, she rubbed them over her hips.

"Want to talk about it?"

Jo turned quickly to find Jamie behind her in full clown gear. She knew her preoccupation had been deep for her to be caught so completely unaware. "Oh, Jamie, I didn't see you."

"You haven't seen anything but Prescott since you stepped out of the cage," Jamie pointed out.

"What are you doing in makeup?" she asked, skirting his comment.

He gestured toward the dog at her feet. "This mutt won't

respond to me unless I'm in my face. Do you want to talk about it?"

"Talk about what?"

"About Prescott, about the way you feel about him."

The dog sat patiently at Jamie's heels and thumped his tail. Casually, Jo stopped and ruffled his gray fur.

"I don't know what you're talking about."

"Look, I'm not saying it can't work out, but I don't want to see you get hurt. I know how it is to be nuts about somebody."

"What in the world makes you think I'm nuts about Keane Prescott?" Jo gave the dog her full attention.

"Hey, it's me, remember?" Jamie took her arm and pulled her to her feet. "Not everybody would've noticed, maybe, but not everybody knows you the way I do. You've been miserable since he went back to Chicago, looking for him in every car that drove on the lot. And just now, when you saw him, you lit up like the midway on Saturday night. I'm not saying there's anything wrong with you being in love with him, but—"

"In love with him?" Jo repeated, incredulous.

"Yeah." Jamie spoke patiently. "In love with him."

Jo stared at Jamie as the realization slid over her. "In love with him," she murmured, trying out the words. "Oh, no." She sighed, closing her eyes. "Oh, no."

"Didn't you have enough sense to figure it out for yourself?" Jamie said gently. Seeing Jo's distress, he ran a hand gently up her arm.

"No, I guess I'm pretty stupid about this sort of thing." Jo opened her eyes and looked around, wondering if the world should look any different. "What am I going to do?"

"Heck, I don't know." Jamie kicked sawdust with an oversize shoe. "I'm not exactly getting rave notices myself in that department." He gave Jo a reassuring pat. "I just wanted you to know that you always have a sympathetic ear here." He grinned engagingly before he turned to walk away, leaving Jo distracted and confused.

* * *

Jo spent the rest of the afternoon absorbed with the idea of being in love with Keane Prescott. For a short time she allowed herself to enjoy the sensation, the novel experience of loving someone not as a friend but as a lover. She could feel the light and the power spread through her, as if she had caught the sun in her hand. She daydreamed.

Keane was in love with her. He'd told her hundreds of times as he'd held her under a moonlit sky. He wanted to marry her, he couldn't bear to live without her. She was suddenly sophisticated and worldly enough to deal with the country club set on their own ground. She could exchange droll stories with the wives of other attorneys. There would be children and a house in the country. How would it feel to wake up in the same town every morning? She would learn to cook and give dinner parties. There would be long, quiet evenings when they would be alone together. There would be candlelight and music. When they slept together, his arms would stay around her until morning.

Idiot. Jo dragged herself back sternly. As she and Pete fed the cats, she tried to remember that fairy tales were for children. None of those things are ever going to happen, she reminded herself. I have to figure out how to handle this before I get in any deeper.

"Pete," she began, keeping her voice conversational as she put Abra's quota of raw meat on a long stick. "Have you ever been in love?"

Pete chewed his gum gently, watching Jo hoist the meat through the bars. "Well, now, let's see." Thrusting out his lower lip, he considered. "Only 'bout eight or ten times, I guess. Maybe twelve."

Jo laughed, moving down to the next cage. "I'm serious," she told him. "I mean *really* in love."

"I fall in love easy," Pete confessed gravely. "I'm a pushover for a pretty face. Matter of fact, I'm a pushover for an ugly face." He grinned. "Yes, sir, the only thing like being in love is drawing an ace-high flush when the pot's ripe."

Jo shook her head and continued down the line. "Okay, since you're such an expert, tell me what you do when you're in love with a person and the person doesn't love you back and you don't want that person to know that you're in love because you don't want to make a fool of yourself."

"Just a minute." Pete squeezed his eyes tight. "I got to think this one through first." For a moment he was silent as his lips moved with his thoughts. "Okay, let's see if I've got this straight." Opening his eyes, he frowned in concentration. "You're in love—"

"I didn't say *I* was in love," Jo interrupted hastily.

Pete lifted his brows and pursed his lips. "Let's just use *you* in the general sense to avoid confusion," he suggested. Jo nodded, pretending to absorb herself with the feeding of the cats. "So, you're in love, but the guy doesn't love you. First off, you've got to be sure he doesn't."

"He doesn't," Jo murmured, then added quickly, "Let's say he doesn't."

Pete shot her a look out of the corner of his eye, then shifted his gum to the other side of his mouth. "Okay, then the first thing you should do is change his mind."

"Change his mind?" Jo repeated, frowning at him.

"Sure." Pete gestured with his hand to show the simplicity of the procedure. "You fall in love with him, then he falls in love with you. You play hard to get, or you play easy to get. Or you play flutter and smile." He demonstrated by coyly batting his lashes and giving a winsome smile. Jo giggled and leaned on the feeding pole. Pete in fielder's cap, white

T-shirt and faded jeans was the best show she'd seen all day. "You make him jealous," he continued. "Or you flatter his ego. Girl, there're so many ways to get a man, I can't count them, and I've been gotten by them all. Yes, sir, I'm a real pushover." He looked so pleased with his weakness, Jo smiled. *How easy it would be,* she thought, *if I could take love so lightly.*

"Suppose I don't want to do any of those things. Suppose I don't really know how and I don't want to humiliate myself by making a mess of it. Suppose the person isn't—well, suppose nothing could ever work between us, anyway. What then?"

"You got too many supposes," Pete concluded, then shook his finger at her. "And I got one for you. Suppose you ain't too smart because you figure you can't win even before you play."

"Sometimes people get hurt when they play," Jo countered quietly. "Especially if they aren't familiar with the game."

"Hurting's nothing," Pete stated with a sweep of his hand. "Winning's the best, but playing's just fine. This whole big life, it's a game, Jo. You know that. And the rules keep changing all the time. You've got nerve," he continued, then laid his rough, brown hand on her shoulder. "More raw nerve than most anybody I've ever known. You've got brains, too, hungry brains. You going to tell me that with all that, you're afraid to take a chance?"

Meeting his eyes, Jo knew hypothetical evasions would not do. "I suppose I only take calculated risks, Pete. I know my turf, I know my moves. And I know exactly what'll happen if I make a mistake. I take a chance that my body might be clawed, not my emotions. I've never rehearsed for anything like this, and I think playing it cold would be suicide."

"I think you've got to believe in Jo Wilder a little more," Pete countered, then gave her cheek a quick pat.

"Hey, Jo." Looking over, Jo saw Rose approaching. She wore straight-leg jeans, a white peasant blouse and a six-foot boa constrictor over her shoulders.

"Hello, Rose." Jo handed Pete the feeding pole. "Taking Baby out for a walk?"

"He needed some air." Rose gave her charge a pat. "I think he got a little carsick this morning. Does he look peaked to you?"

Jo looked down at the shiny, multicolored skin, then studied the tiny black eyes as Rose held Baby's head up for inspection. "I don't think so," she decided.

"Well, it's a warm day," Rose observed, releasing Baby's head. "I'll give him a bath. That might perk him up."

Jo noticed Rose's eyes darting around the compound. "Looking for Jamie?"

"Hmph." Rose tossed her black curls. "I'm not wasting my time on that one." She stroked the latter half of Baby's anatomy. "I'm indifferent."

"That's another way to do it," Pete put in, giving Jo a nudge. "I forgot about that one. It's a zinger."

Rose frowned at Pete, then at Jo. "What's he talking about?"

With a laugh, Jo sat down on a water barrel. "Catching a man," she told her, letting the warm sun play on her face. "Pete's done a study on it from the male point of view."

"Oh." Rose threw Pete her most disdainful look. "You think I'm indifferent so he'll get interested?"

"It's a zinger," Pete repeated, adjusting his cap. "You get him confused so he starts thinking about you. You make him crazy wondering why you don't notice him."

Rose considered the idea. "Does it usually work?"

"It's got an eighty-seven percent success average," Pete assured her, then gave Baby a friendly pat. "It even works with cats." He jerked his thumb behind him and winked at Jo. "The pretty lady cat, she sits there and stares off into space like she's got important things occupying her mind. The boy in the next cage is doing everything but standing on his head to get her attention. She just gives herself a wash, pretending she doesn't even know he's there. Then, maybe after she's got him banging his head against the bars, she looks over, blinks her big yellow eyes and says, 'Oh, were you talking to me?'" Pete laughed and stretched his back muscles. "He's hooked then, brother, just like a fish on a line."

Rose smiled at the image of Jamie dangling from her own personal line. "Maybe I won't put Baby in Carmen's trailer after all," she murmured. "Oh, look, here comes Duffy and the owner." An inherent flirt, Rose instinctively fluffed her hair. "Really, he is the most handsome man. Don't you think so, Jo?"

Jo's eyes had already locked on Keane's. She seemed helpless to release herself from the gaze. Gripping the edge of the water barrel tightly, she reminded herself not to be a fool. "Yes," she agreed with studied casualness. "He's very attractive."

"Your knuckles are turning white, Jo," Pete muttered next to her ear.

Letting out a frustrated breath, Jo relaxed her hands. Straightening her spine, she determined to show more restraint. Control, she reminded herself, was the basic tool of her trade. If she could train her emotions and outbluff a dozen lions, she could certainly outbluff one man.

"Hello, Duffy." Rose gave the portly man a quick smile, then turned her attention to Keane. "Hello, Mr. Prescott. It's nice to have you back."

"Hello, Rose." He smiled into her upturned face, then lifted a brow as his eyes slid over the reptile around her neck and shoulders. "Who's your friend?"

"Oh, this is Baby." She patted one of the tan-colored saddle marks on Baby's back.

"Of course." Jo noticed how humor enhanced the gold of

his eyes. "Hello, Pete." He gave the handler an easy nod before his gaze shifted and then lingered on Jo.

As on the first day they had met, Keane did not bother to camouflage his stare. His look was cool and assessing. He was reaffirming ownership. It shot through Jo that yes, she was in love with him, but she was also afraid of him. She feared his power over her, feared his capacity to hurt her. Still, her face registered none of her thoughts. Fear, she reminded herself as her eyes remained equally cool on his, was something she understood. Love might cause impossible problems, but fear could be dealt with. She would not cower from him, and she would honor the foremost rule of the arena. She would not turn and run.

Silently, they watched each other while the others looked on with varying degrees of curiosity. There was the barest touch of a smile on Keane's lips. The battle of wills continued until Duffy cleared his throat.

"Ah, Jo."

Calmly, without hurry, she shifted her attention. "Yes, Duffy?"

"I just sent one of the web girls into town to see the local dentist. Seems she's got an abscess. I need you to fill in tonight."

"Sure."

"Just for the web and the opening spectacular," he continued. Unable to prevent himself, he cast a quick look at Keane to see if he was still staring at her. He was. Duffy shifted uncomfortably and wondered what the devil was going on. "Take your usual place in the finale. We'll just be one girl shy in the chorus. Wardrobe'll fix you up."

"Okay." Jo smiled at him, though she was very much aware of Keane's eyes on her. "I guess I'd better go practice walking in those three-inch heels. What position do I take?"

"Number four rope."

"Duffy," Rose chimed in and tugged on his sleeve. "When are you going to let me do the web?"

"Rose, how's a pint-sizer like you going to stand up with that heavy costume on?" Duffy shook his head at her, keeping a respectable distance from Baby. After thirty-five years of working carnies, sideshows and circuses, he still was uneasy around snakes.

"I'm pretty strong," Rose claimed, stretching her spine in the hope of looking taller. "And I've been practicing." Anxious to demonstrate her accomplishments, Rose deftly unwound Baby. "Hold him a minute," she requested and dumped several feet of snake into Keane's arms.

"Ah . . ." Keane shifted the weight in his arms and looked dubiously into Baby's bored eyes. "I hope he's eaten recently."

"He had a nice breakfast," Rose assured him, going into a fluid backbend to show Duffy her flexibility.

"Baby won't eat owners," Jo told Keane. She did not bother to suppress her grin. It was the first time she had seen him disconcerted. "Just a stray towner, occasionally. Rose keeps him on a strict diet."

"I assume," Keane began as Baby slithered into a more comfortable position, "that he's aware I'm the owner."

Grinning at Keane's uncomfortable expression, Jo turned to Pete. "Gee, I don't know. Did anybody tell Baby about the new owner?"

"Haven't had a chance, myself," Pete drawled, taking out a fresh stick of gum. "Looks a lot like a towner, too. Baby might get confused."

"They're just teasing you, Mr. Prescott," Rose told him as she finished her impromptu audition with a full split. "Baby doesn't eat people at all. He's docile as a lamb. Little kids come up and pet him during a demonstration." She rose and brushed off her jeans. "Now, you take a cobra . . ."

"No, thank you," Keane declined, unloading the six-foot Baby back into Rose's arms.

Rose slipped the boa back around her neck. "Well, Duffy, I'm off. What do you say?"

"Get one of the girls to teach you the routine," he said with a nod. "Then we'll see." Smiling, he watched Rose saunter away.

"Hey, Duffy!" It was Jamie. "There's a couple of towners looking for you. I sent them over to the red wagon."

"Fine. I'll just go right on along with you." Duffy winked at Jo before turning to catch up with Jamie's long stride.

Keane was standing very close to the barrels. Jo knew getting down from her perch was risky. She knew, too, however, that her pulse was beginning to behave erratically despite her efforts to control it. "I've got to see about my costume." Nimbly, she came down, intending to skirt around him. Even as her boots touched the ground, his hands took her waist. Exercising every atom of willpower, she neither jerked nor struggled but lifted her eyes calmly to his.

His thumbs moved in a lazy arch. She could feel the warmth through the fabric of her blouse. With her entire being she wished he would not hold her. Then, perversely, she wished he would hold her closer. She struggled not to weaken as her lips grew warm under the kiss of his eyes. Her heart began to hammer in her ears.

Keane ran a hand down the length of her long, thick braid. Slowly, his eyes drifted back to hers. Abruptly, he released her and backed up to let her pass. "You'd best go have wardrobe take a few tucks in that costume."

Deciding she was not meant to decipher his changing moods, Jo stepped by him and crossed the compound. If she spent enough time working, she could keep her thoughts from dwelling on Keane Prescott. Maybe.

CHAPTER 7

The Big Top was packed for the evening show. Jo watched the anticipation in the range of faces as she took her temporary position in the opening spectacular. The band played jumpy, upbeat music, leaning heavily on brass as the theme parade marched around the hippodrome track. As the substitute Bo Peep, Jo wore a demure mobcap and a wide crinoline skirt and led a baby lamb on a leash. Because her act came so swiftly on the tail of the opening, she rarely participated in the spectacular. Now she enjoyed a close-up look at the audience. In the cage, she blocked them out almost completely.

They were, she decided, a well-mixed group: young babies, older children, parents, grandparents, teenagers. They gave the pageant enthusiastic applause. Jo smiled and waved as she performed the basic choreography with hardly a thought.

After a quick costume change, she took her cue as Queen of the Jungle Cats. After that followed another costume change that transformed her into one of the Twelve Spinning Butterflies.

"Just heard," Jamie whispered in her ear as she took the customary pose by the rope. "You got the job for the next week. Barbara won't be able to handle the teeth grip."

Jo shifted her shoulders to compensate for the weight of

her enormous blue wings. "Rose is going to learn the routine," she mumbled back, smiling in the flood of the sunlight. "Duffy's giving her the job if she can stand up under this blasted costume." She made a quick, annoyed sound and smiled brightly. "It weighs a ton."

Slowly, to the beat of the waltz the band played, Jo climbed hand over hand up the rope. "Ah, showbiz," she heard Jamie sigh. She vowed to poke him in the ribs when she took her bow. Then, hooking her foot in the hoop, she began the routine, imitating the other eleven Spinning Butterflies.

She was able to share a cup of coffee with Rose's mother when she returned the butterfly costume to wardrobe and changed into her own white and gold jumpsuit. Her muscles complained a bit due to the unfamiliar weight of the wings, and she gave a passing thought to a long, luxurious bath. That was a dream for September, she reminded herself. Showers were the order of the day on the road.

Jo's last duty in the show was to stand on the head of Maggie, the key elephant in the finale's long mount. Sturdy and dependable, Maggie stood firm while four elephants on each side of her rose on their hind legs, resting their front legs on the back of the one in front. Atop Maggie's broad head, Jo stood glittering under the lights with both arms lifted in the air. It was here, more than any other part of the show, that the applause washed over her. It merged with the music, the ringmaster's whistle, the laughter of children. Where she had been weary, she was now filled with energy. She knew the fatigue would return, so she relished the power of the moment all the more. For those few seconds there was no work, no long hours, no predawn drives. There was only magic. Even when it was over and she slid from Maggie's back, she could still feel it.

Outside the tent, troupers and roustabouts and shandies mingled. There were anecdotes to exchange, performances to dissect, observations to be made. Gradually, they drifted away alone, in pairs or in groups. Some would change and help strike the tents, some would sleep, some would worry over their performances. Too energized to sleep, Jo planned to assist in the striking of the Big Top.

She switched on a low light as she entered her trailer, then absently braided her hair as she moved to the tiny bath. With quick moves she creamed off her stage makeup. The exaggeration of her eyes was whisked away, leaving the thick fringe of her lashes and the dark green of her irises unenhanced. The soft bloom of natural rose tinted her cheeks again, and her mouth, unpainted, appeared oddly vulnerable. Accustomed to the change, Jo did not see the sharp contrast between Jovilette the performer and the small, somewhat fragile woman in the glittering jumpsuit. With her face naked and the simple braid hanging down her back, the look of the wild was less apparent. It remained in her movements, but her face rinsed of all artifice and unframed, was both delicate and young, part ingenue, part flare. But Jo saw none of this as she reached for her front zipper. Before she could pull it down, a knock sounded on her door.

"Come in," she called out and flicked her braid behind her back as she started down the aisle. She stopped in her tracks as Keane stepped through the door.

"Didn't anyone ever tell you to ask who it is first?" He shut the door behind him and locked it with a careless flick of his wrist. "You might not have to lock your door against the circus people," he continued blandly as she remained still, "but there are several dozen curious towners still hanging around."

"I can handle a curious towner," Jo replied. The offhand quality of his dominance was infuriating. "I never lock my door."

There was stiffness and annoyance in her voice. Keane ignored them both. "I brought you something from Chicago."

The casual statement succeeded in throwing Jo's temper

off the mark. For the first time, she noticed the small package he carried. "What is it?" she asked.

Keane smiled and crossed to her. "It's nothing that bites," he assured her, then held it out.

Still cautious, Jo lifted her eyes to his, then dropped her gaze back to the package. "It's not my birthday," she murmured.

"It's not Christmas, either," Keane pointed out.

The easy patience in the tone caused Jo to lift her eyes again. She wondered how it was he understood her hesitation to accept presents. She kept her gaze locked on his. "Thank you," she said solemnly as she took the gift.

"You're welcome," Keane returned in the same tone.

The amenities done, Jo recklessly ripped the paper. "Oh! It's Dante," she exclaimed, tearing off the remaining paper and tossing it on the table. With reverence she ran her palm over the dark leather binding. The rich scent drifted to her. She knew her quota of books would have been limited to one a year had she bought a volume so handsomely bound. She opened it slowly, as if to prolong the pleasure. The pages were heavy and rich cream in color. The text was Italian, and even as she glanced over the first page, the words ran fluidly through her mind.

"It's beautiful," she murmured, overcome. Lifting her eyes to thank him again, Jo found Keane smiling down at her. Shyness enveloped her suddenly, all the more intense because she had so rarely experienced it. A lifetime in front of crowds had given her a natural confidence in almost any situation. Now color began to surge into her cheeks, and her mind was a jumble of words that would not come to order.

"I'm glad you like it." He ran a finger down her cheek. "Do you always blush when someone gives you a present?"

Because she was at a loss as to how to answer his question, Jo maneuvered around it. "It was nice of you to think of me."

"It seems to come naturally," Keane replied, then watched Jo's lashes flutter down.

"I don't know what to say." She was able to meet his eyes again with her usual directness, but he had again touched her emotions. She felt inadequate to deal with her feelings or with his effect on her.

"You've already said it." He took the book from Jo's hand and paged through it. "Of course, I can't read a word of it. I envy you that." Before Jo could ponder the idea of a man like Keane Prescott envying her anything, he looked back up and smiled. Her thoughts scattered like nervous ants. "Got any coffee?" he asked and set the book back down on the table.

"Coffee?"

"Yes, you know, coffee. They grow it in quantity in Brazil." Jo gave him a despairing look. "I don't have any made. I'd fix you a cup, but I've got to change before I help strike the tents. The cookhouse will still be serving."

Keane lifted a brow as he let his eyes wander over her face. "Don't you think that between Bo Peep, lions and butterflies, you've done enough work tonight? By the way, you make a very appealing butterfly."

"Thank you, but—"

"Let's put it this way," Keane countered smoothly. He took the tip of her braid in his fingers. "You've got the night off. I'll make the coffee myself if you show me where you keep it."

Though she let out a windy sigh, Jo was more amused than annoyed. Coffee, she decided, was the least she could do after he had brought her such a lovely present. "I'll make it," she told him, "but you'll probably wish you'd gone to the cookhouse." With this dubious invitation, Jo turned and headed toward the kitchen. He made no sound, but she knew he followed her. For the first time, she felt the smallness of her kitchen.

Setting an undersized copper kettle on one of the two

burners, Jo flicked on the power. It was a simple matter to keep her back to him while she plucked cups from the cupboard. She was well aware that if she turned around in the compact kitchen, she would all but be in his arms.

"Did you watch the whole show?" she asked conversationally as she pulled out a jar of instant coffee.

"Duffy had me working props," Keane answered. "He seems to be making me generally useful."

Amused, Jo twisted her head to grin at him. Instantly, she discovered her misstep in strategy. Keane's face was only inches from hers, and in his eyes she read his thoughts. He wanted her, and he intended to have her. Before she could shift her position, Keane took her shoulders and turned her completely around. Jo knew she had backed up against the bars.

Leisurely, he began to loosen her hair, working his fingers through it until it pooled over her shoulders. "I've wanted to do that since the first time I saw you. It's hair to get lost in." His voice was soft as he took a generous handful. The gesture itself seemed to stake his claim. "In the sun it shimmers with red lights, but in the dark it's like night itself." It came to her that each time she was close to him, she was less able to resist him. She became more lost in his eyes, more beguiled by his power. Already her mouth tingled with the memory of his kiss, with the longing for a new one. Behind them the kettle began a feverish whistle.

"The water," she managed and tried to move around him. With one hand in her hair, Keane kept her still as he turned off the burner. The whistle sputtered peevishly, then died. The sound echoed in Jo's head.

"Do you want coffee?" he murmured as his fingers trailed to her throat.

Jo's eyes clung to his. Hers were enormous and direct, his quiet and searching. "No," she whispered, knowing she wanted nothing more at that moment than to belong to him.

He circled her throat with his hand and pressed his fingers against her pulse. It fluttered wildly.

"You're trembling." He could feel the light tremor of her body as he brought her closer. "Is it fear?" he demanded as his thumbs brushed over her lips. "Or excitement?"

"Both," she answered in a voice thickened with emotion. She made a tiny, confused sound as his palm covered her heart. Its desperate thudding increased. "Are you . . ." She stopped a moment because her voice was breathless and unsteady. "Are you going to make love to me?" *Did his eyes really darken?* she wondered dizzily. *Or is it my imagination?*

"Beautiful Jovilette," he murmured as his mouth lowered to hers. "No pretentions, no evasions . . . irresistible." The quality of the kiss altered swiftly. His mouth was hungry on hers, and her response leaped past all caution. If loving him was madness, her heart reasoned, could making love take her further beyond sanity? Past wisdom and steeped in sensation, she let her heart rule her will. When her lips parted under his, it was not in surrender but in equal demand.

Keane gentled the kiss. He kept her shimmering on the razor's edge of passion. His mouth teased, promised, then fed her growing need. He found the zipper at the base of her throat and pulled it downward slowly. Her skin was warm, and he sought it, giving a low sound of pleasure as her breast swelled under his hand. He explored without hurry, as if memorizing each curve and plane. Jo no longer trembled but became pliant as her body moved to the rhythm he set. Her sigh was spontaneous, filled with wonder and delight.

With a suddenness that took her breath away, Keane crushed her mouth beneath his in fiery urgency. Jo's instincts responded, thrusting her into a world she had only imagined. His hands grew more insistent. Jo realized he had relinquished control. They were both riding on the tossing waves of passion. This sea had no horizon and no depth. It was a drowning sea that pulled the unsuspecting under while promising limitless pleasure. Jo did not resist but dived deeper.

At first she thought the knocking was only the sound of her heart against her ribs. When Keane drew away, she murmured in protest and pulled him back. Instantly, his mouth was avid, but as the knocking continued, he swore and pulled back again.

"Someone's persistent," he muttered. Bewildered, Jo stared up at him. "The door," he explained on a long breath.

"Oh." Flustered, Jo ran a hand through her hair and tried to collect her wits.

"You'd better answer it," Keane suggested as he pulled the zipper to her throat in one quick move. Jo broke the surface into reality abruptly. For a moment Keane watched her, taking in her flushed cheeks and tousled hair before he moved aside. Willing her legs to carry her, Jo walked to the front of the trailer. The door handle resisted, then she remembered that Keane had locked it, and she turned the latch.

"Yes, Buck?" she said calmly enough when she opened the door to her handler.

"Jo." His face was in shadows, but she heard the distress in the single syllable. Her chest tightened. "It's Ari."

He had barely finished the name before Jo was out of the trailer and running across the compound. She found both Pete and Gerry standing near Ari's cage.

"How bad?" she demanded as Pete came to meet her.

He took her shoulders. "Really bad this time, Jo."

For a moment she wanted to shake her head, to deny what she read in Pete's eyes. Instead, she nudged him aside and walked to Ari's cage. The old cat lay on his side as his chest lifted and fell with the effort of breathing. "Open it," she ordered Pete in a voice that revealed nothing. There was the jingle of keys, but she did not turn.

"You're not going in there." Jo heard Keane's voice and felt a restraining grip on her shoulders. Her eyes were opaque as she looked up at him.

"Yes, I am. Ari isn't going to hurt me or anyone else. He's just going to die. Now, leave me alone." Her voice was low and toneless. "Open it," she ordered again, then pulled out of Keane's loosened hold. The bars rattled as he slid the door open. Hearing it, Jo turned, then hoisted herself into the cage.

Ari barely stirred. Jo saw, as she knelt beside him, that his eyes were open. They were glazed with weariness and pain. "Ari." She sighed, seeing there would be no tomorrow for him. His only answer was a hollow wheezing. Putting a hand to his side, she felt the ragged pace of his breathing. He made an effort to respond to her touch, to his name, but managed only to shift his great head on the floor. The gesture tore at Jo's heart. She lowered her face to his mane, remembering him as he had once been: full of strength and a terrifying beauty. She lifted her face again and took one long, steadying breath. "Buck." She heard him approach but kept her eyes on Ari. "Get the medical kit. I want a hypo of pentobarbital." She could feel Buck's brief hesitation before he spoke.

"Okay, Jo."

She sat quietly, stroking Ari's head. In the distance were the sounds of the Big Top going down, the call of men, the rattle of rigging, the clang of wood against metal. An elephant trumpeted, and three cages down, Faust roared half-heartedly in response.

"Jo." She turned her head as Buck called her and pushed her hair from her eyes. "Let me do it."

Jo merely shook her head and held out her hand.

"Jo." Keane stepped up to the bars. His voice was gentle, but his eyes were so like the cat's at her knees, Jo nearly sobbed aloud. "You don't have to do this yourself."

"He's my cat," she responded dully. "I said I'd do it when

it was time. It's time." Her eyes shifted to Buck. "Give me the hypo, Buck. Let's get it done." When the syringe was in her hand, Jo stared at it, then closed her fingers around it. Swallowing hard, she turned back to Ari. His eyes were on her face. After more than twenty years in captivity there was still something not quite tamed in the dying cat. But she saw trust in his eyes and wanted to weep. "You were the best," she told him as she passed a hand through his mane. "You were always the best." Jo felt a numbing cold settling over her and prayed it would last until she had finished. "You're tired now. I'm going to help you sleep." She pulled the safety from the point of the hypodermic and waited until she was certain her hands were steady. "This won't hurt, nothing is going to hurt you anymore."

Involuntarily, Jo rubbed the back of her hand over her mouth, then, moving quickly, she plunged the needle into Ari's shoulder. A quiet whimper escaped her as she emptied the syringe. Ari made no sound but continued to watch her face. Jo offered no words of comfort but sat with him, methodically stroking his fur as his eyes grew cloudy. Gradually, the effort of his breathing lessened, becoming quieter and quieter until it wasn't there at all. Jo felt him grow still, and her hand balled into a fist inside the mass of his mane. One quick, convulsive shudder escaped her. Steeling herself, she moved from the cage, closing the door behind her. Because her bones felt fragile, she kept them stiff, as though they might shatter. Even as she stepped back to the ground, Keane took her arm and began to lead her away.

"Take care of things," he said to Buck as they moved past.

"No." Jo protested, trying and failing to free her arm. "I'll do it."

"No, you won't." Keane's tone held a quiet finality. "Enough's enough."

"Don't tell me what to do," she said sharply, letting her grief take refuge in anger.

"I *am* telling you," he pointed out. His hand was firm on her arm.

"You *can't* tell me what to do," she insisted as tears rose treacherously in her throat. "I want you to leave me alone."

Keane stopped, then took her by the shoulders. His eyes caught the light of a waning moon. "There's no way I'm going to leave you alone when you're so upset."

"My emotions have nothing to do with you." Even as she spoke, he took her arm again and pulled her toward her trailer. Jo wanted desperately to be alone to weep out her grief in private. The mourning belonged to her, and the tears were personal. As if her protests were nonexistent, he pulled her into the trailer and closed the door behind them. "Will you get out of here?" she demanded, frantically swallowing tears.

"Not until I know you're all right." Keane's answer was calm as he walked back to the kitchen.

"I'm perfectly all right." Her breath shuddered in and out quickly. "Or I will be when you leave me alone. You have no right to poke your nose in my business."

"So you've told me before," Keane answered mildly from the back of the trailer.

"I just did what had to be done." She held her body rigid and fought against her own quick, uneven breathing. "I put a sick animal out of his misery. It's as simple as that." Her voice broke, and she turned away, hugging her arms. "For heaven's sake, Keane, go away!"

Quietly, he walked back to her carrying a glass of water. "Drink this."

"No." She whirled back to him. Tears spilled out of her eyes and trickled down her cheeks despite her efforts to banish them. Hating herself, she pressed the heel of her hand between her brows and closed her eyes. "I don't want you here." Keane set down the glass, then gathered her into his arms. "No, don't. I don't want you to hold me."

"Too bad." He ran a hand gently up and down her back.

"You did a very brave thing, Jo. I know you loved Ari. I know how hard it was to let him go. You're hurting, and I'm not leaving you."

"I don't want to cry in front of you." Her fists were tight balls at his shoulders.

"Why not?" The stroking continued up and down her back as he cradled her head in the curve of his shoulder.

"Why won't you let me be?" she sobbed as her control slipped. Her fingers gripped his shirt convulsively. "Why am I always losing what I love?" She let the grief come. She let his arms soothe her. As desperately as she had protested against it, she clung to his offer of comfort.

She made no objection as he carried her to the couch and cradled her in his arms. He stroked her hair, as she had stroked Ari, to ease the pain of what couldn't be changed. Slowly, her sobbing quieted. Still she lay with her cheek against his chest, with her hair curtaining her face.

"Better?" he asked as the silence grew calmer. Jo nodded, not yet trusting her voice. Keane shifted her as he reached for the glass of water. "Drink this now."

Gratefully, Jo relieved her dry throat, then went without resistance back against his chest. She closed her eyes, thinking it had been a very long time since she had been held in anyone's lap and soothed. "Keane," she murmured. She felt his lips brush over the top of her head.

"Hmm?"

"Nothing." Her voice thickened as she drifted toward sleep. "Just Keane."

CHAPTER 8

Jo felt the sun on her closed lids. There was the summer-morning sound of excited birds. Her mind, levitating slowly toward the surface, told her it must be Monday. Only on Monday would she sleep past sunrise. That was the enroute day, the only day in seven the circus held no show. She thought lazily of getting up. She would set aside two hours for reading. *Maybe I'll drive into town and see a movie. What town are we in?* With a sleepy sigh she rolled onto her stomach.

I'll give the cats a good going-over, maybe hose them down if it gets hot enough. Memory flooded back and snapped her awake. *Ari.* Opening her eyes, Jo rolled onto her back and stared at the ceiling. Now she recalled vividly how the old cat had died with his eyes trusting on her face. She sighed again. The sadness was still there, but not the sharp, desperate grief of the night before. Acceptance was settling in. She realized that Keane's insistence on staying with her during the peak of her mourning had helped her. He had given her someone to rail at, then someone to hold on to. She remembered the incredible comfort of being cradled in his lap, the solid dependability of his chest against her cheek. She had fallen asleep with the sound of his heart in her ear.

Turning her head, Jo looked out the window, then at the

patch of white light the sun tossed on the floor. *But it isn't
Monday,* she remembered suddenly. *It's Thursday.* Jo sat up,
pushing at her hair, which seemed to tumble everywhere at
once. What was she doing in bed on a Thursday when the
sun was up? Without giving herself time to work out the
answer, she scrambled out of bed and hurried from the room.
She gave a soft gasp as she ran headlong into Keane.

His hand ran down the length of her hair before he took
her shoulder. "I heard you stirring," he said easily, looking
down into her stunned face.

"What are you doing here?"

"Making coffee," he answered as he gave her a critical
study. "Or I was a moment ago. How are you?"

"I'm all right." Jo lifted her hand to her temple as if to gain
her bearings. "I'm a bit disoriented, I suppose. I overslept. It's
never happened before."

"I gave you a sleeping pill," Keane told her matter-of-factly.
He slipped an arm around her shoulder as he turned back to
the kitchen.

"A pill?" Jo's eyes flew to his. "I don't remember taking
a pill."

"It was in the water you drank." On the stove the kettle began its piercing whistle. Moving to it, Keane finished making the coffee. "I had my doubts as to whether you'd take it
voluntarily."

"No, I wouldn't have," Jo agreed with some annoyance.
"I've never taken a sleeping pill in my life."

"Well, you did last night." He held out a mug of coffee. "I
sent Gerry for it while you were in the cage with Ari." Again
he gave her a quick, intense study. "It didn't seem to do you
any harm. You went out like a light. I carried you to bed,
changed your clothes—"

"Changed my . . ." All at once Jo became aware that she
wore only a thin white nightshirt. Her hand reached instinctively for the top button that nestled just above her bosom.

Thinking hard, she found she could recall nothing beyond falling asleep in his arms.

"I don't think you'd have spent a very comfortable night in your costume," Keane pointed out. Enjoying his coffee, he smiled at the nervous hand she held between her breasts. "I've had a certain amount of experience undressing women in the dark." Jo dropped her hand. It was an unmistakable movement of pride. Keane's eyes softened. "You needed a good night's sleep, Jo. You were worn-out."

Without speaking, Jo lifted her coffee to her lips and turned away. Walking to the window, she could see that the backyard was deserted. Her sleep must indeed have been deep to have kept her unaware of camp breaking.

"Everyone's gone but a couple of roustabouts and a generator truck. They'll take off when you don't need power anymore."

The vulnerability Jo felt was overwhelming. Several times in the course of the evening before, she had lost control, which had always been an essential part of her. Each time, it had been Keane who had been there. She wanted to be angry with him for intruding on her privacy but found it impossible. She had needed him, and he had known it.

"You didn't have to stay behind," she said, watching a crow swoop low over the ground outside.

"I wasn't certain you'd be in any shape to drive fifty miles this morning. Pete's driving my trailer."

Her shoulders lifted and fell before she turned around. Sunlight streamed through the window at her back and poured through the thin folds of her nightshirt. Her body was a slender shadow. When she spoke, her voice was low with regret. "I was horribly rude to you last night."

Keane shrugged and lifted his coffee. "You were upset."

"Yes." Her eyes were an open reflection of her sorrow. "Ari was very important to me. I suppose he was an ongoing link with my father, with my childhood. I'd known for some time he wouldn't make it through the season, but I didn't want to face it." She looked down at the mug she held gripped in both hands. A faint wisp of steam rose from it and vanished. "Last night was a relief for him. It was selfish of me to wish it otherwise. And I was wrong to strike out at you the way I did. I'm sorry."

"I don't want your apology, Jo." Because he sounded annoyed, she looked up quickly.

"I'd feel better if you'd take it, Keane. You've been very kind."

To her astonishment, he swore under his breath and turned back to the stove. "I don't care for your gratitude any more than your apology." He set down his mug and poured in more coffee. "Neither of them is necessary."

"They are to me," Jo replied, then took a step toward him. "Keane . . ." She set down her coffee and touched his arm. When he turned, she let impulse guide her. She rested her head on his shoulder and slipped her arms around his waist. He stiffened, putting his hands to her shoulders as if to draw her away. Then she heard his breath come out in a long sigh as he relaxed. For an instant he brought her closer.

"I never know precisely what to expect from you," he murmured. He lifted her chin with his finger. In automatic response, Jo closed her eyes and offered her mouth. She felt his fingers tighten on her skin before his lips brushed hers lightly. "You'd better go change." His manner was friendly but cool as he stepped away. "We'll stop off in town, and I'll buy you some breakfast."

Puzzled by his attitude but satisfied he was no longer annoyed, Jo nodded. "All right."

* * *

Spring became summer as the circus wound its way north. The sun stayed longer, peeking into the Big Top until well after the evening show began. Heavy rain came infrequently, but there were quick summer storms with thunder and lightning. Through June, Prescott's Circus Colossus snaked through North Carolina and into western Tennessee.

During the long weeks while spring tripped over into summer, Jo found Keane's attitude a paradox. His friendliness toward her was offhand. He laughed if she said something amusing, listened if she had a complaint and to her confusion, slipped a thin barrier between them. At times she wondered if the passion that had flared between them the night he had returned from Chicago had truly existed. Had the desire she had tasted on his lips been a fantasy? The closeness she had felt blooming between them had withered and blown away. They were only owner and trouper now.

Keane flew back to Chicago twice more during this period, but he brought no surprise presents back with him. Not once during those long weeks did he come by her trailer. Initially, his altered manner confused her. He was not angry. His mood was neither heated nor icy with temper but fell into an odd middle ground she could not understand. Jo ached with love. As days passed into weeks, she was forced to admit that Keane did not seem to be interested in a close relationship.

* * *

On the eve of the July 4 show, Jo sat sleepless in her bed. In her hand she held the volume of Dante, but the book was only a reminder of the emptiness she felt. She closed it, then stared at the ceiling. *It's time to snap out of it,* she lectured herself. *It's time to stop pretending he was ever really part of my life. Loving someone only makes him a part of your wishes. He never talked about love, he never promised anything, never offered anything but what he gave to me. He's done nothing to hurt me.* Jo squeezed her eyes shut and pressed the book between her fingers. *How I wish I could hate him for showing me what life could be like and then turning away,* she thought.

But I can't. Jo let out a shaky breath and relaxed her grip on the book. Gently, she ran a finger down its smooth, leather binding. *I can't hate him, but I can't love him openly, either. How do I stop? I should be grateful he stopped wanting me. I would have made love with him. Then I'd hurt a hundred times more. Could I hurt a hundred times more?* For several moments she lay still, trying to quiet her thoughts.

It's best not to know, she told herself sternly. *It's best to remember he was kind to me when I needed him and that I haven't a right to make demands. Summer doesn't last forever. I may never see him again when it's over. At least I can keep the time we have pleasant.*

The words sounded hollow in her heart.

CHAPTER 9

The Fourth of July was a full day with a run to a new lot, the tent raising, a street parade and two shows. But it was a holiday. Elephants wore red, white and blue plumes atop their massive heads. The evening performance would be held an hour earlier to allow for the addition of a fireworks display. Traditionally, Prescott's circus arranged to spend the holiday in the same small town in Tennessee. The license and paperwork for the display were seen to in advance, and the fireworks were shipped ahead to be stored in a warehouse. The procedure had been precisely the same for years. It was one of the circus's most profitable nights. Concessions thrived.

Jo moved through the day with determined cheerfulness. She refused to permit the distance between her and Keane to spoil one of the highlights of the summer. Brooding, she decided, would not change things. The mood of the crowd helped to keep her spirits light.

Between shows came the inevitable lull. Some troupers sat outside their trailers exchanging small talk and enjoying the sun. Others got in a bit more practice or worked out a few kinks. Bull hands washed down the elephants, causing a minor flood in the pen area.

Jo watched the bathing process with amusement. She never

ceased to enjoy this particular aspect of circus life, especially if there were one or two inexperienced bull hands involved. Invariably, Maggie or one of the other veteran bulls would spray a trunkful of water over the new hands to initiate them. Though Jo knew the other hands encouraged it, they always displayed remarkable innocence.

Spotting Duffy, Jo moved away from the elephant area and wandered toward him. She could see he was deep in discussion with a towner. He was as short as Duffy but wider, with what she had once heard Frank call a successful frame. His stomach started high and barreled out to below his waist. He had a ruddy complexion and pale eyes that squinted hard against the sun. Jo had seen his type before. She wondered what he was selling and how much he wanted for it. Since Duffy was puffing with annoyance, Jo assumed it was quite a lot.

"I'm telling you, Carlson, we've already paid for storage. I've got a signed receipt. And we pay fifteen bucks delivery, not twenty."

Carlson was smoking a small, unfiltered cigarette and dropped it to the ground. "You paid Myers for storage, not me. I bought the place six weeks ago." He shrugged his wide shoulders. "Not my problem you paid in advance."

Looking over, Jo saw Keane approaching with Pete. Pete was talking rapidly, Keane nodding. As Jo watched, Keane glanced up and gave Carlson a quick study. She had seen that look before and knew the older man had been assessed. Keane caught her eye, smiled and began to move past her. "Hello, Jo."

Unashamedly curious, Jo fell into step beside him. "What's going on?"

"Why don't we find out?" he suggested as they stopped in front of Duffy and Carlson. "Gentlemen," Keane said in an easy tone. "Is there a problem?"

"This character," Duffy spouted, jerking a scornful thumb

at Carlson's face, "wants us to pay twice for storage on the fireworks. Then he wants twenty for delivery when we agreed on fifteen."

"Myers agreed on fifteen," Carlson pointed out. He smiled without humor. "I didn't agree on anything. You want your fireworks, you gotta pay for them first—cash," he added, then spared Keane a glance. "Who's this guy?"

Duffy began to wheeze with indignation, but Keane laid a restraining hand on his shoulder. "I'm Prescott," he told him in untroubled tones. "Perhaps you'd like to fill me in."

"Prescott, huh?" Carlson stroked both his chins as he studied Keane. Seeing youth and amiable eyes, he felt closer to success. "Well, now we're getting somewhere," he said jovially and stuck out his hand. Keane accepted it without hesitation. "Jim Carlson," he continued as he gave Keane's hand a brisk pump. "Nice circus you got here, Prescott. Me and the missus see it every year. Well, now," he said again and hitched up his belt. "Seeing as you're a businessman, too, I'm sure we can straighten all this out. Problem is, your fireworks've been stored in my warehouse. Now, I gotta make a living, they can't just sit there for free. I bought the place off Myers six weeks ago. I can't be held responsible for a deal you made with him, can I?" Carlson gave a stretched-lip smile, pleased that Keane listened so politely. "And as for delivery, well . . ." He made a helpless gesture and patted Keane's shoulder. "You know about gas prices these days, son. But we can work that out after we settle this other little problem."

Keane nodded agreeably. "That sounds reasonable." He ignored Duffy's huffing and puffing. "You do seem to have a problem, Mr. Carlson."

"I don't have a problem," Carlson countered. His smile suffered a fractional slip. "You've got the problem, unless you don't want the fireworks."

"Oh, we'll have the fireworks, Mr. Carlson," Keane

corrected with a smile Jo thought more wolfish than friendly. "According to paragraph three, section five, of the small business code, the lessor is legally bound by all contracts, agreements, liens and mortgages of the previous lessor until such time as all aforesaid contracts, agreements, liens and mortgages are expired or transferred."

"What the . . ." Carlson began with no smile at all, but Keane continued blandly.

"Of course, we won't pursue the matter in court as long as we get our merchandise. But that doesn't solve your problem."

"My problem?" Carlson sputtered while Jo looked on in frank admiration. "I haven't got a problem. If you think . . ."

"Oh, but you do, Mr. Carlson, though I'm sure there was no intent to break the law on your part."

"Break the law?" Carlson wiped damp hands on his slacks.

"Storing explosives without a license," Keane pointed out. "Unless, of course, you obtained one after your purchase of the warehouse."

"Well, no, I . . ."

"I was afraid of that." Keane lifted his brow in pity. "You see, in paragraph six of section five of the small business code it states that all licenses, permits and warrants shall be nontransferable. Authorization for new licenses, permits or warrants must be requested in writing by the current owner. Notarized, naturally." Keane waited a bit to allow Carlson to wrestle with the idea. "If I'm not mistaken," he continued conversationally, "the fine's pretty hefty in this state. Of course, sentencing depends on—"

"Sentencing?" Carlson paled and mopped the back of his neck with a handkerchief.

"Look, tell you what." Keane gave Carlson a sympathetic smile. "You get the fireworks over here and off your property. We don't have to bring the law in on something like this. Just an oversight, after all. We're both businessmen, aren't we?"

Too overwrought to detect sarcasm, Carlson nodded.

"That was fifteen on delivery, right?"

Carlson didn't hesitate but stuck the damp handkerchief back in his pocket and nodded again.

"Good enough. I'll have the cash for you on delivery. Glad to help you out."

Relieved, Carlson turned and headed for his pickup. Jo managed to keep her features grave until he pulled off the lot. Simultaneously, Pete and Duffy began to hoot with laughter.

"Was it true?" Jo demanded and took Keane's arm.

"Was what true?" Keane countered, merely lifting a brow over the hysterics that surrounded him.

"'Paragraph three, section five, of the small business code,'" Jo quoted.

"Never heard of it," Keane answered mildly, nearly sending Pete into orbit.

"You made it up," Jo said in wonder. "You made it all up!"

"Probably," Keane agreed.

"Smoothest con job I've seen in years," Duffy stated and gave Keane a parental slap on the back. "Son, you could go into business."

"I did," Keane told him and grinned.

"I ever need a lawyer," Pete put in, pushing his cap farther back on his head, "I know where to go. You come on by the cookhouse tonight, Captain. We're having ourselves a poker game. Come on, Duffy, Buck's gotta hear about this."

As they moved off, Jo realized that Keane had been officially accepted. Before, he had been the legal owner but an outsider, a towner. Now he was one of them. Turning, she lifted her face to his. "Welcome aboard."

"Thank you." She saw he understood precisely what had been left unsaid.

"I'll see you at the game," she said before her smile became a grin. "Don't forget your money."

She turned away, but Keane touched her arm, bringing her back to him. "Jo," he began, puzzling her by the sudden seriousness of his eyes.

"Yes?"

There was a brief hesitation, then he shook his head. "Nothing, never mind. I'll see you later." He rubbed his knuckles over her cheek, then walked away.

*   *   *

Jo studied her hand impassively. On the deal, she had missed a heart flush by one card and now waited for someone to open. Casually, she moved her glance around the table. Duffy was puffing on a cigar, apparently unconcerned with the dwindling chips in front of him. Pete chewed his gum with equal nonchalance. Amy, the wife of the sword swallower, sat beside him, then Jamie, then Raoul. Directly beside Jo was Keane, who, like Pete, was winning consistently.

The pot grew. Chips clinked on the table. Jo discarded and was pleased to exchange a club for the fifth heart. She slipped it into her hand without blinking. Frank had taught her the game. Before the second round of betting, Jamie folded in disgust. "Should never have taken Buck's seat," he muttered and frowned when Pete raised the bet.

"You got out cheap, kiddo," Duffy told him dolefully as he tossed in chips. "I'm only staying in so I don't change my standard of living. Money'll do that to you," he mumbled obscurely.

"Three kings," Pete announced when called, then spread his cards. Amid a flutter of complaints cards were tossed down.

"Heart flush," Jo said mildly before Pete could rake in the pot. Duffy leaned back and gave a hoot of laughter.

"Attagirl, Jo. I hate to see him win all my money."

During the next two hours the cookhouse tent grew hot and ripe with the scents of coffee and tobacco and beer. Jamie's luck proved so consistently poor that he called for Buck to relieve him.

Jo found herself with an indifferent pair of fives. Almost immediately the betting grew heavy as Keane raised Raoul's opening. Curiosity kept Jo in one round, but practicality had her folding after the draw. Divorced from the game, she watched it with interest. Leaning on her elbows, she studied each participant. Keane played a good game, she mused. His eyes gave nothing away. They never did. Casually, he nursed the beer beside him while Duffy, Buck and Amy folded. Studying him closely, Pete chewed his gum. Keane returned the look, keeping the stub of his cigar clamped between his teeth. Raoul muttered in French and scowled at his cards.

"Could be bluffing," Pete considered, seeing Keane's raise. "Let's raise it five more and see what's cooking." Raoul swore in French, then again in English, before he tossed in his hand. Taking his time, Keane counted out the necessary chips and tossed them into the pot. It was a plastic mountain of red, white and blue. Then, he counted out more.

"I'll see your five," he said evenly, "and raise it ten."

There was mumbling around the table. Pete looked into his hand and considered. Shifting his eyes, he took in the generous pile of chips in front of him. He could afford to risk another ten. Glancing up, he studied Keane's face while he fondled his chips. Abruptly, he broke into a grin.

"Nope," he said simply, turning his cards face down. "This one's all yours."

Setting down his cards, Keane raked in a very sweet pot. "Gonna show 'em?" Pete asked. His grin was affable.

Keane pushed a stray chip into the pile and shrugged. With his free hand he turned over the cards. The reaction ranged from oaths to laughter.

"Trash," Pete mumbled with a shake of his head. "Nothing but trash. You've got nerve, Captain." His grin grew wide as he turned over his own cards. "Even I had a pair of sevens."

Raoul gnashed his teeth and swore elegantly in two languages. Jo grinned at his imaginative choice of words. She rose on a laugh and snatched off the soft felt hat Jamie wore. Deftly, she scooped her chips into it. "Cash me in later," she requested, then gave him a smacking kiss on the mouth. "But don't play with them."

Duffy scowled over at her. "Aren't you cashing in early?"

"You've always told me to leave 'em wanting more," she reminded him. With a grin and a wave, she swung through the door.

"That Jo," said Raoul, chuckling as he shuffled the cards. "She's one smart cracker."

"Cookie," Pete corrected, opening a fresh stick of gum. He noticed that Keane's gaze had drifted to the door she had closed behind her. "Some looker, too," he commented and watched Keane's eyes wander back to his. "Don't you think, Captain?"

Keane slipped his cards into a pile as they were dealt to him. "Jo's lovely."

"Like her mother," Buck put in, frowning at his cards. "She was a beaut, huh, Duffy?" Duffy grunted in agreement and wondered why Lady Luck refused to smile on him. "Always thought it was a crime for her to die that way. Wilder, too," he added with a shake of his head.

"A fire, wasn't it?" Keane asked as he picked up his cards and spread them.

"Electrical fire." Buck nodded and lifted his beer. "A short in their trailer's wiring. What a waste. If they hadn't been in bed asleep, they'd probably still be alive. The trailer was halfway gone before anybody set up an alarm. Just plain couldn't get to the Wilders. Their side of the trailer was like a furnace. Jo's bedroom was on the other side, and we nearly lost her.

Frank busted in the window and pulled her out. Poor little tyke. She was holding onto this old doll like it was the last thing she had left. Kept it with her for I don't know how long. Remember, Duffy?" He glanced into his hand and opened for two. "It only had one arm." Duffy grunted again and folded. "Frank sure knew how to handle that little girl."

"She knew how to handle him, more likely," Duffy mumbled. Raoul bumped the pot five, and Keane folded.

"Deal me out the next hand," he said as he rose and moved to the door. One of the Gribalti brothers took the chair Jo had vacated, and Jamie slipped into Keane's. Curious, he lifted the tip of the cards. He saw a jack-high straight. With a thoughtful frown, he watched the door swing shut.

*   *   *

Outside, Jo moved through the warm night. With a glance at the sky, she thought of the fireworks. They had been wonderful, she mused, stirring up the stars with exploding color. Though it was over and a new day hovered, she felt some magic remained in the night. Far from sleepy, she wandered toward the Big Top.

"Hello, pretty lady."

Jo looked into the shadows and narrowed her eyes. She could just barely make out a form. "Oh, you're Bob, aren't you?" She stopped and gave him a friendly smile. "You're new."

He stepped toward her. "I've been on for nearly three weeks." He was young, Jo guessed about her own age, with a solid build and sharp-featured face. Just that afternoon she had watched Maggie give him a shower.

Jo pushed her hands into the pockets of her cut-offs and continued to smile. It appeared he thought his tenure made him a veteran. "How do you like working with the elephants?"

"It's okay. I like putting up the tent."

Jo understood his feeling. "So do I. There's a game in the cookhouse," she told him with a gesture of her arm. "You might like to sit in."

"I'd rather be with you." As he moved closer, Jo caught the faint whiff of beer. *He's been celebrating,* she thought and shook her head.

"It's a good thing tomorrow's Monday," she commented. "No one's going to be in any shape to pitch a tent. You should go to bed," she suggested. "Or get some coffee."

"Let's go to your trailer." Bob weaved a little, then took her arm.

"No." Firmly, Jo turned in the opposite direction. "Let's go to the cookhouse." His advances did not trouble her. She was close enough to the cookhouse tent that if she called out, a dozen able-bodied men would come charging. But that was precisely what Jo wanted to avoid.

"I want to go with you," he said, stumbling over the words as he veered away from the cookhouse again. "You look so pretty in that cage with those lions." He put both arms around her, but Jo felt it was as much for balance as romance. "A fella needs a pretty lady once in a while."

"I'm going to feed you to my lions if you don't let me go," Jo warned.

"Bet you can be a real wildcat," he mumbled and made a fumbling dive for her mouth.

Though her patience was wearing thin, Jo endured the kiss that landed slightly to the left of bull's-eye. His hands, however, had better aim and grabbed the firm roundness of her bottom. Losing her temper, Jo pushed away but found his hold had taken root. In a quick move, she brought up her fist and caught him square on the jaw. With only a faint sound of surprise, Bob sat down hard on the ground.

"Well, so much for rescuing you," Keane commented from behind her.

Turning quickly, Jo pushed at her hair and gave an annoyed

sigh. She would have preferred no witnesses. Even in the dim light, she could see he was furious. Instinctively, she stepped between him and the man who sat on the ground fingering his jaw and shaking the buzzing from his ears.

"He—Bob just got a bit overenthusiastic," she said hastily and put a restraining hand on Keane's arm. "He's been celebrating."

"I'm feeling a bit enthusiastic myself," Keane stated. As he made to brush her aside, Jo clung with more fervor.

"No, Keane, please."

Looking down, he fired a glare. "Jo, would you let go so that I can deal with this?"

"Not until you listen." The faint hint of laughter in her eyes only enraged him further, and Jo fought to suppress it. "Keane, please, don't be hard on him. He didn't hurt me."

"He was attacking you," Keane interrupted. He barely resisted the urge to shake her off and drag the still-seated Bob by the scruff of the neck.

"No, he was really more just leaning on me. His balance is a trifle impaired. He only tried to kiss me," she pointed out, wisely deleting the wandering hands. "And I hit him much harder than I should have. He's new, Keane, don't fire him."

Exasperated, he stared at her. "Firing was the least of what I had in mind for him."

Jo smiled, unable to keep the gleam from her eyes. "If you were going to avenge my honor, he really didn't do much more than breathe on it. I don't think you should run him through for that. Maybe you could just put him in the stocks for a couple of days."

Keane swore under his breath, but a reluctant smile tugged at his mouth. Seeing it, Jo loosened her hold. "Miss Wilder wants to give you a break," he told the dazed Bob in a tough, no-nonsense voice that Jo decided he used for intimidating witnesses. "She has a softer heart than I do. Therefore, I won't knock you down several more times or kick you off the lot, as I had entertained doing." He paused, allowing Bob time to consider this possibility. "Instead, I'll let you sleep off your—enthusiasm." In one quick jerk, he pulled Bob to his feet. "But if I ever hear of you breathing uninvited on Miss Wilder or any other of my female employees, we'll go back to the first choice. And before I kick you out," he added with low menace, "I'll let it be known that you were decked by one punch from a hundred-pound woman."

"Yes, sir, Mr. Prescott," said Bob as clearly as possible.

"Go to bed," Jo said kindly, seeing him pale. "You'll feel better in the morning."

"Obviously," Keane commented as Bob lurched away, "you haven't done much drinking." He turned to Jo and grinned. "The one thing he's not going to feel in the morning is better." Jo smiled, pleased to have Keane talk to her without the thin shield of politeness. "And where," he asked and took her hand for examination, "did you learn that right jab?"

Jo laughed, allowing Keane's fingers to interlock with hers. "It would hardly have knocked him down if he hadn't already been tilting in that direction." Her face turned up to his and sparkled with starlight. In his eyes an expression she couldn't comprehend came and went. "Is something wrong?"

For a moment he said nothing. In her breast her heart began to hammer as she waited to be kissed. "No, nothing," he said. The moment was shattered. "Come on, I'll walk you back to your trailer."

"I wasn't going there." Wanting to put him back into an easy mood, she linked her arm with his. "If you come with me, I'll show you some magic." Her smile slanted invitingly. "You like magic, don't you, Keane? Even a sober, dedicated lawyer must like magic."

"Is that how I strike you?" Jo almost laughed at the trace of annoyance in his voice. "As a sober, dedicated lawyer?"

"Oh, not entirely, though that's part of you." She enjoyed feeling that for the moment she had him to herself. "You've also got a streak of adventure and a rather nice sense of humor. And," she added with generous emphasis, "there's your temper."

"You seem to have me all figured out."

"Oh, no." Jo stopped and turned to him. "Not at all. I only know how you are here. I can only speculate on how you are in Chicago."

His brow lifted as she caught his attention. "Would I be different there?"

"I don't know." Jo's forehead wrinkled in thought. "Wouldn't you be? Circumstances would. You probably have a house or a big apartment, and there's a housekeeper who comes in once—no, twice—a week." Caught up in the picture, she gazed off into the distance and built it further. "You have an office with a view of the city, a very efficient secretary and a brilliant law clerk. You go to business lunches at the club. In court you're deadly and very successful. You have your own tailor and work out at the gym three times a week. There's the theater on the weekends, along with something physical. Tennis maybe, not golf. No, handball."

Keane shook his head. "Is this the magic?"

"No." Jo shrugged and began to walk again. "Just guesswork. You don't have to have a great deal of money to know how people who do behave. And I know you take the law seriously. You wouldn't choose a career that wasn't very important to you."

Keane walked in silence. When he spoke, his voice was quiet. "I'm not certain I'm comfortable with your little outline of my life."

"It's very sketchy," Jo told him. "I'd have to understand you better to fill in the gaps."

"Don't you?"

"What?" Jo asked, pausing. "Understand you?" She laughed, tickled at the absurdity of his question. "No, I don't understand you. How could I? You live in a different world."

With this, she tossed aside the flap of the Big Top and stepped into its darkness. When she hit the switch, two rows of overhead lights flashed on. Shadows haunted the corners and fell over the arena seats.

"It's wonderful, isn't it?" Her clear voice ran the length of the tent and echoed back. "It's not empty, you know. They're always here—the troupers, the audience, the animals." She walked forward until she stood beside the third ring. "Do you know what this is?" she asked Keane, tossing out her arms and turning a full circle. "It's an ageless wonder in a changing world. No matter what happens on the outside, this is here. We're the most fragile of circuses, at the mercy of the elephants, of emotions, of mechanics, of public whims. But six days a week for twenty-nine weeks we perform miracles. We build a world at dawn, then disappear into the dark. That's part of it—the mystery." She waited until Keane moved forward to join her.

"Tents pop up on an empty lot, elephants and lions walk down Main Street. And we never grow old, because each new generation discovers us all over again." She stood slender and exquisite in a circle of light. "Life here's crazy. And it's hard. Muddy lots, insane hours, sore muscles, but when you've finished your act and you get that feeling that tells you it was special, there's nothing else like it in the world."

"Is that why you do it?" Keane asked.

Jo shook her head and moved out of the circle of light into the dark and into another ring. "It's all part of the same thing. We all have our own reasons, I suppose. You've asked me that before. I'm not certain I can explain. Maybe it's that we all believe in miracles." She turned under the light, and it shimmered around her. "I've been here all my life. I know every trick, every illusion. I know how Jamie's dad gets twenty clowns into a two-seater car. But each time I see it, I laugh and I believe it. It's not just the excitement, Keane, it's the anticipation of the excitement. It's knowing you're going to see the biggest or the smallest or the fastest or the highest." Jo ran to the center ring and threw up her arms.

"Ladies and gentlemen," she announced with a toss of her head. "For your amazement and astonishment, for the first time in America, a superabundance of mountainous, mighty pachyderms led in a stupendous exhibition of choreography by the Great Serena." Jo laughed and shifted her hair to her back with a quick movement of her hand. "Dancing elephants!" she said to Keane, pleased that he was smiling. "Or you listen to the talker in the sideshow when he starts his spiel. Step right up. Come a little closer." She curled her fingers in invitation. "See the Amazing Serpentina and her monstrous, slithering vipers. Watch the beautiful young girl charm a deadly cobra. Watch her accept the reptilian embrace of the gargantuan boa. Don't miss the chance to see the enchantress of the evil serpent!"

"I suppose Baby might sue for slander."

Jo laughed and stepped up on the ring. "But when the crowds see little Rose with a boa constrictor wrapped around her shoulders, they've gotten their money's worth. We give them what they come for: color, fantasy, the unique. Thrills. You've seen the audience when Vito does his high wire act without a net."

"A net seems little enough protection when he's balancing on a wire at two hundred feet." Keane stuck his hands in his pockets and frowned. "He risks his life every day."

"So does a police officer or a fire fighter." Jo spoke quietly and rested her hands on his shoulders. It seemed more necessary than ever that she make him understand his father's dream. "I know what you're saying, Keane, but you have to understand us. The element of danger is essential to many of the acts. You can hear the whole audience suck in their breath when Vito does his back somersault on the wire. They'd be impressed if he used a net, but they wouldn't be terrified."

"Do they need to be?"

Jo's sober expression lightened. "Oh, yes! They need to be terrified and fascinated and mesmerized. It's all included in the price of a ticket. This is a world of superlatives. We test the limit of human daring, and every day it changes. Do you know how long it took before the first man accomplished the triple on the trapeze? Now it's nearly a standard." A light of anticipation flared in her eyes. "One day someone will do a quadruple. If a man stands in this ring and juggles three torches today, tomorrow someone will juggle them on horseback and after that there'll be a team tossing them back and forth while swinging on a trap. It's our job to do the incredible, then, when it's done, to do the impossible. It's that simple."

"Simple," Keane murmured, then lifted a hand to caress her hair. "I wonder if you'd think so if you could see it from the outside."

"I don't know." Her fingers tightened on his shoulders as he buried his other hand in her hair. "I never have."

As if his thoughts centered on it, Keane combed his fingers through her hair. Gradually, he pushed it back until only his hands framed her face. They stood in a pool of light that threw their shadows long behind them. "You are so lovely," he murmured.

Jo neither spoke nor moved. There was something different this time in the way he touched her. There was a gentleness and a hesitation she had not felt before. Though they looked directly into hers, she could not read his eyes. Their faces were close, and his breath fluttered against her mouth. Jo slid her arms around his neck and pressed her mouth to his.

Not until that moment had she realized how empty she had felt, how desperately she had needed to hold him. Her lips were hungry for his. She clung while all gentleness fled from his touch. His hands were greedy. The weeks that he had not touched her were forgotten as her skin warmed and hummed with quickening blood. Passion stripped her of inhibitions, and her tongue sought his, taking the kiss into wilder and darker depths. Their lips parted, only to meet again with sharp new demands. She understood that all needs and all desires were ultimately only one—Keane.

His mouth left hers, and for an instant he rested his cheek against her hair. For that moment Jo felt a contentment more complete than she had ever known. Abruptly, he drew away.

Puzzled, she watched as he drew out a cigar. She lifted a hand to run it through the hair he had just disturbed. He flicked on his lighter. "Keane?" She looked at him, knowing her eyes offered everything.

"You've had a long day," he began in an oddly polite tone. Jo winced as if he had struck her. "I'll walk you back to your trailer."

She stepped off the ring and away from him. Pain seared along her skin. "Why are you doing this?" To her humiliation, tears welled in her eyes and lodged in her throat. The tears acted as a prism, refracting the light and clouding her vision. She blinked them back. Keane's brows drew together at the gesture.

"I'll take you back," he said again. The detached tone of his voice accelerated all Jo's fury and grief.

"How dare you!" she demanded. "How dare you make me . . ." The word *love* nearly slipped through her lips, and she swallowed it. "How dare you make me want you, then turn away! I was right about you from the beginning. I thought I'd been wrong. You're cold and unfeeling." Her breath came quickly and unevenly, but she refused to retreat until she had said it all. Her face was pale with the passion of her emotions. "I don't know why I thought you'd ever understand what Frank had given you. You need a heart to see the intangible. I'll be glad when the season's over and you do whatever it is you're going to do. I'll be glad when I never have to see you again. I won't let you do this to me anymore!" Her voice wavered, but she made no attempt to steady it. "I don't want you to ever touch me again."

Keane studied her for a long moment, then took a careful drag on his cigar. "All right, Jo."

The very calmness of his answer tore a sob from her before she turned and ran from the Big Top.

CHAPTER 10

In July the troupe circled through Virginia, touched the tip of West Virginia on their way into Kentucky, then moved into Ohio. Audiences fanned themselves as the temperatures in the Big Top rose, but they still came.

Since the evening of the Fourth of July, Jo had avoided Keane. It was not as difficult as it might have been, as he spent half the month in Chicago dealing with his business. Jo functioned. She ate because eating was necessary in order to maintain her strength. She slept because rest was essential to remaining alert in the cage. She did not find any enjoyment in food nor was her sleep restful. Because so many in the troupe knew her well, Jo struggled to keep on a mask of normalcy. Above all, she needed to avoid any questions, any advice, any sympathy. It was necessary, because of her profession, to put her emotions on hold a great deal of the time. After some struggle and some failure, Jo achieved a reasonable success.

Her training of Gerry continued, as did his progress. The additional duty of working with him helped fill her small snatches of spare time. On afternoons when no matinee was scheduled, Jo took him into the big cage. As he grew more proficient, she brought other cats in to join Merlin. By the first week in August they were working together with her full complement of lions.

The only others who were rehearsing in the Big Top were the equestrian act. They ran through the Thread the Needle routine in the first ring. Hooves echoed dully on tanbark. Jo supervised while Gerry sent the cats into a pyramid. At his urging, Lazarus climbed up the wide, arched ladder that topped the grouping. Twice he balked, and twice Gerry was forced to reissue the command.

"Good," Jo commented when the pyramid was complete.

"He wouldn't go." Gerry began to complain, but she cut him off.

"Don't be in too much of a hurry. Bring them down." Her tone was brisk and professional. "Make certain they dismount and take their seats in the right order. It's important to stick to routine."

Hands resting on hips, Jo watched. In her opinion, Gerry had true potential. His nerves were good, he had a feeling for the animals, and he was slowly developing patience. Still she balked at the next step in his training: leaving him alone in the arena. Even with only Merlin, she felt it too risky. He was still too casual. Not yet did he possess enough respect for the lion's guile.

Jo moved around the arena, and the lions, used to her, were not disturbed. As the cats settled onto their pedestals, she once more moved to stand beside Gerry. "Now we'll walk down the line. You make each do a sit-up before we send them out."

One by one the cats rose on their haunches and pawed the air. Jo and Gerry moved down their ranks. The heat was becoming oppressive, and Jo shifted her shoulders, longing for a cool shower and a change of clothes. When they came to Hamlet, he ignored the command with a rebellious snarl.

Bad-tempered brute, thought Jo absently as she waited for

Gerry to reissue the command. He did so but moved forward as if to emphasize the words.

"No, not so close!" Jo warned quickly. Even as she spoke, she saw the change in Hamlet's eyes.

Instinctively, she stepped over, nudging Gerry back and shielding his body with hers. Hamlet struck out, claws extended. There was a moment of blind heat in her shoulder as the skin ripped. Swiftly, she was facing the cat, holding tightly on to Gerry's arm as they stood just out of range.

"Don't run," she ordered, feeling his jerk of panic. Her arm was on fire as the blood began to flow freely. Keeping her movements quick but smooth, she took the whip from Gerry's nerveless hand and cracked it hard, using her left arm. She knew that if Hamlet continued his defiance and attacked, it was hopeless. The other cats were certain to join in a melee. It would be over before anything could be done. Already, Abra shifted restlessly and bared her teeth.

"Open the chute," Jo called out. Her voice was cool as ice. "Back toward the safety cage," she instructed Gerry as she gave the cats their signal to leave the arena. "I've got to get them out one at a time. Move slow, and if I tell you to stop, you stop dead. Understand?"

She heard him swallow as she watched the cats begin to leap off their pedestals and file into the chute. "He got you. Is it bad?" The words were barely a whisper and drenched in terror.

"I said go." Half the cats were gone, and still Hamlet's eyes were locked on hers. There was no time to waste. One part of her brain heard shouting outside the cage, but she blocked it out and focused all her concentration on the cat. "Go now," she repeated to Gerry. "Do as you're told."

He swallowed again and began to back away. Long seconds dragged until she heard the rattle of the safety cage door. When his turn came, Hamlet made no move to leave his

seat. Jo was alone with him. She could smell the heat, the
scent of the wild and the fragrance of her own blood. Her
arm was alive with pain. Slowly, she tested him by backing up. The safety cage seemed hundreds of miles away.
The cat tensed immediately, and she stopped. She knew he
would not let her cross the arena. Outrunning him was impossible, as the distance between them could be covered in
one spring. She had to outbluff him instead.

"Out," she ordered firmly. "Out, Hamlet." As he continued to watch her, Jo felt a trickle of sweat slide down between
her shoulder blades. Her skin was clammy with it in contrast
to the warmth of the blood that ran down her arm. There
was a sudden, vivid picture inside her head of her father being dragged around the cage. Fear tripped inside her throat.
There was a lightness fluttering in the top of her head, and
she knew that a moment's terror would cause her to faint. She
stiffened her spine and pushed it away.

Speed was important. The longer she allowed the cat to
remain in the arena after his cue, the more defiant he would
become. And the more dangerous. As yet he was unaware that
he held her at such a sharp disadvantage. "Out, Hamlet." Jo
repeated the command with a crack of the whip. He leaped
from the pedestal. Jo's stomach trembled. She locked every
muscle, and as the cat hesitated, she repeated the command.
He was confused, and she knew this could work as an advantage or a curse. Confused, he might spring or retreat. Her
fingers tightened on the stock of the whip and trembled. The
cat paced nervously and watched her.

"Hamlet!" She raised her voice and bit off each syllable.
"Go out." To the words she added the hand signal she had
used before he was fully trained to voice command.

As if rebuffed, Hamlet relaxed his tail and padded into the
chute. Before the door slid completely closed, Jo sank to her
knees. Her body began to quake fiercely with the aftershock.
No more than five minutes had passed since Hamlet had de-

fied Gerry's command, but her muscles bore the strain of hours. For an instant her vision blurred. Even as she shook her head to clear it, Keane was on the ground beside her.

She heard him swear, ripping the tattered sleeve of her blouse from her arm. He fired questions at her, but she could do no more than shake her head and gulp in air. Focusing on him, she noticed his eyes were unusually dark against his face.

"What?" She followed his voice but not the words. He swore again, sharply enough to penetrate the first layer of her shock. He pulled her to her feet, then continuing the motion smoothly, lifted her into his arms. "Don't." Her mind struggled to break through the fog and function. "I'm all right."

"Shut up," he said harshly as he carried her from the cage. "Just shut up."

Because speaking cost her some effort, Jo obeyed. Closing her eyes, she let the mixture of excited voices whirl around her. Her arm screamed with pain, but the throbbing reassured her. Numbness would have terrified her. Still she kept her eyes shut, not yet having the courage to look at the damage. Being alive was enough.

When she opened her eyes again, Keane was carrying her into the administration wagon. At the sound of the chaos that followed them, Duffy strode through from his office. "What the . . ." he began, then stopped and paled beneath his freckles. He moved quickly forward as Keane set Jo in a chair. "How bad?"

"I don't know yet," Keane muttered. "Get a towel and the first-aid kit."

Buck had come in behind them and, already having secured the items, handed them to Keane. Then he moved to a cabinet and located a bottle of brandy.

"It's not too bad," Jo managed. Because her voice was tolerably steady, she screwed up her courage and looked down. Keane had fastened a rough bandage from the remains of her sleeve. Though the flow of blood had slowed, there were streaks of it down her arm, and too much spreading from the wound to be certain how extensive the cuts were. Nausea rocked in her stomach.

"How do you know?" Keane demanded between his teeth as he began to clean the wound. He wrung out the towel in the basin Buck set beside him.

"It's not bleeding that badly." Jo swallowed the queasiness. As her mind began to clear, she frowned at the tone of Keane's voice. Feeling her stare, he glanced up. In his eyes was such fury, she pulled away.

"Be still," he ordered roughly and gave his attention back to her arm.

The cat had delivered only a glancing blow, but even so, there were four long slices in her upper arm. Jo set her jaw as pain ripped through her. Keane's brusqueness brought more hurt, and she fought to show no reaction to either. The aftermath of fear was bubbling through her. She longed to be held, to be soothed by the hands that tended to her wound.

"She's going to need stitches," Keane said without looking at her.

"And an antitoxin shot," Buck added, handing Jo a generous glass of brandy. "Drink this, honey. It'll help settle you."

The gentleness in his voice nearly undid her. He laid his big hand against her cheek, and for a moment she pressed against it.

"Drink now," Buck ordered again. Obediently, Jo lifted the glass and swallowed. The room whirled, then snapped into focus. She made a small sound and pressed the glass to her forehead. "Tell me what happened in there." Buck crouched down beside her as Keane began to apply a temporary bandage.

Jo took a moment to draw air in and out of her lungs. She lowered the glass and spoke steadily. "Hamlet didn't respond, and Gerry repeated a command, but he stepped forward. Too close. I saw Hamlet's eyes, and I knew. I should have moved faster. I should have been watching him more carefully. It was a stupid mistake." She stared into the brandy as she berated herself.

"She stepped between the boy and the cat." Keane bit off the words as he completed the bandaging. Rising, he moved to the brandy and poured. Not once did he turn to look at Jo. Hurt, she stared at his back before looking back at Buck.

"How's Gerry?"

Buck urged the glass back to her lips. A faint tint of pink was creeping into her cheeks. "Pete's with him. Got his head between his knees. He'll be fine."

Jo nodded. "I guess I'll have to go to town and have this seen to." She handed the glass to Buck and wondered if she dare attempt to rise yet. With another deep breath, she glanced at Duffy. "Make sure he's ready to go in when I get back."

Keane turned from the window. "Go in where?" His face was set in hard lines.

In response, Jo's voice was chilled. "In the cage." She turned her eyes to Buck. "We should be able to have a short run-through before the evening show."

"No." Jo's head snapped up as Keane spoke. For a long moment they stared at each other with odd, unreasonable antagonism. "You're not going back in there today." His voice held curt authority.

"Of course I am," Jo countered, managing to keep the combination of pain and anger from her words. "And if Gerry wants to be a cat man, he's going in, too."

"Jo's right," Buck put in, trying to soothe what he sensed was an explosive situation. "It's like falling off a horse. You can't wait too long before you get back up, or you won't ride again."

Keane never took his eyes from Jo. He continued as if Buck hadn't spoken. "I won't permit it."

"You can't stop me." Indignation forced her to her feet. The brisk movement caused her arm to protest, and her struggle against it showed momentarily in her eyes.

"Yes, I can." Keane took a long swallow of brandy. "I own this circus."

Jo's fists tightened at his tone, at his careless use of his authority. Not once since he had knelt beside her in the cage had he given her any sign of comfort or reassurance. She had needed it from him. To masquerade its trembling, she kept her voice low. "But you don't own me, Mr. Prescott. And if you'll check your papers and the legalities, you'll see you don't own the lions or my equipment. I bought them, and I maintain them out of my salary. My contract doesn't give you the right to tell me when I can or can't rehearse my cats."

Keane's face was granite hard. "Neither does it give you the right to set up in the Big Top without my permission."

"Then I'll set up someplace else," she tossed back. "But I *will* set up. That cat will be worked again today. I won't take the risk of losing months of training."

"But you will risk being killed," Keane shot back and slammed down his glass.

"What do you care?" Jo shouted. All control deserted her. The cuts were deep on her emotions as well as her flesh. She had passed through a terror more acute than she had known since the night of her parents' death. More than anything else, she wanted to feel Keane's arms around her. She wanted to know the security she had felt when he had let her weep out her grief for Ari in his arms. "I'm nothing to you!" Her head shook quickly, tossing her hair. There was a bubble of hysteria in her voice, and Buck reached out to lay a hand on her shoulder.

"Jo," he warned in his soft, rumbling voice.

"No!" She shook her head and spoke rapidly. "He hasn't the right. You haven't the right to interfere with my life." She flared at Keane again with eyes vivid with emotion. "I know what I have to do. I know what I *will* do. Why should it matter to you? You aren't legally responsible if I get mauled. No one's going to sue you."

"Hold on, Jo." This time Buck spoke firmly. As he took her uninjured arm, he felt the tremors shooting through her. "She's too upset to know what she's saying," he told Keane.

There was a mask over Keane's face which concealed all emotion. "Oh, I think she knows what she's saying," he disagreed quietly. For a moment there was only the sound of Jo shuddering and the splash of brandy being poured into a glass. "You do what you have to do, Jo," he said after drinking again. "You're perfectly correct that I haven't any rights where you're concerned. Take her into town," he told Buck, then turned back to the window.

"Come on, Jo." Buck urged her to the door, slipping a supportive arm around her waist. Even as they stepped outside, Rose came running from the direction of the midway.

"Jo!" Her face was white with concern. "Jo, I just heard." She glanced at the bandage with wide, terrified eyes. "How bad is it?"

"Just scratches, really," Jo assured her. She added the best smile she could muster. "Buck's going to take me into town for a couple of stitches."

"Are you sure?" She looked up at the tall man for reassurance. "Buck?"

"Several stitches," he corrected but patted Rose's hand. "But it's not too bad."

"Do you want me to come with you?" She fell into step beside them as Buck began to lead Jo again.

"No. Thank you, Rose." Jo smiled with more feeling. "I'll be fine."

Because of the smile, Rose was able to relax. "I thought when I heard . . . well, I imagined all sorts of terrible things.

I'm glad you're not badly hurt." They had reached Buck's truck, and Rose leaned over to kiss Jo's cheek. "We all love you so."

"I know." Squeezing her hand, Jo let Buck help her into the cab of his truck. As he maneuvered from the lot, Jo rested her head against the back of the seat and shut her eyes. Never could she remember feeling more spent, more battered.

"Hurt bad?" Buck asked as they switched to an asphalt road.

"Yes," she answered simply, thinking of her heart as much as her arm.

"You'll feel better when you're patched up."

Jo kept her eyes shut, knowing some wounds never heal. Or if they did, they left scars that ached at unexpected times.

"You shouldn't have gone off on him that way, Jo." There was light censure in Buck's voice.

"He shouldn't have interfered," Jo retorted. "It's none of his business. *I'm* none of his business."

"Jo, it's not like you to be so hard."

"Hard?" She opened her eyes and turned to Buck. "What about him? Couldn't he have been kinder, shown even the barest trace of compassion? Did he have to speak to me as if I were a criminal?"

"Jo, the man was terrified. You're only looking at this from one side." He scratched his beard and gave a gusty sigh. "You can't know what it's like to be outside that cage, helpless when someone you care about is facing down death. I had to all but knock him unconscious to keep him out of there until we got it through his head that he'd just get you killed for sure. He was scared, Jo. We were all scared."

Jo shook her head, certain Buck exaggerated because of his affection for her. Keane's voice had been hard, his eyes angry. "He doesn't care," she corrected quietly. "Not like the rest of you. You didn't swear at me. You weren't cold."

"Jo, people have different ways—" Buck began, but she interrupted.

"I know he wouldn't want to see me hurt, Buck. He's not heartless or cruel." She sighed as all the force of anger and fear washed out of her body and left her empty. "Please, I don't want to talk about him."

Buck heard the weariness in her voice and patted her hand. "Okay, honey, just relax. We'll have you all fixed up in no time."

Not all fixed up, Jo thought. Far from all fixed up.

CHAPTER 11

As the weeks passed, Jo's arm lost its stiffness. She healed cleanly. The only traces were thin scars that promised to fade but not disappear. She found, however, that some spark had gone out of her life. Constantly, she fought against a vague dissatisfaction. Nothing—not her work, not her friends, not her books—brought about the contentment she had grown up with. She had become a woman, and her needs had shifted. Jo knew the root of her problem was Keane, but the knowledge was not a solution. He had left the circus again on the very night of her accident. Nearly four weeks later he had not returned.

Three times Jo had sat down to write him, needing to assuage her guilt for the harsh things she had said to him. Three times she had torn up the paper in frustration. No matter how she rearranged the words, they were wrong. Instead, she clung to the hope that he would come back one last time. If, she felt, they could part as friends, without bitterness or hard words, she could accept the separation. Willing this to happen, she was able to return to her routine with some tranquility. She rehearsed, performed, joined in the daily duties of circus life. She waited. The caravan moved closer to Chicago.

* * *

Jo stood in the steaming Big Top on a late August afternoon. Dressed in a leotard, she worked on ground exercises with the Beirot Brothers. It was this daily regimentation that had aided in keeping her arm limber. She could now move into a back walk-over without feeling any protest in her injured arm.

"I feel good," Jo told Raoul as they worked out. "I feel really good." She did a quick series of pirouettes.

"You don't keep your shoulder in shape by dancing on your feet," Raoul challenged.

"My shoulder's fine," she tossed back, then proved her point by bending into a handstand. Slowly, she lowered her legs to a forty-five degree angle, bringing one foot to rest on the knee of the opposite leg. "It's perfect." She executed a forward roll and sprang to her feet. "I'm strong as an ox," she claimed and did a quick back handspring followed by a backflip.

She landed at Keane's feet.

The cascade of emotions that raced through her reflected briefly in her eyes before she regained her balance. "I didn't—I didn't know you were back." Instantly, she regretted the inanity of the words but could find no others. The longing was raw in her to hurl herself into his arms. She wondered that he could not feel her need through the pores of her skin.

"I just got in." His eyes continued to search her face after his hands dropped to his sides. "This is my mother," he added. "Rachael Loring, Jovilette Wilder."

At his words, Jo's gaze moved from his face. She saw the woman beside him. If she had seen Rachael Loring in a crowd of two thousand, she would have known her for Keane's mother. The bone structure was the same, though hers was more elegant. Her brows were golden wings, flaring out at the end, as Keane's did. Her hair was smooth, brushed up and away from her face with no gray to mar its tawny perfection. But it was the eyes that sent a jolt through Jo. She had not thought to see them in anyone's face but Keane's. The woman was dressed simply in an unpretentiously tailored suit that bespoke taste and wealth. There was, however, none of the cool, distant polish that Jo had always attributed to the woman who had taken her son and left Frank. There was a charm to the smile that curved in greeting.

"Jovilette, such a lovely name. Keane's told me of you." She extended her hand, and Jo accepted, intending a quick, impersonal shake. Rachael Loring, however, laid her other hand atop their joined ones and added warmth. "Keane tells me you were very close to Frank. Perhaps we could talk."

The affection in her voice confused Jo into a stumbling reply. "I—yes. I—if you'd like."

"I should like very much." She squeezed Jo's hand again before releasing it. "Perhaps you have time to show me around?" She smiled with the question, and Jo found it increasingly difficult to remain aloof. "I'm sure there've been some changes since I was here last. You must have some business to attend to," she said, looking up at Keane. "I'm sure Jovilette will take good care of me. Won't you, dear?" Without waiting for either to respond, Rachael tucked her arm through Jo's and began to walk. "I knew your parents," she said as Keane watched them move away. "Not terribly well, I'm afraid. They came here the same year I left. But I recall they were both thrilling performers. Keane tells me you've followed your father's profession."

"Yes, I . . ." She hesitated, feeling oddly at a disadvantage. "I did," she finished lamely.

"You're so young." Rachael gave her a gentle smile. "How terribly brave you must be."

"No . . . no, not really. It's my job."

"Yes, of course." Rachael laughed at some private memory. "I've heard that before."

They were outside now, and she paused to look thoughtfully around her. "I think perhaps I was wrong. It hasn't really changed, not in thirty years. It's a wonderful place, isn't it?"

"Why did you leave?" As soon as the words were spoken, Jo regretted them. "I'm sorry," she said quickly. "I shouldn't have asked."

"Of course you should." Rachael sighed and patted Jo's hand. "It's only natural. Duffy's still here, Keane tells me." At the change in subject, Jo imagined her question had been evaded.

"Yes, I suppose he always will be."

"Could we have some coffee, or some tea, perhaps?" Rachael smiled again. "It's such a long drive from town. Is your trailer nearby?"

"It's just over in the backyard."

"Oh, yes." Rachael laughed and began to walk again. "The neighborhood that never changes over thousands of miles. Do you know the story of the dog and the bones?" she asked. Though Jo knew it well, she said nothing. "One version is that a roustabout gave his dog a bone every night after dinner. The dog would bury the bone under the trailer, then the next day try to dig it back up. Of course, it was fifty miles behind in an empty lot. He never figured it out." Quietly, she laughed to herself.

Feeling awkward, Jo opened the door to her trailer. How could this woman be the one she had resented all of her life? How could this be the cold, heartless woman who had left Frank? Oddly, Rachael seemed totally at ease in the narrow confines of the trailer.

"How efficient these are." She looked around with interest and approval. "You must barely realize you're on wheels." Casually, she picked up the volume of Thoreau which lay on Jo's counter. "Keane told me you have an avid interest in literature. In language, too," she added, glancing up from the book. Her eyes were golden and direct like her son's. Jo was tossed back suddenly to the first morning of the season when she had looked down and found Keane's eyes on her.

It made her uncomfortable to learn Keane had discussed her with his mother. "I have some tea," Jo told her as she moved toward the kitchen. "It's a better gamble than my coffee."

"That's fine," Rachael said agreeably and followed her. "I'll just sit here while you fix it." She settled herself with apparent ease at the tiny table across from the kitchen.

"I'm afraid I haven't anything else to offer you." Jo kept her back turned as she routed through her cupboard.

"Tea and conversation," Rachael answered in mild tones, "will be fine."

Jo sighed and turned. "I'm sorry." She shook her head. "I'm being rude. I just don't know what to say to you, Mrs. Loring. I've resented you for as long as I can remember. Now you're here and not at all as I imagined." She managed to smile, albeit ruefully. "You're not cold and hateful, and you look so much like . . ." She stopped, horrified that she had nearly blurted out Keane's name. For a moment her eyes were utterly naked.

Rachael smoothed over the awkwardness. "I don't wonder you resented me if you were as close to Frank as Keane tells me. Jovilette," she said softly, "did Frank resent me, too?"

Helpless, Jo responded to the hint of sadness. "No. Not while I knew him. I don't think Frank was capable of resentments."

"You understood him well, didn't you?" Rachael watched as Jo poured boiling water into mugs. "I understood him, too," she continued as Jo brought the mugs to the table. "He was a dreamer, a marvelous free spirit." Absently, she stirred her tea.

Consumed with curiosity, Jo sat across from her and waited for the story she sensed was coming.

"I was eighteen when I met him. I had come to the circus with a cousin. The Colossus was a bit smaller in those days," she added with a reminiscent smile, "but it was all the same. Oh, the magic!" She shook her head and sighed. "We tumbled into love so fast, married against all my family's objections and went on the road. It was exciting. I learned the web routine and helped out in wardrobe."

Jo's eyes widened. "You performed?"

"Oh, yes." Rachael's cheeks tinted a bit with pride. "I was quite good. Then I became pregnant. We were both like children waiting for Christmas. I wasn't quite nineteen when I had Keane, and I'd been with the circus for nearly a year. Things became difficult over the next season. I was young and a bit frightened of Keane. I panicked if he sneezed and was constantly dragging Frank into town to see doctors. How patient he was."

Rachael leaned forward and took Jo's hand. "Can you understand how hard this life is for one not meant for it? Can you see that through the magic of it, the excitement and wonder, there are hardships and fears and impossible demands? I was little more than a child myself, with an infant to care for, without the endurance or vocation of a trouper, without the experience or confidence of a mother. I lived on nerves for an entire season." She let out a little rush of breath. "When it was over, I went home to Chicago."

For the first time, Jo imagined the flight from Rachael's point of view. She could see a girl, younger than herself, in a strange, demanding world with a baby to care for. Over the years Jo had seen scores of people try the life she'd led and last only weeks. Still she shook her head in confusion.

"I think I understand how difficult it must have been for you. But if you and Frank loved each other, couldn't you have worked it out somehow?"

"How?" Rachael countered. "Should I have taken a house

somewhere and lived with him half a year? I would have hated him. Should he have given up his life here and settled down with me and Keane? It would have destroyed everything I loved about him." Rachael shook her head, giving Jo a soft smile. "We did love each other, Jovilette, but not enough. Compromise isn't always possible, and neither of us were capable of adjusting to the needs of the other. I tried, and Frank would have tried had I asked him. But it was lost before it had really begun. We did the wisest thing under the circumstances." Looking into Jo's eyes, she saw youth and confidence. "It seems cold and hard to you, but it was no use dragging out a painful situation. He gave me Keane and two years I've always treasured. I gave him his freedom without bitterness. Ten years after Frank, I found happiness again." She smiled softly with the memory. "I loved Frank, and that love remains as young and sweet as the day I met him."

Jo swallowed. She searched for some way to apologize for a grudge held for a lifetime. "He—Frank kept a scrapbook on Keane. He followed the Chicago papers."

"Did he?" Rachael beamed, then leaned back in her chair and lifted her mug. "How like him. Was he happy, Jovilette? Did he have what he wanted?"

"Yes," Jo answered without hesitation. "Did you?"

Rachael's eyes came back to Jo's. For a moment the look was speculative, then it grew warm. "What a good heart you have, generous and understanding. Yes, I had what I wanted. And you, Jovilette, what do you want?"

At ease now, Jo shook her head and smiled. "More than I can have."

"You're too smart for that," Rachael observed, studying her. "I think you're a fighter, not a dreamer. When the time comes to make your choice, you won't settle for anything less than all." She smiled at Jo's intent look, then rose. "Will you show me your lions? I can't tell you how I'm looking forward to seeing you perform."

"Yes, of course." Jo stood, then hesitated. She held out her hand. "I'm glad you came."

Rachael accepted the gesture. "So am I."

* * *

Throughout the rest of the day Jo looked for Keane without success. After meeting and talking with his mother, it had become even more imperative that she speak with him. Her conscience would have no rest until she made amends. By showtime she had not yet found him.

Each act seemed to run on and on as she fretted for the finish. He would be with his mother in the audience, and undoubtedly she would find him after the show. She strained with impatience as the acts dragged.

After the finale she stood at the back door, unsure whether to wait or to go to his trailer. She was struck with both relief and alarm when she saw him approaching.

"Jovilette." Rachael spoke first, taking Jo's hands in hers. "How marvelous you were, and how stunning. I see why Keane said you had an untamed beauty."

Surprised, Jo glanced up at Keane but met impassive amber eyes. "I'm glad you enjoyed it."

"Oh, I can't tell you how much. The day has brought me some very precious memories. Our talk this afternoon meant a great deal to me." To Jo's surprise, Rachael leaned over and kissed her. "I hope to see you again. I'm going to say goodbye to Duffy before you drive me back, Keane," she continued. "I'll meet you in the car. Goodbye, Jovilette."

"Goodbye, Mrs. Loring." Jo watched her go before she turned to Keane. "She's a wonderful person. She makes me ashamed."

"There's no need for that." He tucked his hands into his pockets and watched her. "We both had our reasons for resentments, and we were both wrong. How's your arm?"

"Oh." Jo's fingers traveled to the wound automatically. "It's fine. There's barely any scarring."

"Good." The word was short and followed by silence. For a moment Jo felt her courage fail her.

"Keane," she began, then forced herself to meet his eyes directly. "I want to apologize for the horrible way I behaved after the accident."

"I told you once before," he said coolly, "I don't care for apologies."

"Please." Jo swallowed her pride and touched his arm. "I've been saving this one for a very long time. I didn't mean those things I said," she added quickly. "I hope you'll forgive me." It wasn't the eloquent apology she had planned, but it was all she could manage. His expression never altered.

"There's nothing to forgive."

"Keane, please." Jo grabbed his arm again as he turned to go. "Don't leave me feeling as if you don't forgive me. I know I said dreadful things. You have every right to be furious, but couldn't you—can't we be friends again?"

Something flickered over his face. Lifting his hand, he touched the back of it to her cheek. "You have a habit of disconcerting me, Jovilette." He dropped his hand, then thrust it into his pocket. "I've left something for you with Duffy. Be happy." He walked away from her while she dealt with the finality of his tone. He was walking out of her life. She watched him until he disappeared.

Jo had thought she would feel something, but there was nothing; no pain, no tears, no desperation. She had not known a human being could be so empty and still live.

"Jo." Duffy lumbered up to her, then held out a thick envelope. "Keane left this for you." Then he moved past her, anxious to see that all straggling towners were nudged on their way.

Jo felt all emotions had been stripped away. Absently, she glanced at the envelope as she walked to her trailer.

Without enthusiasm, she stepped inside, then tore it open. She remained standing as she pulled out the contents. It took her several moments to decipher the legal jargon. She read the group of papers through twice before sitting down.

He's given it to me, she thought. Still she could not comprehend the magnitude of it. *He's given me the circus.*

CHAPTER 12

O'Hare Airport was an army of people and a cacophony of sound. Nearly losing herself in the chaos of it, Jo struggled through the masses and competed for a cab. At first she had merely gawked at the snow like a towner seeing his first sword swallower. Then, though she shivered inside the corduroy coat she had bought for the trip, she began to enjoy it. It was beautiful as it lay over the city, and it helped to turn her mind from the purpose of her journey. Never had she been north so late in the year. Chicago in November was a sensational sight.

She had learned, after the initial shock had worn off, that Keane had not only given her the circus but a responsibility, as well. Almost immediately there had been contracts to negotiate. She had been tossed into a sea of paperwork, forced to rely heavily on Duffy's experience as she tried to regain her balance. As the season had come to a close, Jo had attempted a dozen times to call Chicago. Each time, she had hung up before Keane's number could be dialed. It would be, she had decided, more appropriate to see him in person. Her trip had been postponed a few weeks due to Jamie and Rose's wedding.

It was there, as she had stood as maid of honor, that Jo had realized what she must do. There was only one thing she truly wanted, and that was to be with Keane. Watching Rose's face as their vows had been exchanged, Jo had recalled her unflagging determination to win the man she loved.

And will I stay here? Jo had demanded of herself thousands of miles away from him. No. Her heart had begun to thud as she had mapped out a plan. She would go to Chicago to see him. She would not be turned away. He had wanted her once; she would make him want her again. She would not live out her life without at least some small portion of it being part of his. He didn't have to love her. It was enough that she loved him.

And so, shivering against the unfamiliar cold, Jo scrambled into a cab and headed across town. She brushed her hair free of snow with chilled fingers, thinking how idiotic she had been to forget to buy a hat and gloves. *What if he isn't home?* she thought suddenly. *What if he's gone to Europe or Japan or California?* Panic made her giddy, and she pushed it down. *He has to be home. It's Sunday, and he's sitting at home reading or going over a brief—or entertaining a woman,* she thought, appalled. *I should stop and call. I should tell the driver to take me back to the airport.* Closing her eyes, Jo fought to regain her calm. She took long, deep breaths and stared at the buildings and sidewalks. Gradually, she felt the tiny gurgle of hysteria dissipate.

I won't be afraid, she told herself and tried to believe it. *I won't be afraid.* But Jovilette, the woman who reclined on a living rug of lions, was very much afraid. What if he rejected her? *I won't let him reject me,* she told herself with a confident lift of her chin. *I'll seduce him.* She pressed her fingers to her temples. *I wouldn't know how to begin. I've got to tell the driver to turn around.*

But before she could form the words, the cab pulled up to a curb. With the precision of a robot, Jo paid the fare, overtipping in her agitation, and climbed out.

Long after the cab had pulled away, she stood staring up

at the massive glass-girdled building. Snow waltzed around her, sprinkling her hair and shoulders. A jostle from a rushing pedestrian broke the spell. She picked up her suitcases and hurried through the front door of the apartment buildings.

The lobby was enormous, with smoked glass walls and a deep shag carpet. Not knowing she should give her name at the desk, Jo wandered toward the elevators, innocently avoiding detection by merging with a group of tenants. Once inside the car, Jo pushed the button for the penthouse with a nerveless forefinger. The chatter of those in the elevator with her registered only as a distant humming. She never noticed when the car stopped for their departure.

When it stopped a second time and the doors slid open, she stared at the empty space for ten full seconds. Only as the automatic doors began to close did she snap out of her daze. Pushing them open again, she stepped through and into the hall. Her legs were wobbly, but she forced them to move forward in the direction of the penthouse. Panic sped up and down her spine until she set down her bags and leaned her brow against Keane's door. She urged air in and out of her lungs. She remembered that Rachael Loring had called her a fighter. Jo swallowed, lifted her chin and knocked. The wait was mercifully brief before Keane opened the door. She saw surprise light his eyes as he stared at her.

Her hair was dusted with snow as it lay over the shoulders of her coat. Her face glowed with the cold, and her eyes were bright, nearly feverish with her struggle for calm. Only once did her mouth tremble before she spoke.

"Hello, Keane."

He only stared, his eyes running over her in disbelief. He was leaner, she thought as she studied his face. As she filled herself with the sight of him, she saw he wore a sweatshirt and jeans. His feet were bare. He hadn't shaved, and her hand itched to test the roughness of his beard.

"What are you doing here?" Jo felt a resurgence of panic. His tone was harsh, and he had not answered her smile. She strained for poise.

"May I come in?" she asked, her smile cracking.

"What?" He seemed distracted by the question. His brows lowered into a frown.

"May I come in?" she repeated, barely defeating the urge to turn tail and run.

"Oh, yes, of course. I'm sorry." Running a hand through his hair, Keane stepped back and gestured her inside.

Instantly, Jo's shoes sank into the luxurious pile of the buff-colored carpet. For a moment she allowed herself to gaze around the room, using the time for the additional purpose of regaining her composure. It was an open, sweeping room with sharp, contrasting colors. There was a deep brown sectional sofa with a chrome and glass coffee table. There were high-backed chairs in soft creams and vivid slashes of blue in chunky floor pillows. There were paintings, one she thought she recognized as a Picasso, and a sculpture she was certain was a Rodin.

On the far right of the room there was an elevation of two steps. Just beyond was a huge expanse of glass that featured a spreading view of Chicago. Jo moved toward it with undisguised curiosity. Now, inexplicably, fear had lessened. She found that once she had stepped over the threshold she had committed herself. She was no longer afraid.

"It's wonderful," she said, turning back to him. "How marvelous to have a whole city at your feet every day. You must feel like a king."

"I've never thought of it that way." With half the room between them, he studied her. She looked small and fragile with the bustling city at her back.

"I would," she said, and now her smile came easily. "I'd stand at the window and feel regal and pompous."

At last she saw his lips soften and curve. "Jovilette," he said quietly. "What are you doing in my world?"

"I needed to talk to you," she answered simply. "I had to come here to do it."

He moved to her then, but slowly, with his eyes on hers. "It must be important."

"I thought so."

His brow lifted, then he shrugged. "Well, then, we'll talk. But first, let's have your coat."

Jo's cold fingers fumbled with the buttons and caused Keane to frown again. "Good heavens, you're frozen." He captured her hands between his and swore. "Where are your gloves?" he demanded like an irate parent. "It must be all of twelve degrees outside."

"I forgot to buy any," Jo told him as she dealt with the heavenly feeling of his hands restoring warmth to hers.

"Idiot. Don't you know better than to come to Chicago in November without gloves?"

"No." Jo responded to his anger with a cheerful smile. "I've never been to Chicago in November before. It's wonderful."

His eyes lifted from her hands to her face. He watched her for a long moment, then she heard him sigh. "I'd nearly convinced myself I could be cured."

Jo's eyes clouded with concern. "Have you been ill?"

Keane laughed with a shake of his head, then he pushed away the question and became brisk again. "Here, let's have your coat. I'll get you some coffee."

"You needn't bother," she began as he undid the buttons on the coat himself and drew it from her shoulders.

"I'd feel better if I was certain your circulation was restored." He paused and looked down at her as he laid her coat over his arm. She wore a green angora sweater with pearl buttons and a gray skirt in thin wool. The soft fabric draped softly at her breasts and over her hips and thighs. Her shoes were dainty and impractical sling-back heels.

"Is something wrong?"

"I've never seen you wear anything but a costume or jeans."

"Oh." Jo laughed and combed her fingers through her damp hair. "I expect I look different."

"Yes, you do." His voice was low, and there was a frown in his eyes. "Right now you look as if you've come from college for the holidays." He touched the ends of her hair, then turned away. "Sit down. I'll get the coffee."

A bit puzzled by his mercurial moods, Jo wandered about the room, finally ignoring a chair to kneel beside one of the pillows near the picture window. Though the carpet swallowed Keane's footsteps, she sensed his return.

"How wonderful to have a real winter, if just for the snow." She turned a radiant face his way. "I've always wondered what Christmas is like with snow and icicles." Images of snowflakes danced in her eyes. Seeing he carried two mugs of coffee, she rose and took one. "Thank you."

"Are you warm enough?" he asked after a moment.

Jo nodded and sat in one of the two chairs opposite the sofa. The novelty of the city made her mission seem like a grand adventure. Keane sat beside her, and for a moment they drank in companionable silence.

"What did you want to talk to me about, Jo?"

Jo swallowed, ignoring the faint trembling in her chest. "A couple of things. The circus, for one." She shifted in her chair until she faced him. "I didn't write because I felt it too important. I didn't phone for the same reason. Keane . . ." All her carefully thought-out speeches deserted her. "You can't just give something like that away. I can't take it from you."

"Why not?" He shrugged and sipped his coffee. "We both know it's always been yours. A piece of paper doesn't change that one way or the other."

"Keane, Frank left it to you."

"And I gave it to you."

Jo made a small sound of frustration. "Perhaps if I could pay you for it . . ."

"Someone asked me once what was the value of a dream or the price of a human spirit." Jo shifted her eyes to his helplessly. "I didn't have an answer then. Do you have one now?"

She sighed and shook her head. "I don't know what to say to you. 'Thank you' is far from adequate."

"It's not necessary, either," Keane told her. "I simply gave back what was yours in any case. What else was there, Jo? You said there were a couple of things."

This was it, Jo's brain told her. Carefully, she set down the coffee and rose. Waiting for her stomach to settle, she walked a few feet out into the room, then turned. She allowed herself a deep breath before she met Keane's eyes.

"I want to be your mistress," she said with absolute calm.

"What?" Both Keane's face and voice registered utter shock.

Jo swallowed and repeated. "I want to be your mistress. That's still the right term, isn't it, or is it antiquated? Is *lover* right? I've never done this before."

Slowly, Keane set his mug beside hers and rose. He did not move toward her but watched her with probing eyes. "Jo, you don't know what you're saying."

"Oh, yes, I do," she cut him off and nodded. "I might not have the terminology exactly right, but I do know what I mean, and I'm sure you do, too. I want to be with you," she continued and took a step toward him. "I want you to make love to me. I want to live with you if you'll let me, or at least close by."

"Jo, you're not talking sensibly." Sharply, Keane broke into her speech. Turning away, he thrust his hands into his pockets and balled them into fists. "You don't know what you're asking."

"Don't I appeal to you anymore?"

Keane whirled, infuriated with the trace of curiosity in her voice. "How can you ask me that?" he demanded. "Of course you appeal to me! I'm not dead or in the throes of senility!"

She moved closer to him. "Then if I want you, and you want me, why can't we be lovers?"

Keane swore violently and grabbed her shoulders. "Do you think I could have you for a winter and then blithely let you go? Do you think I could untangle myself at the start of the season and watch you stroll out of my life? Haven't you the sense to see what you do to me?" He shook her hard with the question, stealing any breath she might have used to answer him.

"You make me crazy!" Abruptly, he dragged her against him. His mouth bruised hers, his fingers dug into her flesh. Jo's head spun with confusion and pain and ecstasy. It seemed centuries since she had tasted his mouth on hers. She heard him groan as he tore himself away. He turned, leaving her to find her own balance as the room swayed. "What do I have to do to be rid of you?" His words came in furious undertones.

Jo blew out a breath. "I don't think kissing me like that is a very good start."

"I'm aware of that," he murmured. She watched the rise and fall of his shoulders. "I've been trying to avoid doing it since I opened the door."

Quietly, Jo walked to him and put a hand on his arm. "You're tense," she discovered and automatically sought to soothe the muscles. "I'm sorry if I'm going about this the wrong way. I thought telling you outright would be better than trying to seduce you. I don't think I'd be very good at that."

Keane made a sound somewhere between a laugh and a moan. "Jovilette," he murmured before he turned and gathered her into his arms. "How do I resist you? How many times must I pull away before I'm free of you? Even the thought of you drives me mad."

"Keane." She sighed and shut her eyes. "I've wanted you

to hold me for so long. I want to belong to you, even for just a little while."

"No." He pulled away, then forced her chin up with his thumb and forefinger. "Don't you see that once would be too much and a lifetime wouldn't be enough? I love you too much to let you go and enough to know I have to." Shock robbed her of speech. She only stared as he continued. "It was different when I didn't know, when I thought I was—how did you put it? 'Dazzled.'" He smiled briefly at the word. "I was certain if I could make love to you, I could get you out of my system. Then, the night Ari died, I held you while you slept. I realized I was in love with you, had been in love with you right from the beginning."

"But you . . ." Jo shook her head as if to clear it. "You never told me, and you seemed so cold, so distant."

"I couldn't touch you without wanting more." He pulled her close again and for a moment buried his face in her hair. "But I couldn't stay away. I knew if I wanted to have you, to really have you, one of us had to give up what we did, what we were. I wondered if I could give up the law. It was really all I ever wanted to do. I discovered I wanted you more."

"Oh, Keane." She shook her head, but he put her from him suddenly.

"Then I found out that wouldn't work, either." Keane turned, paced to the window and stared out. The snow was falling heavily. "Every time you walked into that cage, I walked into hell. I thought perhaps I'd get used to it, but it only got worse. I tried leaving, coming back here, but I could never shake you loose. I kept coming back. The day you were hurt . . ." Keane paused. Jo heard him draw in his breath, and when he continued, his voice was deeper. "I watched you step in front of that boy and take the blow. I can't tell you what I felt at that moment. There aren't words for it. All I could think of was getting to you. I wonder if Pete ever told you that I decked him before Buck got to me. He took it very well, considering. Then I had to—to just stand there and watch while that cat stalked you. I've never known that kind of fear before. The kind that empties you out, body and soul."

He lapsed into silence. "Then it was over," he continued, "and I got to you. You were so white, and you were bleeding in my arms." He muttered an oath, then was silent again. He shook his head. "I wanted to burn the place down, get you away, strangle the cats with my bare hands. Anything. I wanted to hold you, but I couldn't get past the fear and the unreasonable anger at having been helpless. Before my hands stopped shaking, you were making plans to go back into that damnable cage. I wanted to kill you myself then and be done with it."

Slowly, Keane turned and walked back to her. "I saw it happen again every time I closed my eyes for weeks afterward. I can show you exactly where the scars are." He lifted a finger and traced four lines on her upper arm precisely where the claws had ripped her skin. He dropped his hand and shook his head. "I can't watch you go in the cage, Jo." He lifted his hand again and let it linger over her hair. "If I let you stay with me now, I wouldn't be able to let you go back to your own life. And I can't ask you to give it up."

"I wish you would." Solemn eyed, Jo watched him. "I very much wish you would."

"Jo." Shaking his head, he turned away. "I know what it means to you."

"No more than the law means to you, I imagine," she said briskly. "But you said you were willing to give that up."

"Yes, but . . ."

"Oh, very well." She pushed back her hair. "If you won't ask me, I'll have to ask you. Will you marry me?"

Keane turned back, giving her his lowered brow frown. "Jo, you can't . . ."

"Of course I can. This is the twentieth century. If I want to ask you to marry me, then I will. I did," she pointed out.

"Jo, I don't . . ."

"Yes or no, please, Counselor. This isn't an easy question." She stepped forward until they stood toe to toe. "I'm in love with you, and I want to marry you and have several babies. Is that agreeable?"

Keane's mouth opened and closed. He gave her an odd smile and lifted his hands to her shoulders. "This is rather sudden."

Jo felt a wild surge of joy. "Perhaps it is," she admitted. "I'll give you a minute to think about it. But I might as well tell you, I won't take no for an answer."

Keane's fingers traced the curve of her neck. "It seems I have little choice."

"None at all," she corrected. Boldly, she locked her arms around him and pulled his mouth down to hers. The kiss was instantly urgent, instantly searching. Joined, they lowered to the rug and clung. For a long, long moment, their lips were united in a language too complex for words. Then, as if to reassure himself she was real, Keane searched the familiar curves of her body, tasted the longed-for flavor of her skin.

"Why did I think I could live without you?" he whispered. His mouth came desperately back to hers. "Be sure, Jo, be sure." Roughened with emotion, his voice was low while the words were spoken against her lips. "I'll never be able to let you go. I'm asking you for everything."

"No. No, it's not like that. Hold me tighter. Kiss me again," she demanded as his lips roamed her face. "Kiss me." She wondered if the sound of pleasure she heard was his or her own. She had not known a kiss could be so intimate, so terrifyingly exciting. No, she thought as she soared with the knowledge that he loved her. He wasn't asking everything, he was giving it.

"I'm leaving something behind," she told him when their lips parted, "and replacing it with something infinitely more important." She buried her face in the curve of his neck. "When you realize how much I love you, you'll understand."

Keane drew away and stared down at her. At last he spoke, but it was only her name. It was a soft sigh of a sound. She smiled at it and lifted a hand to his cheek. "If there's a way to compromise . . ."

"No." She shook her head, remembering his mother's words. "Sometimes there can't be a compromise. We love each other enough not to need one. Please, don't think I'm making a sacrifice. I'm not." She smiled a little and rubbed her palm experimentally over the stubble of his neglected beard. "I don't regret one minute of my life in the circus, and I don't regret changing it. You've given me the circus, so I'll always be a part of it." Her smile faded, and her eyes grew serious. "Will you belong to me, Keane?"

He took her hand from his cheek and pressed it to his lips. "I already do. I love you, Jovilette. I'll spend a lifetime loving you."

"That's not long enough," she said as their lips met again. "I want more. I want forever."

With slow, building passion, his hands moved over her. Taking his time, he loosened the buttons on her sweater. "So beautiful," he murmured as his lips trailed down her throat and found the gentle swell. Jo's breath caught at the new intimacy. "You're trembling. I love knowing I can make your skin tremble under my hands." His lips roamed back to hers before he cradled her in his arms. "I've wanted to be with you, to hold you, just hold you, for so long. I can't remember not wanting it."

With a sigh washed with contentment, Jo snuggled against him. "Keane," she murmured.

"Hmm?"

"You never answered me."

"About what?" He kissed her closed lids, then tangled his fingers in her hair.

Jo opened her eyes. Her brows arched over them. "Are you going to marry me or not?"

Keane laughed, rolled her onto her back and planted a long, lingering kiss on her mouth. "Is tomorrow soon enough?"